'TIS THE SEASON

It's that time of year again when magic is in the air and the spirit of the season surrounds us. Come celebrate with Arabesque as some of our most popular authors show us 'tis the season for laughter, goodwill toward men . . . and love.

BOOK YOUR PLACE ON OUR WEBSITE AND MAKE THE ARABESQUE ROMANCE CONNECTION!

We've created a customized website just for our very special Arabesque readers, where you can get the inside scoop on everything that's going on with Arabesque romance novels.

When you come online, you'll have the exciting opportunity to:

- View covers of upcoming books

- Learn about our future publishing schedule (listed by publication month and author)

- Find out when your favorite authors will be visiting a city near you

- Search for and order backlist books

- Check out author bios and background information

- Send e-mail to your favorite authors

- Join us in weekly chats with authors, readers and other guests

- Get writing guidelines

- AND MUCH MORE!

Visit our website at
http://www.arabesquebooks.com

'TIS THE SEASON

Donna Hill
Rochelle Alers
Candice Poarch

ARABESQUE
★BET
BOOKS

BET Publications, LLC
www.bet.com

ARABESQUE BOOKS are published by

BET Publications, LLC
c/o BET BOOKS
One BET Plaza
1900 W Place NE
Washington, DC 20018-1211

All Kensington Titles, Imprints, and Distributed Lines are
available at special quantity discounts for bulk purchases for
sales promotions, premiums, fund-raising, and educational
or institutional use. Special book excerpts or customized
printings can also be created to fit specific needs. For details,
write or phone the office of the Kensington special sales
manager: Kensington Publishing Corp., 850 Third Avenue,
New York, NY 10022, attn: Special Sales Department,
Phone: 1-800-221-2647.

First Printing: October 2001
10 9 8 7 6 5 4 3 2 1

Printed in the United States of America

CONTENTS

THE CHOICE

Donna Hill

He was tall, and handsome in an exotic, decidedly sensual kind of way. His warm hazel eyes, an almost identical match to hers, seemed able to peer into her very soul. His shoulder-length dredlocks framed a face of smooth rich chocolate, a face that any woman could fall in love with. And that's exactly what Jewel Avery had done. She'd fallen head over heels in love with Taj Burrell.

A wistful smile tilted her full, bow-shaped lips as she momentarily relived the feel of his mouth trailing tantalizing kisses along her neck. So what was the problem? she asked herself, shaking away the vision with a toss of her dark brown head, as she busied herself making a quick breakfast for her daughter, Danielle. With swift, precise movements Jewel smoothly prepared a plate of scrambled eggs, wheat toast, and a glass of orange juice and placed them on the smoked-glass dining room table.

The problem was, Taj was five years her junior. He was a struggling musician and she was a thirty-seven-year-old independently wealthy divorcée with one of the fastest growing real estate and development agencies in the state of Connecticut. She had yet to introduce him to her family. Her daughter Danielle didn't even know that Taj existed.

Why was introducing him such a problem? she questioned. After all, *age ain't nothin' but a number.* How many times had she heard that line? Yet an admonishing voice echoed in her head that a grown woman with a child did not "run around" with a younger man, and a *musician* no less. What would people say?

Jewel frowned and turned away from the table. Other people's reactions were the least of her problems. It was Danielle who was her greatest source of concern.

She returned to the kitchen and walked toward the polished cherry wood cupboard. Automatically she reached for a jar of coffee. Her slender hand halted in midair and changed direction. She reached instead for a box of herbal tea, hearing Taj's warning about the effects of caffeine. She smiled. He had changed her life in so many ways.

She sighed heavily. It wasn't fair to Taj to keep him a secret from her family. They'd been seeing each other for nearly three months, almost from the first day that they met, when he'd walked into her office and asked for help in finding a loft apartment. Since then, he'd asked her repeatedly to introduce him to her family, especially Danielle. But each time, Jewel made some excuse, and then Taj had just stopped asking. If she didn't quickly come to terms with her dilemma, she knew she would lose him.

She walked to the bottom of the spiral staircase that led to the bedrooms above.

"Dani! Breakfast is ready," she called. "Hurry up or you'll be late for class."

"I'm comin', I'm comin'," fifteen-year-old Danielle yelled back.

Moments later she heard her daughter bounding down the stairs. She turned as Dani bustled into the dining room. Her straight, shoulder-length black hair hung evenly around her pretty, almond-toned face. Her best friend, Kim, had wrapped Dani's hair the night before. Her electric blue backpack was slung over her right shoulder.

Jewel's smile of greeting froze on her face as her large hazel eyes scanned her daughter's attire.

"Must you dress like that every day Danielle?" Jewel cried plaintively, sounding, she knew, much like her own mother.

"Like what?" Dani countered, taking a seat at the table. She frowned at her mother, gearing up for their usual debate.

"Like—like you're ready to go to a yard sale. Your shirts are too big, your jeans are two sizes too large, those sneakers look like space boots." Jewel inhaled, then quickly expelled an exasperated breath as she put her hands on her round hips.

"You'll be sixteen years old in a couple of months. A young lady," she added in a gentler tone. "It's about time you started dressing like one." Jewel turned away and picked up her cup of tea from the counter. Dani rolled her eyes.

"Everybody dresses like this," Dani said. "I don't see the problem. Daddy wouldn't have had a problem with how I dress," she added accusingly.

Jewel swallowed back the lump of frustration that had risen in her throat. Slowly she turned toward her daughter. "Your father isn't here, Dani," she said evenly.

"No, he isn't."

Jewel felt as if she'd been slapped even as she heard the barest hint of pain beneath the angry words.

Danielle sprung up from her seat, tossing her napkin across the uneaten food. "I've got to go," she mumbled. She rounded the table and gave her mother a perfunctory kiss on the cheek. "Bye." She spun away, snatching her backpack from the chair.

Jewel took a calming breath. "Dani," she called softly.

Dani halted and reluctantly turned back. "Yes?"

"It isn't my fault, Dani, that your father moved out." She took a step forward. "I don't know what else I can do to make you understand that. Things didn't work out. It happens, even in the best of families."

Dani sighed. "Maybe if you didn't try to be so perfect and expect perfection from everyone else then Daddy wouldn't have left."

Jewel stared wordlessly at her departing daughter. Perfection. How many times had she had that word thrown in her face?

She sat down heavily in the gold and black chair, unconsciously straightening the place mats and salt and pepper shakers. Then just as quickly, returning them all the way they were. Another Taj Burrell influence, she thought wryly. He had subtly and lovingly tried to exorcise some of the idiosyncrasies that permeated Jewel's life.

Ever since she was a little girl, her parents had demanded her absolute best at everything, from the way she dressed and combed her hair to the straight A's that she maintained throughout her school years.

Any deviation from perfection was met with chilling remarks, withdrawal of affection, and questions about her character. As a result, Jewel had grown up meticulous, afraid of confrontation and starved for affection. So when she met Steven Avery in her freshman year of college, she envisioned him as her knight in shining armor.

Jewel strove to please him in the only way she knew how—by being perfect at everything. But Steven demanded more than even she was capable of giving. When he couldn't get it, he turned to others.

At first he was discreet about his affairs and then he

became blatant with his dalliances. He never really wanted her, Jewel had painfully come to realize; he only wanted someone to warm his bed at night. She could never have done enough to satisfy Dr. Steven Avery.

Jewel slowly rose from her seat and placed her teacup in the sink. She'd promised herself from the day he'd walked out of the door that she'd protect his image in his daughter's eyes. As a result, Danielle believed that Jewel had driven her father away. Jewel had spent the past year, since the divorce, trying to make it up to Dani. Tears welled in her eyes. All to no avail, she sighed.

And now with the Christmas holidays rapidly approaching, she had to find a way to introduce the new man in her life to Danielle. The thought of that confrontation chilled her almost as much as the numbing December air. Deep inside, she knew that Dani would be adamantly against anyone attempting to fill her father's shoes. Dani still maintained the childlike hope that her mother and father would be miraculously reunited.

Jewel slipped on her mint green, wool suit jacket and retrieved her ankle-length mink coat from the hall closet.

As she drove to the office, thoughts of Taj penetrated her troubling musings. Despite herself, she smiled. Taj had planned on an early lunch at his loft apartment for the two of them. Her heart began to race. It was the thoughtful things like that about Taj that had endeared him to her from the beginning.

Moments later she pulled up in front of her office. She stepped out of her BMW and quickly crossed the parking lot, eager to find refuge from the blistering winter wind. She had two houses to show before she could leave for her rendezvous with Taj as well as make some final decisions on the purchase and renovation of a string of abandoned buildings in New Haven. Another full day, she mused.

When she entered her office, she was surprised to find her assistant, Tricia Monroe, already at her desk.

"Mornin' Jewel," Tricia greeted. "You have a visitor," she added. Tricia angled her auburn head in the direction of Jewel's private office.

Jewel frowned. "I don't recall making any private appointments for this morning," she replied. "Who is it?"

"See for yourself."

Jewel stood up straighter and gave Tricia a puzzled glance, then headed down the corridor.

Jewel opened the frosted glass door to her office, ready to apologize for her oversight but was instead swept up in a breathtaking embrace.

Before she had a chance to respond, Taj's strong hands found their way beneath her coat and pulled her solidly against him. His warm mouth found hers, covering it in an intoxicating kiss that left her weak in the knees. His fingers played along her spine, sliding downward to pull her hips closer to his pulsing center.

"I couldn't wait till lunch," he moaned against her mouth. "I dreamed about you all night long."

"Taj," she whispered breathlessly, arching her neck to receive the rain of scintillating kisses as his feathersoft dredlocks whispered tauntingly against her cheek. "What about Tricia?"

"What about her?" he teased. "This is just between us." He looked down into her upturned face and grinned, flashing even, white teeth. Reluctantly he took a step back and slowly released his hold.

Jewel struggled to control the rapid beat of her heart. "What on earth are you doing here?" she was finally able to ask. She pushed the door closed and with much effort crossed the mauve, carpeted floor to her desk, needing to put some barrier between her and Taj if only for a moment.

"I thought I'd surprise you. I know what a stickler you are for order and I just felt that a little spontaneity was way overdue."

"You've certainly accomplished that," she said, slowly regaining control of her breathing as she took in the sight of the gorgeous man in front of her. It took all of her willpower to keep from unbuttoning the tiny white buttons on his pale blue denim shirt and to keep from stroking the hard, muscular thighs that were encased in his blue jeans.

Taj flounced down on the soft, black leather sofa, stretching his long, muscular arm across its length. He crossed his right ankle over his left knee and gave Jewel a penetrating stare. "What's the problem?" he asked, intuitively sensing her uneasiness.

With a long sigh, Jewel slipped out of her coat and hung it on the brass coatrack.

"Dani and I had another falling out this morning." She took a seat behind her desk.

Taj pursed his lips and briefly shut his eyes. "About what?"

"The usual. Her father, me . . . everything."

"Don't you think it's about time that you told her the truth about her father, Jewel?"

"Of course I've thought about it. But knowing my daughter, I'm sure she'd find some way to use that against me as well."

Taj closed his eyes and sighed, then abruptly stood up. "When am I going to get to *know* this daughter?"

She looked up at him, her eyes pleading with him to understand. "Soon Taj. I promise. It's just that—"

"Just what, Jewel?" His voice rose in frustration. "Is it *just* that you're ashamed of me? Is it *just* that I don't fit into your world? What? Because I'd really like to know. Once and for all."

"Taj, please try to understand. It's not easy for me either."

He crossed the short space to her desk, leaned down, bracing his hands against the hard wood, his hair falling on either side of his dark face. The heady scent of his cologne wafted around his body, assaulting her senses.

"We've been together for close to three months now, Jewel," he said evenly. "In that time, you've come up with every excuse in the book to keep me away from your family and your friends. What am I supposed to think? I may be younger than you, but I'm not stupid." He straightened. "I think it's about time that you decided what it is that you want to do about us."

He turned, snatched up his black leather trench coat and his saxophone case, keeping his back to her as he spoke. "I have an audition in an hour. I don't want to be late." He walked toward the door. "You can give me a call when you reach a decision. I'll be waiting." He pulled open the door and left without another word.

Jewel sat motionless. Her heart ached. There was no doubt about it, Taj had finally had enough and had given her an ultimatum. Slowly, she stood up and crossed her arms in front of her. She had a choice to make. Save her relationship by coming to terms with her trepidations and her daughter, or once again, avoid a head-on conflict with Danielle and risk further estrangement and lose the man she loved. She couldn't avoid making a decision any longer.

Jewel sighed heavily, pressing her right fist against her lips. If only she had the same control and self-confidence in her personal life as she did in her business dealings, everything would be so much different.

The ringing of her private line intruded on her thoughts.

"Yes, Tricia?"

"Mr. Hamilton is here with his attorney."

"Send them right in."

Jewel straightened and smoothed down her suit. She had put together a master plan for the development of a stretch of abandoned property that was sure to make the unflappable Donald Hamilton drool with longing. Her problems with Taj would have to wait.

Moments later Tricia opened the office door. Following on her heels was Don Hamilton and his attorney, Sam Connelly.

She'd met Donald Hamilton only on one other occasion and once again, his striking good looks caught her off guard. He was at least six-foot-three-inches tall, with a warm honey-brown complexion. His close-cropped hair was the only indication of his age as it was sprinkled with flecks of gray. However, the gray only intensified his distinguished appearance. It was easy to tell that his suits were custom made and fit as though he were the only man on earth who could wear them. Broad shoulders fanned the dark blue suit jacket, contrasting sharply against a stark white shirt. He moved with an easy grace, yet gave off bursts of energy that seemed barely contained. His wife was a very lucky woman, Jewel thought absently.

"Good morning, gentleman," Jewel greeted warmly, stretching her hand to shake each of theirs in turn. "Please have a seat, we have a lot to talk about this morning."

"I certainly hope so, Mrs. Avery," Don intoned, giving her an appreciative once over. "You peaked my interest with this project. I'm eager to see what you have to offer."

Donald Hamilton was reputed to be one of the wealthiest men in the state. He had holdings in several major corporations around the country and had begun to dabble in real estate over the past year. Word had it that he was determined to buy up as much property as was available. Jewel also knew, from inside sources, that Donald Hamilton was a major player in the President's health care plan. Her vision for the development of the land met all of Don Hamilton's needs.

"In that case," Jewel responded, "let me get right to the point. The land in question is in an ideal location, easily accessible by car or public transportation. What I envision, Mr. Hamilton, is an extensive complex which will include not only major shopping sites but a medical and dental facility and a day care center for shoppers." Before any response could be made, Jewel pulled out a sketch that she'd had an architect draft for her. Expertly, she pointed out the locations of the various buildings and detailed how they would all fit in together.

"This is just the kind of economic boost that Connecticut needs," she concluded.

Don sat back and viewed the sketches. Abruptly he looked across the table at her. "I think you have a marvelous plan. If I didn't know better, I'd say you read my mind." His smile was slow and warm.

Sam Connelly, who had remained silent up to that point, broke in. "Don, I think you need to take these plans over to our people and have them take a look. I wouldn't advise making any decision until then." He looked at Jewel with skeptical green eyes.

The corner of Don's mouth inched up in a grin. "I don't think there will be a need for that, Sam. Mrs. Avery's plan is exactly what I've been looking for." He turned his gaze on Jewel. "Why don't you and I continue this conversation over lunch? I'd also like to take another look at the site. Then, if I still like what I see, just show me where to sign."

"But Don!" Sam sputtered. "You can't just—"

Don turned hard eyes on his attorney. His voice was calm. "I appreciate your advice, Sam. But that's all that it is, advice. The decision is mine to make. And I believe I've made it." He returned his gaze to Jewel. "Lunch?"

She hesitated, thinking of Taj and their aborted plans. "Lunch sounds fine," she said finally.

"Wonderful." Donald checked his watch. "Why don't I pick you up at one o'clock. Is that good for you?"

"Perfect. I have two houses to show, but I should be finished by then."

Both men rose. "I'll see you then." He shook Jewel's hand. Sam gave her a curt nod and they departed.

It took all she had not to burst out laughing from the look of absolute disgust on the face of Sam Connelly. Unfortunately, her brief moment of gaiety was quickly replaced with an onset of nerves. What was she going to do about Taj? She couldn't leave their situation unresolved.

Jewel reached for her phone and punched in Taj's number. The phone rang four times, then the answering machine clicked on. Jewel hung up with a mixture of relief and disappointment. She'd try again later. Mechanically, she straightened her desk, collected her purse and coat and left her office.

"Tricia, I'm going over to pick up my clients to show the house on Melrose. Then it's off to Hudson Street. I should be back by one."

"No problem," Tricia gave a shallow smile.

"Thanks." Jewel turned to leave, then stopped. "Oh,

Don Hamilton is going to stop back by. If he should arrive before I do, just ask him to wait in my office."

"Will do. Anything else?" Tricia asked with an inquisitive glimmer in her eyes.

"Anything like what?"

"Like an exquisitely tall, dark, fine man deserving to be cherished who may call in your absence."

Jewel pursed her lips. "*If* Taj should call, tell him I'll call him back." Without waiting for further comment, Jewel walked out.

Taj had just finished his second set with the band. He put his saxophone back in the case and walked in the direction of the club owner, Nick Hunter.

"That was great, man!" Nick said enthusiastically. Nick slapped Taj's back and shook his free hand.

"Thanks."

"Let's go into my office and talk."

Taj followed Nick into a small back room off the bar. Nick quickly cleared away a stack of music sheets that occupied the one available chair.

"Have a seat," Nick instructed, then sat down behind his cluttered desk.

Taj sat down, stretching his long legs out in front of him.

"Now, this is the deal," Nick began. "I'm only in town one night a week. Which is usually the night that I play," he grinned. "I have another club in New York and one I'm opening in Los Angeles," he added proudly. "What I'd like to offer you are the other six nights." He quoted a salary. "How does that sound?"

"Almost too good to be true," Taj chuckled.

"Hey, listen, I know talent when I hear it, and you've got it. I wouldn't want anybody else snatching you up while I'm haggling over a few dollars. So?"

Taj thought about the offer. If he accepted, it would greatly cut into his time with Jewel. But then again, as things stood between them . . . well, he didn't know where things stood between them.

"I'm in," he said finally.

Nick stood up and stretched his hand across to Taj. They shook in agreement.

"Then it's a deal. I'll have my partner, Neal, get you all of the necessary forms and give you a schedule. You start tomorrow night, seven o'clock."

"I'll be here."

"Glad to have you aboard. Your sound is just the lift the band needs." Nick came around the desk. "Where did you study?"

Taj laughed "I didn't. At least not in the traditional sense. I taught myself."

"No kiddin'?" Nick said, suitably impressed. "You did a helluva teaching job."

"It just seemed like it came natural to me," Taj shrugged. "And it was a way for me to stay out of trouble, especially on Chicago's southside. My mother didn't have the money for lessons, so I just listened and copied from the masters."

"Well, you stick with me and there may be a lot more doors opened for you. I just negotiated a record deal for my wife, Parris. I do all of her management."

"You're Parris McKay's husband?" Taj asked, suitably surprised.

"Yeah." Nick chuckled. "That woman's been ridin' my coattails long enough," he added playfully. "Had to get her those deals or she would have worn me out singing in the shower."

It was all coming together now. Taj recalled reading an article a couple of years back that talked about Parris's debut in New York. And now that he thought about it, her opening night was at *Rhythms* in Manhattan.

"Seems like I'm in pretty classy company," Taj said.

"Yeah, well, we try to keep a low profile. Otherwise life would be unbearable. Next time Parris is in town, I'll make sure I introduce you."

"That would be great."

Nick nodded. "Actually, I've always wanted to get one of the bands really launched but I never found the right combination." He paused. "Until now."

"It's definitely something to look forward to," Taj said.

"Let's talk again later," Nick said. "I'll be back sometime next week. Neal will give me the lowdown on how things went. Any problems, whatever, you go to him. He'll take care of it."

"Thanks, Nick."

"Don't thank me yet," Nick grinned.

Taj was on cloud nine. Things were finally starting to come together. He had a full-time job, paying good money and the possibility of a record deal. What more could he ask for? Maybe now Jewel would take him more seriously. He still believed that although she said she loved him, she still thought of him as someone who needed looking after. Now he could show her that he could make it on his own. He could be all of the things that he felt she needed.

He strolled down Main Street, oblivious to the biting December wind. He spotted a phone booth up ahead and decided to give Jewel a call to share his news.

He dropped a quarter in the slot and started to dial Jewel's office number when something caught his eye. He hung up the phone and stared through the plate glass window of the restaurant opposite the phone booth.

The well-dressed man was looking intensely at his

lunch companion. The man spoke to the woman as if she were the only woman in the world. Jewel looked as though she were enjoying every bit of the man's undivided attention.

Taj's jaw tightened to a point where his head began to ache. He took a step toward the restaurant, intent on just walking in on the apparently intimate meeting. Good sense prevailed and he stopped just short of the door. He wouldn't reduce himself to causing a scene, or worse, risk being humiliated by Jewel and her lover.

Taj turned away and strode across the busy intersection, unconscious of the rush of afternoon traffic. All he wanted to do was get away from the two of them as quickly as possible.

So that was it, he fumed, Jewel was seeing someone else. No wonder she didn't want to introduce him to her daughter. What if she simply used Danielle as an excuse, that her daughter wasn't the issue—the other man was. In the short time they've known each other he really believed that the two of them had something special. Obviously he'd been very wrong.

On the next corner Taj hailed a cab and directed the driver to his apartment. Through the entire ride he replayed the scene he'd witnessed over and over again in his mind. And with each vision his hurt intensified to compete with his anger.

He thought Jewel was different. She made *him* feel different, special, but apparently he wasn't special enough, he thought, sticking his key in the door. He stepped into the enormous space and the first thing that caught his eye was the cozy lunch setting he had arranged especially for the two of them. The small, round table was set for two, with a scented candle as the centerpiece. He had prepared a special vegetarian meal that Jewel had come to love. His anger threatened to overpower him.

He breathed heavily as he took off his coat and tossed it on the overstuffed couch that he and Jewel had selected together. If that's the way she wanted it, then that's the way it would be, he decided. He would confine his energies to his music and let Jewel live her life.

"I didn't mean to lay my troubles on you, Don," Jewel confessed softly. "It—you're just so easy to talk with."

"I've been where you are, Jewel. My second wife, Linda, and I had similar problems with my son. He hated her on sight. It took time but I had to decide that if I wanted to preserve my marriage, I had to put my cards on the table with my son."

"What was the turning point for you?" she asked.

"I don't know, really, I guess it was when I realized that one day my son would be out on his own, living his life. If I sat back and allowed him to dictate my life, I knew I wouldn't have one. I slowly began to understand that it wasn't so much that he hated Linda, but that he was afraid of losing me to someone else."

Jewel stared at her partially eaten lunch. "It's just that Dani's been through so much in the past year. First her father and I break up, then we move to a new neighborhood, she has to change schools and make new friends. I just don't know if I can add any more to what she's already had to deal with."

"You're going to have to decide sooner or later. And whether you believe it or not, kids are a lot more resilient than we give them credit for."

"Thanks," she said softly. She sighed. "Enough of my problems." She forced herself to smile. "We're supposed to be conducting business."

"You're absolutely correct. But," he added, "if you ever need to talk, don't hesitate."

"I'll keep that in mind."

After taking him on a tour of the development site, Jewel returned with Don to his office, where he readily signed the preliminary agreement.

"I'll be in touch after the holidays," Don said. "I'm taking the family down to Florida until the first of the year."

"How wonderful. Have a great time."

"You do the same. And good luck with everything. I'm sure you'll make the right decision. If your instincts for your personal life are as good as they are for business, you won't have any problem." He walked her to the door. "See you next year. And don't forget what I said."

"I won't," she smiled warmly. "And thanks again."

After her meeting with Don, Jewel decided to cut her day short. Suddenly, the holiday spirit had captured her. With Christmas only a week away, there were still so many things she had to do, and the first thing on her agenda was buying something special for Taj. He deserved it.

Jewel spent the next few hours selecting the perfect gifts for her loved ones. She'd found an exquisite jade brooch for her mother, a brilliant piece of African artwork for her eclectic sister, Amber, a CD player for Dani, a silk scarf for Tricia, and for Taj, an original collection of early compositions by Miles Davis.

Satisfied with her purchases, she hurried to the outdoor parking lot and deposited her treasures in the trunk of her car just as the first sprinkles of snow began to fall.

There was still so much to be done, she thought, as

she put the car in gear. She wanted—needed—this holiday to be special. But even as she thought of the plans still to be made, her heart tripped with foreboding. She'd have to prepare Danielle for meeting Taj. She wanted this Christmas season to be extra special and she dare not risk an ugly scene on Christmas day.

Don Hamilton's words of advice ran through her head. "Put your cards on the table." That's when she decided on a plan.

Several times Taj reached for the phone, intending to call Jewel. But each time, he stopped. He'd debated with himself for hours over the scene that he'd witnessed earlier, and had eventually come to the conclusion that he knew Jewel well enough to know that she was not the type of woman who played both sides of the fence. His ego and his pride had temporarily blinded him to that fact. Jewel meant too much to him to let his irrational feelings get in the way of their relationship. They had enough to deal with, without him adding to it with his unfounded assumptions.

Taj reached for the phone again, but at the last minute he changed his mind. He was never one for discussing private matters over the phone. Today would be no exception.

With newfound resolve, he called the local cab service, grabbed his coat, and took the ten minute ride to Jewel's office.

Tricia had just finished inputting the agency's most recent sales figures into the computer when Taj walked through the door.

When Tricia saw him, her pulse immediately quickened. Over the past few months, her secret attraction to Taj had grown by leaps and bounds. Each time that she saw Taj and Jewel together her heart constricted as if the very life was being squeezed out of it.

She knew Jewel was trying her best to keep Taj a secret from everyone, including her. That fact irked Tricia to no end. Taj was the kind of man that deserved to be flaunted. If only she had a chance, she would show him how he deserved to be treated.

"Taj," Tricia greeted with an inviting smile. She stood up and instantly wished that she'd worn something more revealing, rather than her winter white knit pantsuit. The full jacket and flowing pants successfully hid the voluptuous curves beneath. "What a pleasant surprise."

Taj stepped fully into the warm reception area. "Hi, Tricia," he said in a slow, lazy voice. He returned her smile and her stomach did a slow somersault. "I thought I'd surprise Jewel. Is she here?"

"No, she's not," Tricia replied almost too enthusiastically.

"Then I guess the surprise is on me." He tried to laugh it off but it came out hollow. "Do you know where she is?"

Tricia intentionally avoided his gaze. "I would guess she's still with Don Hamilton. They had lunch together." Her eyes finally met his. "I can't imagine what's taking her so long. They've been gone for hours."

Taj fought the urge to allow his imagination to shift into overdrive. "I see," he said tightly. "Maybe the weather is holding her up," he said, giving himself an explanation as well as Tricia.

"You're probably right," Tricia replied. "Well, I was getting ready to lock up, but I'd be happy to stay awhile if you want to wait."

"That won't be necessary. I'll catch up with her later. It wasn't important." He turned to leave.

Tricia thought quickly. "Can I give you a lift? The weather is starting to look pretty bad."

Taj turned back in Tricia's direction and hesitated a moment. "Sure. I'd appreciate it. That's if it's not out of your way."

"No problem. I'm in no real hurry. Let me just get my coat."

By the time Taj and Tricia had left the office, the ground was blanketed with at least an inch of brilliant white snow, making walking treacherous.

"My car is around the corner," Tricia said, pulling her wool coat collar up around her neck. She took a step and slipped. Taj instinctively grabbed her around the waist to steady her.

"That was a close one," he grinned.

"I wouldn't have made a pretty sight sprawled out on the ground," she laughed back, immensely enjoying the pressure of his arm around her waist.

He gave her an appraising once over, taking in her full head of bouncy auburn curls, brown eyes and full pouty lips.

"You would make a lovely sight no matter what," he assured her simply.

"There's my car over there," Tricia pointed, her words sounding breathless to her own ears.

Behind the wheel she tried to recover her composure, but Taj's close proximity only heightened her anxiety.

"I'm over on Auburn Avenue and South Street," Taj offered as he buckled up.

She nodded knowingly as she maneuvered the sky blue Jetta into traffic.

By this time, the snow was coming down so heavily that visibility was near zero. They crawled through the streets at no more than ten miles per hour. A trip that would have normally taken ten minutes, took a half hour.

"I usually see you with a music case," Tricia commented, needing to break the long silence that hung between them. "What do you play?"

"Saxophone," he said with a hint of pride.

"Really? Are you any good?" she teased.

Taj chuckled. "Some people think so. As a matter of fact, I just got a full-time gig playing with the band at Rhythms." His voice took on an empty tone. "That was one of the reasons why I stopped by the office. I wanted to tell Jewel. She was the one who suggested that I check out some of the local clubs," he added, realizing that he'd said too much. Although Tricia had seen him and Jewel together, it was never outside of the office and they always maintained a sense that his visits were business related. However, Taj sensed that Tricia knew exactly what was going on, whether Jewel wanted to believe that or not. He looked off toward the swirling snow.

"I'm sure she'll be sorry she missed you," Tricia said.

"Hmm."

"Well, I hope you'll accept congratulations from me." She smiled.

"Of course. Thanks."

Tricia swallowed. "I'd love to hear you play sometime."

"I start tomorrow night. You're welcome to stop by. Bring your boyfriend."

She flashed a tremulous smile. "I'll be by myself." She paused for effect. "I'm not seeing anyone right now."

"Sometimes that's best," he replied absently. He peered out of the snow-encrusted window. "Well, this is where I get off."

Tricia pulled the car to the curb. Taj turned to her and caught a look of longing in Tricia's eyes that startled him with its intensity. Maybe he was just imagining things he reasoned. "Thanks for the ride, Tricia. I really appreciate it. Maybe I'll see you at the club." He reached for the door handle and felt Tricia's hand on his thigh.

"Wait, Taj," she said softly.

Taj looked down at her hand then upward to her eyes. Before he had a chance to respond, Tricia leaned over and kissed him full on the mouth.

"I've wanted to do that for a long time," she said breathlessly. Her eyes roved longingly over his face as she silently prayed that he would somehow feel the same way.

Taj's jaw clenched. He clasped her shoulders in his hands. "Listen, Tricia," he began gently, "I'm in love with someone, and I wouldn't want to mess that up."

"Jewel," she said in a flat voice.

He nodded. "She means a lot to me, Tricia." As the words came out, he realized the truth in them more than ever.

"We could be good for each other," she nearly pleaded. "I know we could."

Damn. What had he walked into? "Tricia, please." He shook his head as he spoke. "I'm sorry, but it just couldn't work. Jewel is too important to me."

"It'll never work between you and Jewel," Tricia cried, struggling against her tears. "Else she wouldn't hide her relationship with you."

That jab hurt more than he wanted to admit. "I'm sorry Tricia," Taj said gently. "I hope that this incident won't interfere with your work. We can just put it aside and go on from here." He opened the door. "Thanks for the ride. Drive carefully." He gave her a parting smile and darted for the doorway.

Tricia sat for several moments after Taj had entered his building. She was trembling all over. She kept reliving the feel of his lips against hers. It wouldn't end here, she determined. It couldn't. She firmly believed that, given time, Taj would realize that he and Jewel would never last and that only she could love him like he deserved. If only there was a way to rush the inevitability . . .

Taj stepped into his apartment and took a shuddering, relieved breath. The last thing he had expected was a declaration of love from Tricia! He shook his head in disbelief, pulled off his coat and tossed it on the chair. What was he going to tell Jewel? He paced across the hardwood floor. *Nothing.* He wouldn't tell Jewel a thing about this. It would just make things very uncomfortable for everyone. Tricia was a sensible woman. Obviously she thought there was a clear path or else she would have never come on to him like that. He ran his fingers through his dreds, tossing them behind his ears. "I just hope I handled it right," he said out loud.

Jewel eased her BMW into the garage, then quickly unloaded her purchases and stashed them away from Dani's prying eyes. She entered the house through the door that connected the garage to the house.

"Dani! I'm home." Jewel put down her purse and hung up her coat on the brass coatrack.

Dani emerged from the living room looking dreamy-eyed and yawning. "Hi," she mumbled. "I fell asleep on the couch. The last thing I remember was Oprah introducing a woman who was acquitted of stabbing her husband by blaming it on PMS." She yawned again.

"Hmm. Heavy topic. I think I saw that one. How was your day?"

"Not bad. We had a Spanish exam, but I know I aced it."

"Don't you always? Language and every other subject just come naturally to you."

Danielle had skipped grades twice. At fifteen, she was already a senior in high school. She looked and spoke like a twenty year old. That was one reason it was so difficult for Jewel to remember that Dani was biologically still a girl. Intellectually, Dani had the mind of an adult, but emotionally she was still a child in many respects.

"I suppose," Dani shrugged dismissively. "Ma," she began.

Jewel turned toward her, a questioning smile on her lips. "Yes?"

"I just wanted to apologize about this morning. I was way out of line."

"It's all right, angel. I know it's hard sometimes." Jewel kissed Dani's cheek and stroked her hair.

"Yeah. Maybe it was PMS or something," she joked.

Jewel laughed softly. "May-*be*. Worse things have been known to happen."

"Is it all right if I spend the night at Kim's house? Today was the last day of school for the Christmas break. Her mother said it was fine with her."

"So that's what that apology was all about. Trying to soften me up," Jewel chided playfully.

"Oh, Ma. Come on."

"Sure you can go. Do you want to eat first?"

"No. I'll have dinner over there. I think Kim's ordering pizza."

Jewel thought of her impending free evening. "In that case I think I'll go out, myself, for a while," Jewel said, thinking of an uninterrupted evening with Taj.

"Are you going to aunt Amber's house?"

"No. Believe me, I can wait to see my dear sister on Christmas and not a minute before."

They both laughed. Amber Sinclair was a bundle of nervous energy. Anytime she was in your presence for more than ten minutes you began to feel as though you'd been on a wild roller coaster ride.

"So, where are you going?" Dani asked as she walked toward the hall closet.

"Maybe I'll take in a movie, or do some Christmas shopping. This place could use some cheering up."

"Well, have fun." Dani retrieved her coat from the closet.

"Don't you need your overnight bag?" Jewel asked.

"Already packed," Dani grinned, pulling the large tapestry bag out of the closet.

Jewel shook her head in amusement. "See you tomorrow."

"Bye."

As soon as Dani had departed, Jewel dialed Taj's number and prayed that the answering machine wouldn't pick up.

"Hello?"

The simple sound of his voice traveled through her like a good brandy, warming her thoroughly.

"Taj. It's me, Jewel."

"Hey baby," he crooned. "I was hoping that you'd call."

Her heart skipped in relief. "I'm free tonight. Feel like some company?"

"I can't think of anything I'd like better," he said in a decidedly intimate voice.

Jewel felt tingles creep through her veins like a thief in the night. "I can be there in an hour."

"I'll be waiting."

Jewel took a quick shower and selected a brand-new

set of lingerie that she'd ordered from a catalog. She dabbed Taj's favorite body oil, Volumpte, behind her ears, her wrists and all of the very private places that never remain private with Taj. She selected a canary yellow silk shirt and matching straight-legged pants. She accented the outfit with a wide, soft brown and gold scarf which she draped around her hips, leaving the loose ends to trail at her right side, and covered her feet in ankle length calfskin boots.

Jewel took a final look in the full-length mirror, ran a comb through her precision haircut and dabbed her lips with coral lipstick. Satisfied, she hurried downstairs, grabbed her coat and was about to walk out of the door, just as the phone rang.

She hesitated, debating on whether or not to answer. It could be important, she concluded. She quickly crossed the gleaming wood floors and picked up the phone on the fourth ring.

"Hello," she answered in a rush.

"Sounds like I caught you at a bad time?" responded the voice that instantly unnerved her.

"Steven."

"You remember," he chuckled sarcastically. "How are you, Jewel?"

"Fine, thank you," she answered in a strained voice. She hadn't heard from her ex-husband in nearly six months. And she especially didn't want to hear from him now. "What is it, Steven? I'm in a hurry."

"Then I guess I'll get right to the point. I'll be in town next week and I want to spend some time with Dani, take her shopping, whatever she wants."

Jewel blinked back her disbelief. "You what?" she exploded. "How dare you call here as though nothing has happened and casually ask to see your daughter," she railed, completely losing the control she struggled to maintain. "Where have you been for the last six months of her life?"

"I know it's been a while, but I wanted the dust to settle first," he said in the cool patronizing tone that she despised. "Are you saying that I can't see her?" he asked calmly.

She knew that tone all too well. Steven was ready to go for the jugular. If it took wearing her down in anyway he saw fit, he'd do it to get what he wanted.

Jewel swallowed. This was the last thing she needed. Tonight she planned to tell Taj that she wanted him to meet Dani to break the ice before Christmas then ask if he'd like to share Christmas dinner with them. Now, Steven pops out of the woodwork. His reappearance in Dani's life was sure to ruin any chance that Taj and Dani would hit it off. But she couldn't, in good conscience, refuse to let Steven see his daughter. He may have been a bastard of a husband but he loved Danielle and was always good to her.

"Jewel? Are you there?"

"Yes," she said weakly. "When did you want to see her?"

"I'll be driving down to New York on Monday evening. With Christmas being next Sunday, I wanted as much time as possible."

"Will you be coming alone?" she asked cattily, unable to resist the barb.

Steven let out a hearty laugh. "Come on, Jewel, what kind of man do you think I am?"

"It's best if I don't answer that question, Steven."

His joviality quickly changed. He said in a menacing voice, "Let's not dredge up old soil. If you were half the woman you pretended to be, we wouldn't be having this conversation."

Jewel bit back a response, knowing that retaliation

was futile. Steven would just dig and dig at her emotions until she was raw. She forced calm into her voice.

"I'll have to speak with Dani first and see what she says."

"I can't imagine that she wouldn't want to see me," Steven replied with his usual confidence.

"I've got to go, Steven. Where can you be reached?"

He gave her the number of the hotel he'd registered in. "Are you planning on the big, family Christmas dinner, as usual?"

"Yes."

"I hope I'm invited," he taunted.

"Good-bye, Steven."

"I'll be expecting your call Monday night." He broke the connection.

Jewel's hands were shaking when she finally replaced the receiver. What was she going to do? Burning tears of frustration threatened to overflow. She blinked them back and took deep, cleansing breaths.

Mindlessly, she made her way to the garage and headed, at a snail's pace, to Taj's apartment.

Jewel plastered a smile on her face as she stood in front of Taj's apartment door. Taking a deep breath, she rang the bell.

Seconds later the door was flung open and Taj stood before her in all of his magnificence. Immediately, her spirits lifted and her plastered smile took on real life.

He was bare from the waist up, wearing only a pair of faded gray sweatpants that did nothing to camouflage his bulging thighs. His entire upper body formed a perfect V, tapering to a board-flat stomach and narrow hips. His broad chest was clearly defined by his rigid exercise and martial arts regime. The muscles of his chest and forearms rippled like undulating waves as he reached across the threshold and captured her in his embrace.

Painfully slowly, his mouth descended and covered hers, tentatively at first, and then deepening with every beat of her heart. Her lips opened like a blooming flower, receiving the sweet nectar of his kiss.

"I'm sorry about this morning, baby," he whispered against her lips. "It's not my style to issue ultimatums." He took a step back and looked down into her up-turned face without completely letting go of his hold on her.

"Maybe that was the push that I needed," Jewel said softly.

Taj searched her face, then took her hand and walked her to the couch, closing the door behind them.

"Did something happen?" he asked once they were seated. He draped his arm across her shoulders.

"I came to a decision today." She smiled wistfully. "With the help of Don Hamilton."

Taj felt his muscles tighten at the mention of Hamilton's name. "Really. Who's Don Hamilton?" he asked as if he didn't know.

"He's a new client. I thought I mentioned him to you." She shook her head. "Anyway, he's buying that abandoned property. We had lunch today, and before I knew it, I was telling him about my problems with Dani. I came to find out, he went through the same thing with his son and his second wife." Jewel looked deep into Taj's eyes. She took his hand in both of hers. "He said that I had to put my cards on the table and that soon Dani would be on her own and my life would be mine again."

She stroked his cheek and he captured her hand and held it against his lips. "I decided that I want you to meet Dani—before Christmas—and come what may, I'll deal with it."

He kissed her palm. "I guess I owe Don Hamilton a favor," he said, realizing what a fool he'd been to have been jealous of the man. At least he wouldn't have to make that confession to Jewel.

"I don't want to ever lose you, Taj."

"You won't. I promise you that." He leaned closer and lightly kissed her eyes, her cheeks, her lips, then trailed downward to her neck, causing a soft moan to break through her parted mouth. All the while his deft fingers unbuttoned the tiny white buttons of her shirt to expose the satiny skin beneath.

Taj buried his head deep between the swell of her breasts as his own breathing became one with the rapid beat of her heart. He peeled away the lacy yellow bra, slipping it beneath the full, heavy breasts causing the tender mounds to jut out before him, taunting him to take each one in turn.

The hot and cold contact of his mouth made Jewel cry out with shocking pleasure, his own deep moans of longing blending with hers in perfect harmony.

"I've missed you, Jewel," he groaned against her breast, his warm mouth encompassing the hardened bud.

Jewel's eyes slammed shut, her head involuntarily dropped back as she clasped her fingers behind his head, urging him further.

Skillfully, almost magically, he slid her blouse from her shoulders and down her arms, never once ceasing his assault of her heated body.

The force of his body edged her down onto the couch. Taj kneeled beside her, his dark eyes raking over her, continuing to stoke the flames of passion that raged within. Slowly, Taj removed the last remnants of her clothing until she lay bare and beautiful before him.

He stood up and loosened the tie at the waist of his

pants. Jewel reached out and finished what he had begun. Her breath caught in her throat as the full power of his virility loomed before her.

Gently Taj lowered himself above her, resting the full force of his weight on his hands. "It's been too long, baby," he said softly. He lowered his head. His mouth teasingly caressed her lips. The silky strands of his hair brushed her cheek, sending tingles of electricity ripping through her.

"Taj," she cried, as the initial moment of union broke through the final barrier.

Jewel's long, slender fingers dug into his back as Taj buried himself deep within the liquid fire that bathed him, enveloped him. Together they found the perfect, age-old rhythm that held them captive within and around each other.

To Jewel, the act of being with Taj was more glorious than with any man she'd ever known. He, with every word, every breath, every movement, made her feel worthwhile, needed, and truly loved for the first time in her life.

Jewel was everything Taj had ever wished for or dreamed about. He wanted to give her more than just physical love. He wanted to give her all of himself—the best that he could be. She made him feel that he could move mountains. And with her at his side, he knew that he could.

The snow continued to swirl, buffeting all in its path, seeming to summon the forces of nature within the confines of the torrid room. Jewel and Taj merged with the heavens, building in tempo with the beat of the howling winds. Nature released an outpouring of purity that exploded between them in crystalline synchronism.

***

They found their way to the enclosed area that Taj had sectioned off for his bedroom. On the king-sized bed, they lay nestled in each other's embrace, quietly relishing the afterglow of their loving.

Taj tenderly brushed the damp tendrils of hair from Jewel's face. "I have some good news," he said softly into her hair.

Her eyes fluttered open and rested on his face. "What? Tell me."

"I got that job today."

Jewel sprung up and then planted herself solidly atop of Taj. "Really? That's fabulous. Where? When?" she rushed on.

"Over at Rhythms on State Street."

"Nick Hunter's place?" she asked with renewed enthusiasm.

"The very one," he grinned.

"I love that place *and* the music," she exclaimed.

"You know Nick?"

"As a matter of fact, I do. I helped him locate that space and connected him with the designer who did the layout."

"No kiddin'. I should have mentioned your name. Maybe he would have upped the pay scale," Taj joked.

Jewel tapped him playfully on the head. "You got this job on your own, without any name dropping. Why didn't you tell me that's where you were going?"

"Well, I didn't want to get my hopes up or yours."

"When are you going to realize just how talented you are? Your music is about as close to heaven as you can get." Then she smiled wickedly. "Except for your other talents. Now that's heaven." She kissed him solidly on the lips.

"You think so, huh?" he said, grabbing her bottom and pressing her firmly against his growing arousal. "You ain't seen nothin' yet."

* * *

Tricia sat alone in her apartment, curled up on the sofa, stoically drinking a glass of wine.

She couldn't seem to shake the vision of Taj out of her head. The harder she tried, the worse it became. Maybe if she just had another chance to talk with him she could make him see the light. She sighed heavily and took another sip of wine.

She sat straight up as a plan began to materialize. Maybe there was something she could do. She sprung up from the couch and dashed to her bedroom to the small section she used as an office.

Sitting behind her computer she switched it on and brought up the database file. Quickly she scanned the files until she found the name she wanted. Steven Avery.

Taj and Jewel sat at the dining table finishing off the last of the meal they'd prepared together.

"That was delicious," Jewel announced. "If I may say so myself."

"Compliments to the *chefs*," Taj added.

"We make a great team," she said, looking at him with loving eyes.

"I know. And it can only get better with time." Taj sat back and looked squarely at Jewel. "Now that you've been loved and fed, do you want to tell me what's on your mind?"

Jewel shook her head in disbelief. His intuitiveness never ceased to amaze her. No matter how hard she tried to camouflage her emotions, Taj saw through every barrier that she erected.

"Am I that transparent?" she asked, stalling for time.

"Not at all. But I can always sense the tension in your

body even when that gorgeous smile is planted on your lips. You give off vibrations, and I happen to be very attuned to your vibes." He gave her a wink that made her laugh in spite of the seriousness of her dilemma.

"Steven called me this evening," she blurted out. She looked at Taj to gauge his reaction, but got nothing more than an arched eyebrow. "He wants to see Danielle. He'll be in town next week," she added quickly.

"Is that a problem?" Taj asked calmly.

Jewel's shoulders slumped. "Right now it is. When Steven gets Dani back under his fatherly spell, I know it will be nearly impossible for her to accept you in my life." She took a breath. "And then he had the audacity to ask if he was invited to Christmas dinner!"

"I think you're making this more complicated than it is. You made a decision. All you have to do now is follow through. Give Dani some credit, Jewel. Me, too, for that matter," he said evenly.

"You're right," she said with conviction. "And the sooner the better." She looked at him with a gleam in her eye. "Are you free for dinner tomorrow?"

"Let me just check my social calendar." He put his index finger to his temple. "It just so happens that I am totally at your disposal."

Jewel laughed. "Then dinner it is."

Jewel arrived back at her house just after sunrise. Although she knew that Dani wouldn't be back before noon, she wasn't quite ready for Dani to discover that she'd spent the night out. She felt that it was essential that she be a credible role model and exhibit a sense of discreetness about her relationships.

With Dani blooming into womanhood, it was important that she get the right messages. Jewel may not have done a great job with Steven, in Dani's eyes, but she had no intention of making the same mistakes with Taj.

Between the two of them, Taj and Jewel had decided to form a united front with Dani. It was not going to be open season on either of them.

With that notion in mind, Jewel plunged into preparing for the evening. She did a thorough cleaning of the house, which was totally unnecessary, as she always kept the modest home in immaculate condition. Some old habits are hard to break, she thought as she took a final look at her handiwork.

Next on the agenda was planning the meal. She sat down at her antique Queen Anne desk and made a list of the necessary items she needed from the market. As Taj didn't eat red meat, she planned a sumptuous seafood menu with a crab meat, shrimp, and scallop soufflé as the main course. She wanted everything to be perfect.

It was nearly noon by the time Jewel returned from the market. Loaded down with packages, she was happy to find her daughter home. Dani hurried to the door when she heard her mother.

"Wow, Christmas dinner shopping already?" Dani asked as she helped bring in the array of bags.

"Something like that," Jewel replied.

"Hi, Mrs. Avery," Kim greeted as Dani and Jewel entered the kitchen.

"Hello, Kim," Jewel responded to the pretty teenager. "How are you?"

"Fine. My mom put us out," Kim complained. "Hope you don't mind me hangin' out over here for a while."

"Of course not. You know you're always welcome." Jewel began putting the groceries away. "As a matter of fact, why don't you stay for dinner?" Jewel asked, the beginnings of a plan germinating in her head. If

Kim was around for dinner, she thought, the whole event wouldn't appear so formal and no one would be put on the spot.

"Love it," Kim responded enthusiastically.

"Just let your mother know."

Kim shrugged. "Believe me, she won't care," she said, her voice taking cynical edge. "Some guy she's dating is coming over and I know she won't want me around." The hurt was so evident in Kim's voice that Jewel turned quickly toward Kim to see her looking dejectedly at her sneakers. Dani had a comforting hand on Kim's shoulders.

Jewel took a cautious step forward and tilted Kim's chin up with the tip of her finger. Kim's dark eyes glistened with unshed tears.

"Kim, sweetheart, I know your mother cares about you. Just because she has someone in her life doesn't mean she loves you any less." She intended the statement as much for Kim's benefit as for Dani's.

"It doesn't seem that way," Kim said in a shaky voice. "Whenever *he's* around she barely gives me the time of day. And he acts like I'm in the way."

"Maybe you should give them both a chance, Kim," Jewel said gently.

"For what?" Dani jumped to her friend's defense. "What kind of chance have they given her?"

"Dani!" Jewel admonished.

"Well, it's true," Dani added with a touch of vehemence.

This was not going well, Jewel realized with alarm. Instead of Kim being the support system that she had hoped for Dani, Kim's situation would only complicate her own.

"Maybe you should talk with your mother about how you feel," Jewel said gently.

Kim shrugged. "I guess."

"That's better." Jewel patted Kim's shoulder, then looked at Dani. "Dani, I need to talk with you for a minute." It was now or never, Jewel thought.

Jewel walked through the archway into the living room. Danielle followed moments later.

"What's up?"

"Sit down a minute, angel." Jewel took a deep breath. "There's someone I want you to meet," she began, measuring her words carefully.

Dani tensed. "Who?"

"His name is Taj Burrell."

Dani frowned. "Who's he?"

"Someone who's become very important to me," she said softly.

Jewel saw her daughter's face change expression from bewilderment to anger.

Dani sprung up from her seat. "Well that's just great. Sure, Ma, do what you want. It's your life."

"Danielle," Jewel started.

"I don't want another father," Dani continued.

"Danielle, no one is going to try to take your father's place."

"I don't understand," Dani's voice took on a childish tone. "I don't know why you and daddy can't work things out, Ma," she cried. "I don't want to end up like Kim." She angled her chin in the direction of the kitchen.

"I'd never let that happen, baby," Jewel assured, taking Dani's hand in her own. "I thought you knew me better than that."

Dani pressed her lips together and turned her head away.

Jewel pressed forward. "Taj will be here for dinner tonight and he's anxious to meet you. I've told him wonderful things about you."

"Where'd you meet him?" Dani asked in a flat voice.

"At my office. I helped him find an apartment."

"Mmm." She kept her gaze from Jewel. "What does he look like?"

Jewel grinned despite herself. "Why don't you be the judge of that this evening?"

Dani heaved a sigh and nodded.

"There's one more thing, Dani."

"I know, be nice."

"That too, but that's not what I meant." Jewel took a deep breath. "Your father called last night."

Dani whirled around, her eyes lit up like two Roman candles. "He did! What did he say? Where is he?"

"He's still in Chicago, but he'll be here next week." She paused. "He wants to see you."

Dani's smile nearly broke Jewel's heart, knowing how Steven had literally abandoned Dani. Yet she still worshipped the ground he walked on.

"I can't wait," Dani gushed. "I'm gonna tell Kim." She ran out of the room before Jewel could say anything else.

All Jewel could do now was hope for the best.

Steven put the last of his clothing in his suitcase. The phone call from Tricia the previous night had put a new spin on things.

So his dear ex-wife was sleeping around with some long-haired musician who was young enough for Dani. What kind of an example was Jewel trying to set? He may not have been a lot of things, he admitted grudgingly, but he was always a decent father. The last thing he wanted for his daughter was to see a string of men running in and out of her mother's life.

It was apparent that he was going to have to step back into the picture. He'd even go so far as to sue

Jewel for custody if that's what was needed. He'd do whatever he had to in order to protect Danielle.

Jewel had obviously gone over the edge after the divorce and this was her way of asserting her independence. "We'll just see about that," he said.

He snatched up his coat and his suitcase and headed for the door. He'd put a stop to this quick, fast and in a hurry.

"I spoke to Dani," Jewel said to Taj over the phone.

"And?"

"It went better than I expected. No histrionics."

Taj laughed. "Great. I told you to give your daughter some credit. What time do you want me there?"

"About five?"

"Sounds good." Then he remembered. "I have to be at the club tonight at seven."

"Hmm. That doesn't give us much time."

He thought about some options. "How about this? We have an early dinner and then you all come to the club and hear me make my debut."

Again Jewel was struck by Taj's sensitivity and smiled brightly. "Perfect! Then why don't you come over at four, help me with dinner and get acquainted. We can eat about five-thirty."

"No problem. I'll be there. And Jewel . . ."

"Yes?"

"Don't worry. I hear the anxiety in your voice. Believe me, if I can charm you, I can charm anybody."

"Gee, thanks," she laughed.

"See you later, baby." He hung up.

Jewel replaced the receiver, a contented smile framing her lips. She sighed softly. She really did love that man. She turned away from the phone and walked to the bottom of the staircase.

"Dani! Kim!"

"Yes!" they replied in unison.

"Come down, I have some errands I need for you to run."

"Listen, girls," Jewel began when they'd both arrived in the kitchen. "I need you two to go down to the mall and pick up some holiday decorations."

"Okay," Dani agreed.

"And," Jewel continued, "I have a treat for you young ladies. We're going out for a night on the town after dinner."

"Where?" they squealed in unison.

"To a club called Rhythms."

"You're taking us to a club, Mrs. Avery?" Kim asked in astonishment.

"Yes, missy. A friend of mine is playing there tonight for the first time. I want to give him some moral support."

"Who?" Dani asked, her face clouding over.

"Taj."

"He's a musician?" Dani asked, plainly surprised. Jewel nodded.

"What does he play?" Dani asked.

"The sax."

"Oh man, sax players are so cool," Kim said.

"Well you'll both get to meet him in a few hours. He's coming for dinner."

"Mrs. Avery," Kim teased, giving her a sidelong glance.

"Don't 'Mrs. Avery,' me," Jewel tossed back with a smile. "Come on you two. I want to get this house in a festive mood. So hurry up."

After Danielle and Kim had left for the mall, Jewel took a moment to assess the situation. Although Dani was unusually quiet after the news, everything was turning out better than she'd expected. Things were going to work out just fine. She hoped.

The telephone call replayed in Tricia's mind. Calling Steven Avery was a desperate move. At the time, she'd felt compelled. Now all she felt was guilt. Even though Steven had sworn to her that he'd never reveal what she'd told him, her conscience still nagged at her. Steven had sounded furious. She wanted to talk with Taj before things got out of hand. But then again, maybe she should just leave things alone, yet something told her, she'd made a big mistake.

By the time that Kim and Dani had returned from the mall, the aroma of dinner filled the air.

"Smells good, Ma," Dani said.

"Why, thank you," Jewel answered, relieved at Dani's casual tone of voice. "Were you able to get everything?"

"Yep. We went to this really great store with all sorts of African art and stuff. I thought we could do something a little different this year."

"Like what?" Jewel asked with interest, knowing that Dani had an innate talent for creativity.

"Decorate in kente colors for Christmas. Maybe we could carry it through to Kwanzaa. It might be nice."

"Sounds fine with me. Maybe Taj could help," Jewel offered. "He celebrates Kwanzaa."

"I see. Taj seems to do everything," Dani said, her tone sarcastic.

Kim poked her in the ribs. "Chill," she said through the corner of her mouth.

Dani sucked her teeth. "Come on. Let's get busy."

She snatched up the bags and marched off to the living room.

Jewel watched Dani's departure and her spirits slowly sunk.

Kim lingered behind. "Mrs. Avery?"

"Yes, Kim," Jewel sighed.

Kim looked over her shoulder to see if Dani was out of earshot. "Me and Dani were talking and, well, she's real upset about meeting your . . . friend. Even though she's trying to hide it."

Jewel pursed her lips as she noted Dani wasn't hiding it well. "Could you tell me why? I had really hoped that she was all right with this."

"She thinks things are gonna be different."

Jewel sat down on the stool at the counter. "Different how?"

"Well, like how things are between me and my mother. And"— Kim lowered her eyes—"she still wants you and her father to get back together."

Jewel sighed and patted Kim's shoulder. "Thanks, Kim. I'm sure everything will work out for the best. Go on and help Dani."

Jewel watched Kim depart, but before she had the opportunity to think about what she'd been told, the doorbell rang. Instinctively she checked the overhead clock in the kitchen. Taj was an hour early, she mused. Her pulse beat faster as she turned toward the living room.

She was on her way to the door, but Dani beat her to it. Instead of the subdued greeting that she'd expected to hear, the screams of joy from Dani caused Jewel to race into the foyer.

Steven looked over his daughter's head, as she held him in a bear hug embrace.

"Hello, Jewel," Steven said as though standing in her

living room, unannounced, was the most ordinary thing in the world.

Jewel felt as if she'd been slammed against a brick wall. She took a deep breath, willing the trembling in her body to cease. She took one step forward and then another until she stood no more than a foot away.

The look of absolute adoration glowing from Dani's face was almost more than Jewel could stand.

"Steven," she said in a flat monotone, her eyes defiant and cold. "I wasn't expecting you today," she added, enunciating every syllable.

Steven's lips curled into a sheepish grin as he gave Dani a kiss on the cheek. He stepped out of her embrace and over to Jewel. Jewel's heart thudded madly.

Steven bent down and kissed her chastely on the lips. She did everything she could not to visibly cringe at the contact.

"You know me, Jewel, when the spirit hits me, I just go with it." His grin widened. "You, on the other hand, were never so creative or impulsive," he said in a voice so low only she could hear the mocking words. "Maybe that's what our problem was."

Jewel stood stiffly before Steven wondering if Dani could feel the tension and hostility that snapped and sparked between them.

Jewel took a step back. "We're—I'm expecting a guest for dinner, Steven. I don't think this is a good time."

Dani quickly jumped into the conversation, took her father's arm and looked imploringly into his eyes. "Stay, Daddy. Please. There's plenty of food." She turned to Jewel. "Ma?" She hadn't heard from her father in six months and she wanted him to share Christmas more than anything.

Jewel swallowed hard, knowing that the minutes were ticking away. If she said no, she'd immediately be seen as the heavy. If she gave in, there was sure to be a fiasco when Taj arrived. She was trapped.

"Fine," she said finally. "Stay. But just for dinner." She turned away, halting any further discussion, and almost ran up the stairs to her bedroom.

Leaning against her closed bedroom door, she shut her eyes and tried to calm her rapid breathing. Her thoughts raced in confusion. What in the world was she going to do? And what was Steven doing here nearly three days early? This was the type of nightmare that only happened in romance novels and soap operas— not to real people!

Taj put his sax in its carrying case and reached in the closet for his jacket. He'd decided to wear all black for his debut at the club. He checked his watch. Three-fifteen. If he left now, he'd reach Jewel's house right on schedule.

All night he'd struggled again with the notion of telling Jewel about his encounter with Tricia. Again he'd decided against it. There was no need to stir up trouble.

He put on his jacket and loosened an extra button on his shirt. Feeling confident about his appearance, he picked up the small bouquet of flowers that he'd purchased for Jewel. He'd debated about getting something for Danielle but thought that it would appear that he was coming on too strong. He really wanted to make a good first impression on her. So much hinged on how she would react to him.

He took a deep breath, and grabbed his coat and his sax case. "It's show time," he said to his reflection in the hallway mirror.

Just as he opened the door, the phone rang. He didn't have time for a conversation. He'd let the machine pick it up then call in for his messages later. With a dismissive wave of his hand, he closed the door behind him.

Jewel listened to Taj's phone ring until the answering machine clicked on. She hung up. There was no point in leaving a message. It was too late now to warn him. Was there any chance of a freak earthquake? she wondered morosely.

She stood at the top of the staircase, listening to Danielle, Kim, and Steven engaged in animated conversation below. Jewel was so nervous, she nearly fell down the staircase when the doorbell chimed.

"I'll get it," Dani called out.

Before Jewel had the presence of mind to react, Dani had the door opened. Jewel suddenly felt as if everything was moving in slow motion. She stood stock still on the stairs as Taj and Dani met for the first time. She wished she could see Dani's expression.

"Hi. You must be Dani," Taj said. "You look a lot like your mother." He gave her his most engaging smile.

Dani felt her cheeks flame, and she couldn't find her voice.

"Dani," Jewel said, walking briskly toward the door. "You're letting all of the cold air into the house."

"Sorry," Dani mumbled.

Jewel walked closer to Taj and he immediately saw the panic in her hazel eyes as they darted between him, Dani, and the living room. "Come in, Taj."

"These are for you," he said softly, giving her the bouquet of flowers. He stepped across the threshold as Steven rose from the couch and turned in his direction. If he thought Dani looked like her mother, that idea was swiftly eliminated. Even at a brief glance there was no denying that this was Dani's father. Steven Avery and Danielle bore a striking resemblance from the same chiseled features, wide eyes, to the strong chin defined by an unmistakable cleft.

Taj crossed the foyer in long measured strides until he was within breathing distance of Steven. He stuck out his hand. "Taj Burrell."

"Steven Avery," came the modulated response.

If Steven expected to spark a reaction at the mention of his name, he didn't get one, Jewel noted in silent pleasure. The hard set to Steven's chin was a familiar indication that he was ticked off by that fact.

"I've heard a lot about you," Taj said evenly, looking Steven straight in the eye.

Steven's eyebrow's arched. "Is that right?" He released the hand that gripped his. "I can't say the same."

Taj shrugged nonchalantly. "It happens," he smiled. "I guess it all depends on the level of communication."

Steven looked like he wanted to explode. But before he could toss back a response, Taj turned his attention toward Jewel who had watched the exchange with her heart lodged firmly in her throat.

"Something smells great," Taj said, flashing Jewel a smile that said, *I have everything under control.* She released a long held breath. "Is there anything I can help you with?" Taj asked, slipping out of his coat, which Dani quickly took from him. Jewel raised her eyebrows in surprise.

She swallowed hard. "There are just a few things left to do, if you wouldn't mind."

"Of course not. Lead the way."

As soon as they were out of range, Jewel nearly burst into tears as she tried to explain her ex-husband's impromptu appearance.

"Oh, Taj, I'm so sorry. I had no idea that Steven was

going to show up today. This is just a mess," she cried
in a strangled voice.

Taj gently pulled her into his arms and brushed comforting kisses across her face. "It's okay, Jewel," he whispered into her hair. "We'll handle it."

"This is not the way it was supposed to happen," she
continued, apparently unmoved by Taj's reassurances.
"Did he say why he's here so early?"

" 'Oh, you know how I am, Jewel,' " she mimicked
in Steven's patronizing tone, " 'when the mood hits me
I just go with it.' "

Taj wanted to laugh at the brilliant rendition, but
fought off the impulse. He eased her away, holding her
at arm's length. He looked down into her brimming
eyes. "We'll get through this, babe. It's no big deal."

"Damn it, Taj!" she shouted, breaking free of his
hold. "He just makes me so furious, as though he has
some right to just saunter in here and commandeer
my life like he's always done."

"Maybe it's about time you stood up to him, Jewel,"
Taj said calmly. "Instead of venting your anger out into
the air, let him hear it once and for all. Otherwise, he'll
always think he can do whatever he wants to you."

She went back into Taj's embrace. "You're right,"
she said weakly, then with more conviction. "You're absolutely right. This has got to stop. Tonight."

Taj smiled broadly. "Now that's the woman I know
you can be."

Taj was the center of attention at dinner. From every
direction he was bombarded with questions; from why
he decided to grow dreds to his musical career. All of
which he graciously answered with a touch of his usual
humor and charm. Surprisingly, most of the questions

came from Danielle, Jewel noticed with a sense of relief. Maybe things would work out after all, she thought.

Steven also noticed the flurry of attention that his daughter directed at Taj. How could Danielle fall for this musician's smooth talk? And what about me? he thought jealously. Although she sat next to him, all of Dani's attention seemed to be on Taj. He'd put a stop to this once and for all.

Steven loudly cleared his throat and pushed his chair away from the table. "Dinner was delicious, Jewel. I see you haven't lost your touch."

"Thank you," she answered graciously.

He leaned toward Jewel, who sat at the head of the table. "I'd like to speak with you briefly before I go," he said in a near whisper, intentionally giving the impression that they still maintained an intimate relationship. His gaze included everyone at the table. "If you'll excuse us for a moment."

Jewel glanced at Taj, who gave her a reassuring wink. She excused herself and walked into the kitchen.

Practically before she could turn around to face him, Steven began his attack. "What the hell is going on around here, Jewel?" he hissed. "You have some *boy* coming in here to see you and your daughter falling all over him as though he were some *god* and you just sit by and allow it! What's happened to you? Have you lost your mind?"

"I haven't, but apparently you've lost yours!" she tossed back with a vehemence that surprised them both. "How dare you come in here and talk to me that way. How I run my life or who I see is not up for discussion, Steven. Taj is not here for you to approve or disapprove of. No matter what you may conclude about him, he makes me happy, which is more than you were ever able to do." Her eyes narrowed into two slits. "Maybe *that* was our problem," she added nastily, giving him a taste of his own venom. "And another thing," she continued, finally feeling the power of her emotions, "this is *my* house. I pay the mortgage. The next time you decide you want to visit, I strongly suggest that you call first."

Her heart was pounding so loudly she thought it would explode. But she refused to back down. Her eyes locked firmly on his as they continued their staring contest.

Steven was so taken aback by Jewel's outburst, he was at a loss for words. Never in their seventeen years of marriage had she ever stood up to him. If he wasn't so furious and, he hated to think it, jealous, he could actually admire her newfound backbone. This wasn't the same woman he left over a year ago. It was obvious that this new man in her life had had a great impact on her.

"This isn't the end of it, Jewel," he said, finally finding his voice. "I won't stand by and have you traipse one man after another in front of my daughter. What kind of example is that? If I have to file a suit to get Dani away from you in order to protect her, then I will." He knew he'd hit home when he saw the lights in her eyes suddenly go dim.

Jewel felt the floor sway beneath her feet.

"I'll prove that you're unfit, Jewel. And you know I'll do whatever I have to, to get what I want."

Jewel's fury rose again. "What is it that you want, Steven? Do you want me to always be the meek, subservient woman that you married? Do you want me to never have love again? Do you want to make sure that no one else ever cares about me? Are you that selfish, Steven? You don't want me, but you don't want anyone else to have me. Fine. If it's a fight you want, then it's a fight you're going to get. I'm not backing down from you, Steven." She spun away from him, the tears of anger ready to overflow. But she wouldn't give him the satisfaction of seeing her cry. She took a deep breath, and pushed open the kitchen door.

"This isn't over, Jewel," he tossed at her back. "Not by a long shot. You better decide what it is you want; that man or your daughter. Or else I'll be happy to make the choice for you."

Jewel's back stiffened. She pushed through the door and back into the dining room, relieved to see that only Taj remained at the table.

Taj immediately rose when he saw her enter. Although she wore a smile, he knew it was empty. He could feel the pent up tension vibrating around her body, ready to explode.

"Are you all right?" he asked softly.

She nodded. "We'll talk later. Where are the girls?"

"They went upstairs to find something to wear for tonight."

Steven came through the swinging door. They both turned in his direction.

"I guess I'll be going." He stuck out his hand. "It was a pleasure to meet you, Taj. Good luck with your musical career."

Jewel felt nauseous.

"Thank you."

He inclined his head in Jewel's direction. "Jewel, I'll be in touch. Tell Dani I'll pick her up tomorrow around one o'clock."

Taj put his arm protectively around Jewel's shoulder as they watched Steven put on his coat and leave.

Jewel nearly collapsed when the door closed behind Steven. Taj ushered her over to a chair, while taking glances over his shoulder toward the staircase. The last thing Danielle needed to see was her mother falling apart.

He stroked her face as the tears rolled unchecked

down her cheeks. "I didn't want to eavesdrop, so tell me what happened? What did he say to you?"

Jewel sniffed back her tears, her body trembling. "He threatened to take Dani away if I didn't get you out of my life."

"Jewel, listen to me," Taj said gently, brushing away her tears with his thumbs, "I can't let you make a decision like that. I love you. You know that. But I'd never be so selfish as to jeopardize your relationship with your daughter for my sake."

She looked lovingly into his eyes. "I can't back down. You taught me that. This is too important, Taj. If I let Steven threaten me every time he doesn't like something, I'll never have any peace."

"You know I'm behind you a hundred percent, no matter what you decide to do."

Jewel nodded sadly then brightened. "Well, it seems as though Danielle liked you."

Taj smiled. "She's a brilliant girl." He knew that Dani had lavished him with attention, but as dinner progressed her interest became genuine, not flamed by some teenage infatuation. He really believed that they had hit it off.

"I've made up my mind, Taj. If it's a fight Steven wants, then he's got it." She stood up and wiped her eyes. "Now, let's get ready to get out of here before you're late for your opening night." She walked over to the bottom of the staircase. "Dani! Kim! Hurry up or we'll be late. I want to be out of here in the next fifteen minutes."

Jewel turned away to see Taj smiling broadly at her. "What?" she asked suspiciously.

Taj walked right up to her. "You're an amazing woman, Jewel Avery." He lowered his head until his lips brushed hers. "I'm happy that you're mine." His mouth covered hers, tempting her lips open with the force of his tongue. His hands slid up and down her back, the strong fingers kneading out the knots of tension and replacing them with a tingling warmth. She slid her arms around his neck, pulling him closer to her, their bodies melting into one. For those brief moments that they clung to each other, nothing else mattered.

"So, how did you like the show?" Jewel asked, as she stood at the door to Dani's bedroom.

"It was great," she reluctantly admitted. "I didn't even realize that I liked jazz," she grinned. She sat on her bed and looked up at her mother. "Ma?"

"What baby?" Jewel stepped into the room and sat on the edge of the bed.

"You really like him?"

Jewel nodded.

"Well, Taj is all right. I mean, I didn't intend to like him, but I do. He's real. When we were talking at the dinner table he really listened to the things I was saying. He didn't treat me like a kid, but a real person. Even when I tried to trip him up with a bunch of hip hop talk, he was right there with me understanding every thing I said. Even you don't understand half the things I say sometimes." She looked up at her mother with a *you're hopeless* expression. "He just might do you some good," she grinned. She sighed and studied her entwined fingers. "It's just that," she hesitated, "I don't want to neglect Daddy. He's still my daddy." She looked up at her mother and twisted her lips in concentration. "But I guess the most important thing is that *you're* happy."

Jewel moved closer to Danielle. "The important

thing is that we're *both* happy. Taj is a decent man. He cares a great deal about me and it's important to me that you like him, too."

"If I ask you a question, would you tell me the truth?" Dani asked.

"Sure."

"Suppose I didn't like Taj. Would you have kept on seeing him?"

Jewel breathed deeply. "That's a question I've been wrestling with for the past three months. I finally came to terms with it yesterday. If you were really dead set against him, and had legitimate reasons, I wouldn't keep seeing him. But, I just prayed that you were really growing up and would see what a good man he is."

Danielle smiled at her mother's glow as she spoke about Taj. She leaned back on her elbows and eyed her mother skeptically. "How old is Taj?"

"None of your business, young lady," Jewel teased, tweaking Dani on the nose.

"I know he's younger than you, Ma. Come on, tell me. This could be my big break for television. Older woman dating younger man. Daughter tells all, today on *Oprah!*"

"Danielle Nichole Avery! Don't even think about it."

Danielle fell back on her bed in a fit of laughter. "I wonder if they'll pay airfare for friends of the guests?"

Jewel shook her head. "You're impossible. Good night." She gave Dani a kiss on the cheek. "And don't forget, your father is planning on picking you up at one o'clock tomorrow."

"I'll be ready. Kim wants me to go with her downtown in the morning. But we'll be back in time."

"Where is Kim?"

"In the bathroom taking a shower."

"All right. See you in the morning." Jewel closed the door and walked slowly to her room. Taj had been right when he said to give Dani a little credit. She had certainly underestimated her daughter. All things considered, what could have been a fiasco turned out to be a wonderful evening. She was definitely looking forward to Christmas and sharing it with her family and the man she loved.

As soon as she reached her bedroom, she went for the phone and dialed Taj's number. He answered on the third ring.

"Hello?"

"You were wonderful tonight. On stage and off," Jewel said.

"I'm glad you approve," he chuckled. "Listen, it's still early," he coaxed in his most persuasive voice, "why don't you come over?"

She ran the possibility over in her head. The office was closed until after the holidays. Plus, she had no pressing engagements for the next day. Finishing off the night with Taj would be the perfect ending to an almost perfect evening.

"I can't stay long," she hedged.

"I know. It's no problem. But I'd still love to spend some quiet time with you. To celebrate."

"Well, it's eleven-thirty. I can be there by midnight. Kim is here to keep Dani company."

"So I'll see you shortly?"

"I'm on my way."

Jewel went back to Danielle's room and told her that she was going out with Taj for a while. The girls were more than happy to have the house to themselves and were already making plans to stay up all night watching videos before Jewel stepped out of the room.

Steven sat in his hotel suite, silently fuming over the events of the evening. He still couldn't get over the change in Jewel. And to think that she found a younger man to replace him was almost more than he could tolerate. He had to find a way to put a stop to this once and for all. His pride was at stake. He had prided himself on his playboy persona and for others to see Jewel with the likes of that musician, even though they were no longer married, would make Swiss cheese out of his reputation. Besides, Danielle liked him just a little too much.

Well, he'd have his chance with his daughter tomorrow. Jewel may have changed in some respects, but he knew that Danielle was the most important person in her life. If he could convince Dani that her mother was making the wrong decision, his battle would be won without a fight. His daughter adored him and he was confident that she still believed every word he said. He sighed. He didn't relish having to resort to suing for custody although he knew he could make a winning case. However, a victory was not what he really wanted. While he loved and missed Dani, having full custody would put a serious crimp in his own life. Yet he was sure he wouldn't have to go that route. Not after talking with Danielle.

"You handled Steven beautifully," Jewel said, wrapping her arms tightly around Taj's bare waist.

"You didn't do too badly yourself," he returned. "I'm proud of you." He kissed the tip of her nose. "Do you really think Steven is serious about his threat to sue for custody?"

"I wouldn't underestimate him. It may have been a scare tactic, but when Steven is pushed, especially when his ego is at stake, he's liable to do anything."

She released him and turned away. Taj clasped her shoulder and spun her around to face him.

"It's your call, Jewel. Whatever you decide, I'm behind you."

She smiled tightly. "And I love you for it. But I don't want to think or talk about Steven. I'm just so happy that you and Dani hit it off. She really surprised me. I think she surprised herself."

"Dani is really a together young lady. You've done a great job with her, Jewel."

She smiled at the compliment.

"I promised her that she and Kim could come down to the club on Sunday for brunch and hear the band rehearse. I hope that's okay."

Jewel smiled in amazement. "You two really *did* hit it off."

Taj shrugged, the beginnings of a smile tilting his lips. He winked at her. "I told you I was a charmer."

"We'll see about that. The next hurdle is the rest of family—particularly my mother."

"Oooh, the dreaded mother-in-law," he said, twisting his face into a feigned grimace.

They both laughed at the image.

"She's not that bad," Jewel admitted. "Just set in her ways."

"Well"—he brushed her lips with his—"if she produced something as special as you, she can't be all bad."

His warm hazel eyes gently caressed her face, telegraphing the depth of emotion that beat inside of him. Each and every day he realized how much Jewel meant to him, how much he needed her.

Jewel gave him something that no woman had ever been able to give him, a sense of being needed. She filled a void that had been a part of his everyday existence. Before meeting her he'd only lived for his music and the moment. Now, he had really begun to think about the future and a family—permanency. Jewel had become his anchor. Without her, he knew he would be adrift again. And although he'd projected the gallant image, he really couldn't imagine what he would do if she chose to let him go.

He pulled her tightly against him, needing to feel her nearness and force away the shadow of foreboding that he'd struggled to keep at bay. Unceremoniously, he picked her up, cradled her against him and carried her to his bed.

When her body arched and trembled in fulfillment and the last shuddering pitch sprang from his body, he knew that together they could conquer anything.

Jewel sighed and snuggled closer to Taj's warm body. Absolutely perfect, she thought. Maybe one day soon they wouldn't have to settle for stolen moments, but could wake up in each other's arms every morning. They hadn't talked about marriage, specifically, but she knew that she wasn't quite liberated enough to have a live-in relationship. With the lifestyle that Taj was used to living, that may be all that he expected or wanted. It was something that they would have to discuss at some point.

"It's almost two a.m.," he whispered into her tousled hair.

"I know," she replied with a hint of regret filtering through her voice. "I should be getting home."

"I'll turn on the shower for you."

"Are you going to join me?" she asked, turning to him with a wicked gleam in her eyes.

"I guess you don't intend to leave anytime soon," he said in a low voice that vibrated through her veins.

"I wish I didn't have to."

"One day, you won't." He kissed her slowly, stirring the embers that still glowed hot between them. "I promise you that. But until then," he patted her bottom and got up, "it's off to the showers with you."

He popped up out of bed and strode across the hardwood floor, giving Jewel an ample view of what she was leaving behind.

She pulled the sheet up to her chin and sunk deeper into the fluffy pillow. Did he really mean what he said? she wondered. And what exactly did he mean?

Moments later she heard the rush of water and Taj's deep voice humming a tune over the rushing water. She pulled herself into a sitting position, just as the phone rang.

"Taj! Telephone!" she called, but he couldn't hear her. She'd never answered his phone before and she wouldn't start now although she couldn't help but wonder who would be calling at this hour?

On the fourth ring the machine picked up.

"Hi, Taj. It's me, Tricia." Jewel sat as if frozen as the all too familiar voice continued. "I know I shouldn't be calling you, but I just wanted to say that I didn't mean for anything to happen between us yesterday. It just did. I guess it was the only way I could show you how much I cared." Jewel's head began to pound. "I feel foolish. I know I can't face Jewel, not after what I've done. I'm sending in my letter of resignation. There's no way that I can continue to work with Jewel, see the two of you together, and the both of us knowing how I feel. Please take care and I hope that when you think of me, it will be kindly."

Jewel felt as if she were going to faint. *Taj and Tricia. Yesterday. It just happened* . . . What did she mean? Suddenly she didn't want to hear Taj's explanation. She didn't have the strength to stand there and watch him lie, just like Steven had always lied. Like a robot, she found her clothes that were scattered around the room, dressed and was out of the door by the time Taj returned.

She felt as if someone had her by the throat. Jewel struggled for air as she made her way to her car. Behind the wheel she momentarily squeezed her eyes shut and forced herself to calm down long enough to start the engine and get the car onto the darkened streets.

How long had it been going on? her mind screamed in agony. Maybe Tricia was really what Taj needed. Her own life was so complicated. Tricia was young, attractive, single, and didn't have the responsibility of a child.

Her throat constricted. She shook her head and wiped away the tears with the back of her hand. How could she not have known? The question tumbled around in her head clashing viciously against the realities. Taj seemed so sincere. He showed such an interest in Danielle. "He told me he wanted to be a part of my life," she shouted to herself. "The way he made love to me . . . Oh God." The tears streamed down her cheeks unchecked.

She took a shuddering breath. Maybe all the months of secrecy had been too much for him and he just never admitted it, and he turned to Tricia. Or worse, maybe this was just the way Taj was.

Even with all of Steven's infidelities, she had never felt so betrayed as she did now. She thought Tricia was her friend. She thought that Taj loved her totally. How wrong she'd been. And to think that she was willing to do battle with Steven in defense of her relationship with Taj, and all the while he was . . .

A sense of hopelessness settled over her like a blanket as she pulled up in front of her house. All of her dreams seemed to melt away like the snow that ran in puddles on the ground.

***

Taj returned to the bedroom with all the intentions of fulfilling Jewel's earlier request to join her in the shower. The teasing smile on his face dissolved by degrees when he returned to the bedroom alcove.

"Jewel?" He quickly scanned the expanse of the loft. He walked into the enclosed kitchen sure to find her busying herself with something. Nothing.

"What the . . . ?" He ran his hands across his face in frustration. "Why would she leave just like that?" He expelled a breath. It was too late to call her house at that hour. He'd wait until morning—bright and early—and he truly hoped she had something to tell him that would explain her abrupt departure. Confused and annoyed, he stomped back to the bathroom and turned off the steaming shower.

It wasn't until he stretched out on the bed and saw the flashing light of the answering machine that the pieces began to fit together.

By the time that Jewel walked through her door, stripped out of her clothes, and scrubbed her body free of all traces of Taj, her hurt at his betrayal had transformed itself into anger.

She'd been a fool. She'd been taken in by his sweet words and attention. She'd been so starved for affection after her divorce that she was easy prey.

She sat down in front of her vanity and stared at her reflection, angry at herself for being so naive. At her age, she should have known better, been more aware. But what did she know? she thought miserably, some of the self-condemnation ebbing. Steven was the first man she'd ever been with. After the divorce there had been brief, platonic dinners with business associates, but she'd been wary of any relationships because of Danielle. Until Taj. Her throat tightened.

Slowly she rose, suddenly bone weary. She crossed the room, switched off the ringer on her phone and stretched out on top of the bed, not even bothering to turn down the quilt. For several moments she just stared sightlessly up at the ceiling. She flung her arm across her eyes, but it didn't stem the tears from trickling down her cheeks.

For hours she drifted in and out of sleep with images of Taj and Tricia playing havoc with her head. Realizing that sleep was not hers to have, she got up when Danielle's and Kim's laughter drifted to her room. Then reality struck another blow. What would she tell Danielle?

"Ma!" Dani called from downstairs. "Telephone!"

Jewel's heart thumped. It was Taj. She just knew it. He'd try to explain and she didn't want to hear it. But then again, she did.

She walked to her bedroom door and opened it. "Thanks, hon." She retraced her steps and for several seconds she stood staring at the phone. She let out a shuddering breath and snatched up the receiver, ready to administer the verbal lashing that had cemented itself on her tongue.

"Yes," she snapped.

"That's a fine way to greet your mother," Nora Sinclair replied.

Jewel's shoulders slumped and she sat down on the edge of her bed. A flash of disappointment swept through her. She rested her head on the palm of her hand.

"Mom, I'm sorry. I was just getting out of the shower," she lied easily. "How are you?"

"Wonderful. I was just calling to find out if you needed me to do anything for Christmas dinner."

"I can't think of anything," she said in a distant voice. Christmas was the last thing she had on her mind at the moment.

"Are you all right, Jewel? You don't sound like yourself."

"I'm fine," she answered almost too quickly, forcing cheer into her voice. "Maybe a little tired, but I'm fine."

Nora could easily detect the false note of gaiety in her daughter's voice. Jewel never believed that she understood her, but Nora knew her daughters better than they knew themselves, especially Jewel. Maybe this wasn't a good time to share her news. Hopefully Jewel would be in a better mood on Christmas.

"Well dear, if there's anything you need, just call me. I know that no-cookin' sister of yours won't be any help."

Jewel chuckled. Her sister Amber's ineptness in the kitchen was the family joke, although her mother never thought it was very funny. "Ma, be nice."

"No harm intended, but that Amber doesn't have a drop of domesticity in her. No wonder she can't keep a man for a hot minute. She probably starves them to death." Nora laughed lightly.

"Anyway, sweetheart, you take care. You're probably working too hard. Tell that granddaughter of mine to give you a hand. You know how lazy teenagers can be if you're not firm."

"Yes, mother, I know," Jewel said in a singsong voice.

"Ugh, there's that tone that I hate. I'm hanging up. See you next week, sweetie. And Jewel?"

"Yes?"

"This too shall pass," Nora said gently.

Startled, Jewel paused before speaking. "Thanks. Bye, Mom."

* * *

After Nora had hung up the phone, she remembered that she didn't tell Jewel to set an extra place. Oh well, the surprise would do her good.

He didn't even bother to call, Jewel fumed. He probably didn't have any explanation. That was just fine! The hell with him. She wasn't interested in any of his lame excuses anyway. If and when he did call, she would be unavailable. Furious with herself for feeling that momentary sensation of disappointment, and furious at Taj for creating the problem, she stomped out of her room, slamming the door in the process.

She entered the kitchen to find Dani and Kim at the table huddled over enormous bowls of cereal.

"Hey, Ma," Dani greeted with her mouth full.

"Hey, baby. Morning, Kim." She tried to smile but it felt more like a grimace. Thankfully, neither girl seemed to notice.

"How was your date with Taj?" Danielle asked.

Jewel bit down on her lip and turned toward the cupboard. She put the kettle on to boil. "Fine," she said tightly.

Dani and Kim gave each other a quick, "wonder what happened" look.

"If he should call, I'm not in," Jewel said in a tone that left no room for discussion.

Dani's eyes widened in surprise, but she knew her mother well enough to know not to pry.

Jewel pulled open the cupboard door and in an act of defiance she snatched up the jar of coffee, scooped up a heaping teaspoon and dumped it into her cup. Somehow she felt mildly satisfied.

"Ma, is it okay if I go to Kim's house for a while before Daddy comes?"

Damn. She'd forgotten all about Steven. He was the next to last person she wanted to see.

In that same short, snapping tone she replied. "Go ahead. Just be sure to be home in plenty of time. I may go out and won't be here to let your father in."

The girls got up from the table and put their empty bowls in the dishwasher. Dani eased up next to her mother. "Are you all right, Ma?" she asked gently.

Her daughter's concern nearly did her in. She felt the tears that rested just beneath the surface sting her eyes with warning. She swallowed and blinked quickly. "Sure," she answered in a steady voice that surprised her. "You go ahead."

Dani gave her mother a last questioning look, then kissed her cheek. "Um, maybe this isn't a good time to ask, but is it still okay for me and Kim to go to the club tomorrow? If not," she added quickly, "it's no problem."

She'd forgotten that, too. She couldn't very well say no. But of course she could. Dani didn't need to be around him anyway, having one philanderer in her young life was enough. But then again, she really wasn't prepared to explain her sudden change of attitude toward Taj. Denying Dani would only draw attention to a problem that she wasn't ready to handle. She sighed.

"Sure you can go. But don't make it a habit. Understood?"

Dani nodded. "Thanks, Ma. See you later." Dani dashed out.

"Don't forget your keys," Jewel called. She looked up at the kitchen clock. Nine-fifteen. She had absolutely nothing to do today, except think about things she didn't want to think about. The kettle began to whistle in concert with the ringing phone. She felt the hot flush of nerves envelop her. She stood in front of the kitchen phone staring at it as though it were a foreign object. The phone rang for the fourth time and the answering machine, connected to her bedroom phone, clicked on. She ran up the stairs to her room.

"Please leave a message after the tone."

"Jewel, if you're there, please pick up."

Jewel listened to the voice that was still like a song in her heart. She trembled with hurt and anger. But she couldn't—wouldn't pick up the phone, even as the sound of his voice seemed to magically erase the stream of accusations and condemnations that she'd planned. She wasn't willing, emotionally, to allow herself to fall victim to his words of explanation.

He waited several seconds, willing her to pick up the phone. "Please, Jewel, call me."

The pleading sincerity of his voice almost convinced her, but she held her ground.

"We have to talk, Jewel. It's important. I can explain everything. Call me."

"Explain!" she yelled as if he could hear her. "What is there to explain?"

He called three more times within the next two hours, sounding more urgent with each call. Jewel couldn't bear to hear anymore and she certainly didn't want to be home when Steven arrived. What she wanted was to turn back the clock before everything got so ugly. But that was impossible. What she could do was get in her car and drive as far away as possible. At least for a while.

She erased the telltale messages from the machine, put on an old sweatsuit and sneakers, got her coat and went out.

Taj's mood shifted between misery and outrage. If he'd only followed his instincts and told Jewel what had happened with Tricia, none of this would have happened. He could kick himself for being so stupid! Now Jewel thought the worst. He couldn't really blame her. If he'd heard a similar message he would have undoubtedly jumped to conclusions. But at least he would have given her the opportunity to explain. That's what infuriated him the most, the fact that Jewel had so little confidence in him—in their relationship—that she would think he was capable of cheating on her.

He sat down heavily on the couch. Maybe the relationship wasn't all he thought it was. Maybe he'd just wanted it so badly he couldn't see it for what it was. Talk about love being blind.

Well, he wasn't going to run behind her like some lovesick puppy. If she wanted to be stubborn, so could he. He hadn't done anything wrong.

He sprung up from the couch, grabbed his sax case and coat. He needed to get her off of his mind and the only way he knew how was through his music. He'd go over to the club for a while and warm up for the early dinner crowd.

Steven picked up Danielle promptly at one o'clock.

"So, what would you like to do today, sweetheart?" Steven asked as they pulled out of the driveway.

"I could really use some new clothes," she said coyly.

Steven grinned. "Is that right? So I guess it's the mall, then."

"Sounds good to me."

"I bet it does." Steven drove in the direction of downtown New Haven. He cleared his throat. "So what do you think about your mother's new friend?"

Dani shifted uncomfortably in her seat. Her shoulders lifted then dropped. She kept her eyes glued to her knees. "He's nice."

"Does your mother really like him?"

Dani thought about her mother's earlier behavior. Based on that she really didn't know anymore. But no one gets that upset over somebody if they don't really care, she decided. "I guess."

Steven pursed his lips. "I've seen his type before, and believe me, he's nothing but trouble."

Dani turned her head to look at her father. Steven kept his eyes on the road.

"I can't understand what your mother could possibly see in him. He's young enough to be your older brother, for Chrissake," he added, his injured ego inciting him. "He's the type of guy that will come and go. You know musicians. And if your mother's hooked on that type then who knows how many men she'll be involved with. I don't want you in that kind of environment. Your mother is obviously too blind to see what's going on. If I have to," he paused for breath, "I'll take you out of there and bring you to Chicago."

"What?" For the first time Dani thought about her situation. Her mother had done everything possible to make Dani happy and all she did was complain about a father who had totally disappeared out of her life for the past six months. While she missed her father desperately, she would not have him cast judgment on her mother.

"Mom is happy for the first time in I don't know how long and she deserves it. I like seeing her happy." she said clearly. "Taj is not that kind of man. Not at all. You haven't been around. You haven't even called and suddenly you want me to go live with you? You don't have a clue, Dad."

"Dani, honey," he said in his most cajoling tone, "I just want what's best for you—to protect you."

She looked at him with new eyes. "Did you want what

was best for me when you had all of those other women in your life?"

The question was so unexpected, he nearly lost control of the car. "Dani, what are you talking about?"

"You think I didn't hear the arguments, or hear Ma crying to Aunt Amber on the phone?" She swallowed hard and tried to control the trembling that had taken over her body. "I wanted to believe that it was Ma's fault. I blamed her when you left because I didn't want to believe those things about you. But you know, no matter how horrible I was to my mother she never said an ugly thing about you! Ever."

Steven had never felt so small as he did at that moment. He'd always wanted his daughter to see him as a knight in shining armor. Even though she had known the real him, she had loved him anyway. And Jewel had never allowed her own pain to cloud Dani's opinion of him. How wrong he'd been.

"I'm—sorry Dani. For everything," he said humbly.

Dani swallowed down the knot in her throat and sniffed back her tears. Now that she had finally gotten the words out, she realized that the person she was angry with for so long was not her mother, but her father. She'd only lashed out at the person who was available. She sucked on her bottom lip and turned to face the window. "Forget it," she said in a strained voice.

"I can't do that. It's about time I admit that I was wrong. I was wrong, Dani. I allowed your mother to take the blame for everything, just so that I could keep up a good front with you." He blew out a heavy breath. "I never allowed myself the opportunity to appreciate what kind of woman your mother really is. You're right, your mother deserves to be happy. I'm sorry I'm not the one to do it."

Dani's lip trembled as she struggled not to cry. "Can you take me home, please?" she asked in a tiny voice.

Steven pulled the car to the curb and unfastened his seat belt. He reached over the stick shift and gathered Dani, gently into his arms. "I'm sorry, baby," he said softly into her hair, stroking her back as he spoke.

Dani nodded feebly against his chest, then eased herself away. "Can we go now?"

"Are you sure?"

"Yes."

Steven turned the car around. They made the return trip in silence. When they pulled to a stop in front of the door, Steven turned to Danielle. "Listen to me a minute. Okay? I might have really blown everything between us. But I hope that, in time, you'll find a way to forgive me, Dani. I wouldn't ever do anything to intentionally hurt you. You know that. I've made a lot of mistakes, maybe sometime soon you'll give me a second chance."

Dani turned shimmering eyes on her father. "I know things can't be the way they were," she said sadly, giving him a crooked smile, "but maybe they can just be different."

He returned her smile and gently stroked her hair. "Deal," he agreed softly.

"You still owe me a shopping trip," she added with a wavering grin.

"Call in your I.O.U. whenever you're ready."

"Will I see you before you leave?"

"Of course. Do you think it would be all right if I stopped by on Christmas? I think I owe your mother a big gift and a big apology."

"You'd better ask Ma."

"Put in a good word for me."

She smiled. "I will." She leaned over and kissed his cheek then turned to open the car door.

"I'll call you during the week."

"Okay," she said, shutting the door behind her. She stood on the curb and waved as Steven drove away and quietly realized that she had grown up quite a bit.

"Taj," Nick greeted, walking up to the bottom of the stage. "I'm glad you're here. I have a proposition for you."

Taj put down his sax and hopped down off of the stage. "Hey, Nick" he stuck out his hand for Nick to shake. "I didn't expect to see you until tomorrow night. What's up?"

Nick put his arm around Taj's shoulder. "Come on in my office so we can talk in private."

Once they were inside, Nick wasted no time in getting to the point.

"There are some people in New York that I want you to meet," he began, taking a seat on the edge of his desk. I told you that I'd been thinking about getting a group together to cut a record deal."

Taj nodded and took a seat opposite Nick's desk. He crossed his left ankle over his right knee. His adrenaline began a slow, steady buildup.

"A couple of guys are interested in hearing what I've got. They offered me studio time to cut a demo tape." He paused for effect. "And I want you in on it."

A slow smile eased across Taj's face, even as he tried to contain his growing excitement. "You don't waste any time," he chuckled, shaking his head.

"There's no time to waste. So what do you say?"

"I say, if you want me, I'm in," Taj said without hesitation.

"Now, when I said there's no time to waste, I meant that. We have to be in New York by tomorrow night."

Taj's eyes widened in surprise. "Tomorrow?"

"Is that a problem?"

He thought about his unresolved situation with Jewel. Leaving now would only widen the bridge between them. But if he didn't go, he may ruin a chance of a lifetime. "No. No problem. I just didn't think you meant immediately."

"I promise to have you back before Christmas. How's that?"

Christmas. He didn't even want to think about it. "Sounds fine."

"Great. That's what I was hoping you'd say." Nick hopped down from the desk, smiling broadly. He clasped Taj's hand in both of his. "I have a good feeling about this," he said, his dark brown eyes sparkling with excitement that was barely contained. "It's what I've been dreaming about."

So have I, Taj thought. I had only hoped that I'd have someone to share that dream with.

Jewel drove for hours, stopping occasionally at the boutiques along the shopping district to pick up additional gifts for her family to put under the tree. Valiantly, she'd tried to push thoughts of Taj to the back of her mind, but images of him nipped at her as powerfully as the biting December wind.

By the time she began the long drive back home, a light snow had begun to fall. All around her couples huddled together, twinkling lights glistened against the darkening skies, music could be heard in concert with the gay voices of the holiday crowds. All painful reminders of how alone she felt.

The shock of what had transpired between Taj and Tricia had yet to wear off. She still vacillated between anger and impending tears. *This too shall pass,* she kept reminding herself, playing her mother's favorite phrase in her head like a mantra. But when? she asked of her reflection in the rearview mirror. When?

Entering the house Jewel was surprised to find that Dani had already returned and was stretched out on her favorite spot on the couch, fast asleep. Then her antennae went up. She quickly scanned the living room as she crossed the foyer and deposited her bundles then took a quick peek in the kitchen. No sign of Steven. Thank heaven.

She walked over to the couch and lightly tapped Dani's shoulder. "Hi, hon," she said softly.

Dani's eyes fluttered open. She gave a sleepy smile.

"How was your day?" Jewel took off her coat, hung it on the rack and stepped out of her boots. "I didn't expect you home so early." She plopped down on the love seat facing Danielle.

Dani pulled herself up into a sitting position. "I've been home for a while."

Jewel's brow creased. "That doesn't sound like you. You can shop for hours. I assume that's what you'd planned."

Dani cleared her throat. "We didn't go shopping."

"So what did you do?"

"We talked."

Jewel leaned back, angling her head speculatively. "Do you want to tell me about it?"

"Let's just say we got a lot of things straight." She looked away and then let her eyes rest on her mother. "I made a big decision today."

Jewel felt her pulse quicken. *Please don't let her leave me*, she thought frantically, Steven's threat reverberating in her head. "What decision was that?"

"That I have to stop pretending that I don't know what really went on before Daddy moved out. That I had to decide if I was going to be a grown-up and face it, or stay a little girl and believe in fairy tales."

"Dani . . . I—" Jewel leaned forward, her throat burned with the tears that she held in check. Danielle got up and squeezed next to her mother on the love seat. Jewel wrapped her arm around her, hugging her fiercely. "You knew?"

Dani nodded. "I didn't want to believe it."

"What—what made you change your mind?"

"When I was faced with the choice of having to decide if I would defend you, or listen to Daddy."

Jewel squeezed her eyes shut as joy washed over her. "Thank you," she whispered.

"Dad and I got a lot of things aired out. He finally admitted how wrong he had been. He also said he never really appreciated you." She looked up into her mother's face. "And that you deserved to be happy. He just wasn't the one to do it."

Jewel blinked back her surprise. "Your father, Steven Avery, actually said that?"

Dani smiled. "Yep."

"Will wonders never cease?"

"He asked me to put in a good word for him. He wants to stop by on Christmas. Would that be all right?"

Jewel instantly thought about Taj. "How could I say no?" she answered.

Dani hesitated a moment. "What about Taj?"

Jewel got up. "What about him?"

"Is he going to be here?"

"I really don't know," Jewel answered tightly, turning away.

Danielle watched her mother's reaction and knew that something was definitely wrong. If her mother didn't tell her, maybe she'd find out for herself when she went to the club. It seemed like the adults were having a hard time communicating.

* * *

After his last set at the club, Taj returned to his apartment, charged with the excitement of anticipation. A budding new career loomed on the horizon. All of his years of struggling to perfect his craft may finally pay off.

He tossed his coat on the chair and followed behind it, kicked off his boots and stretched out his long legs in front of him. Automatically he looked at the answering machine that sat on the small table by the couch. No message.

He heaved a sigh, and was tempted to call Jewel again. But, he reasoned, it was apparent that she had no intention of returning his numerous calls.

It continued to irk him that Jewel thought so little of him. He'd never been the type of man who ran around. If anything, he was the complete opposite. He'd spent most of his adult life trying to carve a niche for himself in the music world. His social life had taken a backseat as a result. Sure, there'd been women. Occasionally, but never anything serious. He'd never met anyone who could compete with his first love: his music. Until Jewel.

She'd changed him. She gave him reason to want to plant roots, to have a family. All of the things he hadn't had since he was ten years old and woke up to find that his mother had left him alone, in a cold, shabby apartment to fend for himself. Neighbors had found him wandering in the street and had contacted the authorities.

Sure he'd told Nick that his mother couldn't afford lessons. It was just a story that he'd brainwashed himself to believe over the years, as he was shuttled from one foster home to another. His mother's desertion had made him feel unworthy and he carried that burden with him throughout his life. The only stable thing he'd had was the beat-up saxophone that he'd found in an alley. It had comforted him when he felt alone in the world. It was his constant companion. But there was still that great big hole in his soul that all of the music in the world couldn't fill. Until Jewel became a part of his life.

He stood up. He'd gotten over other hurts and disappointment. He'd get over this too, he tried to convince himself. In time.

Jewel lay in bed and stared up at the ceiling. So many things had happened in the past few days. Her mind was reeling. It was at times like this that she would reach out to call Taj and share her thoughts. He would ease her troubles away with his earthy wisdom and genuine concern.

It was remarkable, she thought, that a man with such a troubling beginning could have turned out to be so compassionate to others and so giving of himself. She expelled a shuddering breath and closed her eyes. That's probably what attracted Tricia, she thought miserably.

Jewel knew that at some point she would have to confront him, let him know how much he'd hurt her. But she dreaded the moment. But maybe she should give him more credit, as she should have with Dani.

You've got to put your cards on the table. The words rang so clearly in her head that she flinched in surprise.

"Yes, I will," she said out loud. "How soon, is the question."

"Ma! Kim and I are leaving now," Dani called out from the bottom of the staircase.

Jewel came to the top of the landing, still dressed in her nightgown. She'd debated all night whether or not to accompany Dani and Kim to the club, but finally decided that the club was not the place for a personal discussion. And she didn't want to be a distraction to Taj while he played. Once she'd finally made up her mind to talk with Taj, she decided to wait until he'd returned home.

"Be home before dark," Jewel instructed.

"See you later."

"You two be careful."

"Any messages for Taj?" Dani asked hopefully.

"You've done enough delivering for a while," Jewel said lightly, referring to Dani's request on her father's behalf.

Dani shrugged. "Bye."

Jewel returned to her room, got dressed and went downstairs. She opened the cupboard and reached for a jar of coffee. Momentarily, she hesitated. She took the box of herb tea instead. A fleeting smile curved her lips. Somehow she knew that things were going to be all right. She took the jar of coffee and dropped it in the garbage can.

Taj joined Dani and Kim at their table. "I'm glad you two came down," Taj said, surprised that Jewel had allowed it. "How did you like what you heard?"

"Great," Dani said, between bites of buffalo wings. "I was telling my mother that I didn't realize that jazz was so cool."

The mention of Jewel caused Taj's jaw to tighten. "How is your mother?" he asked with hesitation.

"Excuse me," Kim interrupted. Taj and Dani turned their attention toward Kim. "I'm going to the ladies' room. Be right back."

"She likes to make announcements," Dani explained, looking down at her plate of food. "Maybe you should call and find out," she said quietly, easing back to his question with finesse.

Taj leaned back and gave Danielle a long assessing gaze. His instincts told him that she knew more than she would tell, and he wouldn't push her. It would never be his style to pry her for information about her mother. Now or in the future. If there was a future.

"Do you think that's a good idea?" he asked in a slow, probing voice.

"Absolutely." She looked across at him from beneath long, thick lashes. "Sometimes people need a push. Know what I mean?"

"I think I get the picture," he said, struggling not to smile. "Uh, in your professional opinion, would a personal visit be too pushy?"

The corner of her lip quivered in a grin. "Sometimes personal is best."

His smile was open now, enveloping Dani in its glow. He reached across the tabletop and placed his hand over hers. "Thanks," he said softly.

Dani brought a wing to her mouth with her free hand. "No problem," she said giving him a conspiratorial wink.

Taj pushed away from the table and stood up just as Kim returned. "You two should be getting home. It'll be dark soon."

"Yeah," Dani said, finishing off the last of her soda. "Aren't you coming with us?"

"No." He shook his head. "I've got to go home and pack."

"Pack?" Dani asked. Her smooth brow creased in bewilderment.

"I'm leaving for New York tonight. My boss is trying to put together a record deal. I should be back by Sunday."

"A record deal!" Kim piped in. "So you mean we'll see your video on *Video Music Box?*"

Taj tossed his head back and laughed heartily. "That's probably a long way off," he said.

"So when are you coming over?" Dani wanted to know.

"Let's say soon. How's that?"

Dani twisted her lips. "Whatever," she said dismissively, feeling disappointment. "Come on Kim, let's go." She got up from her seat, avoiding Taj's watchful eye. "Thanks for inviting us," she said to her shoes.

Taj tipped her chin up with the tip of his finger and peered down into her face. "Everything's gonna be cool. Okay?"

She nodded. "Sure." All she could think about was that she should have stuck to her convictions. She allowed herself to like him and now he was going to wind up being like all the other guys that her friends complained about. How could she have believed he was special? She hated him!

She pulled her head away from his touch. "Bye," she said sullenly. She snatched up her coat from the back of her chair and stomped off toward the door with Kim on her heels.

Taj watched them leave and tried to figure out where he'd gone wrong.

"How'd it go?" Jewel asked, almost too anxiously, when the girls returned.

"Fine," Dani said shortly.

Jewel came to stand beside Danielle, her face clouded with concern. "Dani? Are you all right?"

"I'm fine," she snapped, her dark eyes burning when she looked at her mother.

"Dani." Jewel reached out and braced her shoulders. "What is it?"

"Just forget it. Okay?"

"No. I won't forget it. That's your response to everything you don't want to discuss. Now you tell me what happened," she demanded, her panic rising as thoughts of Steven's accusations about Taj raced through her mind.

"It's nothing," Dani insisted. "Sometimes you just let your guard down and it isn't worth it." She pulled away from her mother and ran upstairs.

"Dani!" But the only response Jewel got was the sound of the slamming door.

"What on earth happened, Kim?" Jewel asked, whirling toward Kim like a top.

"I don't know, Mrs. Avery. She's been pissed off—I mean, upset—since we left the club."

Jewel pressed her palm to her forehead. "If he did anything to hurt my child. I swear . . ." she seethed under her breath.

"I guess I'd better go and let my mother know I'm back."

Jewel nodded absently as Kim slipped soundlessly out of the house. She looked up the staircase, debating on whether or not to go up, or give Dani some time to collect her thoughts. She was sure that whatever was bothering her daughter, Dani would eventually tell her. It was the waiting and the not knowing that was so difficult. Then suddenly she made up her mind. She marched over to the phone and punched in the seven digits. Somebody was going to tell her something, she fumed.

The phone rang until the machine clicked on. Jewel slammed down the receiver and issued an expletive just as the doorbell rang.

Kim probably had forgotten something. She briskly

crossed the room and snatched the door open, ready to send the girl back home to her mama.

"Taj!" A million thoughts and feelings converged and collided into one large lump in her throat that seemed to keep her from breathing. She tried to swallow but her mouth went dry when she saw the suitcase that rested at his feet.

"I know I should have called," he began slowly, prepared if she slammed the door in his face, "but I didn't want you to hang up on me."

Jewel folded her arms protectively beneath her breasts as if the act could somehow contain the torrent of emotions that tumbled within her.

"Can I come in, or should we talk right here? Because we *are* going to talk," he said in a tone that left no room for argument.

Jewel tugged on her bottom lip with her teeth and stepped slightly aside. Taj picked up his bag and brushed past her, the scent of him rushing to her brain and scrambling her thoughts.

He walked halfway into the living room, then turned abruptly around, nearly colliding with Jewel on her approach. He instinctively reached out and grabbed her by the shoulders. The instantaneous flash of heat raced from her body and shot straight up his fingers to his heart.

She shuddered and it wasn't from the cold, she realized, staring up into the eyes that matched hers. Her heart fluttered and pounded as if she'd been running and was desperate for air.

"Jewel," he said in a strangled whisper. His hand slid up her shoulders to stroke her cheeks, then angled upward through her hair, pulling her forward until they were only a breath apart. He looked down into her eyes, his own slowly caressing her face. "I love you," he said softly. "I'd never do anything to hurt you. Nothing happened between Tricia and me. Nothing ever could."

"But the phone call," she said between tiny gulps of air. "She said—"

"I don't give a damn what she said. I know what she meant." His lips brushed tantalizingly across hers and her knees weakened. "She was apologizing for kissing me."

"What?" She tried to pull away, but Taj tightened his grip, locking his body to hers.

"Yes," he said huskily, "a kiss. Like this." She held her breath. Taj pressed his lips almost dispassionately against hers, and released her mouth, but not his hold. He looked down into her startled eyes. "Not like this," he said, in a throaty whisper. He lowered his head by degrees, until his lips fluttered across her eyelids, slid down to her cheeks, seared her long neck, raised up to her chin where he nipped her with the tip of his teeth. He cupped her face in his hands and grazed her lips with the pads of his thumbs. Languidly his tongue traced a pattern across her parted mouth. She let out a gasp of pleasure as the slow heat of desire built a fire in her belly.

His mouth captured hers in a total act of possession. He delved deep into the warmth that awaited him. A moan rose deep from within him as she clung to him, curving her body to match his. All of her worry and hurt seemed to evaporate like melting crystals of snow.

Dani stood at the top of the landing, peeking down at the scene below. Slowly she smiled and tiptoed back to her room. Maybe he wasn't so bad after all, she smiled happily.

Taj and Jewel were settled on the couch, with Taj's arm draped across her shoulder. He played with her hair as he spoke.

"You have a very special daughter. I hope you know that. She was in there pitching for you. Indirectly, of course."

"Every time I think I understand Danielle, she surprises me. I truly underestimated her. She's growing up so fast, it's frightening."

"You've done a great job. You don't have anything to worry about." He turned her head to face him. He looked steadily into her questioning eyes. "I don't ever want anything to come between us again," Taj said softly. "Have faith in me. I'm not Steven."

Jewel looked away. "I know that now. I guess my confidence in relationships has been trampled on so badly that I just ignored my better judgment." She curved closer into his embrace and looked up at him. "Don't ever worry about my mistrusting you again."

"If you promise me that if you ever have any doubts, any fears, and flashes of jealousy, you'll tell me."

"I promise," she said smiling. "I promise."

"That's better." He kissed the tip of her nose, and reluctantly pulled himself up, just as Dani entered the room.

"What's the big grin for?" her mother asked.

"Just wondering if it was safe to come in now?" she teased.

Jewel felt the hot flush of embarrassment sweep through her. She worried just how much Dani witnessed.

"The coast is clear," Taj said, grinning. He walked over to where Danielle stood and chucked her under her chin. "Thanks for the advice, Doc."

"My bill is in the mail."

"Ugh."

"What are you two whispering about?" Jewel crossed the room and boldly slipped her arm around Taj's waist. She looked suspiciously from one to the other.

"Family secret," Dani said.

Taj smiled warmly at her. "I like the sound of that."

Dani grinned at them both and skipped back up the stairs.

"See you when I get back," Taj called out.

"Bring me something!"

Taj chuckled, then turned his full attention back to Jewel. "I hate to say this, baby, but I've got to go. Nick is picking me up at the club in a half hour."

"I'll drive you."

Taj winked. "I knew you were going to say that."

She swatted him on the shoulder. "Oh, yeah. Don't get too comfortable in predicting my behavior," she challenged, taking her coat from the rack.

"Ooh, sounds like a threat," he countered, following her to the door.

"Trust me. It's a promise. I intend to keep you on your toes."

He spun her around and into his arms. His eyes burned down into hers. "You'd better," he warned, before his lips covered hers.

The next few days were a race against the clock. Every hour seemed to be crammed with activity as Jewel and Danielle prepared for Christmas dinner.

"Taj told me he doesn't really celebrate Christmas," Dani said, dipping her finger in the chocolate icing that Jewel lathered on the three-layer cake. She shooed Dani's hand away.

"I know. His holiday starts the day after. But he said he'll come for dinner. He just won't be exchanging gifts."

"I like seven days of getting gifts. Maybe we should start celebrating Kwanzaa," Dani suggested hopefully.

Jewel gave her a sidelong glance. "You would," she

said, her tone ripe with sarcasm. "But Kwanzaa is a lot
more than just receiving gifts for a week."

"I know," she said in a singsong voice. "I've been
reading up on it."

"Good. Now pass me that apple pie so I can put it
in the oven," Jewel instructed. "Is Kim coming over
tomorrow?"

"She said she was, after she gets back from her grandmother's house. Speaking of grandmothers, did you tell
grandma about Taj?"

Jewel sighed "No. But I will."

"When?"

"When she gets here."

They both laughed, imaging the look on Nora's face.

Jewel surveyed her kitchen. Every available counter
space was covered with prepared dishes ready for the
oven or the refrigerator. She had something for everyone. Collard greens seasoned hot and sweet for her
mother. Candied yams loaded with maple syrup and
marshmallows for Amber. And for everyone, french cut
string beans and carrots, a huge garden salad, macaroni
and cheese, a twenty pound turkey, her seafood casse-
role, and enough dessert to send everyone into diabetic
shock.

The house was filled with the fragrant scent of evergreen. Poinsettias decorated in kente colors adorned the
tabletops. Brilliant African fabric, twisted into intricate
knots, draped the banisters of the staircase and twinkling
lights gave the entire scene a picture postcard appeal.

Instead of the traditional tree, the stacks of gifts were
arranged in front of the fireplace. Everything looked
beautiful, she thought, pleased with herself and her
talented daughter's handiwork. Now for the grand fi-

nale. The arrival of her family. Her heart skipped in anticipation of what tomorrow would bring.

When she finally settled down for the night, she felt every muscle of her body give a relieved sigh. As she lay there, she replayed her last phone conversation with Taj. She smiled. The executives from the record company were thrilled with what they'd heard, and were ready to sign them on the spot. "Nick wants his lawyer to look everything over first," Taj had said. "He doesn't want us falling into any traps."

"I'm so proud of you," she'd said, her own excitement for him barely contained. "You're going to really make it. I can feel it."

"I needed to hear you say that. That you believe in me."

Her heart pinched. She knew how desperately he had longed for someone to really feel that way about him. And she promised herself that she would do everything in her power to keep reminding him of just how important he was.

"So I hope you won't mind being married to a superstar. You don't look like the live together type."

Shock slammed against her and her hand began to shake. "What?"

"You heard me." She could feel the laughter in his voice. "We'll talk about it when I get back tomorrow. Think of me until then."

He'd hung up before she had a chance to catch her breath and respond. Her heart was racing so fast she thought she was going to have one of those conniption fits that she'd heard about.

All she could do was repeat the word over and again in her mind, just like she was doing now. Marriage. A smile of pure joy lifted her lips as she drifted off to sleep filled with beautiful dreams of her future.

***

Squeals of delight and the sound of pounding foot-steps pulled Jewel out of her sleep with a start. Seconds later, Dani jumped on her bed and smothered her with kisses.

"Thank you, thank you, thank you," she chanted. "You got me everything I wanted."

Jewel sat up and rubbed the sleep from her eyes. "Hmm. I'm glad, honey," she said drowsily.

Dani plopped a large, beautifully decorated box on her lap. Jewel squeezed her eyes shut then opened them. She must be tired, she thought, she hadn't even seen Dani bring the box in the room.

"Open it," she said, her eyes bright with anticipation.

Jewel did as she was instructed. She gasped with delight as she pulled out the silky pink kimono and matching gown. "Dani!" she exclaimed in awe. "This is beautiful. Where on earth did you get the money for this?"

"I've been saving my allowance," she announced proudly. "You like it?"

"I love it." She slipped the kimono over her arms, relishing the feel of the feather-light fabric as it glided over her skin. She gave Danielle a tight hug. "Thanks, sweetie."

Dani popped off of the bed. "I'm going to hook up my CD player, put on my new coat and boots and *Paarty!*" she giggled.

Jewel smiled. "Go right ahead."

When Dani reached the door she stopped and tossed over her shoulder, "All those skirts and tops were nice, too."

"Right." Jewel immediately lay back down as soon as Dani was out of the door, only to jump back up again when she realized all that she had to do.

She took a quick shower and dressed in comfortable

jeans and a T-shirt. All the better to hustle around the kitchen in, she thought merrily.

In no time, the house was filled with the delicious aromas of Christmas dinner. When she'd finished mixing up the ingredients for the stuffing, she checked the clock. Taj said he'd be back by noon. It was nearly that. Her heart picked up a beat. *Married*. She wanted to change before he arrived.

She quickly cleared her countertops and checked the progress of the turkey. Everything was right on schedule. Except whoever was ringing the doorbell. She wiped her hands on the red and green kitchen towel and went to the door, knowing that it could be none other than her mother, who always arrived three hours early so that she could supervise. Well at least she'd have time to tell her about Taj before he arrived, she reasoned, pushing her stomach back in place with a deep swallow.

She took a deep breath, put on a warm smile of greeting and opened the door.

"Merry Christmas, Jewel."

"Steven." Her smile vanished.

"May I come in? I promise I won't stay. I just wanted to drop these off." He indicated two large shopping bags, that sat at his feet, with a nod of his head.

"Sure. Come on in." She stepped aside to let him pass.

"The place looks real good," he said, turning toward her with a smile that hovered between regret and longing.

He was still so devilishly handsome, she thought, annoyed with the observation. "Thank you. Can I get you something? Apple cider, coffee?" She started toward the kitchen.

"No. But you can sit down for a minute."

"I really have a lot to do," she protested. "If you want to see Dani, I'll get her. I—"

"No, Jewel." He put a restraining hand on her arm. "I want to talk with you. Please. Sit down. Just for a minute."

She nodded reluctantly and took a seat opposite him on the armchair.

"I just wanted to say that I'm sorry, Jewel." Her eyes widened in disbelief. She'd never heard Steven apologize for anything. "Sorry for the way I treated you," he continued. "Sorry for the things that I've done that hurt you. There's no excuse." He looked down at his hands as if searching for answers. He linked them together and looked across at her. "You didn't deserve the things I've done to you. Even though I tried to make you believe it was your fault."

If he wanted a response, she thought wildly, she couldn't give him one. She was stunned into complete silence.

"I know I can never make it up to you. I know we can't go back. I made certain choices in my life and I'll have to live with them. I just wanted you to know that you were the best choice I've ever made."

He stood up, and heaved a sigh. "I want you to be happy, Jewel. You deserve it more than anyone I know." He tried to smile. "Putting up with my B.S. for seventeen years should earn you sainthood."

"Steven, I—"

"Ssh. Please don't say anything. There's no need. I just wanted you to know that at any time for whatever reason, if you need, you tell me. No matter what it is."

Jewel stood up and pursed her lips. "Are you the same man I married?"

"And divorced," he reminded her. He chuckled. "The new and improved version. Now, where's that daughter of ours? By the sound of the racket, she must be upstairs. I want out of here before the troops arrive. You know how they always want to be diagnosed."

"Steven." She took his hand in hers. "Thank you," she said softly.

"For what?"

"For finally setting me free."

The corner of his mouth inched up in a smile as he nodded in understanding. "It's about time. Don't you think?"

Jewel was still reeling from the shock of Steven's confession when the doorbell rang. The Christmas celebration had begun.

Nora Sinclair was a stunning woman in anybody's book. She was a personal testament to self-preservation. She worked out every day. Played tennis twice a week. Saw her doctor regularly. Had her hair always styled in the latest fashion, and shopped for clothes incessantly. And for a woman who knew her way around any kitchen, she was still a size ten. At sixty-three, Nora Sinclair could still turn the heads of men half her age.

Which she'd apparently done.

The tall, handsome man on her arm must have been forty, Jewel thought, as shock gave way to amused bewilderment. Was this her mother, who as far as she knew hadn't dated a man since her father died nearly ten years ago?

"Well, are you just going to stand there with your mouth open, or are you going to let us in? It's freezing out here." Nora did all she could to keep the grin off her face when she saw Jewel's expression.

Nora breezed in with her escort and an armful of

gifts, leaving Jewel standing at the door. Nora spun around.

"Jewel, I'd like you to meet James Monroe." Nora cast adoring eyes on James. "James, my daughter Jewel."

Jewel was finally able to move. She closed the door and stepped into the foyer. James stepped forward and gave her the most engaging smile she'd ever seen, next to Taj's. He extended his hand.

"Nice to finally meet you, Jewel," he said in a voice that sounded surprisingly like James Earl Jones. "Your mother has told me a lot about you."

Jewel took his hand and felt like a complete fool as she kept staring at him trying to frame something coherent to say. She cleared her throat. "I hope it was all good things," she said lamely.

"Most of it," he teased, giving her that smile again.

"I came early to help," Nora said, hanging up her coat. "James, make yourself at home while I help Jewel in the kitchen."

Dutifully, Jewel followed her mother into the kitchen. Before she could get a word in, Nora cut her off.

"I know what you're going to say. He's too young for me. Well, I thought so at first, too. But after ten years of being around men my own age, I found they couldn't keep up with me," she said defiantly. She walked over and took both of Jewel's hands in hers. "I know this is a shock, sweetheart. But I think I'm in love again. And he loves me." Her soft brown eyes begged for understanding.

Jewel grinned with delight and a hint of mischief as she hooked her arm around her mother's shoulders. "Mom, there's something I think you ought to know . . ."

***

Christmas dinner was more than she could have ever hoped for. It was filled with laughter, acceptance and an abundance of love that flowed as freely as the falling snow. Even her sister Amber seemed to have added a new dimension to her character. It was a time of change, for everyone.

Long after the last dish was washed and dried and all of the guests had departed, Jewel and Taj sat in front of the fireplace, finally sharing a quiet moment together.

"You have some family," he said, twisting a lock of her hair around his finger.

"You can say that again. This week has been a true revelation to me. All of my beliefs about everyone I thought I knew were blown out of the window." She shook her head, remembering her mother's parting words, "I'll see you when I get back," Nora had said wickedly. "We're going to the Bahamas for the weekend."

"A new year is on the horizon, baby," Taj whispered softly. "Time to make changes." He looked into her eyes. "Are you ready for that?"

She thought about the person that she had been and the person that she'd become with Taj at her side and she knew what he was asking of her. Was she ready to make that choice?

She cupped his face in her hands and looked at him with all of the love and passion that filled her soul. "Yes," she said without further hesitation. *"Yes."*

FIRST FRUITS

Rochelle Alers

Shelby Carter walked briskly along the snow-covered Manhattan sidewalk toward an Upper East Side luxury high-rise apartment building, trying to escape the gusting, frigid wind sweeping off the East River. She made her way into the vestibule, returning the smile of the young, dark-eyed uniformed doorman.

"Good evening, Miss Carter," he greeted her, touching the shiny brim of his maroon cap.

"Good evening, Henri," she returned.

"Mrs. Morrow is expecting you," he informed her, still flashing his best toothpaste-ad smile.

"Thank you."

She crossed the opulently decorated carpeted lobby to the elevators. Henri's admiring gaze followed her progress. Her short, naturally curly hair was concealed under a bottle-green wool cloche which matched a sweeping double-breasted greatcoat with black frogs. A pair of highly polished black riding boots and a shoulder bag completed her winter ensemble.

Gleaming brass doors opened silently and Shelby stepped into the elevator, pressing the button for the sixteenth floor. The car rose swiftly and quietly, stopping at her floor, and again the doors opened silently. She made her way down a spacious hallway to Naomi Morrow's apartment.

She had accepted Mrs. Morrow's invitation to dinner to discuss what the older woman hinted was a "special project," something art-related.

Two years ago, Naomi Morrow had attended an art exhibit featuring a dozen sculptured pieces of an up-and-coming artist whose work was reminiscent of primitive tribal masks and statues. Mrs. Morrow had purchased the entire collection and a bond between Shelby and the retired school administrator was formed.

Shelby had garnered her share of praise that evening as the purchasing agent for the gallery that had set up the showing. Now, at thirty-four, and fortified with an undergraduate degree in ethnoanthropology, a master's in African studies, and a second master's in art education, she had earned the respect of her contemporaries in the New York City art world.

She rang the bell while admiring the large, fragrant evergreen wreath with miniature red glazed ceramic apples, pinecones, and a red velvet bow hanging outside the door to apartment 16K. It opened and Shelby found herself face-to-face with Naomi Morrow.

She smiled at the petite woman with a smooth honey-beige complexion which complemented her expertly coiffed silver hair. An unlined face and a slim figure belied Naomi Morrow's sixty-nine years.

Extending both hands, Naomi grasped Shelby's shoulders and pressed her lips to her cheek. "How lovely you look. I'm so glad you could make it. Please come in."

She stepped into the foyer, handing her host a decorative shopping bag.

"What's this?" Naomi questioned, peering into a large green bag overflowing with red and black tissue paper.

"An early Kwanzaa gift," Shelby replied. Kwanzaa was

still another three weeks away. She pulled off the cloche and slipped out of her coat, hanging them in the closet in the foyer. Tilting her head, she sniffed delicately. "Is that roast turkey I smell?"

"I remembered it's your favorite."

Naomi led the way down three carpeted stairs and into a sunken living room filled with golden light, a blazing fire in a fireplace, curio cabinets crowded with priceless art pieces, and a glossy parquet floor covered with an Oriental rug.

Running a hand through her hair, Shelby picked out the soft curls clinging to her scalp. "You didn't have to bother."

Naomi waved a delicate hand. "Cooking for you is not what I would call a bother. Why don't you freshen up while I get us something to drink?"

Shelby made her way to one of the two bathrooms in the beautifully decorated two-bedroom apartment. The apartment in the pre–World War II building was designed with towering ceilings, a fireplace, wood floors, and tall windows offering magnificent views of Manhattan's skyline and the bridges spanning the East River.

She compared this view with the one from her apartment on Manhattan's Upper West Side, preferring the panoramic scene of the Hudson River and the New Jersey Palisades from her own living and bedroom windows.

Staring at her reflection in a mirror over a sink in a bathroom decorated in black and gleaming silver, Shelby ran a tube of cherry-red lipstick over her full lips and used a small rounded brush to lift the shiny black curls at the crown of her head. Wetting the brush, she smoothed down the wisps of curls on the nape of her neck and over her ears.

Studying her face, she silently thanked her mother

for her flawless dark brown skin and perfect teeth. Her large, vibrant dark eyes, naturally arching eyebrows, hair, nose, and mouth were her father's. Stanton Carter's good looks had always turned heads, and the similar reaction was repeated with his daughter. Shelby Carter had matured into a beautiful woman whose dramatic face and slender body were certain to turn heads whenever she entered a room.

She adjusted a necklace of large black lacquered beads over a long-sleeved white knit dress which lay with perfection over her firm breasts, narrow waist, and rounded hips. Designing the dress had been a challenge for Shelby because of the slightly flaring bias-cut skirt.

She enjoyed sewing almost as much as she appreciated art. There was a time when she couldn't decide whether she wanted to become a fashion designer or a museum curator; however, after careful consideration, she realized she could study art and design clothes; but the clothes she'd design would be for her own personal use.

Shelby returned to the living room, smiling as Naomi set down two porcelain cups on a coffee table. The aroma of orange and cinnamon tea mingled with the sweet smell of burning wood.

"Everything looks and smells wonderful," Shelby remarked, her dark gaze sweeping the living room. Towering potted ficus trees rose up toward the twelve-foot ceiling. Sparkling pinpoints of light from towering skyscrapers, expansion bridges, and stars in a clear winter nighttime sky provided a glittering background through the floor-to-ceiling windows.

Naomi sat on a white love seat beside Shelby, smoothing down her slim navy blue wool gabardine skirt. Picking up her cup and saucer, she took a sip, nodding her approval. "I think I finally made it right," she said.

Shelby took a sip of her own orange-flavored cinnamon tea. Glancing over the rim, she returned the nod. "Perfect." There was just a hint of orange liqueur in the fragrant liquid.

The two women sipped their tea in silence, both watching the flickering flames in the fireplace behind a decorative screen.

Naomi turned and directed her attention to Shelby. She wasn't certain whether the young woman would accept her offer, but if she did, she knew it would change Shelby Carter's life forever.

"I've given your name to the search committee for the Studio Museum in Harlem for assistant curator."

Shelby went rigid, her hand with the fragile teacup poised in midair. Her head turned slowly as she stared at Naomi. Naomi Morrow was offering what she had dreamt of all of her life.

"I . . . I had no idea you took what I'd said about becoming a curator seriously," she said hesitantly, trying to compose herself. As a part-time lecturer for the Metropolitan Museum of Art, Shelby had often dreamed of becoming a curator for one of the museum's galleries.

Naomi blushed, her bright eyes crinkling with a smile. "I take everything you say seriously, my dear. Besides, with your brains and training, you should've been the assistant curator of the Met's Egyptian galleries a long time ago. But of course, I know everything is political, and I've decided to use my clout just this one time to help you realize your dream."

Naomi Morrow was a trustee with several museums, including the popular Studio Museum in Harlem and the prestigious Metropolitan Museum of Art.

"I don't know what to say," Shelby stated modestly.

"Just 'thank you' will be enough when you're hired."

What Naomi didn't tell Shelby was that her name

was the only one the board had selected for the final round of consideration. Shelby Carter's extensive background in African studies, with a focus on African antiquities and her art education in tribal art, prompted the Harlem museum trustees to label the young woman as an "expert" in her field.

Naomi fingered the single strand of pearls resting on her silk blouse. The magnificent necklace had been in her family for four generations, and she had gained possession of the famous Graham pearls on her wedding day. At twenty-one, she'd married Charles Morrow and shared the next thirty years with him until his sudden death from a massive stroke eighteen years ago. Widowed and childless, Naomi had suddenly thrown all her time and energy into her "causes." Her professional career had spanned schoolteacher, principal, superintendent, and art patron, and retiring at sixty after more than thirty-five years as an educator, she set out to make her dreams a reality.

Shelby took a sip of her fragrant tea, smiling over the rim of the cup. The glint in Naomi Morrow's dark eyes said there were more surprises.

"Something tells me that submitting my name for assistant curator at the museum doesn't have anything to do with the 'special project' you hinted at," she said perceptively.

"You're so bright," Naomi exclaimed with a wide smile, "and you're right. It doesn't. But I'll let my nephew tell you about it when he gets here."

Shelby's smile faded. "Your nephew?"

"Yes. Marshall Graham. He's . . ." The doorbell rang, preempting whatever she was going to say. Naomi placed her cup on the coffee table and rose to her feet. "That must be Marshall. He's always on time."

Less than a minute later, Shelby caught a glimpse of

a tall figure with a pair of broad shoulders filling out the soft wool fabric of a camel's hair overcoat.

Marshall Graham leaned down to kiss his aunt's cheek, but his gaze was directed over her shoulder at the slender young woman sitting on the white love seat in the living room, the light from an overhead lamp ringing her dark head in gold. Even from the distance he noted her beauty immediately.

He removed his coat and hung it in the closet. The fragrance of an unfamiliar feminine perfume clung to the green coat beside his own coat.

Marshall shifted an eyebrow as he caught his aunt's knowing smile. Leaning down, he said softly, "She's beautiful, Naomi."

Naomi winked at him. "I told you she was lovely," she whispered, leading Marshall into the living room.

"Shelby, I'd like for you to meet my nephew, Marshall Graham. Marshall, Shelby Carter. She's the young woman I've been bragging about."

Shelby stood up, extending her hand and tilting her chin to get a better look at the imposing figure above her. "Hello, Marshall."

Marshall grasped her hand in a firm handshake, his large, dark eyes moving leisurely over her face. "*My* pleasure, Shelby."

Shelby felt a tingling sensation race up her arm as a wave of heat suffused her face. Marshall Graham claimed the exquisite good looks of James Van der Zee's photographic subjects from the Harlem Renaissance.

Marshall's ocher-tinged brown skin was smooth and clear, so velvety smooth it appeared nearly poreless. His black hair was cut close to his scalp, and glints of light picked up the shine of gray along his temples.

He smiled, and his teeth shone white against the brush of a neatly barbered moustache. But what transfixed Shelby most was his eyes: they literally sparkled. Laughing eyes framed by thick, lush lashes.

"May I have my hand back, please?" she teased lightly.

Naomi laughed aloud as she stared at the startled expression on her nephew's face when he realized he still held Shelby's hand.

"Of course," he replied, appearing somewhat flustered by the woman Naomi Morrow mentioned every time he called or visited.

"Would you like a cup of tea, Marshall?" Naomi asked, breaking the spell between the couple.

"Yes, please, Naomi."

Naomi retreated to the kitchen, leaving Shelby and Marshall alone together.

Shelby took her seat again while Marshall sat down opposite her on the matching white sofa. Crossing one leg gracefully over the other and picking up her cup of tea, she surreptitiously examined Marshall Graham.

A navy blue suit with a double-breasted jacket, collarless white silk shirt, and black low-heeled boots draped his tall slim physique like a lingering caress. The result was tasteful and totally masculine.

Marshall successfully concealed a smile as he watched Shelby watching him over the rim of her cup. He examined her ringless fingers. They were long, tapered, and professionally manicured. If he had known Shelby Carter was so attractive he would have been more receptive to his aunt's insistence that he meet her. It was only when he and Naomi discussed the need to expand the curriculum to include a cultural arts program at the school where he was headmaster that he'd consented to an introduction.

Naomi returned, carrying a tray with a hand-painted porcelain teapot and matching cup and saucer. Marshall rose quickly, taking the tray from her and setting it down on the coffee table.

Picking up the teapot, he stared at Shelby. "Would you like a refill?" Nodding, she extended cup and saucer, and his free hand held her wrist, steadying her hand as he poured the fragrant tea into her cup.

Shelby's gaze met his and her eyes widened in realization. Marshall Graham had the same effect on her as her ex-husband had had. There was an instant attraction the moment she saw Earl Russell; and that attraction had resulted in her marrying Earl when they both were twenty-two. The attraction and the marriage had lasted six years, and now, six years later, she felt the stirrings of desire for the first time in a very long while.

She was uncomfortable with Marshall Graham—a stranger, a man, she didn't know had the power to make her feel something she had forgotten. She had dated over the years since her divorce, but no man—not a one—had elicited anything but a sisterly hug or a chaste kiss.

Marshall released her wrist, refilling his aunt's cup before filling his own. He took his seat and sipped his tea, eyebrows lifting slightly.

"Excellent tea," he remarked, smiling at his aunt.

Naomi stared at Shelby. "It's Shelby's recipe."

His gaze shifted to Shelby. "My compliments, Shelby."

She nodded. It was only when Marshall said her name that she recognized his Southern drawl. "Virginia?"

"I beg your pardon?"

She smiled. The four words rolled fluidly from his tongue like watered silk. "Are you from Virginia?"

Marshall returned her smile. "D.C.," he confirmed. "You have a very good ear for speech patterns."

"I've done a lot of traveling and I've learned to listen

to the way people speak to see if I can identify where they're from," Shelby explained.

A buzzer sounded from the kitchen. Naomi put down her tea and rose to her feet. "You two talk while I put the finishing touches on dinner."

"Do you need any help?" Shelby questioned.

"No, I don't. And you, Marshall, please stay and explain *your* project to Shelby."

Marshall waited until his aunt walked out of the room before sitting down again. He stared at Shelby, seemingly deep in thought.

"Your project," she began, breaking the silence.

"My project," he replied, absentmindedly.

What Marshall Graham wanted to discuss was Shelby Carter. He wanted to know everything there was to know about her. His father's sister had only hinted that Shelby was "quite lovely" and "very bright," and that she would be the perfect resource person for his latest school project. And after going over her curriculum vitae, which Naomi had forwarded to him, he was certain Shelby would be able to write the curriculum for Nia Academy's cultural arts program.

"Are you familiar with the Swahili word *nia*?"

"Yes, I am," Shelby replied. "It's the fifth of the seven principles of Kwanzaa. It means 'purpose.' "

"For the past four years I've directed all of my energies toward a single purpose, and that is to give young men of color a quality education coupled with social skills that will help them to succeed when they become adults.

"Nia Academy is a preparatory school for grades one through eight with a very strict dress code. All the young men wear uniforms: navy blue blazer, white or light blue shirts, gray slacks, black shoes, and navy blue ties. And what makes Nia Academy so unique is that it's in Harlem."

"Why Harlem?" Shelby asked, wondering why she hadn't heard of the prep school's existence before tonight.

"Why *not* Harlem?" Marshall gave her a knowing smile. "Would you prefer it be in a Massachusetts, Connecticut, or Rhode Island suburb?"

She shook her head. "Not for people of color."

"Exactly, Shelby. Too many of our young people have gone to these prestigious prep schools and into a world that is so foreign to them that when they return to their own neighborhoods they're not able to fit in. They feel as if they're straddling two worlds. There's the one world, where the students are so privileged that their only concern is where they should spend their summer vacation. Should they go back to Switzerland or the Greek Isles?

"Then we have our children who return to their own communities, where they suffer the ridicule of their peers because they talk differently and perhaps act a little differently than they did before they went away. The pressure is always on for them to prove that they're still a homey and can hang."

Shelby was intrigued with the idea of a prep school in a predominantly African-American community. "Why would a prep school in Harlem be any different from a school like Choate or Chapin, except for location?"

"The curriculum may be similar, but the difference is Nia's emphasis on their heritage. My students all know that Columbus sailed to the Western Hemisphere in 1492, but none of them knew that the navigator of the *Santa María,* Pedro Alonzo Niño, was of African descent. Or that when Vasco Nuñez de Balboa discovered the Pacific Ocean in 1513, thirty Africans were with him, and that these Africans helped Balboa build the first ship to be constructed in the Western Hemisphere."

Shelby's eyes glittered with excitement as she leaned forward. "Aside from the academics, what else are they offered?"

"Dance skills. Not the hip-hop and street dancing they can pick up on their own, but ballroom techniques. They never know when it will come in handy," he added, seeing Shelby smile. "I must not forget the very important sex education courses for the upperclassmen, and last but not least, the course on table etiquette—which fork or spoon to use when dining. They've all become familiar with the differences between a water goblet, a fluted glass for champagne, and one for cordials. I don't ever want them to be confused when they sit down to a formal dinner. The social skills training helps to build esteem and confidence."

"Are they receptive to the social skills courses?" Shelby questioned, totally caught up in the activities of the school.

"In the beginning we were met with a lot of resistance, but each year it gets easier and easier," Marshall admitted honestly. He smiled, the expression so sensual that Shelby stared at him in a stunned silence. "They don't mind the ballroom dancing because it's always held after class and they get to invite their sisters, cousins, or girlfriends to practice with them. The upperclassmen have become positive role models for the younger students. And what most of them like is not having the pressure of deciding what to wear each day. The latest style of dress becomes irrelevant between the hours of nine and three."

"I'm certain their parents like the dress code," Shelby remarked.

"Aside from the academics, it's what they like best."

"What else do you plan to offer the young men at Nia Academy?"

Marshall gave her a look that set her pulses racing, and she felt herself caught up in the man and the moment. For a brief instant she had caught a glimpse of his vision for Nia Academy.

Leaning forward and bracing both elbows on his knees, he threaded his fingers together and studied the design of the Oriental rug.

"I want a cultural arts curriculum. A curriculum that will include art, music, literature, folklore, and religion." His head came up slowly and the dark, laughing eyes were serious. "My students know what they are, but they don't know who they are, Shelby. I want them to know that they're descendants of a race of brilliant, creative, and honorable people who built advanced ancient civilizations dating from 4500 B.C. and that their accomplishments have continued throughout the ages up to and including 2000 A.D. And they will know this only if they study their past—every phase of it."

Shelby nodded slowly. "What you want is the main focus of the history of Arabs and Europeans in Africa to be shifted to the Africans themselves. In other words, a history of the blacks *that is a history of blacks*. And the same in the Americas."

"Yes." There was an almost imperceptible note of pleading in the single word.

Shelby had known what he'd wanted the moment he'd outlined the school's purpose, and she was certain she could write the curriculum Marshall wanted. But she had never made it a practice to accept a project without doing her own research.

"Can you write it?" Marshall asked.

"It's not *can* I write it, Mr. Graham," she replied with a slight tilting of her chin, "but *will* I write it."

His eyes narrowed and he sat up, his back becoming

ramrod straight. "You'll be paid well for the project, Ms. Carter."

Shelby compressed her lips tightly, biting back a sharp retort. Marshall thought she was balking because of money. "When do you intend to incorporate the cultural arts courses into your curriculum?"

"Next fall. It's going to take at least three to six months to hire the qualified instructors before everything is put into place. And that includes setting up specialized classrooms for permanent exhibits."

Marshall knew he had done a lot of talking about Nia Academy and he couldn't help himself whenever someone appeared genuinely interested in what had become a priority in his life. He had left a coveted position at Howard University as an associate professor in their history department and had sacrificed his marriage to pursue his dream to establish a prep school for young men of color within their own neighborhood.

Shelby fought her own war of emotions. She wanted to develop the curriculum; she knew the school needed the curriculum; but she also knew that if she undertook the project, it meant interacting with Marshall. His presence reminded her of what she had been denying for so many years.

The stirrings of desire brought back a yearning for an intimacy she had missed for more than six years.

"We'll exchange phone numbers and I'll let you know whether I'll do it," she said, not committing herself.

"When?"

"Soon."

"How soon?" Marshall shot back.

A tense silence enveloped the room, broken only by the sound of crackling, burning wood, followed by a shower of brilliant falling embers. Both of them turned and stared at the fireplace.

Shelby breathed in shallow, quick gasps, trying to ease her tension. Her chest felt as if it would burst. Why was she, she berated herself, getting so worked up over a man whose manner reminded her of her ex-husband's?

Earl Russell had been smooth and confident beyond his years. His friends had referred to him as "slick," yet she saw him as mature; mature and slick enough to get her to marry him within weeks of their graduation.

Act in haste, repent in leisure. Shelby's mother's words came back to haunt her once Earl had revealed his true selfish nature. *And I'm still repenting,* Shelby mused.

The tension was gone from her face when she turned to face Marshall. "I'd like to see your school first. Then I'll give you my answer."

"I can give you a tour tomorrow," he said quickly.

"Tomorrow's Sunday, and I've already made plans for the day. Monday would be a better day."

"But classes are in session during the week," Marshall argued.

"I prefer to observe your school in operation. Besides," she added with a bright smile, "I don't lecture on Mondays."

Marshall let out an audible sigh he was certain Shelby heard. He inclined his head slightly. "Then I'll arrange my schedule to accommodate you on Monday."

Shelby smiled at him. "Very good."

Marshall studied her intently before he returned her smile, a gleam of interest in his gaze betraying his polite expression. Only Naomi registered his look as she walked into the living room.

She studied the two people sitting only a few feet from each other and successfully concealed a secret smile. "Dinner is ready," she said softly, turning and walking back to the dining room.

Shelby found herself charmed and thoroughly entertained throughout dinner. Naomi and Marshall kept her laughing with stories about the students they had taught.

"It's unfortunate, Marshall, that when you finally get to work with a younger student population it's not in a teaching capacity. I'm certain you would've enjoyed hearing the 'not having the homework' excuses," Naomi said to her nephew with a warm smile.

"College students aren't exempt from coming up with their share of excuses," he reminded her. "And because they're older, the excuses go a bit beyond 'the dog ate my assignment' or 'my mother lined the bird cage with my research paper.' "

"What's the most original one you've heard?" Shelby asked Marshall.

He lowered his fork of candied sweet potatoes and smiled at her. He was delighted to see amusement flickering in her large dark eyes. The expression softened her mouth and crinkled her eyes slightly.

His mouth ruffled with a smile, then his lips parted with a wide grin as he recalled some of the more ingenious stories he had heard during his tenure at Howard University.

"I think the most original one I heard was when a student claimed his mother used his research notes to drain the fried chicken for Sunday dinner."

Shelby bit back laughter. "If she didn't have any paper towels, why didn't she use a brown paper bag?"

"That's . . . that's because the notes were written down on brown paper," Marshall replied, laughter rumbling deep down in his chest.

"But why would the poor child write his notes on a paper bag?" Naomi questioned, a look of distress marring her smooth forehead. "Couldn't he afford a notebook?"

Marshall stopped chuckling long enough to say, "Because he didn't want to waste writing or typing paper. He said he was an environmentalist and his intent was to save the trees."

"But Marshall, darling, didn't the poor child know that brown paper is also made from trees?" Naomi asked.

Marshall nodded vigorously, holding his chest as tears of laughter filled his eyes. "He had only decided to become an environmentalist that morning."

"How convenient for him," Shelby said, shaking her head and wondering how students, even the ones she'd attended high school and college with, managed to come up with their creatively concocted excuses for not meeting assignments.

"Not convenient enough," Marshall stated, having recovered from his laughing fit. "I took off a full letter grade from his paper when he finally handed it in two weeks late."

"Only a full letter grade?" Naomi asked skeptically. "The rumor around Howard was that Dr. Graham gave out more zeroes than any other professor in college history."

Marshall shrugged his broad shoulders under his jacket. "He caught me at a weak moment." He winked at Shelby.

She gave him a full-mouthed smile. Something told her that the man didn't have too many weak moments. His smile faded slowly as he stared across the table at her. An odd but primitive warning swept through her. There was no mistaking Marshall's curiosity. Her curiosity was also aroused, but she knew the mutual attraction would be perilous—perilous only to her.

The heat that rose from her chest swept up her throat and to her face under the heat of his gaze. Her wildly beating heart was the only audible sound in the room as everything around her faded into a pinpoint of light.

He's nothing like Earl, she thought. Nothing except for an intangible sexual magnetism that made Marshall Graham so much like the man she had fallen in love with on sight and married after a three-month whirlwind romance. At twenty-two, she was going to become a modern-day Margaret Mead. She wanted to be the anthropologist for the twenty-first century, studying tribal people from the continent of Africa.

She had earned her degree in ethnoanthropology and had planned for graduate work in the same field, but Earl had complained that her fieldwork would keep them apart for long periods of time; and not willing to risk her new marriage, she'd conceded, deciding instead to pursue a degree in African studies.

Shelby didn't realize until after Earl had entered medical school that she should have continued her original plan to become an anthropologist because she and Earl had never found time for each other because he seemed to study around the clock; and when he wasn't studying, he was trying to catch up on lost sleep.

It wasn't until Earl had come to her seeking a divorce that she'd realized how much she had sacrificed. She and Earl had decided to wait until they were thirty before starting a family; they were careful, and she was very careful not to conceive; however, once Earl disclosed that a colleague he had been sleeping with since they'd entered medical school together was pregnant with his child, Shelby felt doubly cheated. He had given another woman the child they'd planned to have, and she'd given up her career as an anthropologist.

Shelby Carter had learned a valuable lesson: seek out your own happiness before you try to make someone else happy.

"Is something wrong, Shelby?"

She stared blankly at Naomi, unaware that she had asked her a question.

"I'm sorry," she apologized, her cheeks hot with embarrassment.

"I asked if you're ready for dessert."

Giving Naomi a warm smile, Shelby said, "I don't think I can eat another morsel." She had eaten turkey with giblet stuffing and gravy, a piece of cakelike cornbread, candied sweet potatoes, and a portion of steamed mustard and turnip greens.

"Don't tell me you're going to pass on my deep-dish apple pie?"

Shelby hesitated. Naomi Morrow made the best apple pie. "If you don't mind, I'll take a slice home with me. I'll have it for a midnight snack."

Naomi's smile widened. "Marshall?"

"Like Shelby, I'll also take my portion home with me."

Naomi placed her damask napkin down beside her plate and rose to her feet. Marshall also stood as she began stacking silver onto an empty plate. "Marshall, you and Shelby relax in the living room while I take care of this."

Shelby pushed back her chair, rising to her feet. "No, please. Let me help you."

"Nonsense," Naomi protested. "You're my guest."

Shelby picked up her own silverware, then reached over and removed Marshall's place setting. "I've eaten here so many times that I don't think of myself as a guest."

Naomi's hands stilled. "There's an unwritten rule with the Grahams that says if you don't want to be treated like a guest, then you'll be treated like family."

Shelby gave the older woman, whom she thought of as her mentor, a warm smile. "I'd be honored if you'd consider me family."

"And what would you like to be?" Marshall questioned. "A granddaughter?"

Shelby arched her eyebrows at him. "Your aunt isn't old enough to be my grandmother."

"But I'm old enough to be your aunt. How fitting," Naomi continued, pleased with herself. "Even though I've always doted on Marshall, I've always wanted a niece."

"Aunt Naomi, you may think of Shelby as a niece," Marshall said quietly, "but I find it very difficult at thirty-nine to think of another woman as my sister."

Naomi was slightly taken aback by her nephew's reference to their kinship. It was only on rare occasions that he referred to her as "Aunt Naomi."

"Does it bother you, dear nephew, that I'd like to think of Shelby as a niece?"

Marshall stared at Shelby, and the double meaning of his gaze was obvious even before he spoke. "Not in the least. However . . ." He paused, a teasing smile tilting the corners of his mouth upward under his neatly barbered moustache. "As an only child, I never had the experience of dealing with a younger sister. I hope you'll bear with me, Shelby, until I get it down pat."

"Well, since I do have a brother," Shelby countered, "I'll be certain to let you know when you don't get the older brother-younger sister scenario just right."

Marshall leaned forward. "Is your brother younger or older than you?"

"Four years younger."

"Quite different from having an older brother."

Shelby winced. She remembered her friends when growing up who always lamented about their older brothers being too protective. "Are you certain you want to assume this role?"

Marshall's sensual smile was slow in coming, and there was no mistaking his acquiescence. "This is an offer I can't refuse."

"I remember you saying that once before and it changed your life forever," Naomi reminded Marshall.

His aunt was right. He had accepted her offer to leave Howard to take the position as headmaster for Nia Academy, and the decision had cost him his marriage.

"It's a lot different this time," he said. Different because something told him Shelby Carter was different—very, very different from Cassandra.

"Come, big brother," Shelby teased. "You and I are on kitchen duty tonight while *Aunt* Naomi relaxes."

It took some urging, but Naomi finally retreated to the living room while Shelby and Marshall cleared the dining room table.

"I'll rinse the dishes and you can stack them in the dishwasher," Marshall ordered, removing his jacket and hanging it on a colorful hook along the kitchen wall.

Shelby gave him a saucy smile. "Are you certain you're not an older brother? You sure know how to give orders." Her gaze swept over his broad shoulders under the collarless silk shirt. She stared at his face rather than begin a leisurely visual perusal of Marshall Graham's slim, hard athletic frame.

Suddenly his face went grim. "My mother lost a child the year I turned seven. It was a baby boy—a stillbirth. She never recovered from the loss. After she came home from the hospital I don't ever remember hearing her laugh the way she used to. She'd smile, but it was always a sad smile. In my own way I tried to make her forget the loss. And I did everything I could to make her happy. I earned high grades, helped her around the house, and during the tax season when Dad worked late, used to read the stories of Charles Chestnutt to her."

There was a faraway look in Marshall's eyes as he focused on a spot just above Shelby's head. "The loss was hard on my father, too, because he'd lost not only his second child, but also a small piece of his wife. And although I never heard them talk about it, somehow I knew the intimacy in their marriage had died when they'd buried my infant brother."

Shelby hadn't realized she was holding in her breath until her chest felt as if it would explode. "I'm sorry, Marshall. I'm truly sorry for you, your mother, and your father."

His gaze met hers and he smiled. "Sometimes it takes a little longer than we want it to take, but everyone heals. Last year, for my parents' fortieth wedding anniversary, I gave them a gift of a monthlong cruise on the *QE II.*" His smile widened. "My father confessed the time they spent together was better than their honeymoon."

"You're a wonderful son, Marshall," Shelby said without guile or sarcasm.

"I love my parents very much. All I want is to see them happy."

The conversation ended when Marshall rolled back the cuffs of his shirt and rinsed dishes and silverware before he handed them to Shelby to stack in the dishwasher.

Sharing in the cleaning of the kitchen with Shelby reminded him that his ex-wife never set foot in the kitchen in their Washington, D.C., home. Every social event they'd hosted was a catered affair. Cassandra abhorred housework, yet she hadn't been willing to leave the colonial home to relocate with him to New York.

Marshall left Washington, D.C., giving Cassandra the divorce she sought and leaving her the house she used solely as a showplace for entertaining.

He glanced down at Shelby as she filled the dishwasher cups with liquid, closed the door, and pushed several buttons to begin the wash cycle. There was no doubt that the slender well-dressed woman whose head came just to his nose was more than familiar with the inside of a kitchen.

There was a quiet intimacy of working side by side on a task even as mundane as cleaning up a kitchen. Working together they finished quickly, and smiling at each other, Shelby and Marshall left the kitchen to return to the living room.

"Don't tell me you're leaving so early," Naomi lamented as Shelby glanced down at her watch.

Shelby knew Naomi didn't want them to leave. Whenever she went to the older woman's apartment, they usually spent hours talking about everything from art to the world's political situations.

"It's after eleven, and I have an appointment to meet someone tomorrow morning," she explained.

Marshall stood up, walked over to his aunt, and leaned down to kiss her cheek. "It *is* getting late, and you need your sleep."

Naomi folded her hands on her hips. "Are you trying to say something, Marshall Oliver Graham?"

He smiled down at her, extending his hand and pulling her gently to her feet. "No, ma'am."

Naomi hugged him, her cheek resting on his solid broad chest. "I thought not." She released him, smiling and watching as he retrieved his coat and Shelby's from the foyer.

Minutes later she stood at the door, kissing both of them on the cheek. "Please, Marshall, make certain Shelby gets home safely. And I don't have to tell you to see her to her door," she whispered in a quiet tone.

"I'll take good care of her," he confirmed just as quietly.

Naomi closed the door, smiling and humming "Matchmaker" from *Fiddler on the Roof.* It had taken her more than a year to bring her nephew and Shelby together; and what she had suspected would happen did happen. It was more than obvious that Marshall was intrigued by Shelby; however, it was up to him to realize that he wasn't destined to spend the rest of his life alone.

Shelby pressed her back against the supple leather seat in the vintage Mercedes-Benz sedan while Marshall expertly maneuvered his car through the nighttime traffic. He waited for a traffic light to change and she felt him studying her profile.

"Do like living here in the city?" he asked, accelerating smoothly after the driver of the car behind him tapped lightly on his horn.

"Very much," she replied. "Everything is right here at your fingertips: restaurants, movie theaters, museums, and art galleries." It was now her turn to stare at his strong profile. "You don't like the city?"

Marshall signaled, then turned off the avenue to the lane leading crosstown through Central Park. "I love it."

"Where do you live?"

"White Plains."

"That's not the city," Shelby countered.

"It's a suburban city."

"It's not New York City, Marshall."

He gave her a quick glance. "Only the five boroughs can be New York City, Shelby."

"You're right about that." Shrugging, she turned to stare out through the window at the passing landscape. A full yellow moon cast an eerie glow on leafless branches reaching skyward like grotesquely shaped skeletal fingers. Gnarled tree trunks took shapes of hulking black bears and crouching felines, and boulders the shape of grazing buffaloes.

"Central Park at night becomes a magical fairyland," she said quietly.

Marshall slowed, permitting her to savor the scenery. "Only if you're not on foot."

She smiled.

"Have you ever taken a hansom ride through the park?"

Turning her head slowly, Shelby looked at Marshall. "No. I've lived here for sixteen years and I've never done it."

He smiled, flashing white teeth. "Don't tell me you're not a native New Yorker."

"I'm a native Californian. My parents and my brother and his family live in the Bay Area, but I have relatives all over the state."

There was a moment of comfortable silence before Shelby spoke again. "Do you miss D.C.?"

"Yes and no," he replied, his tone filled with a strained emotion he couldn't disguise. "I sometimes miss the milder weather and the small-town flavor of a cosmopolitan city. But what I miss most of all is . . ."

"What, Marshall?" Shelby prompted, when he did not finish his statement.

"The food and the jazz clubs," he replied in a half-lie. There was no way he'd admit openly to Shelby that what he felt was loneliness and estrangement. He was more lonely than he was willing to admit—even to himself.

Marshall didn't equate loneliness with celibacy because he hadn't been celibate since his divorce. He'd gone out with women, but he found that they bored him. However, his sense of estrangement had begun when he'd uprooted himself from his hometown, left a position he'd wanted ever since he'd entered Howard University as a freshman, then sacrificed his marriage because he wanted to pursue the second phase of his lifelong dream to head or teach in a specialized school for young men of color. It was only since he'd spent the past four hours in Shelby's presence that his feeling of loneliness had intensified tenfold. He had become so involved with Nia Academy that he hadn't thought of his own personal needs.

"I don't know how many restaurants there are in White Plains that serve Southern cuisine or clubs that offer jazz," Shelby replied, "but I know quite a few of them here in the city. If you want a listing, I'd be more than willing to put one together for you."

"I'd like that very much." What he didn't say was that he'd prefer that she accompany him.

He exited the park, continuing westward until he turned north onto Riverside Drive. "Which apartment building is yours?" he asked, once he neared 112th Street.

"The first one." There were two apartment buildings on the street, both with canopies shading the entrances.

"I may have to circle the block before I find a parking space."

Shelby placed a hand on his arm. "Don't bother to park. Please let me out in front of the building."

He continued past her building and pulled into a space at the corner. "I'll see you to your door."

Shelby opened her mouth to protest, but closed it quickly once she registered the frown set into his features.

By the time she had gathered her handbag and the small shopping bag with a plastic container filled with apple pie, Marshall had opened the passenger door.

She placed her gloved hand in his, permitting him to pull her to her feet. He didn't release her hand as he walked with her to the entrance of her apartment building. Handing him her keys, she waited until he unlocked the door leading to the lobby.

Shelby pushed the elevator button and the door opened. Marshall glanced in, then stepped aside to let her enter before he did. She pressed the button for her floor and both of them stood side by side as the car carried them quickly to the twelfth floor.

"The building has nice art-deco furnishings," he remarked as they left the elevator and walked to her apartment.

Shelby smiled at him. "The buildings on this street are cooperatives and are beautifully maintained. Many of the tenants have lived here for more than thirty years, so when the opportunity came to buy, they snapped up the offer."

She unlocked the two locks and pushed open the door. Heat and the soft glow of pink light lit up the entry. Turning slightly, she glanced up at Marshall. "Thank you for seeing me home."

Inclining his head slightly, he let his large dark eyes examine her face. "I'll call you tomorrow evening to set up a time for your tour of the school."

Something intense flared through Shelby with his lazy appraisal of her features. A warning flag in her

brain snapped up with the word printed in bold red
letters—*don't!*

*Don't see him again! Don't accept his offer to write the
cultural arts curriculum for Nia Academy!*

He took her silence as acquiescence, saying, "Good
night, Shelby."

"Good night," she mumbled to his broad-shoul-
dered back as he turned and made his way to the elevator. She watched until he disappeared into the
elevator, then closed and locked her door.

Letting out her breath slowly, she pulled off her hat,
slipped out of her coat, and hung it in a small closet
near the front door. Walking through the living room,
she placed the small shopping bag on a table in the
dining area. She stood at the window spanning the living room and dining area, staring out at the black surface of the Hudson River and the tiny lights winking
back at her from New Jersey.

Marshall Graham had walked into Naomi Morrow's
apartment at exactly seven-thirty and he had walked
away from hers at eleven-thirty. Four hours. It had
taken only four hours to remind her that the memory
of distrust and infidelity hadn't vanished completely.

Pulling back her shoulders, she smiled. She would
write Marshall's cultural arts curriculum, then she'd
move on to the next stage of her life. And hopefully
that would be as assistant curator for the popular Studio Museum in Harlem.

Shelby sat on a tall stool examining several small
pieces of sculptured jewelry. Her eyes narrowed as she
picked up a pendant and turned it over on her palm.

"Gold?" she questioned without looking up.

"Gold leaf over bronze."

This time she did glance up. Her smile matched that

of the tall, thin artist who had secured a profusion of curling dreadlocks with a leather thong at the nape of his neck.

"Do you recognize it?" Shumba Naaman asked.

"It's Aztec." Shelby held it closer. "This guy looks like Mictlantecuchtli, Lord of the Dead. And if he is, I would place this little beauty somewhere in Oaxaca around the fifteenth century."

"Right on all accounts, Shelby Carter."

She weighed the pendant, which nearly spanned the length of her hand. "It's an exquisite replica."

"Do you think you can sell it for me?"

She picked up another pendant in the form of a monster with a human head, the body of a snake, and a tail shaped like a bird's beak. The pendant was about six centimeters in height and had been crafted with such precision and skill that only an expert would be able to tell it was a replica.

She examined a golden bell in the form of a monkey. This piece was copied from a sixteenth-century original crafted by the Mixtec. The Mixtec had been the most talented craftsmen in ancient Mexico. They'd lived around the valley of Oaxaca, southeast of the lake. They had carved jade, made exquisite painted pottery, and worked gold with a skill that was unexcelled in the whole of pre-conquest America.

Shumba leaned closer to Shelby, inhaling the sensual fragrance of her perfume. "What do you think of this one?" He held up a pendant in the form of a skull with movable jaws hung with bells.

She took the skull from his long, skillful fingers. Holding up the pendant, she shook it gently. The bells tingled musically. "He's cute, but the movable jaws don't excite me too much." She handed it back to Shumba. "Are all of these cast in bronze?"

"Mr. Jaws is cast in copper. I tried using the same

method of casting as the Mixtec. I mixed the copper
with an alloy the Spaniards call *tumbaga*. It turned from
dull red to yellow after I melted it, then I rubbed it
until the copper dissolved from the surface, leaving a
spongy film of pure gold which was consolidated by
burnishing. It's an expensive method because the *tumbaga* must contain at least ninety percent copper to glis-
ten to a convincing yellow."

"Starving artists don't make pieces in gold,
Shumba," she teased.

"I only look as if I'm starving."

Shumba was right. At six-foot-three, he weighed 170.
There was a time when he'd weighed in at 210, but
after he'd changed his name from Francis Humphries
to Shumba Naaman and let his hair grow into dreadlocks, he had become a vegetarian. He'd left his very
lucrative position as a stockbroker for one of the top
Wall Street firms to be an artist. And as a starving artist
he worked out of the spacious SoHo loft which he'd
paid for in full from the bonuses he'd earned during
the ten years he had "gambled" with the investments
of his clients.

Daylight streamed through the windows, highlight-
ing the gold undertones in Shumba's skin and the red-
dish strands in his sandy-brown hair. His gold-brown
eyes were humorous and tender.

There had been a time when Shumba had confessed
that he was in love with Shelby. She'd laughed, saying
she didn't want to spoil their friendship by becoming
involved with him. He had only shrugged, saying she
was probably right. Afterward, they'd promised to see
each other every other month over Sunday brunch.

"I can sell every piece and you know it," she said,
examining a golden replica of a sixteenth-century Inca
woman. Putting it aside, she picked up the matching
one of a man.

"Those two are solid gold. The little guy is yours."

"No, Shumba."

He took the tiny figure from her fingers, wrapping it in a soft cloth. "I made it for you, Shelby. It's my Kwanzaa gift to you." He grasped her hand and placed the cloth-covered sculpture in it. "Take it. Now the only other thing you have to do is represent me again at my next showing."

Her eyes glistened with excitement. "When do you want to show these pieces?"

"As soon as possible. I'd like to sell everything before I go to Benin."

"If I can get the gallery to set up the showing within two weeks, will that be soon enough?"

"Perfect. I'm scheduled to leave the second week in January."

Shelby spent the entire Sunday afternoon cataloging Shumba's pieces, while he prepared a sumptuous meal of steamed vegetables with homemade sourdough bread and a crisp salad. They toasted each other with several glasses of an excellent dry white wine before Shelby gathered her coat to leave.

Shumba escorted her down to the street, hailed a taxi, paid the driver, then kissed her mouth lightly before he waved her off.

Shelby's thoughts were filled with planning the exhibit for Shumba, and she wondered how many pieces Naomi would buy from this showing.

Pulling out her appointment diary, she scribbled notes on a pad of blank pages at the back of the small spiral book. Using the waning daylight, she jotted down days and dates. She lectured Tuesday, Wednesday, and Thursday at the Met, and usually worked at the gallery on Monday and Friday afternoons.

Flipping open to Monday, she winced. She was scheduled to go to Nia Academy. She hadn't planned to spend the entire schoolday at Nia, which meant she could make it to the gallery before it closed. She wanted to set up the showing as soon as possible.

Closing the diary, she mentally outlined what she had to do before the end of the year. She had done all of her holiday shopping early, mailing off gifts to her parents, her brother, her sister-in-law, and her nieces and nephew. She returned to California for the holidays every even-numbered year. This year, an odd-numbered one, would find her spending the season in New York.

Shelby unlocked the door to her apartment, registering the soft chiming of the telephone. She rushed into the living room and picked up the receiver. "Hello?"

"Did I catch you at a bad time?"

"No, Marshall," she answered quickly, her pulse starting up an erratic rhythm at the sound of his softly drawling voice.

"I'm available to meet with you at any time you wish tomorrow."

She wanted to cover as many of the school's activities as she could in one day, and she had to get to the midtown gallery by three.

"I'll be there at nine and stay until two."

"I can provide transportation for you," Marshall offered.

Shelby laughed. "That's all right. I have the address and I believe I can find my way to the school without getting lost." Nia Academy was less than a mile from where she lived.

"If that's the case, then I'll expect you tomorrow morning at nine."

"Good night, Marshall."

"Good night. And, Shelby . . ."

"Yes, Marshall?"

"Thank you."

"You're welcome." She hung up, sinking down into the sofa. She had committed herself.

As she stared across the room decorated in black, off-white, and tan, something clicked in her mind.

She knew nothing about Marshall Graham other than that he was the headmaster of a preparatory school and the nephew of an acquaintance. She didn't know whether he was married or single, and if he was single, whether he was involved with a woman.

Their conversation over last night's dinner had covered topics of a general nature. They'd discussed sports, the results of recent elections, and the evolution of popular music.

And now, only after she'd spoken to him over the telephone, did she know what had had her off balance with Marshall. There was something about him that reminded her that she *was* a normal woman with normal desires.

Without him knowing it, Marshall had become her conscience, reminding her that although her life had undergone an evolution, emotionally, she hadn't.

It was she who should have done the thanking.

Rising to her feet, she took off her coat and laid it over the arm of the sofa. She examined the furnishings in the apartment she'd occupied for the past five years. It was as if she were seeing everything for the first time: the comfortable sofa covered in off-white cotton, a throw rug covering the wood floor in a mud cloth pattern, and matching throw pillows she had bought during a trip to Mali, and the many pieces of sculpted primitive art she had purchased were nestled on off-white glass-topped rattan tables. Lush, live green plants and cacti added a splash of color to the living room, dining area, and bathroom.

She was alive—truly alive. She wanted to be loved, and she wanted to be *in* love; and more than anything, she wanted to share the special intimacy she hadn't had for more than six years.

"Thank you, Marshall Graham," she whispered to the full moon shining in a clear, star-littered winter nighttime sky.

Shelby stood outside the three-story townhouse. A large plaque in gold letters on a black background identified it as Nia Academy. The school was on a quiet residential West Harlem street lined with trees, town houses, and brownstones. It was an ideal location for a private school.

She noticed one side of the street was restricted to school personnel parking only, and she was able to appreciate the full beauty of Marshall's stately dark-gray vintage 1975 Mercedes for the first time in the bright daylight.

It was ten minutes to nine when she made her way into Nia Academy and to a front office where two women sat close together, talking quietly over mugs of coffee.

One glanced up and smiled. "Good morning. May I help you?"

"I'm Shelby Carter. I have an appointment with Dr. Graham for nine."

The woman's smile faded slowly as she glanced at a telephone console on the table in front of her. "Dr. Graham's line is busy. As soon as it's free, I'll let him know you're here. Please have a seat, Miss Carter." Her voice was pleasant, her manner professional.

Shelby nodded. She removed her gloves, pushed them into the pockets of her coat, and sat down on a tufted chair in a blue and gold kente-patterned design.

The reception area was spacious, the pale walls covered with the framed prints of Romare Bearden, Jacob Lawrence, and Faith Ringold, and Henry Tanner's *The Banjo Lesson.*

Shelby examined the Tanner print, remembering the Met had recently offered an exhibit of Henry Ossawa Tanner's work. The response to his best-known paintings, *The Banjo Lesson, Daniel in the Lion's Den,* and *The Resurrection of Lazarus,* had been one of the highlights of the museum's year.

"Miss Carter, Dr. Graham will be with you momentarily."

She turned and smiled at the receptionist. "Thank you." The words were barely out of her mouth when Marshall walked into the reception area, smiling.

"Good morning, Shelby."

The smooth, resonant voice brought a smile to her face and she rose to her feet. Seeing him again was like a punch to the solar plexus. This was the real Marshall Graham—in his universe.

He was dressed in what he'd described as the school's uniform: a navy blue double-breasted blazer with a patch on the pocket in the same navy and gold kente pattern as the one covering the chairs in the reception area, gray slacks, white button-down shirt, and navy tie. His footwear was a pair of black loafers. He looked every inch the preppie. Her sculpted eyebrows arched; her gaze fixed on the pin on his blazer lapel.

"Good morning," she replied, her smile mirroring confidence and pleasure at seeing him again.

His right hand cupped her elbow. "Please, come into my office and I'll let you know what I've planned for us."

Marshall led her into a large, sun-filled room, his hands going to her shoulders. "I'll take your coat." Lowering his head, his warm, clean breath swept over the back of her neck, eliciting a slight shudder, then a smile from Shelby as his hands caressed her shoulders before he eased the black wool garment from her body and hung it on a brass coatrack in the corner near the door.

Turning around to face her, it was Marshall's turn to gape at the pin on over Shelby's left breast. A slow, sensual smile parted his lips before they inched up, displaying his beautiful white teeth.

"Where did you get yours?" he questioned.

"At the Black Expo last year."

"That's quite a coincidence, because that's where I bought mine." Moving closer, his gaze was fixed on what had been labeled the Middle Passage Holocaust Pin. He and Shelby had each elected to purchase one in pewter.

Most people who saw the pin for the first time were transfixed with the piece of jewelry designed in the shape of the hull of a slave cargo ship. Closer examination showed the outline of human bodies, lying in spoonlike fashion, head-to-toe, commemorating the importation of Africans through the Middle Passage.

"I see you elected to buy the one with the cowrie shells," Marshall said, staring at Shelby's pin.

She nodded. "And you went for the tiny heads." The five tiny heads, each face different, were suspended from nooses. The five tiny cowrie shells shook delicately when her fingers caressed her pin. The pin's designer had selected the number five because it represented "justice" in African forklore.

"Dr. Graham, I have a call from Ms. Pierce." The receptionist's voice came through the intercom on his desk.

Marshall moved over to the desk and pushed a button on the telephone. "Please take a message, Angela."

"I told her I'd take a message, but she insisted that

I put her through. She said it had something to do with a date for the fund-raising dinner dance."

Marshall hesitated, not wanting to, but knowing he had to take the call. His gaze was fixed on Shelby's face. Motioning, he held up one finger. She nodded and he picked up the receiver.

"Good morning, Nadine." He only half-listened to what Nadine Pierce said as he watched Shelby study the framed diplomas, awards, and certificates on a wall, and several photographs on a credenza facing the desk. "Yes, Nadine, I'm listening," he drawled. His gaze was fixed on Shelby's shapely legs, outlined in a pair of black opaque stockings and mid-high suede pumps.

He found the slim wool black skirt she had paired with a matching long-sleeved tunic flattering to her slender feminine figure. The severe color was offset by a challis scarf in a brilliant orange-and-black paisley. Her neatly coiffed hair was brushed off her forehead and over her ears, and his gaze drank in the delicate symmetry of her features. Tastefully exquisite. The two words summed up everything he had observed in Shelby Carter.

Shelby leaned closer, studying the photographs of a very young Marshall with Naomi Morrow. There was also a photograph of him with people she thought were his parents, on the day he'd graduated from college. There were no photographs of children or of a young woman, and she assumed that he had elected to keep that part of his personal life private.

Marshall ended the call, jotting down a date on the appointment book on his desk. Nadine could have given the information to the receptionist. He punched the button on the intercom. "Angela, please take messages. I'm going to be out of my office for most of the day. So if there's an emergency, page me."

"Okay, Dr. Graham."

He crossed the room, and as he neared Shelby, she turned and smiled up at him. "Where do we begin, Dr. Graham?"

He arched an eyebrow. "There's no need for us to be so formal, Shelby. The faculty and staff maintain a level of formality for the students because many of them lack discipline when they first arrive at Nia. It'll usually take a couple of months before they conform, and when they do, they're exemplary."

Taking her elbow, he guided her out of his office and down a navy blue carpeted corridor away from the front office. "All of the offices are on the main floor," he explained. He pointed out the offices of the school's psychologist, nurse, and guidance counselor. A modern theater, designed with a center stage and seating in the round and doubling as the auditorium, was also on the main floor.

Shelby followed Marshall up a flight of carpeted stairs to the second level. "Grades one through four are on this floor," he explained, walking slowly and stopping to peer through the glass on the doors of several classrooms.

Shelby stared at a class of eight second-graders who were listening intently to their teacher as he pointed out countries on a wall map.

A tender look softened her gaze. The young boys were so small, yet appeared mature beyond their years. "Do you employ only male instructors?" she asked quietly, still staring through the glass.

"No," Marshall replied close to her ear. "We have a few female instructors."

"Do you ever intend to admit female students?"

"Hopefully, one day."

Shifting slightly, Shelby glanced up. "Won't that change your *raison d'être*?"

"No. By that time there won't be a need for special-ized or alternate schools for young men of color."

Shelby lost track of time when she sat in on a fourth-grade science class that was conducting an experiment on dissection. The class of twelve young men were di-vided in teams of two as they dissected frogs. Most of them barely noticed her, while acknowledging Marshall with smiles and nods.

Marshall had to urge her to leave as they made their way to the third floor and the upperclassmen. The floor was quiet and the halls empty except for a tiny figure huddled near a classroom door. Dark, round eyes in a chubby face grew larger and rounder when the boy spied Marshall.

"What are you doing up here, Malik?"

"I . . . I wanted . . ." His little chin wobbled.

Marshall hunkered down to the child's level. "You wanted what?"

Malik pulled a strip of navy from his blazer pocket. "I wanted to see LaVarr. I . . . I couldn't tie my tie."

Marshall took the tie from the boy. "Does your teacher know you're up here?"

Malik shook his head. "I told him I wanted to go to the bathroom."

"You're not to lie to your teacher, Malik," Marshall scolded softly. He pulled up Malik's collar and slipped the tie under it. "If you wanted your brother to help you with your tie, you should've told your teacher that." Quickly and deftly he tied the tie, adjusting its length. "I'll get your brother to take you back to your class-room."

Malik nodded vigorously while staring up at Shelby. She smiled at him and he lowered his gaze. She waited with Malik until Marshall returned with a boy of about thirteen, an older version of his little brother.

"Good morning, ma'am," he said, nodding at

Shelby. His dark, intelligent eyes shifted to Marshall. "Will Malik get in trouble, Dr. G?"

Marshall managed a slight smile. "Not this time, LaVarr. But I want you to practice with him until he's able to tie his own tie. We can't have him buying clip-on ties when he's twenty-five years old and vice-president of a family-owned company, can we?"

LaVarr's smile was one of relief. "No way. Thanks, Dr. G." He gave Marshall a high-five before he led Malik back to his classroom.

"Dr. G," Malik called out. He rushed back to Marshall, also giving him a high-five. "Thanks for tying my tie."

Marshall struggled not to smile. "You're welcome, Malik."

"He's truly adorable," Shelby remarked, staring at the two boys as they made their way down the hall to the staircase.

"Malik's a charmer, Shelby. He manages to wrap all of us around his little finger." Although he'd spoken about Malik, Marshall's gaze was fixed on Shelby's animated features. "Do you have any children?"

"Why, no," she answered quickly. She hadn't expected him to ask about her. However, she had to admit she was more than curious about the private Marshall Graham. "How about yourself?"

His mouth tightened noticeably under his moustache. "I don't have any, either." He studied her thoughtfully for a moment. "Just in case you're wondering, I wanted children, but my ex-wife didn't." He watched her lush lips part slightly with a soft intake of breath. Unknowingly, he had read her mind. "I've been divorced for five years."

Shelby couldn't ignore the buildup of heat in her face. Her thickly lashed eyes were fixed on his Windsor-knotted tie.

"I've got you beat by a year. It's been six years for me," she admitted.

Marshall seemed to move closer while not taking a step. "How long were you married?"

"Six years." She smiled up at him. "And in case you're wondering, we planned on having children, but decided to wait until we were thirty before trying. Then my ex-husband decided he didn't want to wait and . . ." Her expression hardened as her voice trailed off.

This time Marshall did move closer to her, his chest nearly touching her shoulder. Shelby wanted him to take her in his arms and hold her until she healed completely; until she could learn to trust again.

"And what, Shelby?" His voice was low, coaxing.

Her eyelids fluttered slightly, then she tilted her chin and gave him a direct look. "He couldn't wait for me. He'd been sleeping with another woman and she got pregnant." She noted his black eyebrows slant in a frown and she forced a weak smile. "How did we get on the topic of failed marriages?" she asked, glancing down at her watch. It was nearly noon.

Marshall looked at his own watch. "We'll break for lunch before I show you the rest of the school."

He led the way to an elevator at the far end of the hall and a minute later they stepped out to the building's lower level.

The remainder of the afternoon sped by quickly. After sharing a lunch of grilled chicken and a Caesar salad in the lower-level cafeteria, Marshall showed Shelby a modern gymnasium with the latest exercise equipment, an Olympic-sized swimming pool, and a library with an extensive collection of books, ranging from contemporary popular literature and fiction to rare and out-of-print editions donated from private collections.

"Nia has only been as successful in its curriculum and philosophy because of donations," Marshall continued. His right hand cupped her left elbow as he guided her back to his office. "We do a big fund-raiser once a year in the spring, and with wonderful results. We have several very generous donors and one benefactor who prefers to remain anonymous. His donation underwrites the administrative overhead expense line in our annual budget."

"Do you offer scholarships?" Shelby asked, sitting down on a love seat covered in what she had now come to recognize as Nia's navy-and-gold kente-cloth pattern.

Marshall removed his blazer and hung it on the coat tree. Shelby's mouth went a little dry as she stared at the outline of his shoulders against the fabric of his shirt. The tailored gray slacks fit his waist, hips, and long legs with proportioned precision, and his powerful, athletic body moved with an easy grace that made him look as if he floated through a distance of space. She wondered about the woman who had let this brilliant, handsome, well-groomed man slip through her fingers.

"Most of our upperclassmen are offered scholarships because their parents need to save the money for college." Marshall sat down behind his desk, ignoring the stack of telephone messages he would return later that day. "Our children come from professional, working-class, and poor families. There is a very stringent admissions policy, so we don't and can't take every young man who applies. But if a child is accepted, the fact that his family can't make tuition is never a factor. If we have to underwrite the entire cost of his tuition, then we do it."

Shelby crossed one leg over the other and chewed

her lower lip. The ideas were tumbling over themselves in her head. "How involved are your parents with their children?"

"Not as much as I'd like. They come to the traditional open school nights to talk to the teachers about their sons' progress."

She stared directly at Marshall and was successful when she didn't succumb to the intensity of his gaze. It was as if his dark eyes had caught fire and singed her. "How would you like to begin your cultural arts curriculum a little early?"

He rose to his feet, eyes glittering. "You'll do it!" His voice was barely a whisper.

Shelby's smile was dazzling. Marshall reminded her of a little boy opening gifts on his birthday. But she had to remind herself that the tall man was anything but a little boy. "Answer my question, Marshall."

"Hell, yes. I mean, yes," he said, correcting himself.

She rose to her feet and walked over to him. "What do you think of the students at Nia hosting a 'Kwanzaa Expo' for their families and the neighborhood?"

Marshall stared at Shelby, a look of complete surprise on his face. What had been so obvious, too obvious, had never entered his head.

Shelby noted his indecision, wondering if he was opposed to her suggestion, if it had been too preposterous for him to consider.

"Marshall?"

He blinked, then smiled his sensual smile. "That's a wonderful idea."

Her expression matched his. "I take that to mean . . ."

"I mean yes," he cut in. He slipped his hands into the pockets of his slacks to keep from reaching out and clasping her tightly to his body. He found Shelby composed and controlled, yet there was something about her that elicited spurts of passion from him . . . not the physical, sexual passion, but one that made his emotions whirl and tilt until he lost his grip on his rigid self-control.

Shelby crossed her arms under her breasts. "You're not going to have much time to pull it off. I take it the school closes for a holiday recess?" He nodded. "I suggest that you hold it a week before the recess. That way, the students are familiar with all that will go into a Kwanzaa celebration before the holiday arrives. Then they'll be able to duplicate it at home with other friends and relatives."

"That's just what Nia needs to affect a holiday mood after a week of final exams."

"Then the timing is perfect. I have a lot of books and the props you'll need to help you celebrate Kwanzaa."

"When can we get together?"

"Tomorrow," Shelby replied, knowing Marshall would not have a lot of time to organize everything he'd need to host a schoolwide exhibition. "You can pick everything up from my apartment."

His gaze dropped from her face to her breasts, then back to her face. "What time do you leave the museum?"

"Five."

"Then I'll pick you up at the Fifth Avenue entrance."

Shelby noted the clock on his desk. It was nearly two o'clock. "Thanks for the tour. I'm more than impressed with Nia." Turning, she walked to the coatrack.

Marshall was only two steps behind her and reached to retrieve her coat. He held it out while she slipped her arms into it and secured the swingy wrap with a wide matching belt.

"Does this mean you're going to write the curriculum?" he asked, his breath sweeping over her neck.

Shelby looked up at him over her shoulder, unaware

of the tempting picture she presented as Marshall lowered his head until his mouth was only inches from hers.

"Yes."

His smile was dazzling while his eyes glittered with excitement. "Thank you." The two words spoke volumes.

Shelby rode the downtown bus, thinking about Nia Academy's commitment to academic excellence, social development, parent involvement, and student goals for continuous self-renewal. Focusing on the school's philosophy temporarily suppressed the awakening realization that she was more than attracted to Marshall Graham.

It hadn't been just his intelligence and overall good looks, but it was the man as a *male;* and seeing him again evoked feelings she recognized as a very strong passion within herself.

How had she, she thought, been able to repress passions which at one time had been as volatile and sometimes unquenchable as an oil field fire, a passion so encompassing that she was stunned when Earl left her marriage bed for another woman's? It was then that Shelby had doubted her role as a wife, and wondered if she had been indeed woman enough to hold on to her man.

The doubts and questions had attacked her relentlessly for a year, and she second-guessed her role as a wife and lover whenever she asked herself if she had demanded too much. Had she not given enough in return? Had she been too conservative in her lovemaking? What was it Earl had wanted that she hadn't been able to give him and he'd found with another woman?

The questions and the self-doubt led to withdrawal. She dropped out and hid herself away from the social circle she had spent years cultivating and became very selective whenever she accepted a date.

The healing process was slow, but she healed; and with the healing came a realization that she had been woman enough; that she had given Earl all he'd needed from a wife and lover; and most important, the fact that she had been concealing a great deal of anger and resentment that she had accommodated Earl when she'd given up her goal to become an anthropologist.

Once and only once had she permitted a man to make her decisions for her, and with disastrous results. Her delicate jaw hardened. It would never happen again.

The tightness in her face eased as she stared out the bus window, noting how easy it was for her to identify different neighborhoods without reading street signs by the types of shops open for business along the avenues. Manhattan was truly the ethnic mecca of the world.

Shelby walked through the door of the trendy East Side gallery and was the recipient of a dazzling smile from a tall, strikingly handsome man with a natural ash-blond ponytail sweeping down his back to his waist.

Hans Gustave's smoky gray eyes swept over her like a quick flash of lightning. "I know that look," he said confidently. "You have something for me."

Shelby made her way through the spacious Madison Avenue art gallery to a back room. She hung up her coat, then withdrew the stack of five-by-eight cards from her leather portfolio.

"What I have is eighteen pieces of exquisite sculpted pieces from Shumba Naaman."

Biting down on his lower lip, Hans pressed his palms together. "Tell me what you've got."

Shelby handed him the cards with detailed descriptions of each piece of sculpture. "They are incredible replicas of Aztec, Mixtec, and Inca amulets and totems."

Sitting down behind a priceless Louis XVI desk, she watched Hans read each card in quick precision. His grin grew wider as he read and shuffled each one. After the sixth one he glanced up. "I want every piece."

"But you haven't gone through all of them."

"I've seen enough. When can I show these?"

"Shumba wants a showing ASAP."

Hans took a matching chair, tapping the cards against the open palm of his left hand. "I can get invitations printed and in the mail by tomorrow, which means if I set it up for a week from this Friday, that'll give everyone on our mailing list a week and a half to clear their calendar and get their checkbooks in order. How does that sound to you?"

"It's a go, Hans."

Shelby spent the next three hours going over the large index cards, editing descriptions for a printed brochure before she and Hans agreed on the list price for each piece.

It was after seven o'clock when she walked into her apartment and flipped on a news cable channel on the television in an alcove of the bedroom. She undressed slowly, trying to digest the events of the world as her brain had shifted into overdrive when she thought of the three projects which would take up all her spare time over the next three weeks.

She had a lot on her plate: assisting the planning and coordination of the Kwanzaa Expo for Nia Academy, setting up the showing for Shumba, *and* writing the cultural arts curriculum for Marshall.

She was going to be very busy; too busy to think

about Marshall and how she felt whenever she was in his presence.

Marshall. The thought of his name brought a smile to her lips. *Mr. Perfect.*

So perfect, she mused, that his wife had left him. Or had he said he'd left her?

It didn't matter, she thought, shrugging a bare shoulder. Her association with Marshall was strictly business, and *only* business.

At five-fifteen Shelby walked out of the Met and glanced down from the top of the stone steps, looking for Marshall. Vehicular traffic along Fifth Avenue had slowed to a crawl as buses, taxis, and cars inched along. Christmas and Chanukah lights glowed from many windows in the apartments of the buildings facing Central Park.

She had taken only a step when a figure moved behind her from the shadows. "Marshall." His name had escaped her lips in a whispered wonderment before she turned around.

"Do you have eyes in the back of your head?" Marshall asked near her ear.

Shelby shivered slightly, turning and staring up at him. "No. I recognized your cologne," she confessed, her gaze racing quickly over his face. Her breath caught quickly in her lungs. Despite the darkness of the hour and the diffuse glow coming from streetlights, she still was able to register a flicker of interest in Marshall's intense eyes.

He was casually dressed in a pair of dark slacks, a charcoal gray and white patterned pullover sweater, and a short gray wool jacket.

"Is that how you identify *men*—by their cologne?"

His fingers curved around her upper arm, leading her down the steps.

"Not *all* men," she teased.

Lowering his head, Marshall let his mouth touch her ear. "That's encouraging to know."

"Why?"

"Because . . ." He grasped her hand, guiding her to the street and between lanes of stalled traffic. "Because," he repeated, once they crossed the street, "I don't want to be lumped into the category of the *insignificant* ones."

"What makes you so certain you're not one of, as you say, the insignificant ones?"

Marshall squeezed her gloved fingers slightly. "I say that because I think you like me as much as I like you."

Shelby stopped short, and Marshall nearly lost his balance. "Hold on there, mister. Who are you kidding?"

Tightening his grip on her hand, Marshall pulled her to him until her torso was pressed against his sweatered chest.

"Do you want me to show you how much you like me, Shelby?"

"No!" she gasped, glancing around her and hoping that the passing couples hadn't overheard him.

His hands went to her shoulders and he cradled her to his body. "I thought not, Shelby."

"Marshall." Her voice was small and muffled in his sweater. They were standing on 82nd Street, embracing like so many other lovers on New York City streets did every day.

"Loosen up, Shelby. I was only teasing you. Isn't a *big brother* entitled to tease his sister?"

Pulling back, she stared up at his smiling face. "Of course you are."

Marshall's arms fell away from her body and his smile

faded, and even though he had released Shelby, she hadn't moved. They stood, inches apart, their warm breaths mingling in the crisp night air. Seconds stretched into a minute before he spoke again.

"Shelby."

The quiet sound of her name coming from his lips left her tingling. The tingling increased until it was a surging wanting. Her heart pounded in her ears, and amazingly, she felt Marshall's, too. Her gloved right hand went to the middle of his chest at the same time Marshall folded her gently against the solid hardness of his body.

"It's not going to work, Shelby. As much as I try, I can't treat you like a sister or think of you as one."

The spell was broken. The warm wanting was replaced by an icy chill, a chill that began around her heart and spread outward, touching every nerve and fiber of her being.

Had Marshall recognized her attraction to him and decided to establish the rules for their working relationship?

Why hadn't she noted his unyielding self-control before? She was aware of the strict rules and regulations he had set down for Nia, and there was probably no doubt his private life was also maintained by the same strict codes.

Extracting herself, Shelby forced a smile. "That's quite all right. Having one brother is enough for me," she replied, her voice filled with indifference.

Marshall's brow furrowed. "I promised my aunt I would take care of you, and I will."

"There's no need for you to take care of me," Shelby retorted. "At thirty-four I'm quite able to look after myself."

"That's not what I mean," he countered. "I . . ."

"There's no need to explain," she interrupted.

"But Shelby . . ."

"Marshall. I've been on my feet all day, and you and I have a lot to cover tonight. Let's not waste time talking about who you're responsible for."

This time when Marshall's hand went to her arm, his grip was firm, but not friendly. "I thought we could talk over dinner. I wanted to take you to a favorite restaurant of mine."

Shelby had to quicken her step to keep up with Marshall's longer legs. "Perhaps some other time. We can either order in, or pick up something on the way."

Marshall clenched his teeth. Shelby wasn't making it easy for him. He wanted to go over all he needed to celebrate Kwanzaa with the students and their families, but he also wanted to know all there was to know about Shelby Carter.

He knew the professional Shelby from the information he had gleaned from her curriculum vitae; but his aunt had refused to elaborate about Shelby Carter the woman, other than that she was single.

He could still hear Naomi's voice: *"You've spent so much time at Nia that you've lost all the famous Graham male charm, dear nephew. I introduced you to Shelby. Now you're on your own. If you want the woman, go after her!"*

And he *did* want Shelby. He wanted to see her, to talk to her . . . and he wanted to kiss her.

He wanted to taste the moist lushness of her mouth and discover if the flesh covering all of her was as soft and smooth as the skin on her beautiful face.

He wanted Shelby Carter with the same intensity he had once wanted to become a Howard University professor and either a teacher or the headmaster of an all-boys school for young men of color.

"What would you like to eat?" Shelby questioned, breaking into his thoughts as they stopped next to his car.

"It can be your call tonight."

"There's a wonderful Chinese takeout on Broadway, several blocks from my place."

"Chinese it is." Marshall opened the passenger door and waited until she was seated. After he'd settled himself behind the wheel, he stared at her profile. Slowly and seductively, his gaze traveled a downward path, mirroring approval. Beautiful, intelligent, feminine, and sexy. Those were only the first of many other adjectives he had attributed to Shelby Carter as he started up the car and pulled away from the curb and into traffic.

Shelby unlocked the door to her apartment and pushed it open with her shoulder, balancing her shoulder purse and a large bouquet of snow-white lilies. "I can't believe you ordered practically everything on the menu."

"I couldn't decide what I wanted to eat," Marshall replied, following her into the foyer carrying two large bags filled with containers of Chinese food and a third bag with a bottle of wine.

He took several steps into the living room and stopped, feeling as if he'd stepped into a lush, verdant rain forest. All of the white, tan, and black furnishings were set against a backdrop of lush green plants.

Shelby, placing the calla lilies on the dining table, glanced back over her shoulder at Marshall. "Is something wrong?"

He smiled, shaking his head as he made his way to the dining area and placed his packages on the table. "I'm just a little taken aback by your place. It's so beautiful."

Soft pink light from the foyer and from several lamps on the tables in the living room bathed the apartment in a cool, rosy glow. Floor-to-ceiling lace panels in eggshell permitted a view of the Hudson and the New Jersey coastline from the picture window that spanned an entire wall.

The gleaming parquet floor was covered with several area rugs in what he recognized as a mud cloth print. Natural woods and cotton fabrics covered tables, sofas, and chairs, and straw and terra cotta planters held massive banana, colorful coleus, gloxinia, cyclamen, and towering flowering cactus plants.

Shelby shrugged out of her coat. "It's home and it's comfortable."

Marshall agreed with her. Her apartment *was* a home. It was warm and filled with an aura of life. It was tastefully furnished with a combination of the old and the new. The furnishings were contemporary, while the pieces of sculpted art were reminiscent of a time long gone and of people who also were long gone, except for some of the lingering customs, which would remain alive as long as the griots passed along the oral histories.

Her place was so unlike the house where he lived. The house he had had professionally decorated with every convenience possible was large, cold, and empty, now that he was aware of what had been missing. His home was missing the love of a man and a woman—a family.

How, he thought, had he seen to the needs of so many others without seeing to his own? What did he have to prove, playing the selfless martyr?

Shelby watched Marshall as he slowly surveyed her apartment. His reaction was similar to most who were impressed with her collection of primitive artifacts.

"Marshall," she called softly. "Take off your jacket and stay awhile. Make yourself at home." He spun around to face her, his eyes crinkling in amusement.

"You may come to regret that invitation," he said,

removing his waist-length gray wool jacket. He turned back to the window. "This is truly a room with a view."

Shelby took his jacket from him and scooped up her coat from the back of the dining chair, heading for the closet in the foyer. "I'll invite you back again when there's a prediction of snow," she said glibly. "I sit on the floor, with all the lights off, and watch it fall for hours," she explained. "It's a natural stress reliever."

She returned to the dining area, watching Marshall as he slipped his hands into the pockets of his slacks. His gaze was fixed on the window.

"Is that an open invitation, Shelby?"

The quiet timbre of his voice served as a warning to remind her of what she'd just offered.

"I . . ."

"Is it?" he repeated, stopping whatever she was going to say. He was frozen in place, only the rising and falling of his chest indicating he was still alive.

"Yes. Of course," she replied, as glibly as she had offered the invitation. "Please give me a few minutes to change my clothes, then we'll eat and go over what you'll need for your Kwanzaa Expo."

Walking past Marshall, Shelby didn't let out her breath until she made it to her bedroom and closed the door behind her.

Fool, she chided herself. What was she doing? How could she invite the man back to her place when all she wanted to do was complete her projects for him and move on? Move on to another man she found less disturbing . . . a man who didn't remind her of Earl.

She exchanged her skirt and sweater for a pair of black silk lounging pajamas with an abstract print of gold. She had fashioned the outfit of a long shirt with extended cuffs and side slits and loose-fitting pull-on pants with an elastic waist and drawstring tie. She quickly cleansed her face of all makeup, smoothed on a moisturizer, then brushed her curling hair off her forehead and over her ears. Slipping her bare feet into a pair of black leather ballet slippers, she returned to the living room.

Shelby walked into the darkened living and dining area, only the flicker of candles placed strategically on side tables illuminating the space. The sound of Jean-Pierre Rampal playing Vivaldi's *The Four Seasons* filtered through the apartment. The coffee table was set with a vase of lilies, two crystal wineglasses, several plates, the bottle of wine, and the containers of Chinese food.

Marshall stood with his back to the window, waiting for her. He saw her gaze sweep around the room in the flickering candlelight. The haunting sensual fragrance of vanilla lingered in the space. The fat candles were scented with a similar ingredient in Shelby's perfume.

"You said to make myself at home, and I did."

She bit back laughter. "So you did. Everything looks beautiful."

Floating across the room with his fluid stride, Marshall met her, extending his hand. "Dinner is served." She permitted him to seat her on the floor in front of the coffee table. Marshall also knelt, sitting down with his sock-covered feet tucked under him. He waited until she picked up a pair of chopsticks before he filled her wineglass with a chilled white Zinfandel.

"What would you like to begin with?" he asked.

Shelby's large eyes glittered with anticipation. She had thought of Marshall Graham as conservative and stodgy. How wrong she was, because he'd shown her he was anything but stodgy when electing to sit on the floor to eat. The candles, wine, flowers, and classical music revealed a lot about the man: he was a romantic.

She tried to remember all that he'd ordered. "I'll start with a steamed vegetable dumpling."

Each of them ate a dumpling before sampling a medley of stir-fried seafood and vegetables, chunks of lightly fried chicken with a hot spicy sauce, and sliced boneless duck bedded in snow peas, broccoli, red bell peppers, and water chestnuts. Her gaze met his over the rim of her wineglass as he balanced a portion of white rice on his chopsticks.

"Your students should be made aware that Kwanzaa lasts for seven days—December twenty-sixth to January first. They also should learn about twenty words and phrases in Swahili if they're to make the celebration an authentic one," she said, before taking a sip of the delicious chilled wine.

"Class projects can include making or buying the seven symbols of Kwanzaa. They can make a *mkeka,* or placemat, by hand from strips of cloth or paper," Shelby continued. Marshall had lowered his chopsticks and stared intently at her.

"Nia should purchase a big cup or goblet. The Swahili word for the cup of togetherness is *kikombe cha umoja.* Everyone who takes part in the celebration sips juice or wine from the *kikombe.*"

"What else do we need for the celebration?" Marshall questioned, taking a sip of his own wine.

"*Mazao,* or fruits and vegetables. *Mazao* represent the harvest for all work. When these are placed on the *mkeka,* African Americans honor themselves and the work that they do.

"The *muhindi,* or corn, represents our children. A family places one ear of corn on the *mkeka* for each one of their children."

"What about us, Shelby? We don't have any children."

"We would still put corn on our *mkeka.*"

Marshall couldn't pull his gaze from Shelby's face. The golden light from the candles flattered the delicate bones of her jawline, illuminated the brightness of her eyes, and made her appear ethereal, almost unreal.

"What else?" he asked softly.

Shelby felt her heart racing. It was as if she were poised on the top of a mountain, waiting to plummet back to earth.

"The *kinara,* or candle holder, is the center of any Kwanzaa celebration," she replied breathlessly. "The *kinara* represents our ancestors, who lived many years ago in Africa. The *kinara*'s seven candles are called *mishumaa saba.* The candles are a beacon because they light the way. A black candle is at the center, with three red candles on the left and three green on the right."

"Shouldn't they know what the colors stand for?"

"I saw a *bendera* in one of the history classes. I'm willing to bet every student at Nia knows that black stands for black people staying together, red for their struggle for freedom, and green for their future."

"Only some of them may remember."

"If that's the case, then I'll be certain to include it when I write up the lecture."

"What's the seventh symbol?"

"The *zawadi,* or gifts. The *zawadi* are usually for the children."

"Can the *zawadi* be for adults?"

Shelby nodded. "Children, parents, siblings, or loved ones. On the first day of Kwanzaa, a child lights the black candle in the center of the *kinara.* One more candle is lit each day, beginning with the red candle, then the green candle, closest to the center. When the day's candle is lit, the child talks about one of the reasons for Kwanzaa.

"These reasons are called the *nguzo saba*—the seven principles. The principles are goals for African Americans to strive for. Posters defining the *nguzo saba* should be put up around the school during the weeklong celebration."

A clock on a table chimed the hour and both Shelby and Marshall turned to stare at it. It was eight o'clock, and she marveled at how quickly the time had passed.

Marshall turned back to look at her, his mind filled with an eager excitement that he would see her again. He'd formulated a plan, but what he had to be careful of was that she not suspect his intentions.

"It's getting late, Shelby, and tomorrow is a workday—at least, it is for me."

"It is for me, too," she confirmed.

"Then, if you don't mind, we can go over the seven principles tomorrow. At what time are you scheduled to leave the museum?"

"Wednesday is my late night. I don't leave until six-thirty. What I can do is write up a draft of everything we've covered tonight. I'll also include the seven principles, their translations, and what each represents."

"You don't have to do that."

"I think it would be best," she insisted.

Marshall showed no sign of relenting, saying, "I have to see you anyway."

"Why?" Marshall didn't answer her, and she felt increasingly uneasy beneath his scrutiny. The look he gave her was familiar and disturbing. It was as if he could look inside her and see the real Shelby Carter.

He could see a woman who had hidden her emotions behind a facade of indifference to men; a woman who successfully hid her passions and emotions from every man who'd shown an interest in her; a woman whose body screamed silently for a release of the leashed sexuality she had repressed for years.

"I need you to sign the contract for the project. The contract's language reads that you'll be paid one-third on signing, a second third when you submit a draft of the proposed curriculum, and a final third on the approval of the curriculum committee."

Shelby knew she had to complete the cultural arts curriculum for Nia Academy quickly. She couldn't afford to spend many more "dinner meetings" with Marshall and not succumb to his charm and blatant masculinity.

"Okay, Marshall," she said quietly. "I'll meet you at six-thirty."

He stood up, coming around the table and helping her to her feet. "I'll help you clean up."

"No!" she nearly shouted. "It's all right. You have a long ride ahead of you. I'll clean up. Thank you for dinner." *Go home, Marshall Graham,* she said to herself.

Marshall slipped his feet into his loafers. "I should be the one thanking you." He moved closer until he left her no room at all to escape. The backs of her legs were pressed against the coffee table.

Lowering his head, he held her shoulders in a firm grip and brushed a gentle kiss across her ear. "Good night, Shelby."

Her fingertips grazed her ear after he'd released her and walked to the closet to retrieve his jacket. The thick brush of his moustache was intoxicating, and at that moment she wished her ear had been her mouth.

"Good night, Marshall." He glanced at her over his shoulder, smiled, and then opened and closed the door.

Shelby stood staring at the closed door for a full minute before she locked it. The warning voice in her head taunted her again. *Don't see him again. He's dangerous. He's trouble.*

But how could she not see him if she had committed herself to writing a curriculum proposal for him? She had given her word, and to her, her word was as bind-ing as a contract.

Contract! The word slapped at her. Marshall wanted her to sign a contract and they'd never discussed or negotiated a fee.

She shook her head. She was slipping. In the past, she'd never committed herself to a project unless she had negotiated a fee that she felt was comparable to her experience and training.

"Get it together, Shelby," she whispered, making her way back to the living room to clear away the remains of dinner.

Everything she'd shared with Marshall was put away, except for the vase of lilies. After Marshall had paid for the food, she'd waited at the restaurant for it to be prepared while he'd left to pick up what he'd referred to as a "few things." The few things turned out to be a bottle of chilled wine and a bouquet of flowers.

A wry smiled twisted her mouth. If she had been looking for the "perfect" man, she probably wouldn't have been able to find one. On the other hand, Mar-shall Graham came close to what she defined as "per-fect," and she was afraid. Not afraid of Marshall, but of herself and what she felt whenever they were to-gether.

Had she really matured emotionally in six years? Was she really ready to become involved with a man again?

Sitting in bed with a pad and pencil and outlining the Kwanzaa celebration for Nia, she pushed the ques-tions to the recesses of her mind, but they attacked her relentlessly as she slept.

Her dreams were filled with visions of Marshall—his smooth ocher-tinged brown skin, his close-cut graying black hair, the brilliance of his large, laughing dark eyes, his cologne, and the silkiness of the thick black moustache that concealed most of what appeared to be a sensual male mouth.

She woke up two hours before her alarm went off, exhausted and disoriented. She stayed in bed, staring up at the ceiling until sleep claimed her again . . . this time without the disturbing dreams.

Shelby sat across the table from Marshall in his favorite restaurant. The Garden was an atrium-designed restaurant with an abundance of live plants and flowers that reminded her of an oasis. The fragrance of pale orchids hung from planters filled the air.

Marshall watched Shelby's expression as she glanced around the private alcove. The space contained only four tables, with seating for two at each.

Her gaze met his. "I can see why this is your favorite restaurant. It's beautiful."

He nodded. "A beautiful setting for a beautiful woman." His penetrating gaze and compliment were as soft as a caress, and what Marshall was unaware of was that he'd stoked a gently growing fire in Shelby.

Her lashes shadowed her eyes for a quick second, the gesture demure and provocative. "Thank you." Her voice was a breathless whisper.

Marshall smiled, his arching eyebrows inching up. It never occurred to him that there was an innocence in Shelby that wasn't apparent when he was first introduced to her. There was no doubt she could hold her own professionally, but it was the woman that entranced him.

He stared at the commemorative pin she wore on the orange wool dress over her left breast before bringing his gaze back to her face. Reaching into the breast pocket of his jacket, he withdrew an envelope and handed it to her.

"There're two copies of the contract. I need you to sign both and give them back to me. You'll receive one copy and a check for your first installment after the school board meets Monday night."

Shelby noted the dark blue and gold embossed logo of Nia Academy on the thick sealed envelope. "Is it all right if I bring this back to you on Monday?"

"Perhaps you can get it to me over the weekend."

Her brow furrowed. "What's this weekend?"

"My aunt's birthday is Saturday, and I've planned something very special for her big 7-0. I know she's quite fond of you, and I'd like for you to help me host a party in her honor."

"Where?" She was too startled by his suggestion to flatly reject his offer.

"At my house. I've sent out invitations to all her friends and former colleagues and hired a caterer and a small combo for the musical program."

Shelby's eyes sparkled. "Is this a surprise?"

"Yes. I told her I was taking her out for her birthday, so she believes it's going to be only the two of us."

"How are you going to get her there if you have to be home to greet the guests?"

"I've arranged for a car service to pick her up. I told her I was taking her to a place where black tie is the norm for dinner and dining. She's prepared to stay overnight."

"It sounds like a wonderful surprise."

"I'm hoping it will be. Well, Shelby?"

"Well, what?"

"Will you be my hostess?"

All her uneasiness regarding Marshall Graham slipped back to grip her. What she wanted to do was throw the envelope back at Marshall and walk out of the restaurant. She wanted to forget he'd ever existed. But she couldn't. An invisible thread bound her to him through Naomi

Morrow, the kind elderly woman who had become her mentor, friend, and surrogate aunt.

"Yes."

Her reply was wrested from a place where logic and reason ceased to exist, and she murmured a silent plea, praying fervently she would not make the same mistake twice.

Reaching over the table, Marshall held her hands possessively between his large, well-groomed fingers. Shelby stared at his hands covering hers, and if she had glanced up she'd have recognized his caressing gaze making passionate love to her face. However, neither of them noticed the woman approaching their table.

"My, my, my. Isn't this a touching scene?"

Shelby's head came up quickly. She stared up at a woman whose attractive face was marred by a sneer pulling down the corners of her lush mouth.

Leaning over, the woman placed her gloved hand on Marshall's while kissing him flush on the mouth. "Hello, sugar."

Marshall released Shelby's hands, rising to his feet. A muscle ticked in his lean jaw, and there was no mistaking his annoyance. He glared at the woman with straightened hair pulled tightly off her toffee-hued face. "Nadine."

Nadine arched an eyebrow. "Oh, so you *do* remember my name. You said you would call me, but it looks as if you've been occupied with other *things.*"

Shelby's back stiffened. She'd never been referred to as a *thing*. Her gaze met Nadine's dining partner, and he offered an apologetic smile.

Nadine slipped her arm through her date's, pulling him to her side. "Cameron, this is Marshall Graham. He's the headmaster for Nia Academy. Marshall, Cameron Porter."

The two men shook hands, murmuring the appro-

priate polite responses. Marshall turned and stared
down at Shelby.

"Shelby, this is Nadine Pierce. Ms. Pierce is chairperson for our fund-raising committee. Nadine, Shelby
Carter."

Shelby nodded. "Nadine." She extended her hand
to Cameron. He grasped it firmly and held her fingers
a moment too long for propriety. "Cameron."

Cameron Porter placed a hand in the center of
Nadine's silk-covered back and steered to her toward a
table in the alcove. "Let's not tarry, Nadine. You know
I'm starved."

Nadine gave him a dazzling smile, then glanced back
at Shelby. "That's a darling little dress you have on. I'd
love to carry something like that in my boutique.
Would you be so kind as to tell me where I can pick
up a few like it?"

"I'm so sorry," she replied facetiously. "It's a one-of-
a-kind original." There was no way she was going to
tell her that she had designed the dress.

"Such a pity," Nadine crooned.

Shelby's smile was wide and false. "Isn't it?'

Marshall took his seat, letting out his breath as
Cameron steered Nadine to their table. "I'm sorry
about that," he apologized softly.

Shelby fingered the large gold hoop in her left ear,
remembering he had taken a call from Nadine Pierce
on Monday. There was no mistaking the woman's venomous hostility and jealousy.

"Are you in some way involved with Ms. Pierce?"

Marshall's eyes flashed anger, and for a long time he
stared at her. "My involvement with Nadine is strictly
business."

"Does she make it a practice to insult every woman
she sees you with?"

"Well . . . no."

Shelby raised her eyebrows. "I see."

"Do you really?" Marshall shot back.

"I'd have felt better if she'd referred to me as *Miss Thing.*"

"I've never known Nadine to be overtly rude to anyone." He waved away the waiter who'd approached the table to take their order. "Nadine's involvement with Nia serves as a vital link between the school and the business community. Her methods may be unorthodox at times, but her efforts have generated more than a half million dollars in contributions from business organizations. If you want, I'll talk to her about her being rude to you . . ."

"Don't bother, Marshall," Shelby interrupted. "I can defend myself."

"I bet you can, Shelby Carter."

She registered a smile crinkling his eyes. "You've offered to protect and defend me. What else is left for you to do for me?"

Make love to you, he mused. Thinking of making love to her elicited an instant response in his groin. "I don't think you'd want to know at this juncture, Miss Carter." His smile had turned into a lecherous grin.

Explosive currents raced through her body, heating and melting away her resolve, and leaving in its wake a slow, drugging wanting.

From the moment she was first introduced to Marshall there had been a strange waiting: waiting to discover whether he was married or single, and waiting to find out whether he was involved with another woman; it was more than apparent he wasn't, if he asked her to be his hostess for his aunt's seventieth birthday celebration.

"I don't think so," she replied, reading his mind. "I'm not interested."

His grin vanished, replaced by an expression of innocence. "Now, what did you think I meant?"

Rather than reply, Shelby picked up the menu, studying the selections. "How's the lamb, Marshall?"

"The lamb's great. But you didn't answer my question. What did you think I meant?" He enunciated each word.

She prayed she was right, saying, "You want . . ."

He leaned closer. "I want what?"

Her lashes shadowed her eyes, sweeping down and brushing her high cheekbones. The light from the small table lamp was flattering to her features. It glimmered on her flawless sable-brown skin and soft, moist mouth.

"You want me," she said in a small voice.

Marshall nodded. "To do what with?"

Her head came up, and there was fire in her challenging gaze. "What every man wants to do to a woman."

"I'm not every man, Shelby," he stated, so quietly that she had to strain to hear what he'd said. "But you're right. I *do* want you, but only on your terms. The choice has to be *yours.*"

"Aren't you gallant? Why make me responsible for everything, Marshall?"

"Then it'll be my way."

"No way, Marshall Graham."

He eyed her critically. "What's it going to be? Take your pick . . . my way? Or yours?"

Shelby realized Marshall was offering her the chance of becoming whole again. He wanted her to trust not only him, but men in general.

"My way," she said, after a long silence.

Marshall picked up his glass of water and touched it to hers. "I'll drink to that." He drank half the glass of water, then reached for his own menu. "The grilled lamb with mint jelly looks good." Glancing up, he winked at her and she smiled back at him.

He gave their orders to the waiter, Shelby ordering
club soda with a twist of lime, while Marshall opted for
mineral water.

Over dinner she outlined the *nguzo saba* for each day
of the celebration, translating the Swahili and describing
the seven principles in detail.

"The fifth day should be of great significance to the
students because their school is named for the principle Nia," Marshall said solemnly. "And that's what Nia
has tried to do. It's purpose being to make our young
men as great as they can be."

"You seem to be doing a wonderful job with them."

He bit down on his lower lip, seemingly deep in
thought. "It hasn't been easy. Everyone connected with
Nia has made a lot of sacrifices to make it a success. I
think of myself as twice blessed to have a selfless and
dedicated faculty and staff."

The evening sped by quickly and Shelby felt completely at ease with Marshall for the first time. It would
be up to her to determine where their relationship, if
there was to be one, would go.

He drove her home and saw her to her door. Shelby
smiled at him. "Thank you for a wonderful evening."

"My thanks to you, too. I'll pick you up Saturday
afternoon at one. Be prepared to spend the night."
Leaning over, he kissed her ear, then spun around on
his heel and retraced his steps to the elevator.

"What are you talking about? Marshall!"

"Good night, darling," he answered, without turning
around, and disappeared into the elevator.

Damn, she swore to herself. He'd tricked her. He'd
gotten over on her without her being aware of it. Next
time, Marshall. Oh yes, there would be a next time.

Shelby spent three hours in the area adjoining her
bedroom, completing the proposal for the Kwanzaa Ex-

position. When she'd taken possession of the apartment five years ago she'd hired a carpenter to remove the folding doors to a walk-in closet, creating a spacious alcove where she'd set up a table for her sewing machine, television, and computer workstation.

Pushing a button, she printed out what she had saved on a disk. Duplicate copies of the contract Marshall had given her earlier that evening lay on the bedside table.

She had to read the fee Nia offered her to complete the cultural arts curriculum twice before she realized the amount was more than half of what she earned annually at the museum. She remembered Marshall saying, *"You will be paid well for the project."* He had not lied to her.

She was expected to submit a preliminary draft within sixty days of signing, and a final copy by April first. Shelby smiled. She could make both deadlines easily. She always took a leave from the museum and the gallery the last week of the year. Yes, she thought, she had plenty of time to complete the project.

Shelby ticked off the listing of things to do on a page in her appointment diary. She'd made arrangements for a pickup from Shumba and delivery to Hans of the sculpture with a bonded messenger service that specialized in transporting precious gems and priceless art. The completed Kwanzaa packet and signed contracts were in an oversized envelope, along with a book of recipes for an African American celebration of culture and cooking and a large *mkeka* in a kente-cloth pattern she'd made as a donation to Nia for Kwanzaa.

She had also chosen a dress to wear for Naomi's party and packed a bag containing clothes she'd need to spend the night at Marshall's house.

The clock in the living room chimed one at the exact moment her intercom buzzed loudly. Marshall was always prompt. She buzzed him into the building.

It was a very different Marshall who walked into her apartment. He was dressed in a pair of worn jeans, a black wool turtleneck sweater, and jogging shoes. She stared openly at the dark stubble on his unshaven cheeks, finding him even more stunningly virile than before.

Marshall was equally entranced as his gaze swept over Shelby. It was the first time he had seen her not wearing a dress. She had paired black tailored wide-wale cords with a bulky white ski sweater and black leather hiking shoes. He smiled at the neat feminine figure she presented.

"I'm ready," she announced, walking back to the living room. She picked up a ski jacket and slipped her arms into it. She hadn't missed Marshall's obvious examination and approval.

Marshall picked up her overnight bag by the door. "Did I tell you to pack a swimsuit?"

Shelby spun around and stared at him, her expression mirroring surprise and shock. "I thought I was going to White Plains, not White Sands."

"You *are* going to White Plains," he confirmed.

"But why would I need a swimsuit, Marshall? It's all of twenty-eight degrees, with a prediction of sleet later tonight. Sorry to disappoint you, but I happen not to be a member of the Polar Bear Club."

Marshall set down her bag and walked over to her. Reaching out, he cradled her face between his hands, giving her no choice but to stare up at him. All that she didn't know she felt for him swept over her at that moment.

There was no way she could resist the man cradling her so gently. She had known him exactly one week, and in that week he had unwittingly forced her to examine herself.

She couldn't continue to live in the past. Earl was Earl and Marshall was Marshall. How could she ever have thought that they were anything alike?

Earl had done nothing to her that she hadn't permitted him to do. He hadn't forced her to give up her study of anthropology—she'd done it willingly to please him; and she didn't have to agree to wait until she was thirty before becoming a mother—she'd also agreed to that willingly.

Marshall had permitted her a choice: her way or his way, and she had opted for her way. It was up to her to see him; it was up to her to permit him to kiss her; it was up to her to share her body with him. And most important, she would have the freedom, without doubt or guilt, to offer Marshall her love.

"Do you own a swimsuit, Shelby?" His voice was soft and seductive. She nodded numbly. "Then, please go and get it." His hands moved to the back of her head, his fingers threading through the short curls. He lowered his head slowly and deliberately, then did what he'd wanted to do ever since he'd first seen Shelby Carter. His mouth moved over hers, exploring and tasting her lush, moist lips. He felt her hands curl into fists against his ribs, slacken, and finally open to close again, grasping the back of his sweater as she parted her lips to his searching, demanding tongue.

Shelby inhaled the familiar cologne on his clothes and body, felt the heat searing her body through his clothes, and marveled in the feel of the thick, silky hair on his upper lip. She was soaring, floating, and drowning all at the same time. Her tongue met the velvet warmth of his.

Marshall's hands swept down her back and his fingers

curved under her hips, pulling her closer. He felt her trembling and his passion grew stronger.

Blood pounded in his brain and the heat and fire seared his loins. He wanted Shelby Carter with a longing that was totally foreign to him. He wanted her not for a cause or reason or because of a lifelong dream. He wanted her for himself. She was the first woman he wanted because she was wholly woman. All of the other women he'd known were his sexual counterpart—female.

Shelby pulled back to catch her breath, and in that moment, sanity returned. She pushed against Marshall's thick shoulders, breathing heavily. "Stop! Please."

He raised his head, but he didn't release her. He folded her gently against his chest, permitting her to break the hold if she chose to. The sound of their heavy breathing echoed in the stillness of the apartment. Marshall closed his eyes, sighing in relief as she pressed her cheek against his shoulder.

Shelby smiled as one of Marshall's hands came up and cupped the back of her head in a comforting gesture. His heartbeat throbbed wildly against her ear before slowing to a steady, measured rhythm.

A deep feeling of peace entered her, and she wondered if she should feel some guilt. Marshall was the first man she had kissed who was able to summon the passion she had hidden away for six long years.

Pulling out of his loose embrace, she smiled up at him. "I think I'd better get that swimsuit now."

Marshall watched her walk toward her bedroom, hoping the swimsuit was not a bikini.

"The house is at the top of the hill," Marshall informed Shelby, as he downshifted the four-wheel-drive vehicle up a steep, winding road.

Shelby was unprepared for the panorama unfolding before her eyes. She turned in her seat and stared out the back window at the Hudson River and a magnificent view of the Tappan Zee Bridge, but it was the sight of the house on the hill that stunned her.

Marshall's house was a series of connecting modern pale-gray structures with what appeared to be two floors of glass and skylights. The house reminded Shelby of the nooks, crannies, twists, turns, turrets, and charm of a nineteenth-century Connecticut farmhouse-turned-bed-and-breakfast she had once stayed in.

Puffs of smoke drifted from several chimneys, disappearing in the raw late-fall air. Towering pine and blue spruce trees provided the only color on a hilly landscape dotted with starkly bare maple, oak, and white birch trees. Patches of snow still remained after the first snowfall of the season ten days before, although all traces of it had already disappeared in Manhattan.

Marshall opened the passenger door, curved an arm around Shelby's waist, and swung her effortlessly to the ground. A smile crinkled his eyes as he registered her staring up at him. His smile faded slowly, replaced by a slight frown.

"Do you realize that this is the first time I've ever looked at you in daylight, Shelby? It seems as if we can only get together at night."

Her smile was mysterious. "Maybe we're vampires and we're not aware of it," she teased.

His gaze shifted from her eyes to her mouth. "I think not. I'd prefer to think of you as a witch . . . a beautiful witch who's cast a spell over me where I'm unable to resist your charms."

"What charm, Marshall?" she asked, tilting her chin.

"You haunt my dreams, Shelby," he replied, his words echoing her dreams. "Since I met you, I've undergone the worst case of insomnia I've ever experienced," he admitted. And he was also experiencing another condition he hadn't had since he was a teenage boy.

Marshall's expression was so serious that she wanted to laugh; but she didn't. She placed a delicate hand on the sleeve of his sweater. "You should see a doctor about your insomnia. Perhaps he could prescribe a sleeping aid."

What about my other condition? he asked himself silently.

She stared at him, drowning in the black pools of shimmering velvet staring back at her. "You're going to need more than a prescription for a sleeping aid if you continue to stand out here without a coat," she said quietly.

"If I get sick, will you take care of me?"

"No."

Dropping an arm over her shoulder, Marshall led her toward the house. "You're a hard woman, Shelby Carter."

"And you're not a hard man?"

"Not with someone I care very deeply about."

She was unable to reply to his retort. She cared for Marshall, more deeply than she was willing to admit; however, she couldn't care more for him than she could for herself. She could not give again; she could not give more than she hoped to receive. But on the other hand, if Marshall was willing to offer her what she was willing to offer—trust and fidelity—then she'd consider becoming involved with him.

"I believe in giving sixty-five percent in a relationship, Shelby."

"That would only leave you with thirty-five percent. You'd wind up on the losing end," she protested, wondering if he'd done all the giving in his marriage the way she'd done and wound up the loser—the willing victim.

"Not if you give me sixty-five percent. That way both of us would be winners. We'd both have a hundred percent."

She stared at his sweater-clad back as he unlocked the front door, replaying his equation in her mind. He was willing to give her more than half of himself because he believed if she became involved with him she would give him more than half of herself.

"Did you get sixty-five percent from your ex-wife?"

The broad shoulders under the black wool sweater stiffened, then relaxed. "Yes, Shelby," Marshall replied, not turning around. "She gave me sixty-five percent, but I asked her for something else she refused to give up. And it wasn't until the divorce that I realized she *couldn't* give it up."

He pushed opened the door and pulled her gently into the spacious warmth of his house. "I made a very serious mistake once, Shelby. I *will not* make it again."

She wondered what mistake had been tragic enough to end a marriage. Had he insisted she become pregnant? Had he been unfaithful to her?

The questions regarding Marshall and his ex-wife vanished quickly as Shelby stared up at the cathedral ceiling and a second-story level with roof windows and skylights. Polished natural wood floors, covered with colorful dhurrie rugs, a wood-burning stove off the entrance, and recessed lights provided a warm glow. He had elected to decorate his home in black and pale gray with splashes of peach and coral, and the resulting effect was masculine and visually pleasing.

Marshall placed a large warm hand on her shoulder. "Make yourself at home while I bring in your bags."

She walked into the living room, drawn to a wall of windows rising to the second story, smiling. She remembered she had said the same thing to him the night they'd dined amid soft music and candlelight.

She had thought the scene from her apartment windows magnificent, but now she quickly changed her mind. The vistas from Marshall's house were spectacular and breathtaking. She was barely able to discern the movement of vehicular traffic crossing the Tappan Zee Bridge to upstate New York. The landscape across the Hudson River revealed roofs and chimneys of houses nestled in verdant evergreen-covered hills.

Marshall returned with her overnight bag and a garment bag containing her dress for the evening's dinner party. "Come with me. I'll show you to your room."

She followed him up a curving wood staircase while trying to take in everything around her. Her professional gaze took in the blending of the mix of styles. Marshall had decorated using Queen Anne–style chairs with glass-topped, very classic modern tables and antique quilts as wall hangings, and everywhere she looked there was a sense of spaciousness and light.

"This will be your bedroom." He stepped aside. She walked into a large, octagonal-shaped room with Palladian windows. A king-sized wrought-iron bed dominated the space. The bedroom was filled with warmth—from the white-and-coral-print bed dressing to the vase of fresh pale pink roses, a rack filled with magazines, a wicker basket overflowing with packets of herbal teas, and another basket filled with rose-scented potpourri.

Shelby glanced up at Marshall over her shoulder. "It's charming."

His gaze widened as he stared down at her profile. Again he was stunned by her natural beauty. Her clean-scrubbed face was exquisite. Aside from the passion he had sampled earlier that morning, Marshall wondered what would make a man unfaithful to a woman who appeared to have it all.

Shelby Carter was not only beautiful, but she was brilliant, totally feminine, interesting, and sensual. She claimed the most sensual eyes and mouth of any woman he had ever seen. She stirred passions he wasn't aware he possessed.

And those passions weren't just physical. She made him feel alive, much more alive than he'd felt in years. He wanted to travel with Shelby, visiting museums while she taught him all she knew about art. He wanted them to concoct exotic dishes, then eat whatever they'd cooked over candlelight and with quiet music. But most of all, he needed her to fill the void in his life, because now he knew he did not want to spend the rest of his life alone.

He wanted to remarry. He wanted to have children.

"Do you want lunch?" he asked quietly.

She shook her head. "No, thank you. I'll wait for dinner."

"I'll let you settle in, then I'll give you a tour of the house."

Shelby was awed by the tour. Built to Marshall's specifications, the connecting buildings contained an exercise and weight room, an indoor pool, and a library housing thousands of books. Some were priceless rare out-of-print volumes on European history. He saved the best building for last—a large modern greenhouse.

"Nighttime temperatures are set for a tropical seventy degrees," he explained, watching Shelby as she inhaled a cluster of *lemona ponderosa*.

She moved on to an area where he had planted fruit trees. The ripe, lush fruits hung heavily from cherry, apple, plum, and pear trees.

Walking slowly along a broad path, she noted a Japanese garden and a twelve-foot topiary of acacia, then stopped and stared at the dark green leaves of several vegetables, recognizing collards, the curling ends of kale, and the large, firm heads of cabbage.

"You're a regular greengrocer, Marshall," she teased. The fruits and vegetables fascinated her, but it was the flowering plants that held her enthralled. The greenhouse held a profusion of fuschia, orchids, hanging geraniums, roses, camellias, and a beautifully delicate yellow flower Marshall had identified as an *allamanda cathartica.*

He grasped her hand firmly as she reached out to touch it. "It's extremely poisonous," he warned. "In all of its parts."

She pointed to a brilliant red flower. "How about this one?"

Marshall tucked her right hand into the bend of his elbow, holding it possessively. "No. That's a begonia. The 'firebrand' is one of the most brilliantly colored of all begonia cultivars. I grow it for the color."

Shelby stared up at him, seeing his gaze sweep lovingly over his plants and flowers. "Who in your family is the horticulturist?"

"No one. My mother's a librarian and my father's an accountant. Some people like photography and others *art.*" He shifted an eyebrow when she smiled. "The architect who designed the house is a friend. And when I told him that I wanted a place with an indoor pool and gym, he also suggested the greenhouse. He explained that the heating and cooling system for each building could be regulated independently, but I could save on heating the pool with a special system using solar panels. He decided to experiment using the same procedure with the greenhouse. It works because the nighttime temperature for the greenhouse and the building with the pool are always the same.

"I sort of fell into growing plants," he admitted. "I started with a single rose bush, then tomatoes, and now, three years later, it's a jungle."

"All that's missing are tropical birds."

"They would eat my fruits and vegetables," he replied solemnly. "And I shudder to think of the mess they'd make in here."

Shelby's gaze swept up the wide spotless paths. "What do you do with all your fruits and vegetables?"

"I give them away to an organization that prepares meals for the elderly and homeless."

"That's wonderful." Shelby kept pace with Marshall as he led her back through the greenhouse and the building containing the shimmering blue tiles lining the pool.

Her body under her corduroy pants and ski sweater was coated with a layer of moisture from the warm, humid air enveloping the two buildings. "At what time do you expect the caterers?" she asked Marshall.

"They're coming at four, the invited guests between five and six, the band at six, and my aunt at seven. Why do you ask?"

"I just want to know how much time I need to get ready."

"It's only two-thirty. You'll have plenty of time. What would you like to do?"

"Swim a couple of laps."

Marshall released her hand and cradled her face between his palms. "Only a couple?" he teased quietly.

Shelby tilted her chin, her gaze caressing his lean, handsome face. "I'll be lucky if I swim a lap. I'm out of practice."

"I'll give you a head start."

"Are we racing, Mr. Graham?"

"Why? Do you want to?"

She took a step closer until her breasts were only inches from his sweatered chest. "Do I look that naive to you? You probably swim *at least* two laps every day."

Marshall didn't tell her that he'd swum a half-dozen leisurely laps every morning since the pool was installed.

"I do all right," he admitted.

Shelby's eyes narrowed. "I bet you do."

"Put your suit on and show me what you've got."

She stared unblinkingly and moved away from him and out of his loose grasp, wondering if he was aware of the double entendre.

"You're on."

Marshall registered her challenge and led her back to the main house. A quarter of an hour later, they stood at the edge of the pool. "You count," he offered, unable to take his gaze off her skimpily clad body in an Olympic-style black tank suit.

The body-hugging Spandex garment was more revealing and provocative than a bikini. It was not the first time he'd been awed by her femininity, but it was the first time it had been displayed so wantonly.

Her body was slender, yet there were no straight lines. Her legs were long and slender, her waist narrow, her hips full and rounded, and her breasts ripe and lush, pushing sensually against the fabric of her suit.

Shelby stared at the opposite end of the pool rather than look at Marshall. She felt the heat of his gaze on her, and even though she didn't return his stare, she could still see his nearly nude body in her mind.

Marshall Graham claimed the body of a swimmer: broad shoulders; long, ropy arms; flat midsection; slim, firm hips; and long, muscled legs. She wondered whether she should've challenged him.

"Ready whenever you are," she said, taking in a deep

breath. She moved closer to the edge, her toes gripping the Persian-blue tiles. Marshall also moved into position.

"Now!" she shouted.

His body cleaved the water quickly, but if he had glanced over at Shelby, he'd have noticed the curving arc of her body and the near splashless entry as she dived into the warm pool water.

It had been nearly sixteen years since Shelby had swum competitively, and the rush of adrenaline spurted through her body, giving her what she needed to overcome Marshall's obvious superior strength. She had barely touched the opposite end of the pool before she pushed off to retrace her smooth-measured strokes.

Marshall began his second lap before the realization set in: Shelby was more than a casual swimmer. He increased his pace but knew instinctively he was no match for her. He swam for exercise and relaxation; she swam to compete.

He was nearly twenty seconds behind her by the time he'd finished. She had hoisted herself out of the water and now sat waiting for him—breathing heavily.

He pulled himself up and sat beside her, shaking his head. "Where did you learn to swim like that?" he asked, his chest rising and falling from the exertion. Reaching over, he pulled her to his side.

Shelby rested her head against his hard shoulder. "I was captain of my high school swim team. It's been sixteen years since I last competed."

His free hand curved her chin, tilting her face to his. Water dotted his moustache and spiked his lashes. The soft, warm light from wall lamps and the gray of the sky through roof windows shadowed his features as he slowly lowered his head.

"You're good, Shelby Carter. Very, very good."

Her own lashes, spiked with moisture, lowered. "You don't mind that I beat you?"

He shook his head. "I only mind that you didn't tell me you were a pro."

"Even if I had," she said, staring at his mouth, "I still would've beat you."

"Only this time," he whispered. "We're going to have to do this again some other time. Meanwhile, I'm going to practice until I *do* beat you."

Shelby had to smile. She had bruised his male ego. "I don't give repeat performances."

"But I do." Marshall didn't give her a chance to ask what he meant when he eased her down gently to the tiled floor and brushed his lips across her ear, registering her sharp intake of breath.

His lips feathered over her jaw and down further to her throat. His body covered hers when her arms moved up and circled his neck.

Shelby lay between Marshall's legs, feeling his heat and the hardness between his thighs. Closing her eyes, she gave in to the rising desire scorching her everywhere he touched, moaning once before his mouth claimed hers in a strong, hungry possession that sucked the breath from her lungs.

His tongue pushed incessantly against her mouth until her lips parted. His mouth was as busy as his fingers, slipping the straps of her swimsuit off her shoulders and down her arms.

The passion she had successfully banked for so many years surfaced, short-circuiting her nervous system where every nerve ending screamed for release.

Marshall's mouth was everywhere. He kissed her throat, her shoulders, and her breasts. Her nipples swelled and ached as his teeth teased them into turgid nodules of dark-brown flesh.

Her own hands swept up his muscled back and over his smooth chest. She didn't trust herself to venture lower than his waist, where his aroused sex strained against the scant covering of Spandex.

Marshall's respiration increased, his breathing heavy and labored, as he moved his hips against Shelby's in a slow, deliberate rotating motion. He wanted her; he wanted her so much that he feared he was going to explode.

"Shelby," he gasped, from between clenched teeth. Raising his head, he stared down at her, waiting for a signal. He needed something—a word, any gesture that would indicate she'd permit him to come to her as her lover.

Shelby struggled to bring her turbulent emotions under control as a shudder shook her body. Opening her eyes slowly, she stared up at the face only inches from her own. How could she have thought that Marshall Graham was anything like Earl? Not only did they not look alike, but their approach to lovemaking was completely different, because somehow she'd sensed Marshall was waiting; waiting for her to give approval for him to continue. Earl would never have waited.

"No." She shook her head for emphasis. "It's too soon, Marshall," she explained, her voice a husky whisper.

Sitting up, he gathered her close and she lay across his lap, her head resting on his shoulder. "I'll wait until you're ready," he replied quietly. Marshall smiled and pressed a kiss to her temple. She had not rejected him.

Shelby extracted herself from Marshall's loose embrace and stood up. He also rose in one fluid motion, staring at her with an expectant expression on his face. If she allowed herself to become involved with Marshall, she knew there was a chance for her to grow whole again, to learn how to trust a man again.

She had only known Marshall a week and she had no intention of making the same mistake twice. Her mother's warning came rushing back—*"Act in haste, repent in leisure."* Six years was a long time to do penance, and she knew the time for being repentant was behind her.

She gave him a warm smile. "I have to get dressed."

Marshall opened his mouth to respond, then closed it quickly as he glanced up. The sound of sleet tapped rhythmically against the roof windows. He moved over to the expansive windows surrounding the poolhouse. Sleet was falling, and a driving wind swirled it in a forty-five-degree slant.

Shelby joined him at the window, watching as the frozen precipitation quickly blanketed the winter grass with a sheet of white.

"It wasn't supposed to snow until late tonight," she said, unable to believe how much wet snow and ice had already accumulated.

Marshall dropped an arm around her shoulders and his fingers grazed the length of her neck in a soothing motion. "If it changes over to all snow, it won't be so bad. But if it's sleet or ice, then that's going to be a problem. The roads up here are treacherous whenever there's sleet."

Shelby noted his frowning expression. "What are you going to do if it doesn't change over to snow?"

His fingers tightened. "I don't know."

Her gaze shifted back to the window. Trees and the open meadow beyond the rear of the house were shrouded in an eerie gunmetal gray, making visibility nearly impossible.

"The caterers are due here at four," Marshall said, breaking the silence. "If the weather doesn't break, then I'll have to make a decision whether to try to go ahead with the dinner party or cancel it."

* * *

It was the catering company who made the decision for Marshall. They regretfully informed him that they were closing early because all the roads were covered with ice, which made it virtually impossible to drive without sliding into other vehicles.

Shelby, who had showered, shampooed, and changed into a pair of jeans with a sweatshirt and running shoes, sat on a tall stool in Marshall's kitchen, watching the weather channel on a small television on a countertop as he telephoned the guests to tell them the evening's festivities were canceled. Most had expressed relief that they wouldn't be obligated to try to navigate the ice-covered roads to help Naomi Morrow celebrate her seventieth birthday. After he'd called the limousine company to inform them not to pick up Naomi in Manhattan, he called his aunt.

He spoke briefly with Naomi and ended the call wishing her a happy birthday. The last call was to the small band he'd contracted for the night's musical program. Replacing the receiver in its cradle, Marshall turned to Shelby.

"I promised you a party, and we'll have a party." He flashed a bright smile. "That leaves me to put together something for dinner. I'm far from a gourmet chef, but I can assure you that you won't come down with ptomaine."

Shelby hopped off the stool, smiling. "I'll help you."

Marshall defrosted and marinated two shell steaks. Then, at Shelby's suggestion, he picked enough kale from the greenhouse garden for them. She steamed the kale with olive oil and garlic and roasted small cubes of red potatoes with dried thyme, dehydrated onions, and parsley until they were done to a crisp golden brown.

Standing behind Shelby and looking over her shoulder, Marshall curved his arms around her waist. "It looks delicious."

She speared a small cube of potato and held it out to him. "Try it."

He ate the potato, chewing slowly and nodding. "It's fabulous." He swallowed, never taking his gaze from Shelby's face. Her naturally curling hair had dried, feathering over her forehead and ears. She usually brushed her hair off her face and the style made her appear older and more sophisticated. With her fresh-scrubbed face, curling hair, and casual dress, he found it difficult to believe she was thirty-four years old.

Sharing the cooking duties with her reminded him of what he'd never had with Cassandra. He hadn't thought of himself as a demanding husband. In fact, he had given in to Cassandra even when he hadn't wanted to. He'd never asked anything from her except that she relocate.

He had told her of his dream before they'd married, and she had agreed to go with him whenever the opportunity presented itself. But in the end, he'd realized she'd deceived him. He'd also deceived and deluded himself, because he had married Cassandra knowing she would never follow him. The lure of D.C.'s social life was too strong for his ex-wife to give up. The influential D.C. Grahams helped the ex-Mrs. Marshall Graham improve her social standing in Washington immeasurably.

"I think the steaks should be ready now," Marshall stated, trying not to think of how he was going to spend the night with Shelby Carter sleeping under his roof only several feet away from his own bedroom.

Shelby turned back to the stove and spooned the potatoes and kale into serving bowls, placing them on the dining room table.

Marshall had already set the table with china, silver,

and stemware. He popped the cork on a bottle of deep purple Cabernet Sauvignon and filled two wineglasses.

A hanging light fixture with an authentic Tiffany shade spilled golden light onto the table, while the familiar haunting voice of Sade filled the downstairs space with music. However, the sound wasn't enough to eradicate the sound of the howling wind and the occasional snapping of ice-covered branches as they cracked and crashed to the frozen earth.

Marshall and Shelby sat at opposite ends of the modern glass-topped table, eating and drinking silently.

Shelby felt the heat from Marshall's gaze on her face each time she glanced up. The flattering light from the fixture highlighted the rich gold in his smooth brown skin and the sprinkling of gray throughout his close-cut, neatly barbered hair. Her gaze lingered on his moustache and mouth, remembering the feel of the thick, silky hair on his upper lip and the mastery of his mouth when he claimed hers.

Marshall's kiss hadn't been just a touching of the lips or a joining of their tongues. It was as if he had known instinctively how much pressure to exert, just where he would kiss her, and when to deepen the kiss or pull back.

Marshall Graham wore his sensuality like a badge of honor, displaying it for every woman who'd have to be blind not to recognize it.

Everything about him was subtle. His self-confidence, exquisite manners, quiet virility, and arresting good looks were impossible to ignore.

Shelby sipped her wine slowly, staring down the table at him. *He could be so easy to love,* she thought. *If only I could trust him,* she mused silently.

She opened her mouth to ask him whether he'd been unfaithful to his ex-wife, but decided against it at the last moment. It was too personal a question to ask.

And she hadn't known him long enough to feel comfortable asking.

She was fully and totally relaxed. The two glasses of dry red wine, the succulent grilled steaks, and the steamed tender kale and crispy potatoes left no room for dessert.

"I went over the Kwanzaa proposal. It looks easy enough to implement without a lot of planning," Marshall said, breaking the silence.

"I tried to keep it simple. The students won't have to make a *mkeka* because the placemat will be my donation to Nia for the celebration. You can either buy several *benderas* or have the students make the red, black, and green flags in their art classes.

"I included the listing of stores where you can buy African artifacts only as a suggestion. All of these stores usually have the *kinara* candles and the *kikombe cha umoja* as a part of their regular stock," Shelby continued.

"Nia's *kikombe cha umoja* will be filled with grape juice instead of wine," Marshall said, smiling. "City regulations won't permit us to have alcoholic beverages on the premises."

"Have you decided to celebrate Kwanzaa the entire week before the school closes for the holidays?"

"We're only going to hold classes for three days that week, so I've decided that we'll celebrate the first principle Monday night and invite the parents, family members, and friends of the students, and anyone else who wants to attend. We'll start it around seven and serve dinner after the opening ceremonies."

"Very appropriate." The first principle was *umoja*, and the aim of *umoja* was to strive for and maintain unity in the family, community, nation, and race.

"Will you be able to make it to our first-night celebration?" Marshall asked.

"I wouldn't miss it," she confirmed.

"Are you doing anything for Kwanzaa?" she asked Marshall.

"I haven't made any plans. Why do you ask?"

"This year I'm staying in New York for the holidays, and when I do, I usually get together with several friends and we always have a big celebration for the first night. I'd like to invite you to come along, if you don't have anything planned for December twenty-sixth."

"What do you do for the next six days?"

Shelby went on to tell him that she and her family always observed the seven days, but in New York, most of her friends were usually too busy to observe more than a day or two.

"I wouldn't mind celebrating all seven days with you," Marshall volunteered.

"Are you certain you want to do that?" she questioned.

"I'm more than certain. I haven't celebrated Kwanzaa since I left Howard."

Shelby offered him a quick smile. "Okay, it's settled. You'll come with me to my friend's place for the first night, then we'll decide about the next six nights."

"Do you and your family usually exchange gifts all seven nights?"

"Only the children get gifts all seven nights. They're normally small, inexpensive items, but the kids are thrilled with the notion of getting something new each night."

Marshall propped his elbow on the table, resting his chin on a fist. "I wouldn't mind getting a gift every night for seven nights."

"My, my, my," Shelby teased. "Aren't we subtle?"

He shifted an eyebrow. "You would also get a gift for each of the seven nights."

"We don't have to exchange gifts," she protested. "Besides, gift-giving is for the children."

"Didn't you say that even if someone doesn't have a child they can still place *muhindi* on their *mkeka*? One ear of corn for each child." She nodded slowly. "If I can put an ear of corn on my *mkeka,* then I can buy a gift for someone I think of as very special for each of the seven days of Kwanzaa."

Shelby stared at him as a new and unexpected warmth swept over her. She knew Marshall liked her and that the liking went beyond their professional working relationship. He had hinted that he cared deeply for her, and now he had admitted that she was special.

Could she really take the chance to lower her defenses, the barriers, she had set up to keep all men at a distance? Could she risk opening up her heart and offering Marshall the love she was certain was there?

It had taken only a week, but Shelby was more than certain that her feelings for Marshall were a combination of attraction, anticipation, and desire.

There was no doubt that she was attracted to him and that she desired him. And if her self-control hadn't been so staunchly in place, she was certain she would've succumbed to his lovemaking beside the pool.

She glanced away, her lashes shadowing the passion in her eyes. "I guess that settles it. You can expect a gift for each of the seven nights."

Marshall pushed back his chair, rising to his feet. He took less than a half-dozen determined steps that brought him to her side. He eased back her chair and helped her rise.

Shelby was in his arms, her face pressed to the clean laundered smell of a shirt covering his solid shoulder. "You've given me all the gifts I'll ever need," he whispered against her ear. "Having you for seven nights is enough."

It was only when Marshall openly verbalized his feelings about wanting to spend a week with her that Shelby admitted to herself that she *was* falling in love with him.

What was there for her not to love? He was attractive, intelligent, and dedicated to his career, and he treated her like an equal. He was secure enough to respect her profession, and he had not asked more from her than she was willing to give.

She, too, had all the gifts she needed for her own first fruits: Marshall Graham.

Her arms tightened around his waist as she pressed closer to his length. She inhaled the familiar scent of his aftershave. She remembered admitting that she could identify him by his cologne.

Pulling back she smiled up at him, admiring the velvet softness of his clean-shaven cheek. Her gaze visually traced the line of his jaw, then moved with agonizing slowness down to his mouth and chin.

"Have you decided to reschedule your aunt's dinner party?"

A sensual smile showed his beautiful teeth. "No, I haven't. But I've decided it won't be a surprise, and hopefully by that time she'll have more than a birthday to celebrate."

His head came down slowly as he claimed her mouth in a slow, burning passion that robbed her of her breath. Shelby clung to him, her body vibrating with liquid fire. It took only seconds before her flame was passed to Marshall, and both of them were awed and trembling when she pulled back. She clung weakly to his stronger body.

She was too caught up in her awakening passion for Marshall to register his statement—"Hopefully by that

time she'll have more than a birthday to celebrate"—
not knowing the words would come back to haunt her.

Shelby spent the night at Marshall's house, sleeping
soundly while he tossed restlessly on his bed in a bedroom across the hall.

She awoke to a scene from a Currier and Ives Christmas card. The storm had left the landscape a winter
wonderland with icicles coating trees, shrubs, and
power lines.

Turning away from the window and pressing her face
into her pillow, she hoped for another hour of sleep,
but sat up quickly when she heard a steady tapping on
the closed door.

"Shelby, are you awake?"

Pulling a down-filled comforter up to her throat, she
called out, "Yes."

"Meet me at the pool in five minutes," Marshall announced, issuing a challenge through the door.

She laughed. "Don't you ever give up?"

"Five minutes, Shelby Carter, or I'm coming in."

She jumped out of bed and raced to the adjoining
bath. Five minutes later she slipped on her swimsuit
after washing her face and brushing her teeth. She
hadn't bothered to brush her hair. She simply ran her
fingers through the curling strands, then went down
the stairs toward the pool.

The house was warm and comfortable, the heat generated from several wood-burning stoves defying the
cold wind and ice claiming the countryside.

Shelby beat Marshall again, this time by a greater
margin. She kissed his grim, tight mouth, patted his
broad chest, then turned on her heel and made her
way back to the main house, leaving him sitting on the
edge of the pool and staring at her trim body.

* * *

Marshall sat at the oval conference-room table, writing aimlessly on a pad. One of Nia's board members read from a typed report outlining the proposed school budget for the upcoming school year.

The woman's voice droned on as Marshall listed several items under a column labeled "Shelby." He had accounted for only three of the seven gifts he planned to purchase for her. He didn't know her dress size, so that meant he could not purchase an article of clothing.

He drew another column and listed several department stores: Barney's, Bergdorf Goodman, and Bloomingdale's. A second column listed specialty shops: Chanel, Tiffany, and Polo/Ralph Lauren. He thought about several mail-order houses with the added feature of ordering and having his purchase shipped overnight. His brow furrowed. He had a little more than a week to complete his list and shop.

He wrote down another three items, then turned the pad over. Six down and one to go. He considered a gift basket of lotions and oils or a gift certificate for a complete beauty makeover at Georgette Klinger, but didn't write it down. The name F.A.O. Schwarz popped into his head and popped out just as quickly. F.A.O. Schwarz would have to wait for another time.

The week passed quickly for Shelby. She shopped for her Kwanzaa gifts for Marshall, began writing Nia's cultural curriculum, and called Hans Gustave every day for an update for Shumba's Friday evening showing.

Marshall had called her late Monday night to let her know that the first installment on her proposal was approved and a check would be mailed to her the following day.

He asked to see her again, but she declined, saying her calendar was booked solid for the week and that she wouldn't see him until the evening of Nia's Kwanzaa celebration. There was complete silence. After he rang off, she could tell by the coldness in his voice that he was not pleased.

She'd hung up, thinking, my way or no way, Marshall.

It wasn't that she hadn't wanted to see him, but she was forced to change her schedule after she'd received a letter from the Studio Museum requesting she be available for interviews the first week of the new year.

Things were happening too quickly, and there was no way she wanted to repeat the mistake she'd made with Earl with Marshall. She had to make certain all the pieces fit.

The elegant Madison Avenue art gallery was ablaze with lights, the murmur of voices, and the crush of art critics, collectors, and the curious; and even though it was the most decorative of holiday seasons, most of the attendees were dressed in black.

Shelby Carter was no exception. She wore a black chiffon dress that flowed fluidly around her ankles. The matching silk slip, jewel neckline, and long sleeves were simple, yet proclaimed an understated elegance. Her jewelry was a pair of large pearl earrings. Sheer black stockings and a pair of black suede pumps with matching satin bows completed her tasteful ensemble.

Marshall spied her before she could turn to stare at him. She held a flute of champagne in one hand while the other was lost in the grip of a tall man who held it possessively.

A swift shadow of anger gripped Marshall's features before he schooled his expression not to reveal what he felt at that moment. In one brief instant he felt a foreign emotion he could identify only as jealousy. The man holding Shelby to his side had the woman he wanted.

He wanted her—not just her body, but *all* of her; and in that moment Marshall Graham knew it was for always.

"There's Shelby," Naomi Morrow whispered quietly. Her fingers tightened on her nephew's arm. "And that's Shumba Naaman, the sculptor." She pulled Marshall toward Shelby and the artist whose entire collection she had purchased at his last showing.

Shelby recognized Naomi and smiled as she walked toward her. The smile faltered slightly when she saw the tall man dressed in black escorting Naomi through the large crowd, but it was back in place by the time he stood over her, scowling slightly.

Extracting her hand from Shumba's loose grip, she curved a free arm around Naomi's shoulder and kissed her cheek. "I'm so glad you could make it."

Naomi returned the kiss. "You know I wouldn't miss this little soirée. You look beautiful," she added, close to her ear.

She released Naomi and extended her hand to Marshall, her gaze taking in everything about him in one glance. He was breathtaking in a black silk shirt with a banded collar, a black wool unconstructed jacket, matching loose-fitting slacks, and Italian loafers. She focused on the commemorative pin on his lapel rather than on his face. His large, dark eyes burned with a strange fire she had never seen before.

"Hello, Marshall." She was surprised her voice was soft and evenly modulated while her insides quivered. She hadn't seen him in nearly a week, and the absence made him more startlingly attractive than she remembered.

Marshall took the proffered hand and brought it to his lips. His gaze locked with hers as he took in everything that was Shelby Carter: her artfully made-up face; her curling dark hair swept up and calling attention to her high cheekbones; and the exquisite shape of her delicate jaw. He inhaled the familiar fragrance of her perfume on her wrist, smiling for the first time. It had taken him more than an hour of smelling every fragrance at Bloomingdale's before he'd found it.

"Shelby." His voice was low and seductive. He released her hand, but not before he'd turned it over and pressed his mouth to her inner wrist.

Shelby felt the heat from his mouth and her eyes widened as pinpoints of desire fired her body. She saw Marshall's gaze shift from her face to her breasts. She felt them grow heavy, felt the nipples swell against the silk of her slip.

Damn you, she raged silently. How could he make love to her in a room filled with people?

Shelby recovered quickly, not seeing the questioning glances Shumba and Naomi exchanged. She managed to introduce Shumba to Marshall without further incident, and she only let out her breath when the two men had greeted each other politely.

Naomi took over as she wound an arm through Shumba's and led him away, saying, "I'm not going to buy everything this time. I've heard that someone called me a 'selfish old woman.' I don't mind being called old, but I do resent the selfish part."

Shumba laughed and patted her hand affectionately. Leaning down from his impressive height, he whispered in her ear that he had put aside something he thought she would truly love.

Marshall stared at his aunt's departing back, then

turned to Shelby. He watched as Shelby took a sip of champagne, then he extracted the glass from her fingers. Slowly and deliberately, he turned the glass and drank from the spot where her lipstick had left a faint smudge of color, his gaze fixed on her mouth. He drained the glass and put it down on a freestanding column that doubled as a table.

Moving behind Shelby, he pressed his chest to her back. "Is he your boyfriend?" he questioned quietly.

Shelby's breath caught in her throat. She felt Marshall's heat, the solidness of his chest and thighs against her. The clean, sensual scent of his cologne enveloped her until she had trouble drawing a normal breath.

"He's a friend."

"How good a friend?" The fingers of his right hand closed on her waist, then inched up slowly until they rested under her breast, grazing and caressing chiffon and silk. Marshall's body responded quickly, hardening when he realized Shelby was not wearing a bra under the thin layers of black.

"A very *good* friend," she whispered. She curbed the urge to lean back against his body, but it didn't stop Marshall as his arm slipped under her breasts and eased her back until she lay against him—her back to his chest, her buttocks to his groin.

"I see." The two words revealed nothing yet said everything.

"Let me go, Marshall."

"Why?" His breath was warm near her ear.

"Because my boss is staring at me."

Marshall raised his head and met the dark gray eyes of a tall man with a blond ponytail. He smiled and waved to Hans. Hans returned the gesture, smiling.

"See, Shelby? No harm done. He approves." He dropped his arm and smiled down at Shelby, noting her frown. "Don't frown, darling. It causes wrinkles," he teased.

"I'm not worried about wrinkles, Marshall Graham. Did you come here tonight to harass me or to embarrass me?"

Marshall sobered quickly. "I came here because my aunt invited me. She told me you were putting on an exhibition she thought would interest me. What she didn't tell me was that the artist would be hanging on to you as though you were a priceless piece of sculpture he couldn't let out of his sight."

Mixed feelings surged through her, and she knew she couldn't vent those emotions . . . not in a room filled with people.

Her gaze narrowed. "Jealous, Marshall?"

Marshall leaned over, his strong fingers gripping Shelby's shoulders. "Hell, yeah!" he whispered savagely, before releasing her and stalking away.

Shelby made it through the evening in a daze, smiling and chatting like a programmed robot. She and Marshall did not exchange another word, even though she found him staring at her each time she turned in his direction. A maddening smile played at the corners of his sensual mouth.

He had admitted he was jealous and the thought thrilled her. He had to feel something for her to be jealous of Shumba. She hadn't slept with either man, and that meant Marshall's feelings went beyond lust or sex.

The showing ended at ten with all of the success Hans, Shumba, and Shelby had wanted and expected. The three sat talking quietly amid tables covered with the remains of fresh melon slices, large, succulent strawberries, varied cheeses, smoked whitefish, salmon, lox, and several varieties of imported crackers and breads. Empty bottles of champagne, red and white wine, and soft drinks were packed in cartons stacked along a wall in the back of the gallery.

"It was a sellout again, Shumba," Hans reported.

Shumba, his long legs propped up on a chair, pointed at Shelby. "Thanks to Ms. Carter."

Hans raised a half-filled glass of champagne. "A toast to Ms. Carter."

Shumba raised his glass of seltzer. "Ms. Carter."

Shelby nodded to both men. "Thank you, gentlemen, but this Ms. Carter is going home. I'm exhausted. Hans, please get me a cab."

Hans called a car service while Shumba gathered Shelby's coat and purse. She took the envelope that contained the commission Hans gave her and pushed it into the purse.

She said her good-nights and slumped onto the back seat of the car as Shumba and Hans stood out in the winter cold, watching her until the driver pulled away from the curb.

She didn't realize she had closed her eyes until the driver pulled up in front of her apartment building.

"Happy holidays," she replied, as she exited the car.

Walking quickly to her building entrance, she stopped short, nearly tripping when she recognized the tall man waiting for her.

"I thought perhaps you had gone home with your *very good friend,*" Marshall drawled.

Her heart pounded in her chest. "What are you doing here?"

He shrugged his broad shoulders beneath his overcoat. "Waiting for you."

"Go home, Marshall," she drawled behind a yawn. "I'm exhausted."

He grasped her arm, taking the keys from her gloved fingers and opening the front door. "I'll put you to bed."

They made their way into the lobby. "I don't need you to put me to bed. I'm quite capable of finding my way, thank you."

"I'm a very good tucker-inner."

She followed him into the elevator, smiling a tired smile. "I bet you are."

Marshall lowered his chin and flashed her a sensual grin. The grin faded when he realized Shelby was telling the truth. She looked exhausted. Her face appeared thinner, drawn. His plan to seduce her where she would permit him to make love to her vanished quickly.

All he wanted to do was to take care of her.

Shelby walked into her apartment, hung up her coat, and walked to her bedroom. She forgot about Marshall standing at the living room window, staring out at the shadowy outline of New Jersey, as she showered and prepared for bed.

She heard the haunting sounds of music coming from her living room before she burrowed under the quilt and drifted off to sleep. It would be the first time in days that she'd be guaranteed more than four hours of sleep.

Marshall sat on the sofa in the dark, knowing he should leave, but he couldn't. Seeing Shelby earlier, watching her graceful and elegant motions, had made him aware of what he had been fighting. He was in love with the woman!

He had fallen in love with a woman who'd deliberately spurned his every advance until he'd thought he was going to lose every shred of his iron-willed control.

He had admitted he was jealous while he couldn't admit that he loved her—at least, not to her face.

Running a hand over his face, Marshall wondered

why he found it so difficult to tell Shelby that he loved her. He never had that problem with Cassandra. But then, Cassandra wasn't Shelby. Cassandra could never hurt him the way Shelby could. He only realized that when he thought about how easy it had been to give in to Cassandra and walk away from her.

But could he walk away from Shelby? Could he give her up, now that he'd found her?

"No," he whispered into the darkness.

He didn't know how long he sat, but the three CDs he'd put on the player were finished. Rising to his feet, he removed his jacket, laid it across a chair, then moved back to the sofa and folded his long length on it, shifting until he found a comfortable position and drifted off to sleep.

He had barely closed his eyes when he found himself awake with Shelby standing over him. Her warm, familiar feminine fragrance wafted to his nostrils.

Her fingertips grazed his jaw. "If you spend the night on that sofa, you'll need a chiropractor in the morning. Come to bed," she said softly.

Swinging his legs over the sofa, he sat up. "What time is it?"

"Don't worry about the time, Marshall. If you need a toothbrush, there's a supply in the wall cabinet in the bathroom."

Marshall stared at her figure, retreating in a silky-looking nightgown trimmed with lace. He couldn't make out the color but knew it was a dark shade because it blended in with her skin coloring.

He undressed in the living room, laying out his clothes on the sofa. He made his way to the bathroom, brushed his teeth, and showered. By the time he walked into Shelby's bedroom, he was wide awake.

He made out the shape of her body under the quilt

as he slipped into bed next to her. She moaned softly and moved into his embrace.

Marshall held her, holding his breath while he dared not move. She had trustingly come to him and he didn't want to do anything to destroy that trust.

She shifted and snuggled for a more comfortable position, her face pressed to his chest. He felt her press against his naked body and he let out his breath slowly.

It was a time for comforting and protecting, and he knew if Shelby had invited him to her bed, she would also invite him to share her body. This was not the time to share their bodies. Closing his eyes, he drifted off to sleep again.

Shelby reveled in the hard male body imprinted on hers. It had been too long since she'd lain in the strong, comforting embrace of a man. There were times when she treasured being held as much as she enjoyed the physical fulfillment she sought from sex.

She tried to explain to Earl that sex wasn't lovemaking, but his carnal appetites were too skewed to differentiate between the two.

She smiled in the darkness, listening to Marshall's even breathing. Marshall had surprised her with his open display of possessiveness at the gallery. She had thought of him as stoic, conservative, and quite in control of his emotions and actions.

Nia's headmaster had nearly lost it!

Bright sunlight inched up the bed, spilling over the two people sleeping in spoonlike fashion. Shelby awoke first, registering the body pressed to her back and the warm breath on her neck. She knew Marshall was also awake because the rhythm of his breathing changed.

"I was wondering what color it was," said the soft male voice near her ear.

"What was?"

"Your nightgown." It was a rich mahogany brown with an ecru lace trim.

She smiled. "I don't have to guess about the color of your pajamas, do I?"

"They are always the same color. Bare-butt dark milk chocolate," he teased.

Shelby's smile widened. "I wouldn't know about that. I've never seen it."

Marshall released her and swept back the quilt and sheet. He rose to his knees, permitting her a side view of his naked body.

She swallowed painfully as she saw what his swim trunks had concealed. She had registered his magnificent erection. He turned and presented her with his back. She pinched his firm hip seconds before he flipped her over and fastened his teeth to her buttocks.

"Stop, Marshall. That hurts," she mumbled.

Marshall's fingers grazed her thighs and eased the silky garment up to her waist. His hands spanned her waist as he turned her over effortlessly until she faced him. Concern filled his dark eyes. "Did I really hurt you?"

Shelby reached up and smoothed away the frown furrowing his forehead. "No. I don't think you'd ever hurt me."

"You're right about that, darling. I would never hurt you." He lowered his body, supporting his greater weight on his elbows. "I would never deliberately hurt you, Shelby, emotionally or physically."

Shelby placed her fingers over his mouth. "Don't talk, Marshall."

He stared down into her large eyes, searching in her gaze for what he knew she could see in his—love. "What do you want me to do?" he asked against her fingers.

"Don't make me beg, Marshall," she whispered.

He needed no further prompting. Covering her body, Marshall cradled her face and kissed her. The pressure of his mouth on hers was gentle as he coaxed her lips apart.

He took his time tasting her mouth and throat while moving down to her breasts as he gathered the silk gown around her waist and pulled it over her head. He felt Shelby tremble and heard the rush of breath from her open mouth when he fastened his mouth to the ripeness of one firm brown breast, sucking until she felt her womb contract.

His fingers inched up her inner thigh and Shelby panted, then turned her face into the softness of the pillow to muffle her moans when his finger entered her celibate flesh.

Marshall was experienced enough to know that he had to prepare her small, tight body before he took her. He wanted to bring her pleasure, not pain.

She closed her thighs tightly against his invading hand. "Easy, darling. I won't hurt you," he crooned quietly. She opened her eyes and stared up at him. "I'll try to make it good, Shelby. For both of us."

Marshall's hands and mouth charted a course over the dips and curves of Shelby's body, lingering at the moist area between her thighs until she was nearly mindless with the passion he had aroused in her. And she did beg him—begged him to take her before she dissolved in a trembling mass of hysteria with the searing need that had been building ever since she'd met him.

Marshall waited until he had aroused Shelby where she was unable to disguise her body's reaction that she had nearly reached the point of fulfillment.

He entered her wet, pulsating flesh, moaning loudly when he felt her claim his own turgid sex throbbing for release.

Their joined bodies set a rhythm that was heard only

by the two of them, and in unison they climbed the heights of ecstasy that shattered into brilliant fragments of fulfillment.

Shelby clung to Marshall, languishing in the flooding of uncontrollable joy and wonderment. Her lips quivered against his as she failed to verbalize that she loved him.

Marshall held onto Shelby, carefully reversing their positions. His heated blood cooled, the lingering throbbing subsided, and he closed his eyes, unable to believe the passion she'd aroused in him. It was as if she had reached deep inside of Marshall Graham to capture what no other woman had ever claimed.

Shelby Carter had wordlessly exacted the awesome, uncontrollable passion he'd erected as a shield against the pain of rejection. He had given her more than sixty-five percent of himself; she had claimed the total one hundred percent.

He held her close to his heart until they both succumbed to the sated sleep of lovers.

Shelby walked into Nia Academy and was greeted warmly by one of the secretaries in the front office. They smiled, handing her a visitor's pass. Then an upperclassman escorted her to the auditorium. The school was decorated with their blue and gold kente print, helium-filled balloons in the same blue and gold, and *benderas*—the red, black, and green flag created by Marcus Garvey for African Americans.

She sat in the amphitheater-styled auditorium with guests, students, parents, faculty, and staff, listening to Marshall as he welcomed everyone to Nia's first Kwanzaa celebration. The overhead spotlight flattered his gray-flecked close-cut hair and his smooth skin.

Shelby smiled, remembering how they had lingered

in bed two days before, leaving only to eat and bathe. They had talked, watched a movie, and made love another two times before she'd suggested he leave so she could complete her weekend chores. He'd kissed her passionately at the door, driven back home, and telephoned her as soon as he'd walked through the front door of his house. He thanked her for the two gifts she had given him: herself and her passion.

She was pulled back to the present when eight students, representing each grade level, advanced to the stage and explained the principles of Kwanzaa.

Shelby felt her heart swell with pride as she observed the composed young men, dressed in their school uniforms, articulately deliver their prepared speeches to their peers, parents, and neighborhood community of what Kwanzaa meant to them.

Tears were visible in the eyes of many of the parents, and pride shone from the expressive faces of the instructors who labored unceasingly to help make the young men at Nia the best they could be.

The fruits and vegetables were placed on the *mkeka*, the candles were lit, the students sipped juice from the *kikombe cha umoja* amid the fruits and vegetables on the placemat. Each boy presented another with a *zawadi*, or gift, and this gesture concluded the Kwanzaa ceremony.

The assembled crowd rose, applauding enthusiastically, then filed out of the auditorium. Students who were assigned to the reception committee escorted everyone to the gymnasium for the remainder of the celebration, which was rumored to be the "real fun part of Kwanzaa."

Long tables set up around the perimeter of the gymnasium sent tantalizing smells wafting into the air. Shelby noted the serving dishes contained hot and cold dishes, all labeled with their countries of origin.

She noted a dish labeled *yassa*—spicy marinated chicken in an onion sauce from Senegal, yogurt-sauced chicken curry from Morocco, *tapo*—a Honduran fish stew with plantains and yucca, and familiar favorites from the United States: Southern fried chicken, Texas-style chili, cracklin' bread, Tuskegee Institute sweet potato bread with raisins and walnuts, duck and smoked sausage gumbo, macaroni and potato salads, cornbread, biscuits, shrimp creole, and steamed collard, mustard, and turnip greens.

Amid the surging crowd of celebrants, Shelby caught a brief glimpse of Marshall as he stopped to greet and talk to parents, students, and staff. She stood patiently in line, waiting to fill her plate with the food being served by the white-clad caterers, who patiently explained the ingredients in some of the less-than-familiar dishes.

Twenty minutes later, Shelby sat on the bleachers, her plate balanced on her knees. She swallowed a portion of Hoppin' John, concluding it was the best black-eyed peas and rice she had ever eaten. The dish had been prepared with spicy pork sausage, shrimp, onion, and red pepper.

She chatted amicably with the father of a student on her right, listening to him extol the excellence of Nia's philosophy of education and socialization. He proudly recanted how his nine-year-old son had begun to cut classes at his former public school because he thought he was "wasting his time listening to a boring old teacher." The father said he'd promptly enrolled his son at Nia. The boy managed to drag himself out of bed to attend classes even when he was sick.

Shelby saw Nadine Pierce walk into the gymnasium with a flair of brilliant red and black sweeping behind her. The stylishly dressed Nadine wore a cape-coat that had been fashioned with exquisite detailed piping and epaulets. Nadine spied Shelby and flashed a wide grin before she slipped an arm around Marshall's waist inside his blue blazer.

She turned away, jealousy racing through her chest, rather than look at the man she had fallen in love with cradling another woman to his body. It was she he had cradled to his body, offering her a second chance for love; she hadn't known when it had happened, but she *had* fallen in love with Marshall. And this love was different from the one she felt for Earl. It contained none of the frantic passion or the smothering possessiveness.

What she'd experienced with Marshall was a strong, secure, and comforting passion that she would never tire of. Marshall Graham was a man she would never tire of and who would never bore her.

Heads bobbed and toes tapped in rhythm to the taped music playing updated versions of classic holiday songs. The sound escalated as several parents raised their voices, singing along with the Temptations singing "White Christmas." The mood became even more festive when everyone joined in to what had become a Motown sing-along.

Shelby looked around for Marshall but did not see him in the crowd. She glanced at her watch. She wanted to congratulate him on a successful Kwanzaa celebration before she left.

Gathering her coat and purse, she smiled and excused herself as she wound her way through the crowd. Students and young people gathered in the halls, talking quietly to one another. She walked into the front office and found it empty. She heard Marshall's voice coming from the direction of his private office—his voice and that of another.

"I can't believe this, Marshall," said a woman in a soft, drawling Southern cadence. "We were married for years, and even though I never wanted a baby, there were times when we got careless. But I never got caught. Now, I'm thirty-eight years old, unmarried, and pregnant. Why, Marshall? Why now, and not five or six years ago? A baby probably would've saved our marriage."

"Cassandra," Marshall replied, his voice soft and comforting. "You know we ended our marriage for different reasons. And being pregnant is not the end of the world. I don't know why you think that having a child is a death sentence. You know how I felt and still feel about fathering a child. I've never changed my mind about having children."

Shelby was stunned, not only from what she'd heard, but because she found herself eavesdropping on what was a private and intimate conversation between a man and his ex-wife. A man she had fallen in love with.

Spinning around quickly, she retreated from the office, biting down hard on her lower lip. She tasted blood by the time she found herself on the sidewalk outside the building.

It had happened again. The man she was in love with had gotten another woman pregnant!

Instead of taking a taxi back to her apartment, she walked. The cold wind chilled her face, but she didn't feel it. She was too numb to do anything except replay what she'd overheard in her head.

Shelby didn't cry because she couldn't. There had been a time when she had shed so many tears that she knew she could never cry or grieve for a lost love again.

Why couldn't she have waited, she chided herself once she found herself in bed. She should've waited to sleep with him. But Shelby knew it still would not have changed anything. Unknowingly, she had fallen in love with Marshall before she'd ever offered him her body.

The telephone on the bedside table rang, startling

her. Her heart pounding in her chest, she counted off the rings before the answering machine switched on.

"Shelby, this is Marshall. I'm sorry I missed you before you left. Please call me when you get in. Love you."

The two words shattered her resolve and the dam broke. She cried, the sobs deep and wrenching. Marshall Graham loved her even though he had gotten his ex-wife pregnant.

How could she have made the same mistake twice?

Marshall felt as if someone had kicked him in the head. Pain and tension had stretched his nerves until he was mindless with the fear that something had happened to Shelby.

He pushed the food around on his plate, seeing and not seeing. She hadn't returned his calls; he was told that she wouldn't return to the museum until after the new year, and he had waited in front of her building for hours, praying she would appear.

"Either eat it or throw it out, Marshall."

His head came up and he stared at his frowning aunt. "I'm sorry, Naomi. I'm not too hungry." He kneaded his temples.

"You're not hungry, you have a headache, and you're too stubborn to tell me what's going on," Naomi shot back.

He pushed back his chair, rising to his feet. "Nothing's going on," he mumbled.

"Sit down, Marshall. Now!"

He obeyed her, glaring across her dining room table at her. His hand was shaking when he reached for his glass of wine. The liquid soothed his dry throat, but only temporarily.

Naomi's dark eyes examined her brother's only child. She saw what she should've recognized three weeks ago: Marshall had changed. There was intensity and restlessness that he hadn't shown in years. The last time she saw it was when he had made his decision to end his marriage and relocate to New York.

"It's Shelby, isn't it?" she questioned perceptively. She hadn't missed the interaction between her nephew and Shelby at Shumba Naaman's showing. There was no doubt that something was going on between her protégée and her nephew.

Slumping back in his chair, Marshall nodded slowly. He couldn't lie—at least, not to his aunt. "Yes."

Naomi shifted an eyebrow. "You really like her, don't you?"

Marshall shook his head slowly. "No. I love her."

"Does she know this?"

"I don't think so."

"You don't think so, Dr. Marshall Oliver Graham. For someone who's earned a Ph.D., you're not too bright. And why haven't you told the lady that you love her?"

He closed his eyes. "She won't let me."

"Why not?"

Marshall's temper exploded. "What is this? An inquisition?"

"Don't sass me, Marshall. Just answer my question."

The set of his jaw indicated his stubbornness. He felt like getting up and walking out of his aunt's apartment, but didn't. They were family. Naomi Morrow was the only family he had in New York. And because she was alone, he had elected not to return to Washington, D.C., and spend Christmas with his parents and cousins.

"Because she won't return my calls," he admitted reluctantly. He went on to tell his aunt all that had happened since the night he was introduced to Shelby Carter. He did not disclose that he had slept with

Shelby, but he suspected Naomi was more than aware of it.

"I don't believe she went to California to visit her family," Naomi said, after Marshall explained his dilemma. "But I do know that she always takes off the last ten days of the year."

Naomi stood up, and Marshall rose with her. "Let *me* call her to wish her a merry Christmas. That should confirm whether she's still in New York."

He paced the length of the dining room while Naomi retreated to the kitchen. What he felt for Shelby was akin to an itch that only she could scratch.

How, he asked himself, had she gotten to him without his knowledge? Why Shelby and not some other woman? What was it about her?

Because Shelby Carter is a challenge, a voice taunted him. He found her beautiful and feminine. She was versatile and intelligent. She was fiercely independent, as well as passionate.

He managed a smile. And most of all, she was uncompromising. She never pretended even to let him win during their swimming competitions.

"Marshall." He stopped pacing and turned to stare at Naomi. "She's at home."

"She's been home all this time?" His voice, though quiet, had an ominous quality.

"Don't lose it, Marshall," Naomi warned. "Shelby said she's been working around the clock to complete your curriculum before the end of the year."

"Today is December twenty-fifth. She doesn't have much more time before the year's over."

"And after that, Marshall?"

The forefinger of his left hand stroked the side of his nose, then something Naomi said registered. "Yes!"

Naomi stared at Marshall as if he'd taken leave of his senses. "What are you talking about?"

His smile was dazzling. "Tomorrow is the twenty-sixth, and the first day of Kwanzaa. We're supposed to spend Kwanzaa together."

"Tomorrow?"

"No. The entire holiday—all seven days." His eyes were glittering with excitement as he threw back his head and let out a burst of laughter.

Marshall reminded Naomi of the serious child he had always been who would on occasion exhibit an effusiveness which never failed to shock his family.

"Do you think seven days is enough time for you to win the young lady over?" Naomi teased, feeling some of his enthusiasm.

Marshall picked her up, swung her around, and kissed her cheek before he lowered her to the carpeted floor. "More than enough." There was confidence in his words.

"If that's the case, then I think I should give you something. Come with me," Naomi ordered, taking Marshall's hand and leading him to her bedroom.

He recognized the dark blue velvet pouch when she extended her hand. "Thank you, Aunt Naomi. It helps to know you have that much faith in me."

Naomi cocked her head at an angle, smiling. "Why not? You've inherited the famous Graham male charm. What else would you need?"

"A Mrs. Marshall Graham." Marshall smiled back, and surprisingly, his headache had vanished.

The ringing of the telephone pulled Shelby from her sleep, and before she could react, she picked up the receiver. "Hello."

"Happy Kwanzaa, Shelby!"

Her somnolence vanished. "Marshall?"

"How many Marshalls do you know?"

She groaned silently. "Only one. Happy Kwanzaa, Marshall." It wasn't fair. He'd caught her when she wasn't fully awake. The glowing red dials on the bedside clock read six-ten. The sun hadn't even come up.

"What time should I pick you up for the get-together with your friends?"

Shelby stared at the faint outline of the gaily wrapped gifts lining the work table in the alcove. There were seven—one for each day of Kwanzaa.

"Six." Her voice was low and flat.

"Is the dress casual?"

"Yes."

"Then I'll see you at six."

Marshall hung up, his call lasting no more than sixty seconds. Shelby replaced her receiver and lay in bed, staring up at the darkened ceiling. It was about to begin, and in seven days, it would be over. She had committed herself to sharing the seven days of Kwanzaa with him, and once the first day of the new year came and went, so would her time with Marshall Graham.

Shelby opened the door for Marshall, stepping aside as he walked into her apartment. He was casually dressed in a pair of charcoal-gray slacks, a slate-blue V-neck sweater, and a dark-gray suede jacket. At first glance the jacket appeared more velvet than suede.

He handed her a flat box wrapped in gold foil. *"Umoja,* and Happy Kwanzaa."

"Umoja." She repeated the Swahili word for "unity" or "staying together." Closing the door, she followed him into the living room and handed him the gaily wrapped box on the coffee table. "Happy Kwanzaa, Marshall." The shape of his gift box was similar to the one he had given her.

Shelby felt a little uneasy. Marshall's midnight gaze lingered on her face before moving leisurely over her blouse and slacks. The last time he was in her apartment they had spent most of their time in bed.

She held up her gift. "Should I open it now?" Marshall nodded and she moved over to the sofa and sat down. She felt, rather than saw, him watching her as she carefully peeled off the decorative bow and gold paper. Her heart started up a double-time rhythm when she saw the silk Hermès scarf nestled in tissue paper. The fabric was exquisite, the print vibrant.

Her head came up slowly. "I don't know what to say," she said breathlessly.

Marshall sat down beside her. His gaze caressed the delicate bones in her face. " 'Thank you' will be enough."

A tremulous smile touched her lips. "Thank you, Marshall."

Leaning over, he pressed a kiss to her temple. "You're quite welcome." He unwrapped his gift, his smile mirroring his approval. He held up a length of fabric for a bow tie and a cummerbund in the same print as the Nia Academy logo.

"Where did you find this?"

Shelby placed her gift on the table and clasped her hands together on her lap. "I made it. I hope the cummerbund fits."

Marshall stood up, removed his jacket, and fastened the cummerbund around his waist. It was a perfect fit. He raised an eyebrow. "You have a good eye—and good taste."

What Marshall didn't know was that it had taken her nearly six hours of browsing through every fabric store she knew that sold kente-cloth patterns to match the one on Nia's letterhead.

"I'm glad you like it, Marshall."

He took off the cummerbund and replaced it in the box with the bow tie. "Where are we going and what time do we have to be there?"

Shelby stood up. "We're going to SoHo. We should be there before seven." What she didn't tell Marshall was that Shumba Naaman was hosting the first-night celebration.

Marshall sighed in relief after spending more than two hours at the sculptor's loft apartment. He and Shelby had attended as a couple while not appearing to be a couple. She was polite *and* estranged.

He had spent hours observing her as she'd talked quietly with Shumba and the other invited guests. She had once referred to the talented artist as a very good friend of hers and Marshall believed that was what they were.

"What do you have planned for tomorrow?" he questioned during the drive uptown.

Shelby turned to stare at his profile. "Nothing."

He bit back a smile. "Would you like to spend days two and three at my place?"

"I can't. I'm trying to complete your curriculum."

"Why the rush?"

"I have other things to do. I can't afford to spend two days away from the project."

"When do you expect to complete it?"

"Hopefully, before the first." What she didn't say was that she was pushing herself to complete his project by January first because then she would be able to walk away from him and erase all memories of the man who'd brought back the pain she had forgotten.

"Would you mind if I make the plans for the next two days of Kwanzaa?"

Closing her eyes, she pressed her back against the

leather seat of his vintage Mercedes. "No. I don't mind."

"Dress formally." Those were the last words he said until he left her at her door, bidding her good night. There was no good-night kiss or embrace.

Shelby spent the night tossing and turning restlessly, her dreams filled with images of Marshall—his caresses, his kisses, and his slow, methodical, and purposeful lovemaking.

She'd missed his dry wit and his occasional jealousy. She wanted to hate him for his infidelity, but she couldn't.

"Why didn't he tell me?" she asked aloud in the darkened bedroom. Why couldn't he have told her that he was still seeing his ex-wife? That he was sleeping with her?

Sighing heavily, Shelby managed a small smile. One down and six to go. She prayed she could make it.

Marshall stared at Shelby, his mouth gaping slightly. He inhaled and let out his breath slowly. "Wow!"

Shelby gave him a sensuous smile. "Should I say thank you?"

He moved closer, grinning. "I'm the one who should say thank you." Shelby was stunning in a gold crêpe de chine dress that clung to every line of her body until it flowed around the toes of her black satin pumps. The garment claimed long sleeves and a high neckline, and when she shifted, it revealed an expanse of bared back to her waist.

Marshall handed her a decorative package with a large black velvet bow. "For you."

The burgundy color on her lips shimmered. "Thank you." She gestured to Marshall. "Please come in."

He walked past her and spied his gaily wrapped gift on the coffee table. Picking it up, he shook it gently. "Do you want to give me a hint?"

Shelby shook her head, visually admiring him in formal dress. His black wool tuxedo fit his broad shoulders with tailored precision and the stark white, banded-collar shirt with onyx studs eliminated the need for a bow tie, even though he had opted for a black cummerbund.

He noted her stare. "I do own a shirt with a wing collar," he admitted sheepishly.

"Open your gift, Marshall." Her command was quiet and filled with laughter.

They sat side-by-side on the sofa, opening their gifts. Shelby laughed. Marshall had given her a large box of assorted Godiva truffles.

"I'll have to swim a dozen laps to work off these calories," she said, staring up at him through her lashes.

Marshall noted the subtle bronze and moss green shadows on her lids and the plum blush accentuating her high cheekbones. His obsidian gaze lingered on her hair, swept off her ears and forehead. A styling mousse had taken most of her curl out of her hair, creating a style that would have been much too severe on a woman with features less delicate than Shelby's.

Picking up a truffle, she held it to his mouth. "What flavor is this one?"

He held her wrist as she fed him the truffle, drawing her forefinger into his mouth and sucking gently. Marshall watched her eyes widen as his tongue moved sensuously up and down the length of her finger.

Everything that was Shelby Carter—the haunting fragrance clinging to her flesh, the shimmering gleam of her flawless face, the soft curves of her body in the silky dress, and the essence of her femininity that lingered with him even when they were apart—swept over him, buffeting him like a tidal wave sweeping up everything in its wake.

"Marshall!"

The sound of her hoarse whisper broke the spell. He released her finger and Shelby sprang from the sofa. He moved quickly, capturing her arm and spinning her around.

"Don't touch me, Marshall!"

He stared down at Shelby, baffled by her vehement outburst and the look of revulsion on her face. "I don't understand what the hell is going on. Perhaps I'm missing something, but I seem to remember that ten days ago you invited me to your bed. And in that particular bed you and I shared something that was very personal, special, and quite intimate. I don't recall, but correct me if I'm wrong, us having an argument or a misunderstanding.

"Fast forward to the present. I'm afraid to touch you, much less kiss you. And I dare not even *think* of making love to you." His fingers tightened around her upper arm. "Talk to me, Miss Carter. What did I do wrong?" He enunciated each word.

Shelby stared back at him, her temper rising in response to his angry statement. "I don't ask for much in a relationship, Marshall . . ."

"What relationship, Shelby?" he countered, interrupting her. "You haven't given us an opportunity to *have* a *relationship.*"

"And don't interrupt me," she shot back. He nodded and she continued, "I repeat, I don't ask for much in a relationship. But I demand respect and fidelity."

Marshall released her arm, frowning. "What are you talking about? I haven't slept with, kissed, or even *looked* at another woman since my aunt introduced us."

"What about before that time?"

His gaze widened and he managed to look sheepish. "I'm not a monk, Shelby. I've slept with a few women since my divorce."

"Do those *few* include your ex-wife?"

"Cassandra?"

"Is that her name?"

"Yes. Why?"

"Have you slept with her since your divorce?"

"Of course not." His eyes narrowed and he stared back at her in silence. "What does Cassandra have to do with us?"

At that moment Shelby wanted the floor to open up and swallow her whole. How could she tell Marshall that she had eavesdropped on his conversation with his ex-wife? That she suspected the baby in Cassandra's womb was Marshall's?

"Shelby?"

She jumped slightly at the drawling sound of her name. Turning her back, she wound her arms around her waist in a gesture of protectiveness. There was complete silence except for the soft, even sound of breathing. There came another foreign sound and she spun around.

Her mouth gaped, then snapped closed. Marshall had kicked off his shoes and slipped his arms from his tuxedo jacket.

"What are you doing?"

"What does it look like?" He answered her question with one of his own, removing his cummerbund.

"Put your clothes back on."

"Why, Shelby? I'm not going anywhere until I get some answers. It sounds as if you've tried and found me guilty without a fair trial. And the sentence appears to be exile. You've deprived me of my right to be made aware of the charges leveled against me *and* the right to defend myself. Governments have been toppled from their very foundations because of similar practices, Shelby Carter."

He removed the studs from his shirt, dropping them on the coffee table before he shrugged out of his shirt. His hands went to the waistband on his dress trousers and Shelby panicked.

"No."

Marshall stalked her, unzipping the trousers. "Talk fast, Shelby, or I'm going to *live with you* until you do."

She did, leaving nothing out. She told Marshall what she had overheard when she'd gone to his office, while he stared at her in stunned relief. The heat in her face swept lower and her entire body burned in embarrassment.

Whatever anger or annoyance Marshall had experienced vanished quickly with Shelby's confession. The laughter started in his chest and bubbled up until he nearly collapsed with relief. The more he laughed, the more her humiliation increased.

"It serves you right," he stuttered. "Being nosy is not an admirable trait."

"I wasn't being nosy, Marshall Graham. I just happened to overhear a private conversation."

He sobered quickly. "But if you'd stayed long enough to hear the rest of the conversation, you'd have heard me tell Cassandra to marry her child's father because they did love each other."

Reaching out, he pulled Shelby to his bare chest. "Cassandra and I have remained friends. She came to me because she needed another opinion from a friend. I don't love her anymore, but I don't hate her, either. Both of us finally realized we married for all the wrong reasons. I knew she never wanted children, even though I did, and she knew what my professional aspirations were. She told me flat out that she would never leave D.C. Most of us delude ourselves, believing we can change the other person."

"Are you hoping that perhaps I might change my mind and let you win whenever we swim?" she teased. Shelby was certain he could feel the runaway beating of her heart through the fabric of her dress.

He pressed his mouth to her ear, inhaling deeply. "Of course. Have you no pity for my bruised male ego?"

"No," she whispered, smiling.

"Was there even the slightest chance that you might have been a little jealous of Cassandra?" he crooned.

Shelby smiled, planting light kisses on his broad chest. "Hell, yeah," she replied, repeating the very words he'd uttered at the art gallery.

He pulled back, examining the sensual smile on her lips. "You care?"

She nodded. "I care a lot."

"How much?"

"This much." She wound her arms around his strong neck, pulling his head down. Her lips parted as she kissed him with all the love she could summon for Marshall Graham.

He moved his mouth over hers, devouring its moist softness, drinking deeply to replenish the love he felt for her.

The kiss ended, both of them breathing heavily. Marshall's dark eyes crinkled. "That's a whole lot of caring." One hand came up and covered her breast. "What are we going to do tonight? Dine in or out?"

Shelby was unable to hide the love she felt for him. She was certain it showed in her eyes. "Dine out. Days four and five are mine, and I've planned two very special nights of dining in."

Marshall released her, successfully concealing his disappointment. "May I open my gift first?" She nodded.

The box contained a Vermont teddy bear wearing a blue blazer, gray slacks, a white button-down shirt and navy blue tie. Marshall's unrestrained laughter filled the apartment for the second time that evening.

"It's perfect, Shelby."

"So is its owner."

Marshall nodded modestly. "Thank you, darling. For the bear and the compliment."

The next four nights became a blur with the exchange of gifts and the evening celebrations. Shelby gave Marshall a bottle of his favorite cologne, Eternity for Men, a leatherbound appointment book for the next year, engraved with his monogram, a supply of scented beeswax candles for their candlelight dinners, and a subscription to a magazine for horticulturists, along with an exquisite bonsai plant.

Marshall's exceptional taste was reflected in his gifts to Shelby: a bottle of Shalimar perfume, an illustrated anthology of art and poems of love from the Metropolitan Museum of Art gift shop, a double strand of delicate gold links dotted with tiny diamonds, and the tiny gold sculptured woman he had purchased at Shumba's exhibition. He admitted to Shelby that Shumba had told him that she had the matching male counterpart.

The seventh and final night was celebrated at Marshall's house, the living room ablaze with the scented candles.

Shelby lay on the rug in front of the fireplace, staring up at the shadowed face of the man she loved.

"I didn't think I would finish the curriculum in time, but I wanted it out of the way so that there wouldn't be anything between us if we couldn't work out our differences."

Marshall ran his forefinger down the length of her nose. "What differences, darling? The only problem was that you overheard something you didn't understand. And it's taken me nearly two weeks of penance to pay for that!"

"I had to make certain what I feel for you is real, Marshall. I couldn't sleep with you again until I worked out my problem of learning to trust a man again."

"I would never be unfaithful to you." He punctuated each word with a light kiss on her mouth. "You're everything I'd ever want or need in a woman."

"Imani," she whispered. "Faith, Marshall. The faith to believe in ourselves, our people, and those we love."

"Imani," he repeated.

Shelby reached into the pocket of her dress, handing Marshall a tiny box. "Happy Kwanzaa." He opened the box and removed the sculpted gold Inca man and woman. "She missed you," she said quietly. "But it was her decision to come back with her husband."

Marshall closed his hand around the sculpted pieces, smiling. "Thank you. I think she'll be very content with her husband."

He handed Shelby the velvet pouch by his feet. "Happy Kwanzaa, darling. I love you."

She opened the pouch and removed the strand of magnificent pearls she had seen many times around Naomi Morrow's neck. Her gaze mirrored confusion. "Why?"

"The Graham pearls have been worn around the neck of a beautiful Graham woman for more than a hundred fifty years."

Shelby's lower lip trembled. "But I'm not a Graham woman."

Lowering his head, Marshall gave her a hopeful smile. "You could be, if only you'd marry me."

Her eyes filled with tears of joy. "Are you proposing to me?"

"It sounds like a proposal to me," he replied in a smug tone. "I want to be able to celebrate the next fifty first fruits of the harvest with you, if you'd have me."

Her smile was dazzling. "I love you, Marshall."

"I think you're supposed to say yes, Shelby."

She threw her arms around his neck, whispering, "Yes, yes, yes!"

A New Year, A New Beginning

Candice Poarch

Prologue

As the sun cast its last hour's glow of the day over the cragged formations, Amanda Burns looked into the vast picturesque scene of the Grand Canyon. A sudden sadness, in contrast with the bright colors of orange, red, yellow, and gray, washed over her as the late September day displayed signs of the autumn season.

What should have been tender evenings of relaxing and conversations, sweet kisses and hand holding, that rejuvenation of love she'd planned for years with her husband, had turned into a solitary vacation.

Amanda was not supposed to be here alone. It should have been her first honeymoon with her husband of twenty-two years. She'd pleaded and begged for this trip so many times until he finally gave in. Since that time, five years ago, Brian had postponed it year after year saying he and Adam Somerville needed to work on this project or that one until it was much too late.

She'd grown to have a keen dislike for the unreasonable amount of time Adam had demanded from her marriage. If she heard it once, she'd heard it a thousand times. "Adam thinks they need to do this" or "Adam needs to do that," especially around the time they had made special plans. The man had even called her, asking her not to take her trip alone. As if it were any of his business.

Now, as Amanda stood overlooking the vast beauty of the Grand Canyon, her eyes misted and she unlocked the tight grip she held on her purse strings.

Brian was gone forever. He died in June last year. She'd gone through the "firsts." The first time doing any number of things as half of a pair. The lack of warm, sweet memories to lift her spirits still disturbed her. And worst yet, she considered for the first time, if they were together what would they do? Special intimacies had left their marriage long ago. They had each gravitated to their own little worlds. Their separate worlds. On his deathbed, Brian had gripped her hand and said he loved her. And she wanted to scream, "Don't tell me now." Why didn't he show her all those lonely days and nights when he'd cast her away and she'd had to create a world of her own if only to maintain her sanity. High school dreams of peace and love ever after had been destroyed, dying with Brian's last breath. It was too late now.

As she stood in her little piece of the vast canyon, Amanda tried not to slump into the gloom of why they hadn't shown each other that love while he was here. "Why did your friends mean so much more than your own wife? Why did Adam mean more?" Amanda whispered as warm tears washed a line down her cheeks.

Why weren't we each other's best friends?

As the sun slowly slipped away, the few warm memories she did have seemed a lifetime away.

Shaking her head and trying to clear it, she thought of their son, Josh. He had called just before she came to ask her if he could vacation during the holidays in Montana with his roommate. Trying not to be a clinging mother, she'd responded with a "yes."

With a touch of selfishness, Amanda wondered exactly where that left her? Spending Christmas and New Year's alone. She sighed with the loneliness and the burdens of single parenthood. Brian had handled all the finances in the past but had left nothing for Josh's education. She'd been forced to sell the Land Rover that Brian loved so much to pay for Josh's junior and senior years of college.

Now Josh wanted to go to veterinarian school and she didn't have the money to send him. Brian had willed the insurance money to the business to compensate for the loss of his position. He had built up only a very small savings through the years, since most of the money went back into the business. He'd said over and over that the company needed to keep up with technology to stay on top. Even the house was more a business venture than a comfortable haven. She'd been the perfect corporate wife, entertained more clients, thrown more business New Year's parties, and since many times Brian couldn't make it back from his business trips in time to attend, she had given them alone more times than she cared to think about.

Now she was at loose ends. Adam Somerville, Brian's partner for the last fifteen years, mailed her a monthly check that covered her expenses and small extras, but not enough to cover the enormous fees of veterinarian school.

The volunteer work she did at church was emotionally rewarding but not economically practical right now. At least the senior's center she helped plan and the entertainment drive she'd engineered were successful endeavors. They wouldn't continue to require the enormous hours.

As the last of the sun disappeared into the horizon, Amanda started back to her car. It was time she found her place in life alone. This trip marked the beginning of her new independence, even though it was painful.

Now, she needed to provide for Josh's future.

Chapter 1

"Think positive" was her decree. Amanda looked at her numbered items in her Day Timer. This call was step one. Soon she'd be able to scratch a line through it. Mission accomplished. She took a deep breath before speaking.

"I want to sell my share of the business to you," she told Adam Somerville. Her positive resolve lasted all of five seconds as she listened, tight-lipped through the satellite connection, hating having to go to that man for anything. The Day Timer and lists weren't doing their job the way they were supposed to. Irritated by the prolonged silence that greeted her announcement, she tightened her hand around the phone as she held it to her ear and, with nothing to do with her other hand, drummed her fingertips against the blue tiled kitchen countertop.

"We're in the process of expanding. I don't have the money to buy you out right now." In her mind's eye, she could almost see the creases in his forehead from concentration. He usually gave his undivided attention to the problem at hand. "If you could give me a year or two . . ."

How many times had she heard that line from Brian, *Wait a year for this Amanda, or Wait a year for that,* Amanda thought as she drowned Adam's voice out. No more waiting. "I need the money now." Life was much too short to wait. If she'd demanded more from Brian, maybe. . . .

"Is something wrong? Can I help you with anything?" came his conciliatory reply.

"No, just buy out my share of the company." She knew she sounded like a shrew, but couldn't stop herself. He made her feel incompetent, like a child begging for an allowance. It was her money after all. He had no right to make her feel this way.

She flipped the Day Timer to another page for the affirmations she'd jotted down to help her day go more smoothly. *Stay calm,* she read.

"As I said . . . ," came his reasonable voice, as if he were soothing a troubled client. It only fueled her temper more.

"Then you can find a buyer. Or I can sell to the Blakes. Joel Blake approached me again a week ago." She wouldn't actually sell to the competition, but he didn't need to know that.

"I hope you won't do that. I can't raise the spare cash right away. I need a little time for this new expansion to take place. If you need money for anything, I can get it for you, but not enough to buy you out. The company is your son's legacy . . ."

Line two of her affirmations said *Take calming breaths.* She took two. It didn't help. Her hand was cramped by its stranglehold on the phone. He didn't have a twenty-year-old son to worry about.

"He's part of the reason I need the money." Her calm voice belied her inner turmoil. She hadn't meant for that to slip. Adam had a way of rattling her even at the best of times. Amanda sighed. Now that she'd started, she knew she had to finish the thought. "He wants to attend veterinarian school. He isn't interested in satellite communications. Without Brian, there's no reason for me to stay in the business." She wasn't about to elaborate that her husband hadn't provided the funds to cover Josh's continued education. She didn't have the money to send him to vet school. But money was money. The sale of her stock would work just as well. The company had always come first with Brian. Not so with her.

Amanda could imagine Adam's thick black brows furrowing. His hand swiping across his stern, thoroughly masculine face in irritation with her. His tone contained barely leashed annoyance. Even though they rarely saw each other, his dark brown features, sharp eyes, and controlled smile were so imposing they were impossible to forget.

"I can raise the money for his college education. He is Brian's son, after all, and my godson."

"This isn't your concern. If I sold my shares, I'd be able to afford it." She wanted to sever all connections with the past. As Brian's family had done to her. They blamed her for his heart attack and refused to have anything to do with her.

She heard a voice in the background.

"Look, I'm coming there soon. Josh is a junior this year. We have some time to work things out. We'll have the money for his education." He chuckled in a familial way. "We've worked as partners for the last fifteen years . . ."

"You and Brian were partners," she interrupted.

"Same thing. We can work this through. You don't have to want for anything. I'll see to that."

"I'm not your responsibility." Amanda gritted her teeth.

"Look, Brian was my best friend, as well as my partner. I wouldn't be much of a friend if I didn't see that your needs were satisfied. Let's talk about this when I get there. Don't make any hasty decisions." Someone called out. "We'll talk when I get there. I'll see you New Year's."

Contemplating his last statement, Amanda hung up the phone on the kitchen wall. *I'll see you for New Year's.* Brian had made that very same statement year after year when he had to travel to the Ivory Coast just before the holidays. He'd said it before their last Christmas together. Tears misted her eyes with the memory of her past anticipation of his arrival. And she didn't know if the tears were from the loss of him or a loss of her dreams. Dreams she'd hoped would come true once Brian wasn't so busy anymore.

She had nothing to look forward to this year.

Amanda expected the pain to stab as it had before. For some reason, it wasn't quite as sharp as it had been last year, a short few months after his death. Still, the loneliness had worsened. And Christmas was closing in, the worst season of the year for someone alone.

At a glance around the kitchen, she knew she should be counting her blessings instead of wallowing in self-pity. She had a house that most women would love to have, in an upper middle income neighborhood in Fairfax, Virginia, a short drive from D.C. And a monthly check arrived to cover the expenses. A check she didn't work for. Still, she craved more. Those were all material possessions. She needed something—perhaps something for her soul. She needed to accomplish something meaningful for herself.

Arms swinging back and forth, Amanda speed-walked on the neighborhood track, her breath expelling in cloudy puffs.

"Hold up some, will you?" Struggling along to catch up, Lottie Rodgers wore hot pink, form-fitting spandex covered with three layers of sweats on her upper body

A NEW YEAR, A NEW BEGINNING   237

to keep in the heat. "What're you doing? Trying to win a marathon?"

Amanda slowed her pace and turned while marching in place, not realizing that while so deep in thought, she'd left the woman behind. "Sorry. You're a little slow today, aren't you?"

Finally reaching her, Lottie bent over to catch a breath. "What the hell is wrong with you today?" Air whistling through her teeth, she straightened and they resumed their five-mile walk at a more leisurely pace. "You act like you've got a bee in your bonnet."

"In the name of Adam Somerville," Amanda huffed, barely taking in the brown leaves of the massive oak. She usually enjoyed her commune with nature on these walks.

"What's he done now?" Lottie asked as one who'd heard it all before and then some.

"I called to tell him I wanted to sell my stock last night. With the big expansion, he wants me to hold off. I can't sell anyway for a year. The bylaws say I have to give him that long to purchase before I offer it to someone else." Amanda's teeth gritted. Yesterday at this time she thought it would all be settled by now. Her life would be on the right track with a straight line drawn through item number one.

"Do you really want to sell that stock? It's a great company." It wasn't often that Lottie made sense, this was one of those rare occasions. Under any other circumstances, Amanda would hold on.

"It isn't a matter of choice. I need the money for Josh's education."

"Oh, that's right. He wants to be a vet now," was her dubious reply.

Amanda looked sideways at her friend, suspicious of her tone. "Why did you say it like that?"

"He's a junior. He'll probably change his mind at least a dozen times before he graduates."

"I don't think so. He's so goal-oriented and he's always loved animals." He was the exact opposite of Lottie's two children who'd changed majors with the end of each semester. Poor Henry finally put his foot down and demanded they choose one major or else.

"Still, it would be nice if you can hold onto the company. You did get some insurance money to tide you over after Brian died, didn't you?"

"The insurance went to Worldwide Satellites. Nothing for Josh and me to live off of."

"That worm!" The woman stopped and Amanda had to pull on her arm to get her moving again. Lottie came up with too many reasons for rest stops during their walks. This wasn't going to be one of them.

"I'm looking for a job after the new year, but it's going to take a while for me to work my way up in the company."

"A job!" A particularly big cloud puffed out as Lottie slowed and placed hands on her hips. "Hell, you own half the company, don't you? Just hire yourself on. You couldn't be in a better position. Think up some job you'd like to do and tell that stiff lip what salary you want for the job you decide to hire yourself on as."

Leave it to Lottie to think she could railroad herself into the company. "It's not that easy. Adam's the CEO. I have to go through him."

"Last time I heard, fifty percent means you've got as much say as he does. Lord, child, what the hell would you do without me?" Throwing her arms in the air, Lottie sighed. "This way we can still do the things we enjoy like torturing ourselves three times a week in twenty degree weather so you can stay slim."

"You wouldn't be dieting so much if you didn't eat a box of chocolates after every walk."

"It's my reward for this torture," she sputtered as she plodded on, leading Amanda now. "This way we can continue these idiotic walks."

"I'll be working. It's time I put the degree I got when Josh was a baby to work for me. I won't be able to take off in the middle of the morning to exercise."

"Why not?"

Amanda had forgotten for a moment that Lottie went through jobs the way a child went through cookies. She got a new one at least once a year. And if she was lucky—very lucky—she'd last two weeks. The last time she was fired, Lottie was incensed when her boss had taken exception to what he called her "excessive breaks." She told him that she needed a ten-minute break every half-hour. It just wasn't humanly possible to sit behind the desk and answer phones for three-hour stretches without one. He'd kindly told her she could break the entire day from then on.

Fortunate for Lottie, her husband was vice-president of a local brokerage firm. She really didn't need to bring in an income, but felt, with all the women getting into careers, to be a whole woman she needed one, too.

She was still working on the perfect career for herself. Her children had at least completed something, even though they were now working on their doctorates. And Lottie's husband had learned long ago, to have a peaceful household, to let her explore without comment from him.

All in all, they had a wonderful marriage. Henry loved Lottie immensely and she loved him in return. Amanda still didn't understand how a solid man like Henry could be attracted to a scatterbrain like Lottie.

They walked silently for minutes, each in her own thoughts.

"If you didn't get any insurance, how are you taking care of yourself?"

"I get a monthly check from the company."

"Well, what do you need to work for? You're getting money anyway. You're just thinking up problems. Had me thinking you were on the verge of bankruptcy."

"I need some stability, some purpose in my life. Can you understand that?" Frustrated, and holding back tears, Amanda clamped her jaw tight and stared.

"Honey, you've got purpose," Lottie said softly. "You do all that volunteer work at church with Everett. You care about people. You stay busy. There's only one of you." She patted Amanda on the arm, geared up for the last two miles. "My brother has been lucky to have a worker like you in church." Amanda knew that Everett's career as a minister still baffled Lottie, though after all the years, she accepted it and helped him.

"I feel like I'm getting paid for nothing. I'm not working for that check. And I should be."

"It's the least your husband could have left you. You did work for it. All those business dinners. The New Year's party you plan every year. Don't forget you raised your son almost single-handedly. You do plenty." The silence stretched a moment. "I know we don't value what we often do, but that's work, too. It builds up a good rapport with the clients and the employees. You work very hard for that money."

"I guess." Uncertainty cloaked her voice as much as it had cloaked her life this last year.

"There's no guessing about it. Just count yourself lucky that if anything happens, you can fall back on that stock. In the meantime, just be cool, and as my brother would say, 'Count your blessings.' "

Amanda laughed and shook her head. "There's still Josh's education."

"I've already told you the solution for that."

"There's no need for me to hold onto the company. Josh isn't interested in it. And with selling it, I'll have more than I need for the rest of my life. I don't need that much to live off. I could even sell the house and get something smaller." The maintenance and lawn were only a small fraction of the work required to maintain a home. A condo would be less work.

"Sell that beautiful house?"

"It's too big for one person. I've been thinking about it a lot lately." She'd miss the neighborhood, the familiar surroundings and people. Change was the most difficult of challenges.

"Now don't go making major decisions when you're down in the dumps. Take small steps at a time. Tell you what. They're having a makeover for women at church tomorrow night. Now that I've lost a few pounds, I'm looking forward to some new makeup and clothes."

They waved to a neighbor walking his dog on the opposite side of the street.

"My spirits and clothing are just fine, thank you." Her closet was filled with serviceable suits and church dresses.

"I know, I know, but it wouldn't hurt to try something different. If for nothing else, think of the charitable cause. It's to help displaced women get on their feet."

That did the trick. "Well, we could try it out." She could always use a new sweater or something to lift her spirits.

Amanda soaked in the Jacuzzi after her walk, then dressed and ambled into the foyer. It was a week after Thanksgiving and time for her to put up Christmas decorations. With a glance at the boxes full of ribbons, bulbs, and garlands for decorating scattered on her living room floor, a bit of nostalgia hit her. This would be the last company New Year's party she would host. In the last week, the cleaning crew had washed every window and dusted every cranny in preparation for the holidays. The company employees, along with their spouses and business acquaintances, would attend. For years, she'd prepared the lavish dinner and cleaned the house herself. Until one year Adam had, on a rare occasion, traveled back with Brian for the holidays and requested that she hire a cleaning crew for the house and a caterer for the food. She'd marveled at how uncharacteristically thoughtful he seemed.

Amanda dug into the box and pulled out a star that Brian topped the tree with each year. That had been the finishing touch. After they'd gathered glasses of wine and Josh a warm cup of hot cider before turning the room lights out and the tree lights on. Brian had laughed and toppled on the unsteady ladder they never seemed to replace. Awash in contentment, they sat back to digest and enjoy the rewards of their loving labor. She relished it so because those occasions were rare.

She untangled a string of bulbs to hang on the twelve-foot tree, which stood in a prominent place in the foyer. It was best to keep busy.

Across the Atlantic Ocean, in the Ivory Coast, Adam shook hands with Gil Macklin and walked him to the office door, wishing he'd dare take the rest of the morning off to enjoy the perfect sunny weather outside. Instead he stalked back to his own office where Sheryl Weber, his office assistant, was rearranging chairs. Expansions didn't happen and business didn't move by shirking his duty.

"All right," she said in a stern voice, hands on hips. "You may as well tell me about it. Something's been worrying you all afternoon." Her colorful mauve dress with delicate needle work reached midcalf. She wore slacks beneath it. He enjoyed the colorful African fashion all the women wore.

Adam dropped into the leather chair behind his desk.

"That bad, hum?" She raised an eyebrow.

"Worse." He sighed. "It's that flighty wife of Brian's."

"What's she done?" With coffee cup in hand, she took the chair across from him.

He leaned forward, elbows on the desk. "Now that I'm practically down to bare bones in finances with the expansion, she wants to sell the company." Beyond disgusted, he rose and stalked to the window, half turned and pounced on Sheryl again. "You'd think she'd have *some* sense of responsibility, some respect for the hard work Brian and I've sweated to make this company what it is today!" His hand sliced the air.

"And *worse,* if I can't buy out her share, which I can't, she wants to sell to the Blake brothers. How long do you think the company will survive then? They're a resale company. They don't care who they hurt when they sell parts of it away. Half the employees would be out of jobs within the year. But do you think she'll worry about that? No, she'll have her fat bank roll put away without giving a care about anyone else. She owns half the business. She can do anything she wants to." He sank into his seat, drawing out a long sigh.

"Oh, Adam, she wouldn't really sell, would she?"

He shook his head. "I don't know. Brian always said she was flighty. Didn't have a head for business. No telling what she'd do." Sheryl had worked for Adam for years and had his complete confidence. He knew anything he said would stay with the two of them.

"You and Brian got along so well together. You wouldn't find a partner like that again."

"I really miss him. His cousin raised me after my parents died."

"Really? You never talked about your family," she said softly.

"No." He opened his mouth as if to say something and changed his mind.

"Don't you think it's time? I've always wondered about that icy veneer of yours."

He grinned that twisted smirk he was famous for. "The original ice man," he knew they called him. But suddenly a warm smile covered his features. "We were very poor and very happy. My dad went from job to job. He was a fun man and he loved his family. My mom," a catch marred his voice, "my mom loved him and me more than anything. Regardless of where we were or what idiotic business venture he got into, she loved him and she believed in him."

"You were fortunate, weren't you?" Her eyes were gentle with understanding.

"I was." He didn't feel fortunate after they died and he had no one. But looking back, he realized he was.

"Adam, Brian always thought too much of himself. Amanda may be a different woman from what you think." She paused as if to weigh her words. "You're going back to the States. You're going to be near her. I have yet to see a better salesman than you. You'll be able to convince her to keep the business. I have complete confidence in you." She rose from her seat and gathered the coffeepot. "I'll bring your mail in."

Adam watched her tall dark graceful form glide out the office and wondered why he wasn't romantically attracted to her.

"Here's the mail." She placed the stack on his desk.

"Thank you, Sheryl. For everything."

"Anytime." She left, closing the door quietly behind her.

The heat was oppressive, but he was glad to be here. Thick emotions clogged his throat. He was going to miss her most of all when he moved back to Virginia where the corporate office was located. Some of the company's most lucrative satellite transmission services accounts were here. His replacement, however, was more than qualified to manage them.

As the CEO, Adam needed to be in the corporate offices. After spending the last ten years here, he was in for a huge readjustment.

He shuffled though business letters and marketing barbs until he recognized a letter from Josh. Putting the others aside, he picked up the silver letter opener to slash the top. A scrap of paper had been hastily scribbled on. He opened it and read.

Hi, Uncle Adam,

Sorry I'm going to miss you for Christmas vacation. I'll be in Montana with my roommate. He lives on a ranch, so I'll get plenty of prevet practice and lots of snow this year.

I'm glad you're coming home so Mom won't be alone. The house is so big and lonely for her and filled with memories. You could stay there until you get your own place. And you can keep her spirits up for the holidays. Otherwise she'd brood. I'm counting on you. Thanks, Uncle Adam.

Got to study for exams. Talk to you over the Holidays.

Josh

Thoughtfully, Adam folded the paper in half thinking fondly of his only godson. Brian had brought the boy to Africa twice on trips and Amanda joined them once.

Adam could stay at the house—or try to.

Amanda was likely to toss him out on his ears. He stroked his chin as he considered. The house was half his, a point he hadn't brought to her attention and wondered if Brian had. She couldn't sell the stock for a year without his approval. Without angering her, that would give him time to find out what was going on in her life and convince her not to sell the stock at all.

Adam dropped the letter on the ebony desk. He was going to miss this place when he left. Vivid woven cloths and masks hung on the wall. Looking outside at the tropical setting, it scarcely seemed like Christmas.

Ten years had passed since he'd celebrated the holidays in the States. Suddenly, Adam was looking forward to it—no matter what mood Amanda might be in.

Chapter 2

He'd always thought Amanda was pretty, but pretty was too bland for the smile that hit just the right angle, the eyes a spark of sunshine on a dreary day, lips that invited a man's kiss, and rounded curves a man's dream.

Feeling like he'd been kicked in the solar plexus, Adam wondered what bomb had suddenly dropped on him. What happened to the homey plain-looking woman, the wife of his partner? Straight suits and subdued lines. The red form-fitting sweater with huge white petals over the shoulders softened her face, outlined generous breasts.

Adam pulled up short. A man did not think of his best friend's wife's breasts. But what else could he think with her so inappropriately attired? It was all her fault, her unconscious sensuality causing him to have indecent thoughts of her. If she'd dressed as she should have, he wouldn't have these unseemly thoughts. That wasn't quite true. He'd always felt some stirring around her he failed to identify. This stirring always brought on the guilt. It was also the reason he jumped at the opportunity in Africa. He didn't have the safety of Brian and distance now. He did, however, uphold common decency.

The red sweater and her cheery countenance made her appear all Christmasy and bright. Added to the form-fitting blue jeans, she was hot. At least until she noticed him at her door.

"Adam." She greeted him in that sweet husky voice that fired his senses no matter how capricious she was. Looking from his face to the suitcase she managed a barely cordial, "Come in." With raised eyebrows, Adam took her comment more as a question than statement. He let it ride as she stepped back to allow him entrance while continuing to glance at his suitcase as he passed her. Adam still hadn't decided how to handle the sticky situation.

But the suitcase was forgotten completely when the magnificently decorated twelve-foot cypress standing proudly in the huge foyer immediately drew his attention. Strains of "Silent Night" floated in the background. It reminded him of his youth. His parents had always decorated huge trees. And they'd seemed so beautiful with strung paper, popcorn, and tin cutouts. Amanda's was decorated more lavishly, but it still exuded the feeling of warmth and caring. To his surprise, the decorations he'd mailed to her through the years were on the tree. Whenever he traveled, he'd purchase gifts for Brian's family. He always choose hanging decorations for Amanda.

A discrete cough from the living room drew his attention. To his annoyance, he saw that she was entertaining company. Male company. He left his suitcase by the door to shrug out of his newly purchased cashmere coat and handed it to the waiting Amanda. An introduction to the frigid temperature in New York the previous day had induced him to make the hasty purchase. As she hung it in the spacious hall closet, Adam advanced into the living room, decorated in discrete antiques. A man dressed casually in a sweater and slacks sat on a comfortable Queen Anne sofa. Gray hair peppered his temples. Adam had often heard it made women go wild. His lips tightened. Was Amanda going wild over those streaks of gray?

The pleasant smile on the man's face further irritated Adam. "Good afternoon." The man rose as Amanda entered behind Adam.

"Reverend Smart, meet Adam Somerville, Brian's partner. I think I mentioned to you he'd be moving to the area."

"Yes, you did."

Adam relaxed a little at hearing the man's title, but not for long once he noticed the rev's ring finger was bare. Adam threw a tight smile as he shook hands with him. The reverend had no business at his home trying to make passes at his best friend's wife. With an outward affable appearance, Adam extended his hand. "How are you, Reverend Smart?"

"Ah, what's this 'reverend' business among friends? Call me Everett." The man passed a secret grin to Amanda that further annoyed Adam. "Welcome back to the States."

"Thank you."

Amanda took the seat across from Everett, so Adam sat on the delicate love seat beside her. Adam frowned as Amanda leaned over to reach the teapot, her V-necked sweater cutting a little deeper than he thought appropriate. "We're having tea. Would you like a cup, Adam?"

"Thank you," he responded, almost regretting his answer when he noticed the direction of the rev's eyes. Adam cleared his throat to divert the man's attention.

"How are your parents, Amanda?"

She looked up from her task. "Enjoying Europe," she answered. "I'm glad they finally took the trip. They delayed it long enough."

"And Josh?"

"He'll be out of school in two weeks."

"I'm going to miss him this year."

"So am I," she said quietly. "Sometimes I wish I'd said no."

Everett reached over and covered her hand. "You did the right thing by letting him go."

"I suppose." A vulnerable smile escaped before she swallowed hard and lifted her chin boldly.

"We'll keep you too busy at church to get lonely." He squeezed her hand and leaned back.

Amanda's smile was more confident this time.

"I won't take up much more of your time. I know you two need to talk." He turned to Adam. "How was you trip, Adam?"

"Long," was Adam's short reply.

She relaxed enough to laugh for the first time. "Oh, yes. Brian often complained about it whenever he traveled so far," she said in the strained atmosphere. The good humor drifted away at the mention of Brian's name, to be replaced with sadness.

Adam wanted the radiance back and could have kicked himself for putting her on the defensive. There was probably a legitimate reason for the pastor's visit, other than his obvious interest in his best friend's widow. A very attractive widow. A very *rich* widow. Adam wondered if the reason Amanda needed the money had anything to do with financing any of the rev's ventures. After all, Amanda was a very wealthy woman, if one considered the value of her stock.

She walked with Everett to the door and the rev used the opportunity to grab her hand and squeeze it before he took his coat from her.

Soft hands, Adam remembered from their shake. Hands that probably never experienced the callouses of manual labor. Adam looked at his own hands. They'd seen many callouses as a teenager, callouses so deeply ingrained they never went away. Those callouses were one of the reasons he'd worked so hard to get into college and again to maintain a 3.9 average once there. Adam swore he'd have a better life. A life that would afford him more than the bare necessities and the many extras for comfort.

Now, all of that was threatened by Amanda's desire to sell her stock. His stomach roiled at the thought of losing the business after pouring his life's blood into it for the last fifteen years. How could he convince someone who'd never had to lift a finger toward it what the company meant to Brian and him? Adam rubbed his forehead, willing away an impending headache. Perhaps if he increased her monthly allotment, she'd at least hold onto the business long enough for him to raise the money to buy her out. But with the expansion, that could take years. He remembered his father, the failed businesses, the lost jobs. At least his dad had an understanding wife who knew what it was to love and stand by a man. Really love a man. Adam only had his business.

The reverend's voice brought him out of his contemplations.

"It was a pleasure meeting you, Adam. I hope you enjoy living in the States."

"I'm sure I will, thank you."

"We'll meet on Friday to purchase the food for the shelter. I'll pick you up," he said to Amanda.

"I'll be ready,'" Amanda said before she closed the door against freezing temperatures that hovered in the twenties.

Adam looked around her living room. She had it all. A designer's dream of decorations and furniture. A loving son in college, and money to spare. She didn't want for anything. What more could she possibly desire? She could keep all her money. He'd pay for Josh's education. He owed Brian that much. Since Adam didn't have children of his own, the closest he'd get to a son at forty-five was Josh. At the same time, perhaps it would buy him time with Amanda.

Flustered, Amanda had to force herself not to pat her hair before stepping back into the room. She hadn't expected Adam for a few days yet.

He always looked perfectly put together, perfectly proper, and at six feet, much too tall and attractive for so cynical a man. The suitcase worried her. There was plenty of hotel space in town. Even when Brian was alive, he'd never stayed at her house, always preferring the freedom and privacy of a hotel room. Why would he arrive with suitcase in hand now?

Uneasy, Amanda eyed the suitcase again. Perhaps it was filled with important papers she needed to see. She had no idea why he didn't bring them in a briefcase as most normal people would have. She would still give him the benefit of doubt. There must be too many papers to fit into a briefcase, she told herself staunchly.

He'd made himself comfortable while she'd seen Everett out. With one arm stretched out across the back of the chair, not even the cable-stitched sweater could conceal the muscled strength in his shoulders and arms. A shiver flashed over her.

She would not be intimidated by him this time. If he thought for one second that she would tolerate his presence under her roof for one night, he had another thought coming. Head held high, she took the seat on the sofa Everett had vacated. Adam's mouth jerked into a half smile. Amanda abhorred being anyone's source of amusement. "So," she said smartly at a loss for words. How did one broach the subject of the suitcase without sounding stupid?

"I must thank you for permitting me to stay here until I find a place of my own." Adam didn't have the same lack of conversational skills.

"Excuse me?" Now, owl-eyed, Amanda looked at him

in horror. Unable to close her startled mouth, she knew she must look like a fish. If she was speechless before, she was even more so now. "You . . . you must be mistaken." She shook her head. "You couldn't possibly . . ."

"Josh's room. He offered it when he wrote to me a week ago. I was sure he got your permission first." Adam leaned forward and scrubbed a hand across tired features. "I was so thankful for the invitation. I've been busy with getting everything in order for the move. And after your call, I moved the date up. It'll also give me a chance to go through Brian's papers. There's so much stored here. It'll save me the time of driving back and forth from a hotel."

"There's one that's not too far from here," came her weak reply.

"You wouldn't want me coming and going, disturbing you at all times of the day and night. I talked to a real estate agent before I left Africa. They should have something soon after the beginning of the year. That should give me ample time to get Brian's papers in order. Even though I own fifty percent of this house, I've always considered it yours and Brian's. I wouldn't dream of imposing on you."

Amanda's head swam. "You own half this house?" Her voice squeaked. "What are you talking about?" If she wasn't already seated, she would have fallen.

"You mean Brian didn't tell you?"

She shook her head no.

"He said you loved it. I was single and didn't need much space. I paid half the down payment and monthly mortgage. After all, we used to have our offices in the basement. Some equipment is still down there, isn't it?"

"Yes . . ."

"Good." He stood. "I'm bushed. If you show me to Josh's room, I think I'll crash for the next twenty hours."

Before Amanda knew what had hit her, Adam had unpacked the car and his luggage was safely ensconced in the spare bedroom upstairs, at the opposite end of the hall from hers, instead of Josh's room, and she was downstairs in her—their—kitchen wondering what tornado had hit her.

Not only had she not thrown him out, she'd quickly fallen into the role of dutiful hostess as she put fresh sheets on the bed and dusted the furniture as he showered, even though it had already been dusted three days ago. Her critical eye made sure everything was in perfect order for him. He could stay the night, but tomorrow he absolutely had to leave.

As Amanda dumped the remains of the tea into the sink, she wondered how she could tell the half owner of her house that he couldn't stay there until he found other accommodations.

How could Brian do this to her? Her shoulders slumped. She was so unnerved, the situation almost sapped her energy as she allowed herself a quick few moments to wallow in the despair stealing over her. Had her husband just once considered her worthy of knowing about her own home? Did he honestly believe her head was filled with fluff? That she couldn't comprehend something as simple as her own living arrangements? What was she to do? She couldn't demand that Adam leave the home he owned. She couldn't find other accommodations for herself immediately. Without a job and money—a great deal of money—a real-estate agent would laugh in her face if she went looking for another house.

She just had to sell her share of the company. She'd approach Adam with it at once. Once the stock was sold, she could afford another home. Nothing as large and elaborate as this one, though she'd grown to love it.

She considered the curtains, furniture, paintings, and wallpaper she'd spent months choosing. The huge kitchen with its eggshell wallpaper with burgundy and blue stripes was a woman's dream. The granite and tiled counter surfaces were so satisfying to work with. The round oak table by the huge bay window overlooking the flowers and trees in the backyard was perfect for relaxing with her family. Often she'd watch the birds and squirrels play as she took a moment to savor a cup of tea with her lunch.

Her neighbors were kind. A sudden sadness stole over her. She'd miss the people she'd come to know, many of them mothers like her, sharing their concerns for their children. They'd conversed many times as they watched their children play.

So much had changed in the last two years. This would only be one of many.

Her thoughts wandered to Everett. What would he think—and the volunteers she worked with? He was a handsome and kind man and she enjoyed his company as a friend. She wondered at the lack of romantic response for him. He'd be an easy man to love. Then she thought of the imposing Adam and the unwanted awareness. She couldn't possibly feel anything for that man. He was Brian's best friend.

As she sat in front of her dressing table, her fingers stilled in the process of spreading the cream over her smooth skin. How many surprises would she encounter before her life was in order again? As hard as she tried not to worry, her thoughts returned to her finances and the house.

This was exactly what happened when women didn't get involved in the family's finances. After Brian died, Adam had taken care of everything for her before returning to the Ivory Coast to train someone so he could transfer back to the States. Exactly as Brian had done during their marriage.

Amanda had been so surprised and devastated by Brian's death, she'd been incapable of taking care of anything. Now that the shock had worn off, she realized she needed to know more about their finances. She'd seen to the personal accounts, but after the day with the lawyer, Adam had taken care of the house and insurance. Half of what he'd said had just melted into grief. Now, she was more determined than ever to start a career and get her life in order. Starting right after the holidays. In the meantime, she'd work on her résumé.

The next morning, Adam awakened refreshed to the smell of home-baked cookies and fresh coffee. A quick shower had him descending the stairs in short order. When he reached the kitchen Amanda was bent over, pulling one pan out of the oven and shoving another one in. He snatched up a cookie and munched, fixating on her shapely rear.

"Adam, you're eating cookies before breakfast," she admonished as she placed the hot pan on a rack.

"That's the kid in me," he said and snatched up another one, looking at the mountain of them on the countertops. "Who's going to eat all of these?" He leaned against a cleared end of the counter.

"They're for the bazaar on Saturday. The proceeds go to entertainment for the senior citizens." Pulling the mitt off, she asked with a tight smile, "What would you like for breakfast?"

"Anything. I usually eat light." Her tone was anything but. It ranked that she disliked him. But why did she? He'd done nothing to warrant that internal hostility under her appearance of cordiality. He turned over backward to ensure her comfort.

"Well, I bought eggs and sausage while I was out this morning. It'll only take a few minutes to fix it."

"I don't want to put you through any trouble," he replied in a mocking tone.

"No trouble at all." Her curt response was muffled as she bent to pull open the stove drawer to retrieve the frying pan.

"What can I do to help?" Adam asked, angry that her acid tone didn't detract from his fascination with her.

Amanda gave him a strange look. She seemed to carry on an inner debate while she glanced at the cookies. Finally, she decided to put him to work. "If you like, you can stack the cooled cookies into the tin over there."

"Okay." He got up to do as she requested.

"The waxed paper is in that drawer, and layer them with the paper sheets," she said as she sliced the sausage into cakes and popped it into the frying pan. "Put two dozen cookies into each container." As the sausage sizzled, Adam felt her scrutiny as he carefully layered cookies into the tins before topping them with the waxed paper and layering them again.

Her brows puckered and her eyes squinted as she surreptitiously watched him. He wondered again at her suspicious nature. So far, Adam realized, he'd done nothing to win her good graces as he'd planned to do.

"You can start in the office downstairs whenever you please. It's all ready for you," she said shortly.

"Thank you. I'll start tomorrow morning. My body is still on Ivory Coast time," he said easily. "I've about burned out on work. The earth won't stop if I take one day for myself."

She looked sharply, her eyes narrowing. "Well, whenever it suits you," she snapped, and turned to flip the sausages.

Now, what had he done? No wonder he never married. "Is something wrong, Amanda?"

"No. How is the new project going?" She cracked eggs in a bowl.

He debated before he decided to let her nonanswer ride for now. "One contract we're trying to get is going to keep me busy through the holiday. We should know something by the end of the year, or the beginning of next year." He topped one container and picked up another one. "How are the New Year's party preparations going?"

"Everything's on schedule."

"Between that and your volunteer work, you're quite busy aren't you?" Adam suddenly wondered just how busy the reverend was keeping her.

"Quite."

When she opened the oven door again, another wave of aromas mixed with that of the sausage. What really held Adam's attention was the yellow apron tied around the bright green blouse that accentuated her waistline. A waistline that had maintained its narrowness even after having a child. Not that he would have held it against her if her waist had thickened a bit during the course of nature. What he didn't agree on was all the tummy tucks and face lifts women had to suffer trying to hold onto the last scrap of youthfulness. Until the silver screen celebrated the old as well as the young, plastic surgery would be here to stay.

Then he caught himself. He was as bad as the reverend. Adam Somerville had no business looking at her derriere and waist.

"Adam have you thought about buying my shares of stock yet?" she asked.

Unprepared for the question, Adam was startled for a few heartbeats.

Chapter 3

"I have." Adam put the last filled canister on a pile with the others and decided to come forward with the idea that had been turning in his head for a week. "I need help with some of the contracts. Since you're looking for new directions—a new career so to speak, I thought you might be willing to help out with the company."

"I've never worked on those contracts before," Amanda said, uncertainty in her voice.

Adam filled in the blanks. "You went to night school and have a degree in business, as I recall, even though you never used it. Most of the work is common sense. You'll be working with Joe at first to learn the ropes." He leaned back assessing her. "Give it a try. Let's say, six months before you make a final decision." Thinking that she was spending too much time with the reverend, he added, "Of course, working for the company would cut into your other activities."

Amanda cleared her throat and looked away. "I realize that, with a career, I'd have less time for my volunteer work. I can do that on the weekends and in the evenings."

"Certainly." It was too much to hope she'd stay away from the man altogether.

"Don't worry about Josh," he added. "I can

scrounge up enough money for his education. And as a working employee in the company, you'll get a regular paycheck in addition to what you're getting now." He didn't want her worrying about Josh's education.

It seemed that an immediate weight lifted from Amanda's shoulders. She had no real idea what she could do. Her career aspirations could come down to what she could get in a tight job market. Wasn't this as good as any other? If she didn't jump at this opportunity, at forty she'd have to compete with others who'd been in their careers for years. Who would take a forty-year-old over a twenty-two-year-old when they could train that person at lower wages? And how much would her volunteer work really count with a company? She could say that she managed funds for the food shelter the church provided, or that she managed the senior entertainment program for a small retirement home run by the church or that she was PTA president for six years. But would they recognize those as legitimate skills when they could get a forty-year-old who has been in the job market for twenty years?

It didn't take her very long to reach a decision after all.

"I'll try it out." She set the plate of warmed, homemade apple sauce, sausage, eggs, and buttered toast in front of Adam, filled a glass with orange juice, and topped his coffee. She had tried not to think about how pleased she was, once again, watching a man eat, even if he wasn't involved with her, and with his affability, he was making it difficult for her to hold onto her acrimony. In the early days of her marriage, Brian and she had enjoyed many companionable mornings together, lingering over coffee to make the intimacy last.

Kitchen work certainly didn't detract from Adam's masculinity, Amanda thought. Her nerves were a tangled glob. Anger was easier than the treacherous desire racing through her.

This might be the longest six months of her life. She only hoped she didn't live to regret this decision. She needed to remember that he was responsible for keeping Brian away from his family. Even though Brian ran the offices in the States, Adam was the leader.

"I think we'll work well together," Adam said as he sliced a piece of the sausage. The phone rang and with Amanda in the process of taking another batch of cookies out the oven, Adam answered it for her.

"Hello?" He listened a moment. "All rested from my trip. She's right here."

Amanda placed the hot pan on a trivet and picked up the phone. "Everett, hi." A smile that touched an unwelcome cord in Adam spread over her face when she discovered the caller's identity.

"No, no. They're almost done. You can pick them up tonight, but you really don't need to. I can see to it." She smiled at something he said. "Really, I'll bring them over. They aren't too much for me." She smiled and blushed again. "All right, I'll see you at church at . . ."—she looked at her watch—"let's see—three-thirty? Sure. Good-bye." Still smiling, she put the phone back on the hook.

"I can help you with the cookies," Adam said shortly. "You're going to have enough for an army." Why was her response so friendly to Everett and cold to him? That rankled. The smile still lingered on her face, the sparkle still lit her eyes. All that put together made her breathtaking when she was happy.

The stab of jealousy that racked Adam was so staggering and unwanted it shook him. She was Brian's wife. His best friend. He shouldn't have designs on her and she shouldn't have sweet smiles for Everett. It was too soon for her to even consider dating again.

"It's not that bad really," she said. "I'll welcome the help, though. But you should be resting. Everett volunteered to pick them up, but his hands are full with other preparations. He really gets involved with everything that happens at the church. We're so lucky to have him."

That was more than she'd offered of her personal life since his arrival. Perhaps it was an indication that he'd done something right. Adam picked up the ball and ran with it.

"Um, I've already had plenty of practice boxing them. I'm a pro now," Adam responded. He'd reserve judgment on Everett.

They worked companionably for another two hours.

Later that day they loaded up the packages of cookies and took them to church. Adam's system still hadn't acclimated to the freezing temperatures and he shivered in his newly purchased coat. A manger display featuring African-American characters and surrounded by soft lights was arranged prominently on the front lawn of the huge brick church that dated back to the late eighteen hundreds.

Adam only took a moment to enjoy the scene before he made quick work of unpacking the car. The church basement was noisy with the chatter of what seemed like more than a hundred volunteers and filled with the colorful lights of Christmas decorations and cheerful spirits. Before they could barely clear the door, Everett was hot on Amanda's heels.

"Amanda," he said, coming to a smiling halt. "You made it." He glanced at Adam. "And you brought Adam. Good of you to help our Amanda out." His tone was filled with possession. "The seniors' drive this year is a resounding success. Indeed, God has truly blessed us."

Everett evidently took pride in a plan well executed. There were enough boxes of cookies stacked in the place to feed a small town. That was all well and good, Adam thought, but the possessive note in the man's voice rankled.

"You actually expect to sell all these cookies?" Adam asked, not believing enough people were around to purchase them.

"Last year we received over one thousand mail orders. This year that number tripled. Between the mail orders and what we'll make from the bazaar tomorrow morning, I don't think we have enough, though we've quadrupled our supply this year. The cookies are becoming more and more popular. Lots of wonderful family recipes."

With a myriad of conversations, one stood out above the others. "Keep your hands off my cookies, Harry," came a sharp voice.

Adam turned toward the harsh reprimand. A gentleman, every bit of ninety, was gingerly trying to snitch a box of cookies from the woman's pile.

The woman was at least five-ten and as spare as she was tall.

"One little box won't hurt, Mary. Give me just one box. You got a hundred here."

Stern, she stared him down with her hands on her hips. Poor Harry bent under the war of wills and slid the box with one arthritic finger back on the pile, his spare shoulders drooping. After winning the battle, Mary reached into her oversized purse, pulled out a huge plastic bag of cookies, and handed them to Harry.

"Ah," Harry groaned with a smile that showed that half his teeth were missing. "Thank you. You're all heart, Mary, to think of an old man."

"Uh-huh. Now go on back home before dark."

Harry got up with his cane in one hand and his bag of cookies in the other and slowly tottered his way out the door while the crowd looked on. The woman clearly had a soft spot for him.

"Brother Cox lives next to the church," Everett explained. "He's lived in this neighborhood all his life. Just loves Sister Mary's cookies though," Everett said. "They go through this every year."

Adam couldn't blame the man. He'd snitched a few of Amanda's while they packed, and made sure she saved a few for him. She promised to make him more. He would hold her to that promise, although she looked as though she regretted the impulse as soon as the words were spoken.

"So, are you all settled in and over the jet leg?"

"I am." Adam focused on the officious minister.

"I hope you were able to find good accommodations." It was a question. He must have noticed the suitcase.

"I was." Adam replied, but offered no more.

"Is it some place nearby?" Everett's brows furrowed.

"I'm staying with Amanda." May as well nip that little tryst in the bud right now.

Everett cast a quick look at Amanda who wouldn't meet his eyes.

"Reverend Smart?" someone called out.

"Excuse me. Yes?" He turned toward the voice.

"We can't get this cash register to work." The puzzled man was clearly at a loss.

"Well," Everett said, as he walked over to the machine, "I'm not an electronic wizard, but let's see."

"Did you have to tell him that?" Amanda snapped once Everett was out of hearing range.

"He asked." Adam shrugged and decided to help the hapless Everett out. After all, his spirits had elevated immensely.

Smarting, Amanda went over to her own cookies and started to pack her boxes into the shipping crates. They now sold almost as many by mail as they did from on-site sales.

Everything was well coordinated. Volunteers printed out the addresses and labeled shipping boxes for the cookies. She merely had to stack hers into the boxes and someone would seal them tonight and ship them off. By tomorrow morning, the room would be set up and readied for Christmas shoppers. She had stuck her pack of cookies into a box and shoved packing paper over it when she felt a hand on her shoulder.

"Amanda, could you help me with something in my office, please?" Everett asked.

"Of course." She knew what he was about to say to her. Wearily, she followed him down the corridor to his spacious office, arranged as a combination sitting room and office. He spent so much time with counseling people that the committee felt he should have appropriate accommodations. The church was lucky to have someone who was willing to work as hard as he was. He'd engineered so many wonderful programs for the needy. The seniors entertainment project was just one of many. He had a true sense of the needs of people. An inner sense of their problems.

He closed the door slowly after they entered as if he needed time to pull his thoughts together.

Amanda geared herself for a lecture on inappropriate behavior in living arrangements. She decided to forestall it by explaining first.

"I know what you're going to say, Everett, but I didn't have a choice. He owns half the house. I can't very well refuse him." The arrangement warred with her conscience and what she thought was appropriate. She had a son to consider.

"I thought it belonged to you and Brian," he stated, perplexed.

"So did I." Amanda sighed and rubbed her brow.

"Come on and sit down." He grasped her hand and led her to the chair in front of his tidy desk, which Mary, as church secretary, always kept in order. He sat on the one next to her. "You know there's space at the seniors' home. You can stay there until you can resolve this problem. He can't expect to live in that house with you."

"He's in the process of finding other accommodations. In the meantime, he's working through a lot of Brian's papers. Adam has been overseas for the last ten years. He's back to expand and take over this part of the business. He shouldn't be at my house for more than a month."

"I hate to see you so upset." His hand touched her brow then ran down her arm.

"It's just that I'm finding out things little by little. I should have been more involved in the details hanging over my life, Everett." Too agitated to sit, she rose and began to pace. Everett stood and leaned against his desk.

"Things happen for a reason. God will see you through this. And you know I'm here to help you if you need it."

She paced over to him and grasped his hand to cover it with her own. "I don't know what I would have done this last year without you. Now that my grief is beginning to abate, it's time I get my life in order." She took a quick breath and sent him a fleeting troubled smile. "He's offered me a job with the company. We'll see how that works."

"It is your business, too. You should be an active participant. We will miss your work here."

"Not entirely, I hope. I plan to continue some of my volunteer work." She offered a uncertain smile.

"Good." He looked at her a good long time.

"Well," she said, uneasy with his scrutiny. "I have to

get back to packing or I'll be here all night." She got up in her usual brisk manner and left the room.

Everett sat where he was for a long time, contemplating as background voices mixed with Christmas music filtered into his office. Amanda was a beautiful woman. She was free and finally getting over Brian. And he was growing to love her immensely. He needed someone like her in his life. A wonderful volunteer in the church, she'd fit perfectly into his life. Even though he was constantly surrounded by people, at night he longed for something more. He was the sounding board and advice-giver for many people. He lived his life according to the vows he'd taken twenty years ago. Just as with Brian, his wife passed away five years ago. She'd been a kind woman, older than he. He never once considered breaking his commitment with God or his vows.

Now, he was ready for love, for a special someone to share his life. Amanda would make the perfect preacher's wife.

Chapter 4

Lottie Rogers, vibrant and effervescent, glided into the house. "So, you're Amanda's friend." Stopping short and sliding the gloves off her delicate hands, she looked Adam up and down, making no attempt at trying to hide her frank perusal.

"I'm Adam Somerville," he said in a no nonsense voice that could cause his worst adversary to tremble in his shoes. He extended a hand.

She raised an well-arched eyebrow, clearly not intimidated. "Uh-huh," reaching out, she barely touched his hand with the tips of her manicured fingers. Obviously she had all the time in the world.

Adam cleared his throat, amused by her frank appraisal. God bless the man strong enough to handle the bold woman.

"Oh, Lottie!" Amanda rounded the corner, rescuing him in the process. "I'm glad you stopped by. I've prepared one of your favorite dinners."

The woman immediately came out of her trance and seemingly forgot Adam was even present.

"Hi, yourself, girl. I'm here to take you out before the madness of the season hits."

Amanda looked down at her jeans and sky-blue angora sweater. "I hadn't planned . . . I'm not dressed . . ."

"You look just fine," she assured Amanda, with a cursory glance. "We're just going dancing anyway. Doesn't she look beautiful, Adam?" She remembered he was there after all.

"Ye . . ."

He obviously spoke too slowly for the tornado who blew in.

"Besides, certain men—better known as my husband and brother—are just about to drive me crazy." The woman dropped her purse beside the sofa and carelessly draped her coat on the sofa arm. "I will not return home until I've burned off some energy. I left them in the kitchen, Everett lamenting about you and the hunk here," she said, raising an eyebrow, "and Henry about God knows what. I learned to tune him out years ago."

"By your tone, nobody could tell you're madly in love with Henry," Amanda said, rolling her eyes and shaking her head at the woman.

"These nights out with you and the girls keep me sane and in love with him." She headed to the kitchen. "What's that smell?"

"Just some barbecued ribs."

"We've got time to eat before we leave." Lottie picked up the phone and dialed. "Glenda, Mandy and I'll be a little late tonight, but we'll be there" A pause, then, "Uh-huh. Yes. Got to go, girl." After hanging up, she flew to the powder room, where Adam heard through the open door, water running. "My diet just flew to hell, girlfriend. Why you ever baked those ribs, I don't know. Everyone can't eat that greasy food and stay slim like you."

"I wonder who's forcing you?" came Amanda's dry reply as she handed china to Adam. In another minute, Lottie joined them. The three of them worked companionably together to ready the meal.

"You always fix too much." Lottie forked ribs on her plate. "So you're the one who has Everett so nervous. He thinks he's in love with girlfriend, here," she said to Adam.

"Don't be silly, Lottie. He's not in love with me." Mortified, Amanda kicked Lottie's ankle. It had no effect on the woman's tongue.

"Of course he thinks he is. But you need someone like the hunk here and Everett needs someone . . . well, he hasn't met her yet." She narrowed her eyes at Amanda as she reached under the table, obviously to rub her smarting ankle.

"Thank you, friend," was Amanda's rueful reply. "You know how to lift a woman's spirits, don't you?"

"Don't start spouting that junk with me. You wouldn't want me to lie, would you?"

Adam knew Lottie and he would be fast friends.

"He sees you as the perfect little preacher's wife, what with all the volunteer work and all. Thinks it goes well with his post. But you don't love him. You'll just make yourselves miserable." She waved a saucy rib in the air. "So I'm kinda glad the hunk moved in here. Without him, you two probably would have talked yourselves into marrying. And that would have been a disaster." She bit into one of the homemade rolls.

Lottie monopolized the conversation during the meal and, knowing Lottie was on his side, Adam had no qualms with Amanda spending the evening with her friends. Not that she actually asked him, or needed to.

"What kept you away so long? And why is someone like you still single?"

"Work. And never settled down long enough." He shrugged. "Unlucky, I guess."

"Um, it's a good thing you stayed single long enough for Mandy here."

"Lottie, he didn't stay single for my benefit."

Since she sat between Adam and Amanda, Lottie's neck swiveled to talk with both of them.

"Fate, Mandy. Don't you believe in fate?"

"No."

They finally completed the meal as Lottie continued to dominate the conversation, as usual. Amanda couldn't leave fast enough. She hastily put her dishes in the dishwasher and wiped down the kitchen.

"So, what time will you all be in?" Adam threw in.

All commotion stopped.

"When we get in, sweetheart," came Lottie's sassy reply. "We haven't been on curfew in years." She patted his hand and rose to stack her dishes in the dishwasher.

Amanda dashed upstairs to change, leaving Lottie and Adam on their own.

Amanda returned home around eleven and she had finally snuggled into bed, exhausted from the dancing, when Josh called.

"Hi, honey," Amanda yawned.

Hearing it, he said, "Oh, Mom, I forgot the time difference."

"It's okay, sweetheart. I just got in."

"Where did you go?"

"Out with Lottie." Amanda plumped her pillow and sat up to lean against the headboard.

"Is Adam back in the States yet?" he asked, with more enthusiasm than Amanda cared for.

"Yes, and in the spare bedroom." She decided not to berate him for his part in that fiasco. He was so protective of her.

"Good. I don't like your being alone in that big house."

"His stay is only temporary. Then I'll be alone again."

"But at least he'll be close by if you need help."

"Honey, I don't want you to worry about me. I can take care of myself." Silence greeted her.

"He offered me a job with the company. I start tomorrow."

"That's great!"

"I'm a little nervous about my first job."

"But you've always worked, Mom. You just didn't get paid for it."

"I know, but still . . ."

"Where's that confidence you always poured into me? You're very capable, Mom. You'll do a fantastic job. Don't worry."

"Thanks, honey. I think I needed to hear that."

"I'm sorry I'm out west and left you alone to face this."

"Oh, don't worry about me. How do you like it there?"

"It's great, Mom. All the animals. Something's always going on."

"I'm so glad you like it there."

"It's great experience. Well, I'll let you get to bed, Mom. Tell Adam I said hi, okay?"

"Sure."

Amanda placed the phone on the hook feeling better about tomorrow. Josh loved it in Montana. At least that was one worry off her chest. She snuggled under the covers and it wasn't long before she was nodding off.

Amanda's first day on her new job started with a burst of energy and with more than a little trepidation. Determined to do the very best she could, she rose at five to dress and eat and opened her first folder for her first contract by five forty-five. Joe had written details for organizing the files in a way she could use it. First, he explained what the company did. She knew they provided video, data, and voice satellite transmission services, but she wasn't aware they offered terrestrial lines as well in some remote locations. They were a satellite resale company and did not actually own any satellites. They purchased huge blocks of space from satellite owners and resold time to smaller companies.

Joe was coming by around nine to spend the day training her. Actually, he was taking part of his day every day this week to train her.

She had read through three folders by the time she heard the shower go off at seven and got up from her work to start Adam's breakfast. Slicing potatoes into the frying pan, she wondered how he looked undressed. It must be the masculine aroma in the house making her so aware of him. That didn't explain why she never had those feelings for Everett.

The potatoes were done and she was pouring the beaten eggs for the omelet into the pan when he came downstairs. As he entered the kitchen she diverted her attention from the omelet long enough to peruse his suit slacks, dress shirt, and tie. After hanging the jacket on the back of a chair, he marched directly to the coffee Amanda had brewed.

"You're up early," he said after his first sip.

"I wanted to get an early start." If he looked wonderful in jeans, he was devastating in navy suit and print tie. "You're going out today?" she asked, as she concentrated on her omelet to slow her accelerated heartbeat.

"I have meetings at the office all day. I should be back by six tonight." He peered at her intently. She could almost imagine he referred to a date.

"Good." Her pitch was unusually high. Every time his gaze met hers, her heart turned over in response.

"Joe is an excellent trainer. He should be able to answer any of your questions. I've made a list of phone numbers for you."

Her fingers trembled as she took the paper from him.

With cup in hand, Adam leaned against the counter. He had a way of just observing and focusing that made a person believe he knew their innermost secrets.

She fervently hoped he didn't know hers. She was so ashamed of feeling like this for Brian's friend. She squeezed her eyes and cleared her throat.

"I'll hold dinner until six-thirty," she said.

After she set his plate on the table she straightened up the kitchen and joined him, with a cup of hot tea for herself, basking in the novelty of having someone to talk to in the morning. She wondered what it would be like to have him here every morning as more than Brian's friend and partner.

"How does baked chicken sound for dinner?" she asked as he forked the last bite of omelet. Thank God he wasn't a mind reader.

"Anything you fix is delicious. If I keep eating like this, I'll gain ten pounds in no time. Then I'll have to join a health club just to keep trim."

Amanda didn't comment on that. He looked trim to her. "I usually walk three times a week, though I haven't been able to lately with the Christmas rush."

"We'll have to walk together then."

Picturing long masculine legs beside her, she knew she was too obsessed with this man. He had so many favorable qualities.

With a penchant for neatness, each morning he made his own bed and picked up after himself. Over the weekend, he'd even helped her with the cleaning and he stacked his own dishes into the dishwasher. He wasn't really that much extra work. It troubled her that she liked having him around the house. She found herself eating healthier now that she was cooking for two. Before, she would sometimes eat out to keep from preparing a meal just for herself.

"Do you need me to pick up anything for you on my way home?" he asked as he shrugged into his coat. She forgot, thoughtful.

"No, thank you. I have everything I need."

She stood at the door as he descended the steps. "I'll call before I leave the office just in case." He waved good-bye.

Surprised that he'd even asked, Amanda closed the door and retreated downstairs to work, promising herself she wouldn't think of him again.

She stopped on the last step. She was a fraud. Where was her anger at him? How could she have unconsciously forgiven him for what he did to her marriage? She knew how false he really was, and yet he had a way of making her forget or at the least feel foolish for holding onto the anger. Which is exactly what he wanted.

Amanda wondered at his offer. Was the job his way of keeping her in line? Adam wasn't above using anyone to get what he wanted. He'd used Brian. Was he using her now?

Then, she thought, her job was real. Even if he was using her for his own reasons, she could use him, too. She was half owner of the company. She had as much right to work in her company as he. Amanda vowed to learn as much about her company as possible. The contracts were an excellent start. Even if his motives were suspect, she'd do the very best job that she could. She'd be a useful component to her company. She lifted her head and marched into the office to attack the files with renewed vigor. Adam Somerville was not the sexiest man she'd seen in the last few months.

* * *

With the first snow of the season, the winter wonderland scene outside Adam's window made it almost impossible to concentrate on work. It had snowed off and on all day, and the snow and ice clinging to the sturdy tree limbs offered a picture-perfect view he'd only appreciated in photos and calendars for years.

He wanted to be out there with Amanda, to wrap his arms around her softness. He barely stopped himself before he reached for the phone to call her. He found himself preparing to search for her several times today, as he'd done when he worked in her house. He actually missed his first day away from her. Many comments Brian had made about her just didn't ring true. She didn't show a propensity to be a spendthrift. In fact, most of her entertainment seemed to be her volunteer work for the church. Thinking of the church threw a damper on his spirits as thoughts of Reverend Smart crept in. The man made it a regular duty to stop by Amanda's house for one thing or another.

"Adam," Joe Cager called from the door.

"Yes?"

"Here're the files you requested. They're all small companies that only require a minimum of services. I worked most of the day with Amanda. She's catching on pretty quickly. Next week I'm going to introduce her to some of the customers. If she wants to work, she should work with me on some of the larger accounts. She's not going to be able to do much with these." He placed the stack on Adam's desk and pushed his wire rims up on his nose.

Adam sifted through the folders giving minimum attention to Joe. "We'll let her work with those for now." His fleeting smile indicated the decision was closed, but Joe didn't take the hint.

"But, Adam, she's not going to be able to do much with them. They don't want any other services."

Adam arched a brow.

"Oh," Joe said, catching the drift at last. For such a brilliant employee, he could be slow on the uptake.

Adam stashed the folders into his briefcase. "These should keep her busy for a while."

Clearly uncomfortable with the subterfuge, Joe shoved his hands in his pockets. "She never seemed interested before."

"With Brian gone, she wants to become more involved."

"Anytime she wants real work, let me know." Joe stuck a pencil in his pocket pack, clearly affronted by the waste of time. "One good thing, you'll get an opportunity to attend the company New Year's party. She can throw a great party."

"Um." Adam looked at his watch. It was time to go home. "I'll see you in two days, Joe. Bring the rest of the files by Amanda's tomorrow."

"Will do." He walked toward the door. "See you later."

Adam reached for the phone then and dialed Amanda's.

"Hi."

Her soft, sweet voice greeting him over the wire was like a breath of sunshine. He could imagine her bright eyes lighting up when she realized it was him. At least he hoped she was as pleased to hear him as he was to call. "I'm getting ready to leave. Do you need anything?"

"No," she said. "Your timing's perfect. Dinner's almost ready."

"I'm looking forward to it." Adam hung up with a smile on his face. Then he stopped cold reminding himself, yet again, that she was Brian's wife. Not his.

Now, where did that notion come from? Thoughtfully, he gathered his coat. But even the thought of Brian didn't take away his eagerness to get home.

The Christmas season was very much in evidence as he walked out of his office. Miniature pine trees decorated several desktops. Decorative foil covered doors outlined with garlands. Colorful lights twinkled in the twilight. Immediately, he was thrown into Christmas cheer. Even the bumper-to-bumper traffic didn't throttle his spirits when it took an extra twenty minutes to reach home.

Everett's car in Amanda's yard accomplished what the rush hour traffic failed to do. Thoroughly irritated at having to put up with the man again, his good mood evaporated. Obviously the work he'd given her didn't keep her busy enough.

As he parked in his half of his garage he remembered that Brian's Land Rover should be around. Perhaps Josh had it, but it seemed an expensive vehicle for a college student.

The laundry room door led in from the garage. As Adam entered the house, he could hear Amanda laughing at something Everett had said. Her laughter was more spontaneous than with him. When he closed the door, she faced him, the laughter dying on her lips.

"Oh, Adam. Hi." Her eyes still sparkled. Adam's gut tightened. That sparkle shouldn't have been for the preacher. This must be how a man felt when he caught his woman with another man.

"Hi." He wanted to go up to Amanda and kiss her. He placed his briefcase by the counter, instead.

"You've got great timing. Everett's joining us for dinner, Adam."

"Oh? Good. Good to see you—again, Everett." Adam felt anything but. So much for his quiet evening alone with Amanda.

Everett merely gave him a smirk, as if to say he knew the score. Well so did Adam. And Adam was presently staying under the woman's roof, so to speak. Territorial rights were suddenly called to order. Besides, who better to look out for Amanda's welfare?

This had been the longest dinner Amanda had ever endured. Carrying on a silent war of wills, Adam and Everett had both gotten on her nerves. Amanda felt pulled into the middle. She was not surprised by Adam's aggressive attitude, as that was his usual nature, but Everett had always been soft spoken and—pleasant. Since Brian's death, she'd seen him as a sturdy, calming rock upon which she could lay her burdens, and yet he expected nothing in return. Through his encouragement, she'd increased her volunteer work, thus taking up the excess time for brooding and grief with Brian's death, and Josh, now away in college.

Tonight, Everett had presented a layer of steel she didn't know was there. She almost wished she hadn't invited him to stay to dinner. When he stopped by, she'd thought he'd be the perfect diversion from Adam. That wasn't fair of her, especially after all that Everett had done for her.

After the meal, the three of them sat in her living room, making small and difficult conversation until almost nine, when Everett finally excused himself to leave.

"The evening with you was pleasant as always, Amanda."

Remembering Lottie's comment, Amanda's unease grew at his comment. Then she stopped herself. This was the same Everett who'd made the same small talk for more than a year. Everett hadn't changed, only Lottie's silly imaginings and her stupid obsession with Adam—temporary obsession.

"I always enjoy your company, Everett."

"I'm glad." He pulled her to him and kissed her on the cheek. A move he'd never made before. "I'll see you tomorrow night."

Amanda hated to admit that perhaps Lottie was on target. But a kiss on the cheek was certainly innocent. She was reading too much into it.

Adam cleared his throat and joined them at the door. They jumped apart.

"I hope you'll join us at church Sunday, Adam," Everett said, releasing her hand, scratching his head, a sign of nervousness, before stepping out into the cold.

"I wouldn't miss it," Adam responded, closing the door in his face and twisting the lock.

Amanda hugged her arms, more from frayed nerves than the cold blast of air that had entered.

"Adam, that was rude." She was sick of men in general and these two in particular. If their posturing continued, at this rate they'd keep her on tenterhooks.

"He overstayed his welcome. We both have work to do tomorrow." He stalked beside her. "Is he coming over to dinner tomorrow night, too? He's not going to make it a nightly routine, is he?"

"Everett has been very kind to me. Having him over to dinner isn't an imposition."

"For me it is."

She stopped and confronted him. He would not run roughshod over her.

"The house is half mine, remember."

"And half mine. And I need to get to bed."

"Who's keeping you? You will not control my life like you did Brian's. We had best come to that understanding immediately."

"I never ran Brian's life. What are you talking about?"

"The only thing you need to remember is that my life is my business, not yours." With hands on hips, she swung around furiously.

He almost shouted, "Maybe you should talk to Everett and limit his visits to Sunday after church," his harsh voice lashed out at her.

"No one asked you to join us in the living room. You could have gone on to bed," she snapped and started for the stairs.

"He needs to respect the fact that you're working a full-time job now. He can't monopolize all your time."

"This conversation has passed reasonableness." Suddenly, it dawned on Amanda that this idiotic conversation had nothing to do with dinner, but the sharp, banked fire that lit the brown eyes glaring at her, and her own sensual awareness of him.

At that instant, she knew he wanted her. Worse, her woman's instincts answered that male call. Before, she had deluded herself into believing her reaction was from her long abstinence. She knew it was from desire for this man. Desire for the last man she wanted anything intimate with. And just as suddenly, the sharp control she knew so well replaced the fire in his eyes. Had she not been staring him in the face, she'd have never know it was even there.

"I'm going to bed." She gave him her back and ascended the steps.

"Just make sure he doesn't show up to dinner every evening."

Amanda stopped on the fourth step and turned to face him. "Well, you won't have that to worry about. Tomorrow night is our night to serve food for people in need. You get to fare for yourself."

"What time will you be in?"

"Too late for you to wait dinner. You'll have to fix your own."

"What time do you leave here?"

"Don't worry. I will put in a full day's work before leaving for my volunteer work."

"That's the least of my worries. It's not safe for you to be out roaming about alone at night."

"Don't be ridiculous. I'm not roaming. I'm always out at night."

"Not anymore. I will take you and return to pick you up later."

"I can drive my own car, Adam. You're trying to run my life and I won't have it." Close to screaming, she counted to ten.

"Look there are high-jackings all over the place now. I don't want anything happening to you. Don't begrudge me that. I can take the time to take you out when I don't think it's safe for you."

"Adam, you can't take me every place I need to go. I've been on my own for a while now. Coming and going day and night. At my choosing. I couldn't stand for you to cramp my style that way. Thank you for your concern though." Amanda climbed the stairs.

Think again, Adam said to himself. He was going to have more to say about her life than she'd ever dreamed. And what did she mean when she said he controlled Brian's life?

What was better for her anyway? Him or someone who would take advantage of her good nature? Amanda was still vulnerable. It was his duty to protect her from men like Everett. She was so trusting and fragile. How could he help but have warm feelings for her? They were nothing more than the warm feelings any man would have for a close friend.

In her hurry to leave him, she'd forgotten to turn out the Christmas lights. Visible from the family room, the warm glow invited him to watch them for a while. He reclined on the overstuffed sofa, mesmerized by the twinkling lights, and deep into thoughts about the changes coming over him. Positive changes, he hoped.

Then he realized he was being unreasonable. Try as he might, he couldn't seem to stop himself. Amanda had a disquieting magnetic pull on him in a way he'd never thought a woman would. She conjured thoughts of family and relationships. Forever crept into his mind at an alarming rate. He didn't know if it was from the Christmas season or from being home. Perhaps this attraction was much more. He could feel his reserve cracking. This change creeping in almost frightened him.

After her shower, Amanda combed out her shoulder length hair and tied a band around it. *That impossible man.* As her hand dropped to the dressing table to arrange things in the proper order before retiring, she wondered what they'd do about this awareness between them. Or was it subterfuge? Could a man check his response that quickly, or was it really a ruse to throw her off the track of what she really should concentrate on? *Her work.*

This would all go away when he moved. Acting as though having dinner with Everett would pose a problem with her working. He had her emotions so twisted, it left her in a state of constant confusion.

Perhaps he really didn't have confidence she could do the job. Panic seized her. It was imperative that she do well on her first paying job. She simply couldn't fail. She vowed to put in more hours. Her work today went well. It was certainly interesting. She could go back downstairs for another two hours tonight.

When she crept out her door, all was quiet. Adam must have already retired to his room. She didn't want to run into him again tonight. She slipped downstairs only to find him fast asleep on the couch.

A softness stole over his features as he slept. The calculating barrier always so much in evidence was gone. Her hand was almost to his forehead before she snatched it back. She'd been alone much too long.

She went to the closet, pulled out a blanket, and covered him. He immediately snuggled deeper into the covers much as Josh did.

Too disquieted to deal with her attraction to Adam, Amanda turned the lights off and continued downstairs to her office.

Chapter 5

Two mornings later, Amanda came downstairs later than usual. Most nights now, she'd slip to the office basement, familiarizing herself with the services the company offered and her accounts. A great sense of pride overcame her at the responsibility Adam was entrusting her with. In a short while she'd learned more than she'd gathered over the last fifteen years. After putting in another five hours before retiring, she rose later than usual.

Adam had already made coffee for himself and tea for her by the time she arrived in the kitchen.

"Bless you." With only six hours sleep under her belt, she desperately needed the caffeine kick of the tea. After her first swallow, she caught her first glimpse of his breakfast.

He crunched on a spoonful of cold cereal Josh had gotten when he was home for Thanksgiving.

She eyed his bowl dubiously. "I'll fix you a more substantial breakfast," she offered while opening the cabinet for a pan.

"This is good. I can't eat lavishly every day."

It must be stale. But Amanda knew hungry men tended not to care. Still the guilt from leaving him on his own two nights ago ate at her conscience. "Oatmeal then. It'll stick to you longer. The perfect breakfast item on cold mornings." She grabbed milk out of the fridge without her usual gusto. Yawning, Amanda pulled out oatmeal and fixed bowls for them both, topping it with cinnamon and brown sugar.

Having quickly adjusted to this new lifestyle, it would be difficult when he moved out in a month and once again she'd be alone. Amanda didn't want to be too comfortable or too dependent on him.

"How is the house hunting going?" she asked.

"A few of the places looked interesting. I'm waiting until after the holidays to make a final decision. This oatmeal is delicious."

"I need to take my car to the shop to get the oil changed and get a few other little things done. I don't want to wait for it. Could you pick me up?"

"I can change your oil. What else needs doing?"

She ran down the list.

"I can do all that this weekend. Can it wait that long?"

"Sure."

"What happened to the Land Rover?"

"I sold it in January to pay for Josh's tuition this year and put the rest away for next year's fees."

He had his coffee halfway to his mouth and checked the motion. "If you didn't have the money for Josh's schooling, why didn't you let me know?"

"Believe me, I got more than enough from the Land Rover to cover the expense. It was new." Amanda had thought it silly to pay such an exorbitant price for a car.

"Give me the tuition bill. I'll take care of it."

"No need. It's already done."

"I'll reimburse you for it. Brian and I had made a deal that we'd find a way to pay for it."

"No. And that's final." She was not depending on anyone else again. "Well, I'm ready to get to work."

"You don't have to rush off. I'll make the repairs on Saturday. In the meantime, I have to go out, but it'll be six before I return. I'll take you to the shelter."

Amanda waved a hand. "Everett's already offered. We're going to pick up the turkeys and other food for Christmas dinner for the shelter and deliver it to the church."

Silence. "What time will you be ready? I'll pick you up from church on my way home then."

She shook her head at his reluctance to give up his overprotective nature. "Seven," she said, shortly averting another argument.

It had been a very hectic day, Adam thought, as he went in search of Amanda. He found her and Everett talking almost secretively in the church kitchen. He didn't realize putting groceries away could be such an intimate experience. He was getting darned tired of catching them like this. As he stomped in, they jumped apart almost guiltily.

"Adam," Everett said, sporting a silly grin. "You didn't have to make the trip. Since she was too busy to cook today, I was planning to take Amanda out to eat before bringing her home. Care to join us?"

Again? "That won't be necessary. We'll just stop some place on our way home."

"Really, it'll only take me a moment to throw something together," Amanda cut in.

Everett grasped her hand. "I won't hear of your cooking tonight. You worked so hard today. Thanks for coming by the seniors' home to help before grocery shopping."

She shrugged it off. "It was nothing. I was glad to help out."

She gathered her coat and purse.

"Really, Amanda. The Chinese restaurant down the street is quiet and the service is quick. We can relax for a while. I need to unwind, too."

"If you worked her that hard, we can pick up something on our way home," Adam cut in.

"He didn't work me hard at all."

"You deserve to be pampered," Everett insisted.

"I'll tell you what, I'll just take a taxi. I'm not in the mood for this bickering." She started toward the door.

"Amanda," Everett called out.

"I'll talk to you tomorrow, Everett."

Adam cut a hard stare at Everett, grabbed Amanda's arm and ushered her to the car.

They picked up Chinese on the way home.

After dinner and preparations for bed, Amanda wasn't ready for sleep. She'd put in long hours all week. It was Friday, a week before Christmas and she wanted a treat. A good romance would do the trick. She retrieved a new novel by her favorite author she hadn't had time to read yet. Romance had been definitely missing in her life. She settled back on plump pillows and read for an hour before she dozed off after a love scene.

Amanda was abruptly awakened by a loud crash. Groggily she got up to investigate.

"Adam?" She knocked tentatively on his door.

"It's okay," he called out.

She opened the door a few inches. When she saw the overturned coffeepot, she ran into the bathroom, grabbed the towel, and wet it. By the time she returned, Adam had righted the pot.

"I wasn't looking at what I was doing," he said dabbing at the stain. Since he'd drank several cups while working on the contract, only a little had soaked his T-shirt and spilled on the floor.

Adam set the pottery on the hamper while she

mopped up the last of the liquid and hung the towel to dry.

Returning to the room, Amanda stopped short as she noticed he had discarded his damp shirt. Cold bumps gathered on his bare chest. Even more disturbing was the fact that he wore only briefs.

Adam, too, finally noticed the cotton gown outlining her pert nipples in the cool room. A thin cotton nightgown didn't hide her lacy panties at all. On her bare feet, shapely calves showed below the nightgown. She stood barely a foot away. He reached out to her and ran a hand up her arm. She stood as if rooted to the spot. Adam pulled her into his arms and did what he'd longed to do unceasingly. He kissed her, forgetting he was kissing his best friend's wife. The soft skin, sweet mouth, and drugging kiss rocked his senses. He wanted to explore her leisurely, but the blood that had boiled in his veins made that impossible. It seemed he'd been in a constant state of need forever. He pressed her tighter against himself and felt her arms encircle his neck. Inching the thin gown aside bit by bit, he strung kisses down her neck and caressed her skin.

Gathering her in his arms, he carried her to his bed and placed her in its center, shoving the papers to the side in a disheveled pile. He removed her thin lace gown and delicate panties. Feeling the heat of her desire, he touched her soft skin, urged on by her sweet moans. He took his time exploring, touching. A fine sheen of sweat enveloped him as he struggled to hold back while her soft hands eagerly scanned his body. And then he was in her tight passage. Ecstasy, sweet, sweet heaven. They moved deep, slow, then fast and slow again, feeling each centimeter of her. Enjoying her tightness, the friction, until he couldn't hold on any longer. Continuing the cadence known since the dawning of time, they erupted in a cataclysmic explosion. He held her, felt her arms and legs around him until the last tremble. Kissing her, he held onto her as they both reached for calm.

He rolled over, turned out the bedside light, and brought the overs over them. With her head on his arm, her body cupped into his, he sought and found the sleep so elusive only an hour go.

As Adam slept peacefully beside her, Amanda slipped off the bed, gathered her discarded clothing, and escaped to her own room, locking the door for the first time since Adam arrived. Pressing one hand to her aching and racing heart, she stood there, unable to move her tense fingers from the knob. Leaning against the door for support, she wondered how she could betray Brian's memory by sleeping with his best friend. And under his very own roof.

Worst of all, how could she act so . . . wantonly? She clutched the collar of her gown, remembering her unrestrained response to his lovemaking . . . how much she enjoyed it. Heat spread throughout her body at her passionate abandon. This passion that had been tormenting her since Adam's arrival.

She and Brian had enjoyed very satisfying lovemaking. But this . . . this had been more than enjoyment. It had been another world.

Adam had to leave. Or she had to. They simply couldn't live in the same house any longer.

"Amanda?" The doorknob rattled.

She jumped at hearing his voice. "Go back to bed, Adam." Apprehension swept through her.

"Not until we talk." He rattled the knob again.

"It's late . . . I can't talk tonight. Please go away," she gasped.

"Amanda. Both of us are single. We didn't . . ."

"I'm not single. I'm Brian's wife." The thought tore at her insides.

"Not any longer," he said softly, not unkindly.

"I can't deal with this . . . Please go away." Tears swam in her eyes.

"I can't leave you like this. Open the door." He showed no signs of relenting.

"No." Panic rioted within her. She wasn't ready for this.

"I'll pick the lock."

Adam heard the lock turn and the door whispered open.

"Amanda."

She turned her back to him. "You have to leave. Or I'll go. We can't live in the same house. This can't happen again."

"There are still papers I have to go through."

Business, always business. "Then I'll go."

He grabbed her and turned her to face him, angry and with guilt about her reaction. "You'll do no such thing. We're adults, we've done nothing wrong. Brian isn't here any longer."

"I know that. You were his best friend. I . . . his wife."

"You're no longer married."

"It still doesn't feel right. In his home."

"In our home, Amanda. Yours and mine," he all but shouted through gritted teeth.

She shook her head. "It shouldn't be this way. Brian and I shared this bed, this house . . . It's not . . ."

"It is right. What we did and what we felt was right. Give us a chance."

"The way you gave Brian and me a chance? Always calling him away so we had very little time together. Calling him away so we couldn't even take a honeymoon together for our twentieth anniversary?"

He dropped his arms. "What are you talking about?"

"Oh, come on." She all but sneered. "Do you think I'll involve myself with another workaholic. Someone who'd care so much about the company he won't appreciate the people around him? No, thank you," she snapped.

Looking at her dumbfounded, Adam was at a loss for words. "Amanda . . ."

"Go, just go." She tilted her head up, gathering strength. "I won't leave, and I won't insist that you go. But don't think for a second there will be a repeat performance. Now, leave my room. That much of the house is still mine."

Chapter 6

Adam wandered back to his room in a daze. She blamed him for keeping Brian away from her. Brian had been his own man. Adam never interfered in his life except on company decisions. Both of them were expected to travel. Why didn't she understand that?

She'd laid the blame for it all at his door. How was he going to handle the responsibility of her loss of the man she loved? She still loved Brian. How was he going to alienate her affections from Brian—or at least help her find a place in her heart for him?

When he'd lost his parents, Adam felt a fear incomparable with anything life ever threw him. He'd grieved, survived, and gone on with his life. Now, as his gut tightened, that same fear was beginning to swamp him again.

He didn't know whether he should leave now to give her temporary space, or stay to try to work out their relationship. Retreat wasn't in his vocabulary.

If he left now, she'd shut him out of her life completely. Now, after so many years of feeling lost, with no sense of family, he couldn't let her get away so easily. For the first time since his mother died, Adam felt like he was home. He felt the sense of completeness that he'd been searching for unconsciously . . . that now felt so right. He'd thought that work would give him all the fulfillment he needed. But dreaming about his own company and having made a success of it didn't accomplish it. What he needed was a special someone to share it with. What he needed was love.

Adam stopped short as he reached for the light.

He was in love with Amanda. And she was running, frightened, in the opposite direction.

"You're in love with him, aren't you?"

Her stricken eyes met Everett's briefly before darting away. "No, I'm just so—confused. I just don't know what's happening with me." She straightened a picture on the wall. "He's bossy and interfering. And . . . and he's a workaholic like Brian. There wouldn't be any room left in his life for a woman."

"Are you sure the intruding isn't, perhaps, concern?" He gave her a half smile. A sad smile. "It's all right you know. Brian's gone. You're a widow and Adam's single. As much as I'd like to have you for myself . . ."

"What!" came the stricken reply, her fingers going to her lips. It was one thing for Lottie, fickle Lottie, to say it, but to hear the same declaration from Everett . . .

"That shouldn't shock you. I'm a single man and you're a single woman. There's nothing wrong with the two of us together."

"Oh, Everett, I—I don't know what to say." Her voice rose with anguish.

"It's okay for you to love Adam," he said with an understanding Amanda could only cherish. Their relationship, such as it was, had crossed a barrier. The easy camaraderie and sharing wouldn't be the same. Everything in her life was changing. She just couldn't love

Adam. Sure, she enjoyed his company, but. . . . Too many changes were occurring.

"Don't say that. We . . . we're not in love!" Her eyes softened with sadness. "You've been so wonderful this last year in your guidance. I don't know how I would have made it without you." She wanted her comfortable little world back. Josh's departure to college, Brian's death, Adam's moving into her house were all huge milestones in her life. Amanda wanted to know what each day would bring. She was uncomfortable with the uncertainty.

Everett advanced to her. Holding her cheeks between his hands, Everett tilted her head and kissed her. She wrapped her arms around his neck, trying to respond, trying to give him some semblance of what he'd given her.

It didn't work and they both knew it. The sparks that ignited with Adam's kisses didn't even begin to generate with Everett. Regret filled her heart as he pulled away from her and a tear slid down her smooth cheek.

He caught it with one gentle finger. He seemed to know it, too. "Just put your trust in God," he said softly. "He'll guide you in making the proper decision. Nothing will happen before its proper time." His brow puckered as if it hurt him to say the words that followed, but thank goodness he was taking it so well. "Take it one day at a time. Perhaps this is why God saw fit to send Adam back now. You weren't ready for him a few months ago, but you are now. I . . . I just had to kiss you just once," he whispered and turned, leaving the room and Amanda in a quagmire of mixed emotions.

Adam dropped the contract on his desk and looked up, squeezing the bridge of his nose. How he'd much rather be working in the office at home. The building was quiet and still. It was Saturday, and only two people were working. He wondered if Amanda was back from her volunteer project yet.

The daunting thought wandered again to the fact that she blamed him for many of the problems in her marriage. How could she believe he chose the times Brian took trips? It was true that he'd been in constant contact and planned some of the trips that Brian took, it was part of the business. He took trips to Europe and parts of Africa. They were responsible for their respective territories. And now that Brian was dead, Adam had to make the trips and chart the course. He'd expected that as part of being a business owner. Now, they had received some long-range satellite contracts that would require less travel. Therefore, it was essential that he get a signed contract on the Scott project.

If she ever discovered the work he gave her wasn't real . . . Maybe he should have given her a legitimate assignment. But Brian had always said she was so scatterbrained.

Adam should have known better than to have believed Brian. He could see, with the volunteer work she did, that she was a hard worker. Everett relied heavily on her skills.

A nervous roiling stirred in Adam's stomach. Everett had always been true to her, respected her talents, while he, Adam, had been so sure of his own worth he hadn't taken hers seriously. According to Lottie, Everett was in love with Amanda. Given a choice, who would she prefer? Someone who trusted and believed in her? Or someone who never respected her or valued her talents? The pencil broke in his hand. Adam picked up the pieces as evidence of his emotions. He tossed them in the trash.

Then his resolve strengthened. Adam Somerville had never given up without a fight. He wouldn't now. The rev was in for the fight of his life and as soon as the New Year started, Adam was going to give her an assignment worthy of her skills.

What he didn't need now was to take a trip. Looking at every angle imaginable, trying to avoid it, he saw it was impossible. At least he could delay it until a day or two after Christmas. He thought he'd have—needed to have—more time with Amanda before leaving.

Knowing he'd be spending the day in the office, Amanda had purposely gotten up late this morning. Every day this week, she'd been up by six. Today when she knew he couldn't linger, she hadn't made an appearance by eight. He'd been worried and knocked on her door to make sure she was all right only to get the response that she'd slept in.

Before getting to know her, he could believe that she was frivolous. Now he knew her to be a warm-hearted, kind, and very intelligent woman.

Even if she would relent enough to let him into her life, she'd more than likely compare him to Brian because, yet again, she's alone for a portion of the holidays. And according to her, they were both workaholics.

Neither did he want to leave her alone, giving Everett an opportunity to make moon eyes at his woman or sitting at her dining room table enjoying candlelight dinners. That notion was enough to make Adam change his plans. If it wasn't imperative that he lock in this contract, he *would* change his plans until their relationship was more established. It never occurred to him that perhaps Amanda wouldn't eventually come to love him.

Mere days before Christmas and he had yet to get her gift. That problem he could solve quickly, Adam thought, as he looked at his watch. Five o'clock in the afternoon so close to Christmas was not the best of times to shop, but there was no avoiding it.

* * *

While passing the Porcelain Gallery he noticed clusters of figurines in the window depicting a tender scene and remembered the knicknacks displayed prominently in Amanda's living room curio cabinet. There was space for others. He had the gift wrapped.

His next stop was a jewelry store. Once there, Adam looked at an array of diamonds and other precious gems wondering what a woman like Amanda would appreciate. The teardrop diamond earrings the salesman displayed to him would look perfect on her. In thirty minutes, Adam walked out with diamond earrings boxed and wrapped, leaving a happy sales clerk behind. Pleased with his purchases, he skirted around enthusiastic and desperate shoppers as he glided through the packed mall.

Since most of the cars were at shopping centers, the traffic was decent in the D.C. suburbs. He slowed to a snail's pace as he drove through the neighborhood, taking in the lavishly decorated homes with sleighs and other holiday scenes. How lovely it was driving through neighborhoods competing for their creativity in producing outdoor displays.

The radio commentator announced a downtown display. Suddenly he wanted to celebrate. Take an evening off. It was Saturday, after all—and Christmas.

The garage door was closing as he pulled up into the drive. Parking in the adjourning space, he soon joined Amanda in the kitchen.

"Dinner will be a little late tonight," she said stashing her purse in the closet and then noticing the blinking light on the answering machine. She punched the button. It was a message from Josh saying he'd call back tomorrow. He'd be out until late helping to birth a calf.

"Let's go out instead."

Amanda didn't look at him. "That's a good idea. You go out. I'm staying in."

Adam grasped her shoulder. "We can't ignore what happened last night. I don't want to ignore it."

"It's not that. I have to fix dinner."

"You've been working all day. Have you been to the Ellipse yet to see the decorated trees?"

"The Ellipse?" She shook her head. "No."

"I'm not really hungry right now. If you can hold off, let's go there and after, have dinner. I want to see the lights. It's been years," he said softly.

Though she knew she should, Amanda didn't have the heart to refuse him. "All right." She sighed.

"First," he started quietly, "we need to discuss last night."

"There won't be any repeat performances," Amanda declared.

He lifted a hand and pressed a feather touch to her cheek. "There's nothing wrong with two people who care for each other to make love."

"Not us," she whispered.

"Exactly us."

"I explained to you last night I wasn't ready. It's all too new." How could he understand that she'd never been with anyone other than Brian. How could she explain she didn't know how to even go about dating anymore? She married at eighteen, right out of high school. Brian had graduated from college that May and as soon as she got her diploma, they married. Brian was the only man she'd ever dated. She didn't know how to start her life over.

One day at a time, Everett had said. Amanda looked at Adam. "I'll only be a minute." She put lotion on her hands and repaired her makeup. In five minutes, they left.

Chapter 7

Hand in hand, they strolled around the sights, Amanda as lighthearted as she was at eighteen. She forced worries from her mind and concentrated on the delightful events happening for her at that moment. They wandered leisurely among trees that had been decorated for each state. Missing this year were the reindeer. Added to the celebratory cheer, the band played Christmas songs and each member of the choir, snuggled into winter coats, sang.

Children exclaimed in awe as they circled the grounds with their parents, too impatient to see the sights to relish the music from the choir, while the younger ones sat in their strollers mesmerized by the lilting voices. Amanda remembered Josh and his impatience at that age. Instead of the pain she expected, she enjoyed the memory. She was basking in many memories, experiencing more than the pain. She'd expected to spend the holidays alone and now she was with Adam, enjoying herself. Life had a way of balancing itself out.

Now Amanda was looking at this holiday as one of hope.

They ate in the Trade, an Ethiopian restaurant in Georgetown. Pictures of Africa graced the walls. Wooden statues sat on strategically placed shelves.

A hostess soon escorted them to a table for two where one candlelight burned in the center.

Amanda's first experience with the delicious food made her wonder what took her so long to try this place. They tore pieces of the Ethiopian bread to use in place of utensils to dish up the succulent and spicy fare. Their selections were served on a silver platter that they shared.

"Um, we have to come here again," Amanda said as she popped *daro watt,* a spicy chicken dish, into her mouth.

"We'll come often." Adam tore a piece of *yebeg alitcha,* lamb cooked in herbs, and slipped it into her mouth. It turned into an intimate gesture that held unspoken possibilities before a shadow wiped the intimacy away. "I have to leave for New York shortly after the New Year. I'd hoped to hold it off longer but, I can't. I hate to leave you right now, Amanda."

She reached out across the small table to stroke his hand. "You work so hard. Have you ever heard of delegating?" Amanda struggled to keep from saying more. She was beginning to nag him as Brian often accused her of. Adam was not her husband. She had no right to tell him how to live his life. *Enjoy the moment,* she repeated to herself.

"I can't delegate everything. This is something I must do."

"All right. Adam, thank you for this evening. I've enjoyed it."

"It's not over yet," he said with a quirk of an eyebrow.

"I want to thank you again for offering me this job. I love the work I'm doing and I feel I have purpose again."

He grew quiet. Contemplating.

Some people were embarrassed by praise. Amanda guessed Adam was one of them. "I know you don't want to talk about work tonight, but I needed that in my life." She hoped she didn't look as giddy as she felt. But she couldn't let the evening go on without thanking him for offering her a purpose in life. She had a reason to get up each morning now, and security. She had to let him know, regardless of how uncomfortable it made him.

"I'm going to add to your duties at the beginning of the year. I'm working on the Scott contract right now. You'll help me with it once we win the bid."

Amanda noticed that he said *once*, not *if*. Another indication of his intentions.

"I think the added assignments will be more rewarding for you." He cast her a fleeting smile. So serious, and cloaked with a soft heart.

"I'm already rewarded. But if you feel I need to do more, I'm more than ready."

Adam reached over and took her soft and greasy hand in his and kissed her palm. "Amanda, we need to talk about last night." He held on when she tried to retrieve it, stroking with his fingers.

"Adam . . ."

"I can't leave this hanging. Why do you blame me for problems in your marriage? You're forty. You knew that Brian had to work, just as I have to work now. And because we have to always seek out new business, we need to take trips now and then. Not too often, but they're a requirement. That doesn't mean that there can't be family time."

She seemed to freeze before his eyes. "You know nothing of my marriage. I don't want to discuss it with you."

"But you put me in the middle of this. We can't go on until this is solved. We have to talk about it, Amanda."

"What happened with Brian and me is none of your business." She grabbed a napkin and wiped her hands.

"We can't hope for any kind of future until this is cleared." Adam threw his own napkin on the table and leaned forward, elbows on the table.

Her head snapped back. "There isn't an us!"

He pinched the bridge of his nose and tried for a reasonableness. "There can be. Last night meant more to me than a one night toss. It's what I want."

She let out a low pitched laugh. "I learned a long time ago, we can't always have everything we want."

The waitress brought them warm, moist towels for their hands when she brought them the bill. Amanda made quick work of cleaning her hands, scooted back in her chair, and stood, ready to leave, thinking that was the end of it.

It was, but only until they arrived home and hung their coats in the closet. "We have to resolve this, Amanda," Adam began again. "Why do you think I'm responsible for some failure in your marriage?"

All his badgering was too much. He baited her like a dog with a bone. Amanda shoved her purse into the closet and rounded on him.

"All right. Since you want to know. Yes,"—she nodded with a taut jerk of her head—"I understood Brian had to work. I understood that we couldn't get away for a honeymoon *one* year, but I *don't* understand why we couldn't get away for *five*. Why did you always have to plan trips for Brian that time of year? I've planned five honeymoons and I've had to cancel five. We needed that time to regroup, to rejuvenate our marriage. We needed *some* time. Worldwide Satellites shouldn't have taken *all* the time."

"I don't think it should have either. Come on in the family room and take a seat so we can talk calmly about this." He grasped her shoulders to steer her.

She flinched away. "Maybe you can be calm. It wasn't your marriage. It wasn't your life. I can't be calm," she said, all but trembling.

"Sit anyway." He steered her stiff form to a couch and faced her on it, grasping both her hands. "Amanda, Brian had to take trips. And I required them. But it was up to him when he went. He should have taken time out for the important things. Maybe I am partly responsible. I've been so focused on the business that I haven't thought about his time with you and Josh. Just that there was a job that needed to be done. And as half-owner it was his responsibility."

"Right. So you can understand why I won't get involved with you and go through this again, don't you?" she huffed, pulling back from him.

Adam grasped her chin in his hand and caught her eyes, "But it was up to Brian, as a husband and father, to take care of his family's needs. There's no reason he couldn't take a honeymoon for five years. Maybe not on the exact date that you wanted to, but he could take some time away from the job. I want you in my life, Amanda. I plan to take the time to cultivate our relationship."

"Just as Brian took the time to cultivate his. In the beginning. There's more to a relationship than just getting a woman. We're here after that, too. And there's more than throwing a business party or two."

"I'm asking you to give us a chance." A look of implacable determination was on his face.

"I'm not going through that a second time. It'll be even worse. Before, there was Brian to take up the slack at Worldwide. Now, there's only you." Her voice caught.

"And you. Josh is in college. You can take a major role in the business.

"Believe me, I plan to."

"There's still room for us. I'll make room, Amanda. You're important enough for me."

Having heard it all before, Amanda smiled with a bittersweet sadness. What was the purpose of continuing with this argument. "It's ten and I'm beat. I think I'll call it a night. Thank you for the evening." She stood on stiff legs.

He escorted her to her bedroom door. "It was my pleasure. Think about what I've said." The light feather touch on her cheek was unexpected. So were the warm lips that replaced it for a second. So quick Amanda didn't get the opportunity to snatch away before the muffled steps on the carpet carried him to the opposite end of the hall.

She stumbled into her own room and closed the door, holding onto the knob, gathering strength for a full two minutes before she stumbled over to her bed and sank onto it.

So many memories, so many failures he'd bought up. Hanging by a thread, Amanda rested her face in her hands as she replayed their heated conversation. But she refused to wallow in self-pity. After Brian's death, she'd had to force herself up, to place one foot in front of the other, until the pain lessened. Now, she got up to shower.

All day she'd been busy enough to avoid concentrating on last night's lovemaking too long. Now, in the quiet of night, the house settling around her, it was impossible not to think of its implications.

Was she using Brian as an excuse to evade a new relationship? How could she love Brian's best friend, especially after he'd been a key factor in their marriage's failure? She sighed in confusion and regret, letting the hot water roll over her. It was time to resolve what had really occurred in her marriage.

Brian and she had grown apart. They shared very

little in the end, an all too often sad reality. This was the main reason she was so cautious. At eighteen, they'd been so in love and they'd shared everything. Brian would come home from his job and discuss his day with her. They planned outings and projects together. They were very happy. Soon after they were blessed with Josh, they did less and less together, talked even more infrequently. And then the arguments started. He'd accuse her of nagging him, of wanting him to be everything for her, while she had wanted them to live as a family, to be part of each other's lives. For her it was more than making love, sharing a house, and raising a child. She had her own interests. She just wanted a sharing marriage. Amanda clutched the washcloth in her tense fingers.

The time came when they couldn't agree on anything anymore. There wasn't any togetherness. The glue that bound them was gradually slipping away. What was the purpose of marriage if you didn't share—if you didn't take the time to nourish it? They'd grown apart and into their own little worlds. Brian into Worldwide Satellite, and she into her volunteer work at church and school.

Amanda knew that Adam wasn't responsible for her marriage's failure. It was easier to lay it at his door and not with Brian and herself. Brian could have found time for Josh and her if he'd wanted to. He didn't consider their relationship important enough.

She could be blamed, too. After a while, she just gave up. Perhaps she could have tried harder to reach him and bring their marriage back to what it had been. She also knew it took two people. She couldn't do it alone.

As she dried off with a soft sunshine yellow towel, she realized her last few years had been as bleak as the dreary, cold night. It was time to get rid of the blame, to leave the past where it belonged—in the past—and start with something new. She knew she couldn't, wouldn't start with another workaholic like Brian. She also knew she wanted that special sharing relationship again. As the towel stroked her tender breasts, Amanda realized that tonight she wanted to wear something that made her feel feminine. She selected a white silk teddy that contrasted with the rich brown hues of her skin. If only she could make her body believe that, she'd be fine.

Tonight, as she pulled on her gown, she thought what a loss it was when two people lost that special something they had to offer each other.

She started at hearing a knock on her door. She donned a robe and opened the door to admit Adam. He'd showered and changed into pajama bottoms but at least he had on a robe, though he'd left it hanging open. Whether he'd keep it on was another matter. Her hands itched to touch the springy hairs on his chest.

He offered her a cup of her favorite tea as a peace offering. "Let's watch a movie together," he said leaning into the doorjamb looking devilishly carefree. "I've discovered I'm not sleepy after all."

"Nothing's playing tonight," she all but whispered.

"I have a tape." He lifted it for her to see. "Wesley Snipes. I missed a lot overseas."

Amanda wavered, and reached out to take the proffered cup. "Thanks for the tea." Her nerves tingling with awareness, they descended the stairs. She discovered that even with a paucity of sleep the previous night, she wasn't sleepy at all. They sat on the couch in the family room, facing the large-screened television from opposite sides.

As the tape rolled the previews at the beginning, Adam said, "This isn't going to work."

"What isn't?" Amanda asked.

He scooted next to her and put an arm around her shoulder. "That's better. Courting couples don't sit a mile apart."

"We aren't courting." The idea stirred around in her head. She'd almost forgotten what snuggling up was like. Perhaps she could court again. *Grow up into the nineties, Amanda. You aren't getting married. You're just enjoying the man's presence.*

"Of course, we are."

Amanda strained against his arm. "We need to settle something. I wasn't ready for what happened last night."

"I can wait until you *are* ready." As Wesley rolled into his first quagmire on the colorful screen, Adam lifted Amanda's chin with his forefinger. "Don't keep me waiting too long, baby. Once a man has tasted heaven, he can't settle for less and waiting can be pure hell."

Regardless of what he said, holding Amanda was a slice of heaven. He'd never taken time out to enjoy relationships. He remembered his mom smiling and singing to herself as she worked or sipped a cup of coffee. He'd ask what she was thinking about. She'd pat him on the cheek and say, "I'm smelling the roses, son." Many times, that was followed by a leisurely hug, and he would get a whiff of lemon and spices for perfume in her warm comforting arms.

He'd never taken the time to smell the roses. Of late, that time was becoming more important to him. He hoped Amanda could come to care enough for him to smell the roses with him, and he hoped she'd forgive him for his part in her estrangement from her husband. Determined not to make the same mistake, he tightened his arm around her shoulder.

Chapter 8

Amanda spent the remainder of the time before Christmas talking to her clients and finalizing details and services they'd need for the next year. With pages of lines drawn through items listed in her Day Timer, she had concrete proof that she was making progress on her assignments. She checked one more item when she hung up from her call to Joe.

Joe hated to hear her voice on the phone because she called him often, very often, to clear up areas she wasn't familiar with and to discern if the company could provide one service or another that a client was interested in.

"Sorry I'm late, Adam, but Amanda calls me at least four times a day." Joe hurried into Adam's office, his expression harassed. "And it's not easy getting her off the phone. For busy work, she's certainly taking it seriously. Maybe you need to tell *her* it's busy work."

"Just keep her happy. She'll be getting real assignments soon. For now, we need to work on the Scott contract. I'm going to New York right after Christmas."

"Don't they lay low between the holidays like most normal people?" He handed Adam some papers and sank into a chair facing the desk.

"Apparently not. And since we want their business,

we won't, either." Adam perused the papers, making mental notes.

As Joe left the office, guilt ate at Adam for the useless work Amanda was doing on the contracts. She worked night and day. Maybe not completely useless. The company needed to stay abreast of small clients' needs and it served to give her a feel for the company.

Thinking of his next encounter with her, which didn't include work, Adam couldn't wait to get home. He'd also get her to lighten up.

Amanda stood at the kitchen sink washing broccoli when Adam entered the room. She looked over her shoulder and smiled, tantalizing him.

"Hi," she said in that saucy voice he loved to hear.

"I hear you're working overtime on these contracts," he said as he placed his briefcase by the counter.

"I'm enjoying it."

"Don't work too hard. I only gave them to you to get a feel for the company. You won't get very much out of them." He went up behind her, slid his hands around her waist, stroking her and nuzzled her neck.

"I beg to differ, Mr. Somerville." Her voice caught when his fingers slipped lower. "I've already tripled our business with them." Her voice was filled with pride.

Hands stilling, Adam stopped his nuzzling, turned her and looked into her eyes. "You've what?"

"I've talked with all the clients and most of them need additional services. Several of them have expanded and were thinking of going to another company for additional services because they didn't know what we provided." She tapped him on the shoulder. "What were you thinking of? How could you stay in business so long if you don't keep current with your clients? Most of those companies don't know what we offer."

"Brian assured me he was on top of these small companies," Adam said and wondered what else had been neglected around the office while he was overseas. "I'm glad I put you on them."

He had been so busy training someone to take his position in the Ivory Coast and the expansion. He knew Joe worked side by side with Brian and kept things going as it had been. It seemed things hadn't been going as smoothly as he'd thought. Brian was great with large companies, but they couldn't afford to let the small ones go.

Amanda had put her hands back into the water.

He nuzzled her ear and stroked her abdomen and slid his hands between her legs, still kissing her neck and ear.

"Adam . . . I've got my hands in water," she whispered. "You want dinner . . . don't you?"

"Dinner can wait." He turned her around, with dripping hands unnoticed and claimed her lips. After missing her all day, he couldn't wait another minute. Without breaking contact, he shucked his jacket and pressed her against the sink.

She felt around behind her for a dishcloth and wiped her hands.

Soft hands on his shoulders and back drove his ardor to the limit. Unsnapping her jeans, he slid them down her hips. At the same time, her hands dealt with his shirt buttons slowly, seductively stroking his chest.

Her warm breath kissed his neck, leisurely explored his chest. His heart skipped a beat as her tongue traced his nipple. Lips parted, her warm breath kissed his neck, chest, nipple. He sucked in a breath in sweet anticipation as her fingers unbuckled his belt as if they had all night to explore, unzipped his pants inch by inch. The mere touch of her hand sent a warm shiver through him. He swelled in anticipation as her fingers leisurely slid inside.

"Umm, baby," he groaned as his hands contracted as they wrapped around her thighs just below the juncture. Her sweet moans were music to his ears as he hooked a finger around her damp panties and slid inside to feel her heat. She moved against his fingers, sliding his pants down. He turned, inched back, and lifted her onto the edge of the granite countertop, then slid her panties and jeans completely off. And impaled her. His groan mixed with her high-pitched sigh as she dropped her chin to his chest. Her trembling limbs clung to him. Her touch firm and persuasive, invited more of him.

He sank deeper into her as she wrapped her legs tighter around his waist, her hands gripping his back as she cried out. They moved together, sensations spiraling. Wanting her to reach ecstasy in time with his own, one of his large hands cupped her buttocks, the other reached and stroked her intimately. Her thighs clenched tighter as he stroked her, impaled her, touched her, engulfed her, her breath whispering against his chest. He slowed their pace savoring their passion—until he couldn't hold on any longer. As she writhed against him, the desire he held at bay broke free. He knew he touched her core as they moved urgently together reaching unnamed heights. They held each other, lost in the aftershocks, trembling, hearts pounding, muscles clenching. It all seemed to go on forever. Adam knew be could stay as he was for eternity.

He also knew he'd never give up this piece of heaven. He'd spend a lifetime trying to convince her that they belonged together . . . were made for each other.

As he absorbed the last of her trembling, for once in the last thirty-three years he wasn't an outsider looking in. He belonged.

* * *

On Christmas Eve, Adam still hadn't found the appropriate time to tell Amanda he was leaving after Christmas. She still thought he'd be with her until after New Year.

He almost felt angry for having to tiptoe around her this way. It would only give her another excuse to compare him with Brian. At this stage of their relationship, he didn't need that.

As Reverend Everett Smart spoke of the purpose of Christmas at the midnight service, Adam gripped Amanda's hand, offering up a prayer for enlightenment.

He compared his life from a year ago when he'd been shut up with paperwork, sipping a glass of wine. And his visits to church, although he was a believer, had been few. His dad was fun loving, but his mom was a staunch worshiper. She dragged him and his dad there every Sunday morning, quite often having to wear the same starched and faded dress over and over and his dad wearing the same bedraggled suit, though it was always pressed. But she was there with her Sunday hat perched on her tight curls, nodding during the sermon, giving the preacher encouragement. The sermon would put cheer in her heart to last through the week, because she'd be humming her songs day after day.

And he remembered he was in every last Christmas play, getting teased afterward by the boys who weren't required to get up in front of the church for the display. But she made sure he participated.

He'd cast those memories aside for years, the pain piercing him too sharply to remember. With Amanda beside him, he wasn't afraid to dwell on the fond times.

As Everett led them through the last prayer, he knew

he had truly been blessed this Christmas season, and he rejoiced in it as they sang "Joy to the World." He felt the joy his mom carried through her week in his heart. He knew why she sang.

Christmas morning was snowy and cold. The fire Adam had made while Amanda cooked breakfast was roaring and toasty. After breakfast, Amanda opened Josh's gift first and exclaimed over the silk scarf and bracelet he bought her. Adam opened his and oohed and ahed over the Washington Redskin's sweatshirt.

Finally, they exchanged gifts.

"You shouldn't have," Amanda said as she tore the paper off to bare the delicate porcelain figurine, her eyes sparkling. "It's so beautiful," she whispered. "Thank you. Oh, Adam, I didn't expect this." She put the delicate piece on the table and hugged him.

Adam used it as an excuse for a lingering kiss. "Had I known I'd get this response, I'd have given you more," he said huskily.

"Oh, you." She sat back and plucked up a small package. "I've got something for you, too."

"To mimic you, you shouldn't have," he said as he tore into the paper to reveal engraved gold cuff links and a snow globe with a Christmas scene inside.

Adam swallowed several times before he could say anything. The gifts he received from Brian and her were the only ones he'd received for years. His throat felt too clogged to utter a word. "I'll treasure it always." His voice cracked. He cleared his throat. "Hey, I've got another one for you." He reached into his pocket for a small package and handed it to her.

Amanda unwrapped it to reveal diamond teardrop earrings. Each was one carat. "This is too much. Oh, Adam." She looked up at him. "Why?"

"They're for a very special lady."

Tears sparkled in her eyes. He was making her believe again. She couldn't afford to do that. Love wasn't forever. But it was Christmas and the magic of it was spinning in waves around her. The fire only escalated the sentiment.

They reached for each other at the same time. The actual gifts didn't matter but the sentiment did. In the season of love, they needed to belong, they needed to love, they needed each other.

"Words can't express how much I need you," he said, pressing a kiss to her lips. She sighed in remembered pleasure as he peeled off her clothes to reveal her glistening skin inch by inch. It was a time to relish, not a time for haste. He brushed his chest against her nipples.

She trailed her fingertips lightly over his skin. He followed the sensuous curves and lines, covering the surface with a carpet of kisses. They stroked, squeezed each other, their arousal undulating like waves in the ocean before they were joined as one.

As the light filtered through sheer curtains covering the windows and the warm heat from the fire kissed their skin, they fragmented into a burst of flame to rival that of the brightest star.

Josh called later in the day. "Merry Christmas, Mom."

"Merry Christmas to you. How is it there?"

"It's wonderful, but," he whispered, "I miss your cooking."

Amanda laughed. "I'll freeze some for you."

"Good. How's work?"

"It's going well."

"And Adam?"

He asked a lot about Adam, Amanda thought. "He's fine. I'll let you speak to him before we hang up."

"I'd like that." An unusual silence, then, "You know, Mom, I never told you, but I always talked to Adam more than I did to Dad. I felt guilty about that after he died."

"Oh, honey."

"Adam was always easy to talk to. He would answer questions and deal with stuff Dad never seemed to have an answer for. I used to call him collect in Africa because Dad never knew what to say about certain things, or never had the time."

"Why didn't you come to me if you felt you couldn't talk to your father?"

"They were men things, Mom. I couldn't talk to you about it."

"Of course you could. I thought you knew you could come to me about anything." Amanda said, feeling hurt, and wondering what she did wrong that her own son who slept down the hall from her, couldn't come to her.

"I knew that, but you're a woman. I needed to talk to another man. It's a guy thing. I'm not telling you to upset you."

"I'm not upset. I just wanted to be there for you."

"You were. Still are. I love you, Mom."

Tears misted her eyes. "I love you, too, sweetheart," she sniffed.

"Okay, don't start crying on me now."

"I just can't help it."

"Oh, God. You okay?"

"Yes I am. I'll let you talk to Adam, now."

Amanda called Adam to the phone and went upstairs to change clothes for the dinner with Everett, Lottie, Henry, and their two sons home from college.

"Hi, Josh." Adam sat on one of the high bar chairs in the kitchen.

"How's Mom?"

"She's great."

"Good. I worry about her."

"You shouldn't. I'm keeping an eye on her."

"Good. Good. Oh, and how are you?"

"Thanks for remembering. I'm fine."

"You're always okay."

Adam wondered why he would think that. But he also needed to talk to Josh about his relationship with Amanda. How did you gracefully tell a woman's son that you had the hots for his mom? "I was wondering, Josh. How would you feel if your mom and I . . . well, if we discovered that we . . . liked each other?"

"You and Mom?"

"Your mom and me, yes." Adam held his breath waiting for the response of a lifetime.

"So you really are going to stay in Virginia."

"That's the plan."

"I think she needs someone like you. Dad was never very sensitive to her needs. And you are. At least you were there for me. You'll be a good change for her."

Adam let out a sigh of relief. "Thanks, Josh."

"Just take good care of my mom," he said as he hung up.

Adam helped Amanda finish the Christmas dinner and by two o'clock, the house was busy with people. This time, however, Adam did not feel even a twinge of jealousy in Everett's presence. And he reveled in this heartwarming Christmas Day. It couldn't have been better.

Chapter 9

The day after Christmas they were snuggled in Adam's bed, warm and contented after lovemaking. Christmas had been magical, both warm and tender. It still lingered as they woke the next morning. She wanted it to last another week. Maybe—just maybe she meant more than Adam's work. Perhaps his words rang true. Their relationship was important to him. She understood that, when they started Worldwide Satellites, Brian and Adam needed to put in the long hours to establish the business. But they'd been in business for fifteen years now. It was well established and they were making great profits. There was no reason he couldn't take a week off for them. She wanted—needed—time for intimacy. Time for just the two of them.

At least Adam wouldn't have to leave before the New Year. Then, he'd be much too busy with the company expansion for the time for them.

Adam gave her one last kiss. Leaning over her, he smoothed her brow.

"Adam, Josh told me how you were there for him. Thank you."

"It was nothing."

She reached up and touched his brow. "In a time when so many children are following the wrong path, it meant more than you'll ever realize."

"He's my godson. It's my job to be there for him."

"Not every godparent takes their responsibility that seriously."

He smiled. "You're welcome."

She reached up and kissed him.

When they came up for air, Adam said, "Amanda?"

"Yes?" Her response was soft, her eyes light.

"I have to leave tomorrow."

"So soon? You can't wait another week?" Disappointment spiraled through her.

Adam sighed. "I'm sorry Amanda, I can't. We have to settle this before the end of the year."

At least they could still be together, even if it was in New York Amanda thought, annoyed that, yet again, work intruded. Perhaps they could see a play on Broadway. She wanted the warm moments to last.

"Some of the contracts I'm working on are based in New York. This would be the perfect opportunity to meet the clients," she suggested, stroking the stubble on his chin. Being together was the important thing here. Then she hit her head with the palm of her hand. "I can't do that. The party! I don't understand why this can't wait a few days."

Adam kissed the top of her head. "I wish it could wait, but it can't."

"I knew this was going to happen," she interrupted him vehemently. "You're turning out to be just like Brian. Most of his trips were around holidays, too. Are you even going to make it back in time for the party? Or do I have to give it alone?"

Amanda didn't immediately notice the subtle stiffness in him. "Don't compare us. I'm not Brian."

"Well, you certainly act alike," she snapped.

He caught her chin in his hand. "Do you pretend you're in bed with Brian when we're together, Amanda?" Adam asked quietly through clenched teeth. Too quietly.

"Do you close your eyes, when you reach your peak and think Brian's name?"

"That's cruel, crude, and undeserved . . ."

"Do you dream that you have your husband all over again in me?" He threw the cover back, stormed out of bed.

"What are you talking about? I know who you are. I know who Brian was. I'm not confusing the two of you and I don't like the implication. You need to accept the fact that both of you live and breathe Worldwide Satellites. Nothing else compares." She glowered at him and turned.

"You don't have to go to New York. Your job isn't real anyway." Too late he realized what he'd said. A sudden thin chill hung on the edge of his words. "Oh, boy!"

"The job isn't real?" Amanda scooted over and pulled the sheet up to her chin glaring at him with burning reproachful eyes. "What do you mean by that statement?"

"Nothing. Forget I said anything." He stiffened, momentarily abashed.

"Forget what, exactly?" She got up, wrapping the sheet around her sarong-style. Shock yielded quickly to fury.

Adam swiped a hand through his hair in resignation. "It was meant to get you familiar with the company and contracts. You've done a great job," he placated. "I never expected you to pull that much out of those contracts. You even plugged some holes I wasn't aware were there."

"Exactly how were these contracts going to familiarize me with the company?" She seethed with mounting rage.

"We don't have to go through this now." He sighed. "You were supposed to get familiar with the company and the services we offer by studying these contracts. I didn't expect you to actually contact them all and go over everything in detail. It's turned into more than I ever expected."

"You lied to me." Her voice trembled.

What was he to say?

"I didn't know you. I couldn't very well set you up with major client's accounts when you knew nothing about the business. I didn't know your capabilities. Especially since Brian . . ."

"Brian what?"

His breath whooshed out. ". . . said you were flighty, if the truth be told."

"Oh, so now you're telling the truth? When it comes back on me!"

"I know you're nothing like what Brian said. Actually, I've been thinking that we need a full-time person for that customer service area."

"A full-time person like whom, may I ask?" She spat out the words contemptuously.

"You. You've done a first-rate effort on them. You have a real feel for the business."

"And the little matter of asking me simply slipped your mind, I take it."

"I had to see how you handled it before I assigned you more challenging duties."

"Oh, so now it's a real job! Which is it—real or toy job, Adam? You know, if there's one thing I can't stand it's lying. If you needed to know something about me, you only had to ask. I have enough sense to know that if I couldn't do something, I needed to come to you for guidance. You aren't talking to a teenager." She patted her forehead. "But now I understand. You did this because I was ready to sell the company, didn't you?"

"Amanda. You are a very responsible woman who has done a magnificent job. I respect your capabilities."

"I asked you. Is this about the stock?"

"All right. In the beginning it was about the stock. I put my life's blood in this company and you were ready to sell it out from under me. I couldn't let that happen. I didn't know you. Now I do."

"Let me tell you something, Adam Somerville. I've changed my mind. I'm not selling my stock, but I'm having equal say in this company. And you don't have to lie to me about trips. I overheard one of Brian's phone conversations where he admitted he didn't really need to take a trip to conduct business after he had yet again canceled one of our family outings. He could have handled it by phone and fax. I don't care about your personal life. Only Worldwide Satellites concern me. Every major decision made will go through me." Amanda dropped the sheet and pulled her robe on, and marched out of Adam's room.

"Like hell it will," he said under his breath. "We have to talk more about it," he shouted after her.

She looked over her shoulder. "I've said everything I need to say."

Suddenly, the beauty of the holidays left and a pall fell over Amanda's heart.

She thought Adam had believed in her, trusted her.

It hit Amanda as she shed the robe and turned on the shower with an angry twist of her wrist. He was merely using her. Standing under the spray didn't have its usual soothing effect but the exact opposite. She tried very hard not to sink into despair.

Male using female stories were rampant in novels, television, and in real life. Safely tucked in marriage, Amanda had thought herself immune. Now she knew different.

At least Everett, who'd been gentle and caring, had been true, but she didn't love Everett.

"Amanda," Adam entreated from her office doorway, hoping to call a truce before he left, knowing his chances were slim to none.

"Yes?" she returned, posture stiff, manner cold. She was unbending, and holding up a sheet of paper with stiff fingers.

"We'll work on us when I return." He advanced into the small office and rounded the desk. He admired the proud stiffness in her shoulders and winced for the hurt in her and the fact that she valiantly tried to shield herself. If he could have rescinded his decision a thousand times, he would have. If this trip didn't mean half of next year's salaries would be covered . . . but it did. No one else could negotiate this contract for him.

Adam felt pulled in two. He loved this woman. Did loving mean having to choose between his work and the woman who should stand with him? It needn't be a contest. Why was she making it into one?

She gave him a cold, fleeting smile. "Sure," and dropped the paper on the desk.

If ever he was greeted with a cold shower, this was it. He glanced at his watch, knowing he had to leave now or miss his flight. He bent, grabbing her in his arms and kissed her long and hard. Surprisingly, she responded to his gesture. "I love you, Amanda," he whispered.

And then he was gone.

Such simple words that held more importance than any combination.

Amanda sat speechless and in doubt, with hope racing through her.

She wanted someone who trusted her, believed in

her abilities. She couldn't, wouldn't, fight the battle with him that she fought with Brian who'd never believed in her.

Adam had shown her he didn't either.

It hurt letting him go with unresolved anger between them. She understood that he had work to do. And that he had to do it now. But she didn't understand why he lied to her.

Why was life so complicated?

Chapter 10

Heart heavy, Adam deplaned. The cold send off he'd received from Amanda rivaled New York's frigid temperatures. How the hell could he have fallen in love with her?

Brian was dead. And he, Adam, was flesh and blood alive. Couldn't she see that? *Did* she think of Brian when she was in bed with him? Adam pulled his collar up. Couldn't she see the love they had to offer one another. How perfectly they fit? It was more than sex. It was a blending of spirits. He felt so much at home. He felt she belonged with him. That he had a real purpose in life other than making a living and surviving. Life was made for love, his father had said before his mom's death. Adam thought of the loving snapshot of his parents and was thinking for once he'd have that love for himself. Finally he'd found a woman he thought could give him all his wildest dreams. A woman worth taking the risk for.

Then he remembered his father's last comments while in his deepest moments of despair. *Be careful of your dreams, son. Deal with what you know. Dreams are for fools.* You weren't wrong to live your life the way you lived it, Dad, Adam thought. His mother was one of the happiest Moms around. To be a Somerville was to be a dreamer. That was what made them so special, so loving with so very much to offer.

What were dreams if not to share? The last few weeks had emphasized how much he needed Amanda. He couldn't go back to a work-only existence.

Adam hailed a waiting taxi. Maybe it had come down to making a choice between work and Amanda. Perhaps he had to consider giving up the company. Giving up Worldwide Satellites would be tantamount to giving up part of himself. Was his love for Amanda that significant?

He'd visit Tiffany's while in New York and he'd ask Amanda to marry him as soon as he returned home. New Year's Eve at midnight. It would be the perfect time to propose.

Adam had a feeling this was going to be the biggest gamble of his life. Amanda could be as difficult to gauge as his most demanding client.

"You've been making yourself too scarce, with that new man, girlfriend," Lottie greeted Amanda with a peck on the cheek at The Little Cafe. They took their seats and the menus the hostess handed them.

"He's gone."

She dropped her menu. "For good?"

"For the week."

Lottie negligently waved a hand then resumed perusing her menu. "That's nothing. You said it like it was the end of the world. Young love." She shook her head. "I'm too old for this."

"It's over between us."

"Oh, Lord. That's horrible. What happened?"

The waitress stepped up for their selections. They quickly scanned the menu. Amanda didn't care what she ordered. Just to order something, she selected a grilled chicken and cheese sandwich. Lottie hastily ordered a ham and cheese croissant and New England clam chowder.

After the woman walked away, Lottie said, "Okay. What happened with the hunk?"

She retold the argument.

"Oh, shoot. I thought he was just the perfect one for you, too. Are you sure you can't work it out?"

"I don't know, Lottie. He swears that he loves me, but . . . I can't trust what he says."

"Well, you did say that Brian told him you were scatterbrained. He should have waited to get to know you before forming an opinion, but he trusted Brian. You know how men are." Lottie reached across and patted Amanda's hand. "Honey, he just might love you. At least give him a chance to redeem himself. Maybe he'll throw in some jewelry in the process." She smiled at her own facetious reply.

Amanda shook her head in exasperation. "How did you and Everett end up siblings? He's down to earth and you're out in left field."

She waved a hand at her. "Girl, please. He's so stodgy. That's why the two of you wouldn't do. You'd bore each other to death in no time."

Amanda ignored Lottie's assessment. "How is he? I've neglected him lately."

"Brooding over you, but he'll get over it," was her perky reply.

Adam looked out at the rush of people passing his window as he had dinner with Price Turner who had been trying to buy Worldwide for years.

"So," Price said as he sliced into his medium-rare steak. "Have you decided to sell Worldwide yet?"

The man looked up when Adam didn't respond immediately. "I'm considering it." He needed to play by ear. With the downsizings and changes occurring at astronomical speeds, an offer made a year ago wouldn't necessarily still hold true.

Price's fork clattered as it hit the plate. "I can't believe it. I thought you'd never sell that company."

"I said I'm thinking about it," Adam warned.

"Anytime you're ready, we are," Price said with a gleam in his eye, rubbing his hands in anticipation.

"I need to know that you'll retain the employees. You won't find a better group."

"Hell, I'm not stupid, man. I'm not about to get rid of good workers. I'll even let you continue to manage it if you want to stay in the business."

Adam took in a deep breath. "Thanks. Give me a month to think about it, Price."

The older man looked at Adam. "I'll give you all the time you need."

Chapter 11

The warm homecoming and the exuberant kisses Adam had hoped for upon his return were at odds with the welcoming he received. Amanda was not waiting with open arms to greet him. If possible, she was even more restrained than when he'd left. He left his suitcase by the stairs.

"Oh, you're back," she managed to say as he entered the kitchen, minus the warm embracing enthusiasm he'd become accustomed to, before turning back to stirring something quite aromatic on the stove. The caterers walked briskly back and forth from the truck to the kitchen and dining room. The house was a flurry of activity. The atmosphere wasn't conducive to ironing out family squabbles.

"Could we talk upstairs?" he asked, hands in pocket.

"Now?" she questioned, wooden spoon hovering in the air.

"Yes, now, please."

"Give me a few minutes to finish this off." She resumed her stirring.

Adam skirted a woman carrying a huge punch bowl as he hauled his things to his room. Once there, to calm his jumping stomach, he unpacked. Ten minutes passed before Amanda knocked on the door before opening it. Warily, she stepped over the threshold.

As his thoughts had been centered around her since he left, he closed the door behind her and hauled her into his arms. Her startled shriek was quickly masked by his lips. He sighed when her arms reached around his neck. Instead of waiting, as soon as their lips parted, he asked, "Marry me, Amanda. I've missed you." The smile lit his eyes.

"Adam?"

"What is it, sweetheart?"

"I . . . I'm shocked. I didn't know you were thinking of marriage."

"Why not? I love you. Whatever our problems, we can work them out."

Oh, Lord. She was old and wise enough to know love didn't conquer all.

"I'm . . . I'm not ready for it. It's not as easy as it sounds. This isn't a fairy tale of happily ever after."

Adam dropped his hand from her arms, turned, and paced to the window. "You're not ready for me."

"For anyone."

Hands on his hips now, he asked, "Why not? Is it Brian again?"

"It's not a matter of comparing. I'm cautious. I don't want to make the same mistakes this time that I made with Brian. I'm a grown woman, able to accept responsibility and deserving of respect. I can't live without respect."

"I have never disrespected you. I know you're a woman."

"I'm not talking about sex."

"Don't insult my intelligence. You're not talking to a sixteen-year-old."

"You have to understand." She advanced farther in the room and sat on his bed. "Brian took care of everything. Bills, insurances, investments. Everything. I was the little stay-at-home wife who raised our son, supported Brian in his business, and did volunteer work in the church. I didn't know anything about the insurance. Everything was for the company, and that is where you are exactly the same." She held up a hand to forestall his comments. "It never occurred to him that Josh and I would need something to live off of in the event that he wasn't here or that Josh needed money for his education. He left everything to Worldwide Satellites. And if it wasn't for you, for the funds coming from the company, I wouldn't have had anything to live on. That's frightening. Not to really know where my next loaf of bread is coming from. That's why it's so important that I have a career. It's why it's so important that I have some control over my life. I can't live with the uncertainty. At forty, I need stability."

"I wouldn't dream of taking all that from you. I don't mind sharing every aspect of the business with you, or our lives. As half of this union, you have a right to know. That isn't unreasonable. Every woman should know where she stands financially. I don't have a problem with that. I prefer having a marriage of sharing." Adam sat beside her and grasped her hand in a possessive gesture. "Don't substitute Brian for me. We aren't the same person. We're different men with different drives, different desires, different ultimate goals. Judge me for who I am. Not for what another man has done."

"B . . . Adam."

He took her face in his palms. "I'm not Brian. You have to remember that."

"I know you aren't Brian. I just need more time. It's too soon."

Amanda left Adam sitting on his bed.

The door closing after Amanda sounded like a bomb in his head.

Adam had always been a strategist. He knew he had

two choices. He could give up Amanda completely, or he could bide his time and convince her they belonged together.

Giving up was not an option for the woman he loved. He'd give her time. As she worked more for the company. As she grew to know him better, she'd see things his way.

By ten that evening, the first floor and basement rec rooms were filled with people. Adam was irresistible in his formal attire. Amanda had been itching to open that tuxedo shirt and run her fingers through that hair for hours. Now, he was talking to the Blake brothers who always managed to crash the party. They also tended to stay low-keyed, offering Worldwide's employees better positions. They lost a few, but none in the last five years. Most of the Blake brothers' employees had moved on to other positions after dismantling companies. Worldwide employees liked having the security of management.

"And here is the woman who has been tormenting me for weeks now." Joe was unsteady on his feet.

"Coffee and soda for you the rest of the evening," Amanda said, disgruntled that the man had already imbibed too much so early in the evening. This was a company affair, after all, and Joe was part of management. She could never tolerate excessive drinking. His inebriated state was at odds with his work ethic. He'd done a tremendous job in training her on the contracts and he was a good addition to the company. Actually, he was tops in his position.

Joe's wife came up behind them. "Is he troubling you already, Amanda? The night's only begun." She tapped him on the arm and she and Amanda both had to balance him as he began to topple.

"I'm not tormenting her. She's tormented me!" he sputtered, outraged.

"Come on Joe," his wife said, disgusted. "Let's eat. It's a good thing I'm driving tonight." She took his hand and pulled him toward the buffet.

None of the drivers were allowed to drink at the party. Worldwide Satellites couldn't afford to get sued for someone's drunken driving. And Amanda was very conscious of safety.

It was ten minutes before midnight and the crowd was getting geared up for the countdown. Amanda donned a coat and stepped out onto the deck for some peace and quiet before the ruckus of the New Year. She paced to the railing, leaned against it, and took a breath of the cold, refreshing air when she heard the sliding door behind her.

"You look beautiful." Amanda turned at hearing Adam's voice. She wore the teardrop earrings he'd given her with her black velvet midcalf evening dress.

"Thank you."

"What's wrong, sweetheart?" Adam asked.

"I just wanted some time alone, that's all. Nothing's wrong."

His footsteps sounded on the wooden boards as he approached her, put his hands on her shoulders, slowly turned her. "Mind if I join you?" The moonlight cast irregular shadows on her face.

"Not at all."

"I've made a decision." He tilted her chin, pressed her close to him.

She leaned her head to the side. "What decision?"

"I've decided to sell the business. I'll have less responsibility, more time . . ."

"You're selling it to the Blakes?" She leaned back in horror, pressing a hand to his chest.

"No, no. You remember Price. I don't want the business broken apart. I want it kept intact for the employees. Price is dependable. He runs a tight ship. He'll do right by the employees."

"You see, that's exactly what I meant." Shoving away from him, she paced away, then turned to face him again. "Why didn't you talk to me about it? Why did you make a decision like that on your own?"

"You know what, Amanda, there's no pleasing you." His angry retort hardened his features. "You don't like the business. Now you want the business. What the hell do you want, woman?"

"I don't want you to sell it. You love that company. How could you think that I could love you and want you to give up something so important to you?"

"You love me." It was a statement, not a question. His anger evaporated, leaving only confusion.

"You haven't learned anything from all this. I want you to communicate with me."

"I am communicating with you." The shock of her announcement almost left him tongue-tied.

"No, you aren't. You're making decisions before you talk to me. You can't read my mind. I want you to talk to me before you make major decisions."

"All right, all right. What do you want? I'm all ears." He crossed his arms to keep from sweeping her off her feet and escaping upstairs.

"First, judge me by your own assessment of me, not by what Brian has said."

"I . . ."

She put a finger to his lips to silence him. "Next, don't lie to me. If you have reservations about my abilities, let me know."

"You're very capable. I know that."

"And last, I want the business. I just want to make sure that there's time for us, too."

"There will always be time for us." He took her face in his hands. "I'll always *make* time for us. We got the Scott contract, and"—he reached into his pocket and pulled out two plane tickets—"in a week we have tickets for a two-week vacation to Fiji. Let this trip be a new beginning for us."

She could barely control her gasp of surprise. "You can get away for . . ."

Their heads turned when they heard the countdown, sixty, fifty-nine . . . "We have to join them." Amanda led him into the house and grabbed noise makers, party hats, and champagne to welcome in the New Year. When Adam's lips touched hers and he gathered her into his arms, she knew the New Year would be a new beginning for their lives together. He was willing to give up the most important part of his life for her. He was willing to contribute toward making their marriage work. And she loved him. What more could she ask for? When their lips parted, she said, "I'll marry you Adam Somerville."

He kissed her again and when they came up for air and were once again aware of their surroundings, Josh was beside them. "I guess you don't need mistletoe." He held a sprig above their heads.

Amanda had to blink twice to assure herself she wasn't hallucinating, that she was actually looking at her son. "Josh?" she asked.

"I couldn't miss your engagement," he said, grinning from ear to ear.

She clasped his cheeks in her hands. He grabbed her in a bear hug.

"I can't believe it!"

"Believe it," Adam said from behind.

"You told him?" Amanda asked.

"Of course. He has to give the bride away. Pardon me, is it all right for your son to give you away? You're not too independent for traditions, are you?"

"I'd love for my son to give me away." She laughed. Then she sobered. "How do you feel about Adam and me?"

"I'm happy for you, Mom. As long as you're happy, go for it. You deserve the best."

Tears filled her eyes.

"How did you grow up so fast?"

"It's a new year, Amanda. Isn't this a wonderful start?" Adam gathered the three of them together. "We're a family."

"Yes." It started with the two people she loved most with her. It couldn't have been better.

Adam slipped his hand in his pocket and brought out a three carat diamond ring and slipped it on her finger.

"Now, now," Everett said. "It's time to bless this engagement." He winked at Amanda and shook Adam's hand. "May God be with you." Everyone bowed their heads as he said a special prayer for them.